A Caine & Ferraro Novel

FORGING
Caine

JANET OPPEDISANO

Forging Caine
ISBN Digital: 978-1-7386998-0-3
ISBN Paperback: 978-1-7386998-1-0

For everyone who adores a good love story

Free Novella

To instantly receive the free romantic suspense novella *The Phoenix Heist*, with cameos by Samantha and Antonio and introducing the Reynolds Recoveries heist crew, claim your copy at https://bf.janetoppedisano.com/smbari40im.

CHAPTER 1

SAMANTHA

The laptop stared back at me, providing no more clues than it had over the past two hours. Photographs, police reports, fire marshal's report. Foster Mutual Insurance had paid over twenty thousand dollars for this fire claim last spring, but something told me it was fraud.

My job was to find the proof.

It was somewhere in the files, but my brain refused to focus.

I pushed back from the oversized dark wood dining table in Antonio's oversized open-concept great room. Next to me sat his oversized kitchen with its granite countertops and breakfast bar with too many bar chairs.

No, that would be *our* oversized everything. I'd been living alone in the penthouse condo for four months while he wrapped up his contract in Naples.

I should have been at the office, but after six and a half years working out of my truck, the cubicle life gave me hives. Besides, all I'd have done there was check my watch, stalk the hallways, and refresh my text messages a million times. No one needed to see my excited pacing while I counted down the final hours until my boyfriend would be home for good.

My phone buzzed in the pattern I'd set for the concierge desk downstairs. The security app showed Lucy Chapman waiting to come up. *Thank god*. Work was done for the day—my much-needed distraction had arrived. I authorized her visit and waited by the door.

"Best graduation gift ever!" Lucy squealed as she stepped out of the elevator. She never dressed up to see me, but her normally straight jet-black hair was curled at the ends. Her eye shadow sparkled under the pot lights, bringing my attention to the wing she'd added with eyeliner.

"What's with the makeup?"

"How much time do we have?" She plopped down on the bench inside the door, hauling off her Doc Martens and ignoring my question. "Because you're going to love this."

A few weeks ago, Antonio and I had found ourselves in Boston for a weekend, visiting the book conservator who was repairing my Christmas gift to Antonio—an ancient leather-bound copy of *The Merchant of Venice* my father had given to my mother. Between the pastedown and the interior board, the conservator discovered a small sheet of paper with strange characters none of us could translate.

I'd shown it to Lucy when I got back from Boston and she couldn't have grabbed it from my hand any faster. She loved a good puzzle as much as I did, so we'd called it a graduation present.

On our way to the dining room, she said, "Antonio gets in at four, right?"

"Not until five. He called from Chicago. His flight was delayed so he's renting a car rather than waiting." I held back as much of a sigh as I could. I wouldn't confess it to anyone but Antonio, but I'd been counting down the days until his return and the final hours were driving me mad. As much as I loved my solitude, I was beyond excited to see him again.

She pulled out a few sheets of paper and pencils while I moved my laptop to the side. "So, I've got five hours to keep you busy?"

"Sort of. I have another friend dropping by." I leaned on the back of one of the dining chairs. "You and I need to talk about him."

She froze. "Him? This can't be good."

"You remember I told you I was in the FBI?"

"And then totally refused to fess up to more than that?" She slid into a seat, arranging the papers in front of her. "How could I forget?"

I feigned a scowl, which was met by her blowing a large gum bubble. "Before that, I did an internship at the FBI field office in Detroit with the Art Crime Team."

"Sounds perfect for you." She wasn't wrong.

Part of me had been dying to go back since I resigned prematurely, but another much more vocal part of me didn't want to go anywhere near the Bureau until last year. "I've kept in touch with the man I interned for, Special Agent Elliot Skinner."

"He's the guy you contacted for that stolen painting at Christmas, right?"

"That's the one." I straightened, rubbing my fingers over the chair back. "He's been after me to rejoin, or at least—"

"Shut up! You're leaving Foster Mutual? But I'm starting in September!"

I ran a hand over my face. This was the same question I'd had swirling around my brain practically every day since I moved to Brenton when my sister got sick in June. First, my job with Foster was supposed to be a short-term position until her treatments were done. Then, Antonio came into my life, along with his threats to make it less short-term. Then Elliot showed up and threw a wrench into everything.

My world had flipped upside down this last year. "I don't know. It's possible. Elliot's been trying to prove to some folks at the FBI that I'd be an excellent addition to his team—as a consultant, working from here."

Lucy pushed one sheet in my direction. "I guess if he's coming over, we should get down to business." While her social boundaries were nearly non-existent, she also respected when I was done talking about something. I loved that about her.

"What did you figure out?"

Her eyes lit up the way they always did when she was about to launch into a story about her traveling days with her parents. "When I was fifteen, we did a tour of The National Museum of Computing, north of London. They've got all these historic computers, but the real highlight was an Enigma machine. You know, the—"

"Machine that coded Nazi messages in World War II."

"Exactly!" She popped a bubble. "While we were there, I met this older guy who was really into codebreaking. He taught me some stuff and we stayed in touch after. He used to send me little cyphers for my birthday, so I sent him a photo of the code when I got stumped. That's okay, right?"

I nodded in the sliver of time she took to breathe.

"He gave me a couple of clues, and I thought we could start with a simple letter substitution." She tapped the sheet she'd moved toward me, on which she'd listed each of the shapes. "There are twenty-seven shapes, so I'm betting each one's a letter, plus the most common one represents a space."

"Letter substitution was the first thing you tried, but you said it wouldn't work."

"Turns out, that's only step one. Step two is where the real magic happens."

We got down to work, assigning values to each shape and jotting them onto her working copy. She also rummaged through the cupboards to find snacks, teased me about how much food had arrived with Antonio's grocery order yesterday, and told four different travel stories which were almost related to what we were doing.

The truth was, figuring out the code hadn't been my priority. It was an excuse to have her visit and chat my ear off to distract me from watching the clock for Antonio's return.

After a couple of hours, we finished step one.

Lucy tossed a fresh piece of gum into her mouth and rubbed her hands together. "Now, we need to find the key word."

My phone buzzed with another notification from the concierge desk. Swiping through to the front desk camera, I spied Elliot Skinner carrying—holy shit, my stomach did a cartwheel—he was carrying a Bankers Box.

Was this really it? Was this a case?

I tapped the authorization button and put up a finger. "Hold that thought."

"Will do, boss."

Shaking my head on my way to the door, I muttered the line Lucy had me repeating at least weekly. "Not your boss, Luce."

As he stepped out of the elevator, Elliot lifted the box toward me. "I come bearing gifts."

He wore a dark suit with a white shirt, highlighting his warm brown skin. He sported the same goatee as the last time I'd seen him but had switched his hair from short sponge twists to a low fade with waves.

I took the box from him, surprised at how heavy it was. "How long are you staying?"

"The gift comes with conditions, but I'll be quick."

"Signature?"

He followed me in and closed the door. "Three of them."

I tipped the box slowly from side to side. A subtle whooshing noise and shift in the balance hinted at paperwork. What could it possibly be? A case. It had to be a case.

We walked from the foyer together, into the large, open living space. Lucy looked up from her work with a smile.

"I'm sorry," said Elliott. "I didn't realize you had company."

"This is—"

"Lucy Chapman, Sam's best friend." She was out of her seat and around the table, hand out to Elliot. "And you're the secret G-man she keeps talking about without telling me the juicy details, right?"

Elliott's eyebrows rose. "Lucy? Sam told me about you once."

I hefted the Bankers Box onto the table. "I did?"

"I believe she referred to you as her 'data genius.'"

Lucy gulped, likely swallowing her gum. "You said that?"

"It's possible." I tried frowning, tried keeping my hard-ass image in place, but it was pointless around these two. They'd become immune to my attitude.

Elliot stepped closer to the end of the table, leaning over the mysterious sheet from the book. "What's this?"

"I got it while I was in Boston." I'd met with Elliot and another agent for a quick consult while I'd been there. Somehow, Antonio and I had fallen into the middle of the other agent's case, so Elliot was well-aware of my trip—and the gunman who threatened us at the conservator's shop. "The conservator found this sheet sandwiched inside the lining of an old book of my mother's I gave to Antonio. I couldn't make heads or tails of it, so thought Lucy might want to try."

He remained focused on the sheet, his gaze drifting over Lucy's notes. "You've made some progress. What's your methodology?"

"There aren't any word breaks, but this symbol..." She pointed to a character on her sheet, unable to hide her excitement—either at explaining the details in general or specifically explaining them to an FBI agent. "It appears more than it should. Normally, I'd start by looking for a character to represent the letter E if it's monoalphabetic."

"Reasonable," said Elliot.

"But this character's even more common than E would be, so we're assuming it represents a space. Shortest number of letters between two instances of this character is two, so it's—"

"Polyalphabetic." Elliot cocked his head at her. "I don't suppose you've ever considered the FBI as a career?"

Lucy scrunched her nose. "That sounds dangerous."

I smiled at the woman who'd once been called my protégé. "She's starting at Foster Mutual in September."

"How does Foster Mutual Insurance get all the brightest minds?" He shook his head. "I may have to start recruiting there."

Lucy gathered her work. "I'm assuming I should make myself scarce?"

"We won't be long," I said. "You can use my desk upstairs."

"Nah, I like Antonio's giant desk in the library better." She held out a hand to Elliot and shook. "Pleasure finally meeting you, Elliot."

"And you, Lucy. That's good work." He pulled out his wallet and handed her a business card. "Just in case."

"Wow, thanks!" She beamed at him before heading down the hall.

My insides continued jumping around like a kid on Christmas morning until the library door closed behind her. "Alright, Elliot, what did you bring me?"

"Files and photos from the pawnshop."

Antonio and I had tracked down some stolen paintings in December which had come from a pawnshop in Detroit. The same pawnshop which had been the source of another stolen painting we found at a gala on our first date and was potentially involved in an art smuggling ring the FBI had been investigating for a few years. I pulled the lid off the box, taking in stacks of folders. "Why not digital?"

He hummed aloud and withdrew a contract with the FBI letterhead. "They won't clear you for VPN access yet, so I can't let you log in to our systems to look at anything. And without a verified, secure connection in here, I can't even give you a thumb drive."

I pulled three folders, each an inch thick, peering inside to see more of the same. "But I can have all this?"

"As much as I'd like to make all the rules, I don't. I need you to sign this agreement, saying you'll store it in a secure location." He plucked a pen from his jacket pocket and handed it to me.

"Antonio's got a safe upstairs it'll fit in." I took the pen and signed where he pointed, then he did the same as witness. "What do you want me to do with it?"

"Review, catalog, see if anything sticks out. Cross-reference intake records with the paintings, figure out what might be missing. You know, do your thing. We recovered most of this data off a hard drive the pawnshop owners thought they'd destroyed, so there's some data loss, but I think your eye for artwork will help identify gaps."

"Have you figured out who was behind the pawnshop?"

His eyes sharpened, the thrill of the hunt radiating from him. "Shell companies, fake identities, and a maze of bank accounts. It's slow going, but I have a feeling we're getting close."

I flipped through one folder, full of photographs of artwork, accounting ledgers, and a few documents listing provenance. "How many people do you have working on this?"

"Not enough." He folded the signed sheet and stuffed it into his breast pocket. "When does Antonio get home?"

"Later today. Bad weather grounded his flight from O'Hare, but he's driving." I stopped at a painting that looked eerily like a Chagall, but the details were wrong. It was too crisp, the colors too muted. Stapled to it, a list of dimensions, photos of the stretcher from the back, close-ups of a gallery tag from a museum in Texas.

"You must be excited. Anything special planned for his grand return?"

"Antonio suggested three weeks of vacation. I said no. He insisted. I caved." I rolled my eyes, thinking back to a full month of his begging. "When I brought it up at the insurance company, they said it was a perfect opportunity to test the processes we've been implementing since I joined the Special Investigations Unit."

"Where are you two headed?"

"Why? Want to get a team assembled wherever it is in case some criminal activity follows us?"

"Wouldn't be the first time."

I laughed, but there was a shred of truth to it. Both of my trips to Naples with Antonio, his trip home to see me at Christmas, plus our trip to Boston last month—criminal activity followed us everywhere we went. "We haven't picked a destination yet. I'm reviewing some of the claims pending for Jimmy's trial. He said he'd planted evidence and I know he glossed over details in his police reports. Once I'm done, I'll have the brainpower available to—"

"Change of plans!" Lucy came rushing down the hall, swinging her backpack up on one shoulder. "I'm heading to a movie."

So much for my afternoon of distraction. "With...?"

From the grin she couldn't contain, it was obvious. She and Antonio's younger brother had been spending a suspicious amount of time together.

"On a Friday? Lorenzo's not working?"

"How'd you know it was him?"

"I'll be right back," I said to Elliot and walked to the door with Lucy. "The makeup gave you away. Plus, you're way too excited."

"I texted him last night this new movie looked interesting." She shrugged and sat to lace up her boots. "I may have dropped a hint or two that I was thinking about going, in the hopes he'd want to come with me."

"And he does?"

She flashed me a smile. "He just called to tell me he bought us tickets."

"I don't get you two."

"Me either." Her smile dimmed and she let out a sigh. "The friend zone is *not* where I want to be, but what else am I going to do? We go to the movies, he takes me shopping when I need something, helps with my groceries—did I tell you he came over to my place last weekend and made me dinner?"

"And nothing?"

"Nothing! I don't understand him." She stood and huffed out a breath. "But I do understand numbers and codes."

"Progress on the letter?"

"Yup." She riffled through her backpack and presented two sheets of paper, each folded into quarters. "I already translated it. Turns out it's an apology from someone named Charles—"

I sucked in air. That was my father's name.

She held out the papers. "—to someone named Deb."

A shiver ran up my spine and my hand halted, unable to take the letters. Deb was my mother, who'd died eight years ago, on the day I graduated from Quantico.

Lucy peered at me, folding my unresponsive hand around the sheets. "And here's a strange coincidence. The letter says Charles was leaving with someone named Elliot. Crazy, huh?"

I fumbled with the sheets—the original and her notes—as the door swung shut behind her, barely registering she'd left. My mother had hidden a letter from my father inside the book? And Elliot? Surely it wasn't the same Elliot who was standing in my dining room?

Something odd churned in my stomach. *No such thing as coincidences.*

My eyes clamped shut before I could read a single word. My father took off when I was five years old. Deserted my mother, sister, and me. Would this explain it? Or make it worse?

Either way, I had to know. I forced my eyes open and skimmed the translated letter.

The churning in my stomach grew into a torrent.

I needed answers.

And I was pretty sure the man in the next room had them.

Chapter 2

Samantha

I walked out of the foyer, reading and re-reading Lucy's translation of the code. Not just a code, but a letter from my father. I had exactly one photograph of him and now this letter. Not even any memories left.

I handed Elliot the coded letter and Lucy's translation. His fingers grazed across the original code with its unintelligible characters. It was an almost tender moment. His free hand covered his lips and his shoulders drew up with a deep inhale.

The last time I saw him like this was on the plane to Italy in January. We were talking about my mother and how she'd secured my internship with Elliot.

"This is your name, isn't it?" I whispered. "You knew him?"

He didn't even look up at me.

I snatched the translation from him and read, unable to keep my voice from shaking. "'Dear Deb, I know we agreed I was finished after my last trip, but something's come up. I'm going back East with Elliot and I'm not sure when I'll be in touch. I'm sorry to do this to you again, but we both knew what I did for a living and went in with our eyes open. Tell the girls I love them, and I hope to see you in a few months. Love, Charles.'"

Elliot slid out a chair and sank into it, no trace of my always-in-control mentor to be seen. And no explanation either.

"He's talking about you, isn't he?" I slammed the sheet down on the table. "Talk to me, dammit! You didn't just know my mother. You knew my father?"

Elliot's hand dragged down to his chest. "I feel like all I ever do is ask you to come back to the FBI and give you difficult news."

My gaze flicked toward the letter and up at him again. "Difficult?"

He placed the original coded letter on the table next to the translation. "Deb and I agreed that when you had sufficient security clearance, we'd tell you the truth."

A shudder ran through me, goosebumps launching up my arms and legs. I was right.

"I was going to tell you after your graduation from Quantico, but when she... I didn't think it was a good time. Then you left the Bureau and I wasn't sure what to do." His relationship with my mother was only a professional one. They'd worked on a case together or so they'd told me. How much more was there? "Did you ever learn to lean on Antonio, like I recommended?"

"What?" Why talk about Antonio when he was supposed to be telling me about my father?

"It's what I told you on the plane in January."

I scrubbed a hand over my forehead, like I could draw out some understanding. "Yeah, I guess."

It wasn't just a guess. I *did* lean on Antonio. More than even my sister.

He nodded as he scanned the grid of letters Lucy and I had written on the bottom of the translation. "I should have known this secret wouldn't stay hidden forever, but as the years went by, I started thinking I'd never get to tell you the truth."

This wasn't going to end with him simply knowing my father. There was more. I eased into the chair across the table from him. "What truth, Elliot?"

"I've been with the FBI for twenty years. I think you knew that, but we never talked about my first career."

"No."

"I did a few internships with the CIA while I was studying finance in college—like you did with me—and hired on after I graduated. I moved into the Clandestine Service pretty quickly."

My head spun. Theories and ideas taking form. What did this story have to do with my father? Why did they go somewhere together? Surely my father wasn't with the CIA. That couldn't be what Elliot was telling me.

"There's only so much control you have over your schedule in that role. Sometimes, they tell you it's time to leave, and they mean that very second. There's no chance for drawn out goodbyes or even for goodbyes at all. So, my mentor taught me this code he learned from his mentor before him."

The churning in my stomach gained such speed I was going to be sick.

"My wife and I used a cypher like that a few times when I had to leave suddenly, so I recognized it. It saved my marriage, but I eventually moved to the FBI so we'd have fewer secrets."

I didn't want to hear this. My father abandoned us and I'd accepted that eons ago. My sister would say I'd never gotten over it, but it was a constant in my life. It was a fact. Him leaving couldn't have been something my mother saw coming. She wouldn't have hidden that from us.

Would she?

"Your father and I worked together for a few years and it was only our second trip together—"

"*He* was your mentor?"

Elliot nodded.

No. I was asleep and dreaming. Having a nightmare. There was no way. "Where was the trip to?"

"East of the United States." He gestured toward the translation. "That's all I can say. Other than the obvious—he didn't come home with me."

I picked up the original, covered in the swirls and shapes that were now letters on a separate sheet. My mother used to curl up with her old copy of *The Merchant of Venice* and a glass of wine at night. Had she been reading the book or sneaking the letter out every time? "I don't understand."

"You do." He slid Lucy's translation across the table to me. "You just don't know what to do with the information."

Not only had my mother hidden this from me, so had Elliot. All the years we'd worked together, all the chances he'd had to tell me what happened, he never did. "Were you with him when he died?"

Elliot let out a long breath. "I wish I could give you details, but even with the additional security I'm trying to get for you, that's where my story has to end."

Screw that!

"Your story *has to* end? Seriously? You drop this bomb on me and that's it?" Energy built up inside of me, pinging around, telling me to move. To get out of there. To do something other than sit still and face this.

"Sam." Elliot put up a hand, probably trying to calm me down.

I shoved back my chair and stalked across to the breakfast bar. "You throw everything I believed since I was five years old on its head and you're *sorry* you can't tell me more?"

He stood as well. "I met your mother a few times before that trip. We kept in touch over the years—I think it was because I was the only one she could really talk to about him, although I had to keep a lot of secrets from her. She never stopped loving him."

That's why Mom never remarried. Never even dated. Did she think Dad was coming home someday?

"I was still in Organized Crime when you started showing signs of wanting to join Art Crime, but as fate would have it, I'd switched a year before your mother brought up the internship idea. And she said—"

I stopped him with a raised finger. "So all this stuff about me and the FBI: The internship, getting me into Quantico early, plumb first assignment? What? All of it was to ease your guilty conscience?"

Elliott's lips tightened and he looked down at the original letter. "I don't know if you've ever heard this, but you're a lot like him. Stubborn, obstinate even, driven. I talked it over with your mother when she suggested the internship. I know what this life can do to people. The lies, the secrets, how hard it is on relationships. But she was right. It's where you belong. Just like the CIA was where your father belonged. And she wanted you to know."

My mother should have been the one to tell me. Not to lock up all her memories of Dad so tightly, I barely knew he existed. "National security is a really shitty reason to raise me believing my father abandoned me."

"But there it is." He shrugged. "How much have you told your family about helping me investigate the smuggling ring?"

I could have thrown the box of photos at Elliot. Tossed a chair over. Kicked him out. I hadn't told them anything about the smuggling ring. Fucking national security. "I can't tell my sister about this, can I?"

"Would it change anything in her life?" He was so goddamn calm. Like fucking always.

"That's not an answer." As much as I hated him for it, he was right. Cass had been older when Dad left. Unlike me, she had good memories of him. What would telling her the truth accomplish? Make her go through it all again? Put her back into therapy?

"Deb told me you took his leaving hard."

I needed to go for a run. That was it. That was what I needed. Get my workout clothes and go to the gym. Or maybe outside.

"She couldn't explain it to you when you were little."

What I really needed was Antonio. The thought of him closed my throat and the emotions threatened to spill over. I should have dropped everything and driven to Chicago the second he called. Skipped whatever work I had left and flown wherever the first plane leaving after the storm could take us.

"Once you were old enough to understand, I expect she was afraid it would be too much."

I swallowed hard and forced the words out. "You need to leave."

Elliot nodded and we walked to the door. "For what it's worth, she wanted to tell you the truth. And she was extremely proud of you for following your passion."

I pulled the door open, refusing to look at him.

He gripped my arm before he left. "I'm sorry if the story came too late."

CHAPTER 3

ANTONIO

I placed one hand on the door handle and took a long, deep breath to center myself. Every cell in my body wanted to break it down, run and scoop Samantha up in my arms, and never let her go again. The drive from Chicago had been spectacular—rain and storm aside—filled with blaring music, singing at the top of my lungs, and dreaming about my girlfriend.

And now I was home.

Sadly, we had a party to attend tonight at her sister's. There wouldn't be enough time for a romantic rendezvous before the party as originally planned, but there would be plenty of time afterward. Then I could pull out the ring I'd hidden in my bedside drawer in December and propose. It was almost time for the rest of my life to begin.

I pressed down on the handle and pushed the heavy door open. The subtle scent of lemon from the cleaners hung in the air, the recently buffed marble floors gleamed, and the sun shone through the glass wall across the great room from the foyer.

"Honey!" I called, biting back a laugh. "I'm home!"

There was no response.

Perhaps she was upstairs or in the bedroom and hadn't heard me.

Or perhaps...

Perhaps she was in the bedroom waiting for me. A shot of heat flew through me. It had only been three weeks since we'd last made love, but that was three weeks too many.

I dropped my duffel onto the bench and kicked off my shoes. Left my suit jacket on rather than slowing down more than necessary.

There was a woman in this apartment who was in desperate need of wooing.

"Bella? Do you have a surprise? Should I cover my—"

When I stepped onto the dark hardwood floor of the great room, she stood up from the couch in front of the blank television.

She neither moved nor spoke. A curious darkness hung around her, despite her white sweater and the gleam of the sun across her hair, which hung in long, loose waves, the way I liked it best.

The heat vanished, replaced by jittering nerves. Was she having doubts about living together? The reality of my return bringing all her stresses and worries about relationships to the forefront? *Time to charm her, Tony.* "This is the part where you're supposed to run to me, jump into my arms, kiss me all over, and tell me how happy you are that I'm home."

I took a step toward her, but there was no reaction beyond her chewing on her bottom lip. This usually meant she was hiding something she knew she should tell me.

"I bought you something at the airport this morning." I hooked a thumb over my shoulder, toward my duffel. "It's still in my bag, if you'd like it?"

Her fingers fidgeted across each other at her sides. That was the panic sign. Pins and needles were running through her hands.

"I know things are very different this time. Perhaps it was easy for you to be here while I was not, and now that I'm home, the commitment is scaring you again?"

Another step closer, and I spotted the red rims around her eyes. She'd been crying. A lot.

"Bella?" I hurried toward her, around the edge of the couch. A Bankers Box sat on the mismatched side table—the one she'd stolen from her hotel before Christmas—next to the coffee table, which was littered with tissues. "Is everything alright?"

Tears collected against her lids and she began shaking her head, the tears spilling down her cheeks.

I took her by the elbows, leaning down the few inches I stood taller than her to look her straight in the eyes. Everything had sounded fine when we were on the phone before I left Chicago. "Samantha, talk to me. What happened in the last four hours to cause this?"

Tears when we were separated, I was used to. When she told me she loved me, when she pushed back against something that held her heart from me, when she was utterly exhausted. But her silence was always the hardest part for me to deal with. Words were my currency, but actions were hers.

"You're late," she finally choked out. Her fingers dug into my forearms and she clamped her eyes shut. The desperation in her voice clawed at my heart.

"We talked about that when I was at the airport."

"I needed you."

"Then why didn't you call?"

"I didn't want to talk." Her chin quivered and she blinked furiously. "I just wanted you here."

This was bad. These were not words that came easily from her. I whispered, "I'm here. I don't know what I'm late for, but I'm not going anywhere."

"My mother lied." Her head tipped forward onto my shoulder, and I pulled her arms around me. "About everything."

I drew her closer, wrapping her in my embrace, while she shuddered through her sobs.

Her breath rattled and she pressed her face against my neck, muffling her voice. "Elliot came by with that stupid box. And Lucy translated the letter that was in the book."

Unsure which one to ask about—Elliot and the box or Lucy and the letter—I simply encouraged her to continue with whichever thing she needed to speak of. "And?"

"The letter was from my dad to my mom. It said he was leaving with Elliot." She pulled away enough that I could see her face. "He was a spy, Antonio. My father was in the CIA, and—"

I drew back further, certain I'd misheard her. "He was what?"

"I don't know what to do now." Her tears continued flowing freely, although from the pile of tissues on the table, she'd been doing it for quite a while. How long ago had Elliot left? "My whole life, I thought he abandoned us. Abandoned me. But it was a job."

How was I going to fix this? "This is a good thing, though, is it not? Your father left out of duty?"

One of her hands left my neck and she clenched it into a fist, knocking it against my chest. "But my mother lied to me. My whole life, I thought he just up and left. Cass always told me I was afraid of getting close to people, because I was afraid they'd leave, just like he did. Like so many other people did. I pushed you away because of it. I could have lost you before I even had you, and it was all a lie."

I caught her fist against me before she grew more frustrated and hit harder. "Does Cassandra know?"

She blinked rapidly, the tears slowing. "She would have told me, wouldn't she? Surely, at some point, she wouldn't have kept the secret from me. If she knew dad left us for something like that and got killed doing it, there's no way she would've encouraged me to join the FBI. She would've tried to talk me out of it."

"Wait." I tipped her chin up to look at me. "Your father died on that job? Mission? Whatever it was?"

She swallowed hard, and I could almost see the logic flickering in her brain, pushing the emotion aside. "He didn't actually say."

"Who didn't say?"

"Elliot."

Unlike usual, I was falling further and further behind in the conversation. "Elliot brought the box. How is he involved? Why was he in the letter?"

"They worked together." She pulled away from me, turning to take a few steps, rubbing her hands over her face. Frustrated Samantha was attempting to break free and replace Devastated Samantha. "Elliot was with the CIA back then. And he was with my father on whatever job he left for when I was five. He says it's too classified to give me any details beyond the fact that my dad didn't come home from the trip."

Elliot had been a near-constant presence in our relationship, always showing up, trying to pull her away from me and back into the FBI. I told her over and over if she wanted to go, I'd follow her. She'd told me about their past, from when she interned with him, but I'd never expected they went back so far.

Although she hadn't known that, either.

She spun back to face me, hands cradling her cheeks, shoulders down. "What am I supposed to do? What do I say to Cass when I see her tonight?"

I took one of her hands and pulled her down to the couch as I sat. Plucking a fresh tissue from the table, I dabbed at her cheeks. What else could I do to make this better? She had so many heartbreaks in her life and we'd been working through each of them. Instead, she was handed one more today. "Do you want to skip the party?"

"I've been in this stupid little town for eleven months, by her side for almost every treatment." She curled her legs up over my lap and pulled my arm around her shoulders. Bringing her sister home after chemo and carrying her upstairs to bed, helping Cassandra shave the last of her hair off, delivering food and groceries so her brother-in-law could focus on his wife. Samantha had told me stories after the worst of it was over, when she felt secure enough in saying things out loud, about how difficult the process had been. Both women had been through so much in their lives, but no matter what, they had each other. "I can hardly skip the party to celebrate her last radiation."

"Do you want to talk about the letter?" I brushed an errant tear away from my own eye.

"I hate talking." She let out a half chuckle. "And now I'm making you cry."

"Talking *is* my specialty, you know?" I kissed her salty cheek, resting my lips there until she relaxed a minuscule amount.

She lay a gentle hand on my chest, against the spot she'd hit. "Sadly, yes."

I plucked up her hand and pressed a kiss against her palm. Her citrusy scent, mingled with a hint of salty sea air—which was somehow not a perfume—overcame me. "Would you prefer a distraction? I'm also quite good at those."

She smiled. Finally. "That's also true."

"Papa called while I was on the drive and he wants me at the studio at 5:30 sharp."

"What time is it now?"

I flipped over my wrist to check my watch. "Just after five. It should only be him and Sofia, if that's alright with you? I told him we had somewhere else to be, but—"

She pushed back to sit straighter, so I could take in her stunning, pale green eyes. "You know, I think your father is exactly the kind of distraction I need."

"Alright." I patted her knees, but she didn't budge. "You need to get changed for Cassandra's party, and I need a quick shower."

A hint of the light sparkled in her eyes—the one I'd been expecting when I got home.

I put up a finger before she could force out any lewd jokes that she didn't really feel. "Don't go there, Ms. Caine. We have somewhere to be, which is more pressing."

She grabbed my finger and pulled my free arm around her waist, snuggling closer. "Give me five more minutes of this."

"If I have to," I said with a smirk she didn't see.

"Mom never talked about him, you know?" Samantha let out a soft sigh. "The letter was him apologizing for leaving again and that he'd promised not to. If that was the last thing she had from him, maybe she always hoped he'd come home."

I kissed the side of her head, squeezing her to me. "She knew he'd never abandon her, you, or your sister."

And I'll never abandon you, either, Samantha. I stroked a hand over her hair, attempting to comfort her, lending her whatever support and calm I could.

Part of me thought to prove myself by pulling out the engagement ring from its hiding space but it was hardly the right time, just before the party. The night was about Cassandra, not about us, not about stealing any thunder from her celebration. The proposal would wait until the right moment, after the party. We would be home alone and there would be nothing but our future together waiting for us.

Samantha took in one deep breath and sat bolt upright, swung her legs off my lap, and stood. She was clear of the pain, just like that. At least, she had it shoved so deep inside her I wouldn't see it again for at least an hour. "Let's go. I need that distraction."

CHAPTER 4

SAMANTHA

Antonio parked his car in front of the Ferraro's Fine Art Restoration and Conservation office and pointed at me with mock-gravity. It was the *Sit still so I can open your door* sign. Normally, I complained or rolled my eyes at the ridiculous show, but this time I stayed comfortable in the buttery-soft leather seat of his Maserati convertible and watched him move.

He'd chosen a gray herringbone blazer over navy pants and a matching dress shirt with the top three buttons undone. His gaze remained locked with mine as he rounded the front of the car, grinning at me the whole time.

I'd known I missed him, but sharing space with him really hit home how much. We *lived* together now. We were making a future together. And the moment Elliot gave me bad news this morning, all I wanted was him.

He opened my door with a flourish and held out a hand to help me out.

"Did I ever tell you this car is too low?" I slipped my hand into his, and he pulled me up into his arms. The studio's front wall was all glass—his father and sister were standing right there. I pushed back lightly. "No PDAs in front of your family."

He held tight, pressed a kiss to my cheek, and whispered into my ear. "Last chance to abandon all our plans and go home, so I can see what you're wearing under that tiny little skirt."

I leaned my torso away from him, hands against his chest, and frowned. "Knee-length is not tiny, and if you keep this up, I'll stay over at Cass's tonight and you'll have to wait until tomorrow."

Sofia hauled the door open. Her thick black hair was up in a twist, highlighting the high neck of her tight emerald dress. "Get in here already! My family's waiting for me at home."

Antonio chuckled and eased his arms away from me, holding them up in surrender. Without turning to see her, he replied, "You always spoil my fun."

"That's my job, little brother." She smiled at me and retreated into the office where Dom was laughing.

A white-washed brick building housed their family business, with a black sign reading *Ferraro's* in bold letters and *Fine Art Restoration and Conservation* underneath. It sat in the middle of Brenton's small Italian neighborhood, where decorative street signs hung from black lamp posts, proclaiming we were on Via Calabria, as Calabria Street would have been called in Italy. Through the floor-to-ceiling windows, Sofia's two-tiered reception desk and the black couches of the waiting area were visible. Behind the couches, another *Ferraro's* sign in metallic gold decorated a wall that separated the lobby from the studio space behind.

As we stepped inside, I inhaled deeply, taking in the familiar spicy scent of irises that Sofia kept on her desk and on the waiting area table. Over the speakers in the ceiling, Vivaldi, as always.

"My love!" Dominico was my height before my high heels, with salt and pepper hair and the broadest smile of anyone I'd ever known. He kissed my cheeks and grabbed Antonio next, giving him a sound hug. "My boy! I've missed you."

"It's good to see you, Papa." Antonio hugged his sister next. "And you, troublemaker."

They spoke for a few moments, teasing and laughing with each other, catching up after not seeing Antonio since New Year's. It was good to see him with his father and sister—they loved each other so much.

Why didn't I get to have that? If Dad said he was done, why go again? I'd never know the truth. Elliot was clear enough on that. Dad's job robbed my family of so much. A father. A husband.

What if I'd had him in my life? Would he have steered me away from the FBI? Or encouraged me not to leave after Mom's death? Been there to walk me down the aisle to Matt?

My throat tightened. *No crying. You've done enough of that today.*

I shouldn't have kicked Elliot out. He could have told me more about—

"Are you coming, bella?"

I studied the ceiling, the best way possible to keep the tears at bay. "What?"

"We're going to see the office upstairs?" Antonio's hand slid down my arm, his fingers intertwining with mine. The softness in his eyes told me he realized this wasn't as big of a distraction as I needed.

"Right." I nodded. "The space you're planning to lease out?"

Dom clapped his hands suddenly and laughed. "I may have changed my mind."

"It's a good thing you're home, Antonio. I have no control over this man." Sofia shot her gaze heavenward and rounded her desk. As she sat, she said, "I have a few things to finish before we lock up, so I'll join you in a few."

Dom waved for us to follow him around the wall, into the studio. Light shone through the windows in the back and the skylights high above. The open, industrial feel of the space had been magnified by the changes. The left side of the studio, where the kitchen and lab once sat, had been pushed back twenty-five feet. They were larger, with more equipment, and better prepared for additional staff.

The ceiling rose two stories, but above the lab and kitchen, there was now a second-floor space, separated from the studio by a railing, through which I could see some desks. An area at the back was walled off.

"A mezzanine?" Antonio looked at me, then to the two offices on the main floor at the front—his father's, then his.

I shrugged. "It was covered the last time I was in."

Dom chuckled and gestured as he walked. "The wood shop and labs are half again as large as they were, we've doubled the storage, upgraded the photography equipment, and we'll have room for three more—"

"Sì, Papa, all of that was in the plans we discussed at Christmas. What about upstairs? Why is it open to the studio?"

Ahead of us, beyond Antonio's office, a wide staircase climbed up the wall, from the front of the building toward the mysterious floor above. If Dom was renting the space, he wouldn't leave it open. This was part of the Ferraro's business now.

Near the base of the stairs was a separate exit to Via Calabria. An inner door, vestibule with security panel, and an outer door.

"Separate entrance, although visitors are still welcome to come through the main lobby," said Dom, as he flicked on frosted sconces lining the stairwell and climbed.

We followed behind him, the stairs wide enough for three abreast, following the wall behind the lab to the non-rental offices above.

At the top, he turned on more lights, showcasing a long office, far narrower than the space below, with three large white desks and low bookcases. Tall windows at the front looked out onto the road, and the walled off room at the back contained a meeting table.

Dom stopped at the center desk, where a white sheet was draped over something. He placed a hand on the sheet and smiled, excitement dancing in his eyes. "Are you ready?"

Antonio nodded. "Sì, of course."

With an overly dramatic flourish, Dominico swept the sheet off of the desk to reveal a black and gold sign similar to the company name outside and on the reception wall. It bore the Ferraro's name at the top, but instead of *Fine Art Restoration and Conservation* like the one downstairs, this one read *Fine Art Investigation*.

Investigation? They were opening an investigation company and—my stomach tightened—and Antonio hadn't told me?

"So? What do you think?" Dom clutched the sheet in front of him, his eyes flashing wide. "I wanted to keep the same style as the parent company, but it has its own flair."

Antonio squeezed my hand, bringing my attention to having almost let go of his.

"It's, um…" was all I could come up with. *Why didn't he tell me?*

"Is it too much?" asked Dom, focused on the sign. "I thought it would go nicely over the new outer door, where the shop entrance used to be. You saw I had a security panel added there for secure access. So the—"

"What is this?" asked Antonio.

"We talked about this at Christmas. It's our new investigation arm."

I blinked rapidly, my grip loosening on Antonio's hand and his tightening. He'd kept this from me since Christmas?

Dom looked at Antonio, then at me, and back again. "You didn't tell her?"

Exactly.

"Tell her about what? You said you were considering backing an investigation company, but… you told me not to tell her about that." Antonio ran his free hand through his hair. "You said not to say anything until you decided."

"Well, I've decided!" Dom smiled at us and back at the sign. "I talked it over with Andrea and he was quite excited, as well."

Another truth these two hid from me. First the Chagall, then Cristian's involvement with the fresco in Pompeii, not to mention that Dom's brother Giovanni was an antiquities smuggler.

Honesty and trust, right, Antonio? Not like my mother, who lied to me my whole life. Or like Elliot, who'd hidden so much from me. I'd told Antonio things I wasn't supposed to—things Elliot told me that weren't supposed to go past my ears. So why would he hide this from me?

"Papa, you didn't even tell me you were changing the architectural plans. We were supposed to be building—"

Dominico waved his hand through the air, brushing aside Antonio's comments. "I'm diversifying and improving the world at the same time. It's wonderful! You thought it was a good idea when we talked about it."

This was what I wanted to do with my life. Did he hide it in case I wanted to work here? He didn't want me around that much? Or didn't think I had enough experience?

"We talked for maybe—" Antonio turned to me and froze.

Maybe he didn't think I was capable enough. Or maybe he wanted to keep me working for Foster Mutual so I wouldn't leave town. My hands were shaking. I withdrew mine from his and folded my arms so he wouldn't know. "I think this is a wonderful idea, Dom. You can do a lot of good."

"Yes!" Dom threw the sheet onto the desk next to the sign and paced to the front of the office. "The view is surprisingly good. I thought about moving my office up here and keeping the investigators downstairs, but Sofia said it would be best to give them a separate area, plus I wouldn't have to be going up and down the stairs all day."

I started to follow him, but Antonio grabbed my waist to stop me.

He pulled me back to his chest and whispered, "You're upset by this?"

"Of course not," I said, attempting to follow Dom. *That's a lie, Sam.*

What was wrong with me? Why did I care? Companies like this existed everywhere.

"I didn't know," said Antonio. "He talks about a lot of wild ideas he never carries through with."

"So, Dom, have you finished hiring? Three desks, three employees?"

Dom stared out the front window. "One thing at a time. Space first, then people."

I stepped away from Antonio more forcefully. "What sorts of things will your investigators do?"

"We're asked to authenticate a lot of pieces, so I thought we'd move some of our catalogs and other research tools up here for that work. They can work in concert with the conservators." He turned, walking back to us, punctuating the story with broad strokes from his arms, his speech quickening. "Also tracking down lost pieces, investigating history other than for provenance purposes, maybe even getting involved in some theft cases, like the stolen piece that showed up at my brother's studio in Rome. We had some investigators track down how it got there, and who the original owner was, but I think if they specialized in art cases, they would have been a lot faster."

I nodded, leaning against the desk with my back to the sign. "Someone who understands how galleries, museums, collectors, and brokers work?"

"Yes!" Dom grabbed me by the forearms, shaking me slightly. "When you understand how a gallerist thinks or how acquisitions and auctions work, it's easier to spot the lies!"

Antonio had once told me that his father was passionate about art crimes—that he was almost as passionate as I was. This was the first time I'd seen that, and it made me like him even more.

It also tore the little hole in my heart wider. "Investigative skills will help."

Antonio sat on the desk next to me, placing an arm around my waist.

Dom let go of me. "I said to Antonio that I should use you to help with the hiring process. Maybe you know some people? You have friends in the police, and in other investigations, right?"

Did he know about my past with the FBI? I hazarded a glance at Antonio, which caused my stomach to tighten further, but he gave a slight shake of his head. Did he know what I was thinking about the FBI?

Or was that a sign he didn't want me involved in providing any advice? But why?

"Yeah, I can help you with that. I have some contacts who might be suitable candidates, if you can convince them to move here." I inclined my head toward the back of the office space. "You should have a separate lock on that room for secure case files. Otherwise, anyone in the Ferraro's office downstairs could just wander up here and gain access to sensitive information."

Dom swatted Antonio's shoulder. "I knew she could help!"

Help.

Sure.

The sound of stilettos clicking against the staircase caused us all to turn to the top of the stairs.

Sofia appeared, holding an envelope. She glowered at Dominico. "Who have you been talking to?"

Their father stifled a laugh. "Everyone, as usual. But what's this about specifically?"

"I was finishing dealing with today's mail and found this." She held the envelope out. "It's addressed to 'Ferraro's FAI' with the wrong street number."

"FAI?" said Antonio. "Fine Art Investigations?"

"We haven't hired anyone yet, Papa. How are we supposed to investigate anything without investigators?"

"This is fantastic!" Dom snatched the envelope from her. "It's proof of what a great idea this is. People trust our family with their art, so of course they trust us with their art investigations."

I had to fight tooth and nail with the FBI to get onto a single case, and here they were, just throwing the idea of starting an investigative branch into the wind, and they had work coming in.

Antonio shifted on the desk, eliminating the space I hadn't realized I'd made between us. "How does anyone know to send you mail about this?"

"Alright, I've talked to a few people." Dom's eyes lit up. His ever-present smile grew and he swatted at Antonio with the envelope. "Or possibly many people. I was so excited, I wanted lots of input!"

"Except from me," muttered Antonio. Maybe he really didn't know about it.

Sofia took the envelope and pulled out a sheaf of papers. "I don't know how amazing it is. I looked at it downstairs and it doesn't make any sense."

She handed the sheets to Dominico. They were thin, allowing some light to pass through and show at the edges when he leafed through them. Not quite white, more of a very pale cream color.

Antonio took one from his father. It sported a random series of lines and swirls, reminding me of the incoherence of my father's original letter. He held it up to the light. "Onionskin paper?"

Sofia nodded. "No words, no letter, no investigation. Just lines and scribbles and dots that mean nothing."

I stood, leaving Antonio's grasp, and approached Dom. "Can I see them?"

He handed me the stack and I took the one Antonio held, holding all of them up to the light. They were thin enough to see from one layer to the next, but the layers at the back became too faint to make out.

"I imagine you have to line them up just right to make something out of it," I said, shifting the first sheet to the right, rotating it, flipping it over.

Dominico stood next to me, looking up at the sheets as I manipulated one. "But why send this? If someone wanted us to investigate something, why not send us a letter with the details?"

It could have been a joke or a taunt. Or, it was—my inner detective did a cartwheel—something so secret it had to be hidden in a code. "Where did it come from?"

Sofia said, "There's no return address."

Antonio took the envelope from her. "But the postmark is New York."

"That's clue number one." I placed the sheets on the desk and folded the stack in thirds, like they'd been when Sofia pulled them from the envelope. Was there a clue in the way they'd been lined up originally?

"We have two choices," said Dom. "Either we file this away until after we've hired our investigators or—"

"No," said Antonio, before his father could finish. "I see the way you two are looking at Samantha."

I took the envelope from him and stuffed the sheets inside. The way they were looking at me was the same way I looked at myself. As an intelligent, capable woman who loved solving puzzles. Not as someone whose boyfriend's father was starting a company that was exactly the sort of thing she would have loved to do. "I still have to go to work on Monday and we haven't even chosen where we're vacationing yet."

Antonio's shoulders sagged, but he didn't argue. He always argued when I started a new investigation. Told me to hand things over to the authorities. Or to be careful. Or some other macho boyfriend line designed to make me feel...

I folded my arms.

His words were designed to make me feel safe.

But I didn't need a protector. I needed movement, investigations, mysteries. I needed to take down criminals who plundered the world's cultural heritage. "After Monday night, I promise I will hand it back to your father. I promise I won't cancel our trip just because a little mystery landed in my lap."

And if it took longer than Monday to figure out, I fully planned to stuff it into my purse and work on it while we were on vacation.

CHAPTER 5

ANTONIO

I eased my car door shut and placed a gentle hand on Samantha's thigh. "I didn't know, bella, I swear."

Her lips had remained tight from the moment Papa revealed the sign. They loosened briefly as she inspected the strange letter, but it was clear she was upset. She wanted to work with Elliot and the FBI, so long as she could do it from Brenton; so it was not that she wanted the job. Was she insulted I'd not asked her opinion about it? Or simply that she wanted to have been prepared with information for Papa when he asked about hiring?

"He told me at Christmas he was thinking about an investment in an investigation company and he thought you could provide some guidance." I ran my thumb along the soft jersey of her skirt and a muscle in her jaw flexed.

She turned her head slowly, staring at me and blinking, like she always did. "We should get going."

My heart gave one tremendous thud of defeat. "You don't want to discuss it?"

Her hand covered mine and gripped tight.

"Wait—I understand." My cell phone buzzed in my pocket and I pulled it out. Unknown number. I declined the call and dropped the phone into the cup holder. "You're comparing this to my father telling me to keep the Chagall a secret? You know there was no malice in this?"

"We're going to be late for Cass's party."

My phone rang again and I declined the call. I drew her hand to my heart and leaned closer, attempting to show her the honesty in my eyes. "This is not a pattern. He'd not yet decided and didn't want to get ahead of himself."

She gave me a weak smile, eyes casting down at our joined hands. "I know. I'm not even sure why—"

My phone rang and I snatched it, ready to hurl it out the window for the interruption. Unknown again. Who could be calling me so insistently with a masked number? Unless it was my Zio Giovanni or someone from that part of the family?

Samantha rolled her eyes and withdrew her hand from mine. "Someone obviously wants to talk to you."

"It's probably Cristian. I'll deal with it." I answered and snapped into the phone, "What?"

An unfamiliar voice responded in Italian, "Is this Dr. Antonio Ferraro?"

It could be a client, a contact I made in Napoli, or still someone from Giovanni's organization. But I had little patience for it now. "I'm sorry, but who is this?"

"You may not remember, but my name is Pasquale Fiori."

My chest constricted and I gripped Samantha's forearm too tightly. I mouthed, *Fiori*.

Her eyes grew wide and she hauled out her phone, unlocking it and typing furiously.

"We met last September outside of Sorrento. You and your girlfriend visited my boat, moored off Capri."

"Yes, of course," I said. "How could I forget your kindness?"

"Good, good. I'm in Detroit for a few days and I remembered you live in the area. I was hoping to see you again."

Samantha showed me her phone, with a note-taking app open. She'd typed, *What does he want?*

I held up a finger, shaking my head.

Fiori continued, "I know it's short notice, but are you free tonight?"

He sounded so calm, so friendly. It was the same as when we'd met him and his doctor had taken care of Samantha's injured ankle after a hike gone awry. Cristian had told me in January that they feared Fiori was after Samantha as revenge, since she'd brought the authorities down on several crimes he'd been involved with. The last we'd heard, she was safe.

Now here he was.

Samantha's face squirreled up, exaggerating the confused reaction I was having underneath the layer of panic.

If he was truly *after* her and wanted to hurt her, why call in advance?

"Tonight?" I asked, staring deliberately at her. "I'm heading over to a friend's house right now, so I can't—"

Samantha jabbed at her phone.

"Are you sure?" asked Fiori. "I was hoping you could bring your girlfriend. Samantha, yes?"

"Yes, it was—I mean, it is—I mean, we have dinner plans with family tonight. Detroit is too far a drive."

Samantha returned to typing and held up her phone. It read, *He wants to see us? Say yes!* She'd been so focused on getting to her sister's earlier, but Investigator Samantha was taking over from Devoted Sister Samantha.

"How about desserts and drinks after that?" said Fiori. Why was he so insistent? What did he truly want? Surely it was not simply to catch up with old acquaintances. "The Ferraro's business is in Brenton, yes? And you live there?"

Samantha gestured with her hands, with her chin, with her whole body.

I tipped the phone away from my ear slightly so she could hear better. "Tomorrow might be better?"

"No, no, tonight. Is there a place in Brenton you think I might enjoy?"

Samantha nodded vigorously and pointed from the phone to her and back again, as though she wished to speak with him. That was not about to happen. Heaven knew what she'd promise.

"Let me discuss it with Samantha. Do you have a number so I can call you back in fifteen minutes?"

"I'll call you back in twenty." Fiori hung up.

I sat still for a moment, while Samantha's eyebrows climbed progressively higher. Fiori—the man behind Samantha's ex appearing at Giovanni's, whose goon tried to shoot me in January, who my cousin feared wanted Samantha dead—he was nearby. On the very day I returned from Napoli.

"Antonio?" Samantha nudged me and I snapped to attention. "He wants to see you?"

"Us," I said. "He specifically mentioned you and was quite insistent it had to be tonight."

"Why?"

I pressed the phone against my chest, as though he were still listening. "I don't know. It can't be a coincidence that the only day he can see us is the same day I get home."

"I don't like this." Yet she tapped her fingers against her lips, one of so many tells I'd learned from her.

"You're excited. You're planning something."

"Are you kidding me?" Her eyes all but twinkled. "He's on our turf now."

I drew closer to her, dropping my voice. "You want to meet with him, don't you?"

She nodded, the corner of her lip curling into the first genuine smile I'd seen from her since I got home. "Of course! But it has to be somewhere public, and we really should call Elliot about this."

"Finally!" That was a miracle. "You're suggesting we call in backup as the first step?"

Her half-smile evolved into a smirk. "I guess you *can* teach an old dog new tricks."

"You're hardly an old dog, bella." My mood shifted with hers, the relief of seeing her happy almost enough to make me forget the topic. "He said dessert and drinks this evening. Are you willing to leave Cassandra's celebration early enough for that?"

"She told me to come and put in an appearance, but insisted we not stay long." The smile softened and a hint of tenderness appeared. "Said I was supposed to take you home and celebrate your return."

I lifted my phone and winked at her. "So, I'll tell him there's no chance we're seeing him tonight?"

She grabbed my wrist. "Don't you dare or there will be no celebration at all."

The untended fire smoldering deep in my core flared hotter. "You're playing dirty, Ms. Caine."

She leaned closer, so I caught a whiff of her heady scent. "Whatever it takes, Dr. Ferraro."

"I'll call The Train Station."

"Good luck!" She snorted a laugh. "Their waiting list is at least two months long."

"You doubt me?"

"Never."

"Good." The Train Station was the best restaurant within a two hours' drive, and she was right about their waiting list. However, she still had not learned how much weight my family's name carried around Brenton and so many other places. I opened the center console and withdrew earbuds to make the call while we drove to Cassandra's. "Do you think the chef's private dining room would work? It's on the second floor and overlooks the kitchen. It's completely closed off from the rest of the diners."

"There's no way you can—" She cut off when I cocked at eyebrow at her. "Okay, fine, let's assume you can pull that off. Is it maybe too private? Do you think he'd try something?"

I started the car and pulled out onto the road. "If by something you mean kill us, he'd either surprise us or he'd be the one making the reservations. He wouldn't let us control the location."

"Good point." She settled back in her seat. "Do you think there might be a link between him and the mysterious letter showing up at your office?"

"Bella, if I were not sitting in this car with you, I'd assume it's a coincidence. When was the letter mailed?"

She pulled the envelope from her handbag on her lap. "The stamp was canceled three days ago. He'd have no way of knowing if it would arrive yesterday or Monday or even a week from now."

"He could have had one of his people send it, coordinating with his visit?"

Samantha withdrew two folded sheets from the envelope, holding them up to the window and the sunshine. "I don't know. If he's approaching us in person, what purpose would this mystery letter serve?"

"One mystery at a time?"

She pressed the sheets against the glass, rotating one slowly, as though searching for how they lined up.

"You're not canceling our trip for this."

She lowered the sheets and mock-frowned at me. "Why would I ever do that? You know how much I love for you to spend way too much money on first class seats and even more on a ridiculously large suite at whatever hotel or resort we end up at?"

"You're cute when you're patronizing me." I pinched her leg and she elbowed my bicep. I swallowed the jolt of pain screaming up my arm—there was no way I'd let her know how much it still hurt all these months after being shot. "We do still have to decide where we're going."

"I thought we already did," she said, focused on the sheets again.

"No, you told me to choose. And I told you we were going to decide together."

What was her problem with making this choice? Was it because I was intending to pay for everything? She didn't want to take the time off work?

"How about a compromise? I'll present the list of ideas my travel agent sent me, and you can accept or decline."

"Mm-hmm."

"The top of the list is a brand new resort in Tahiti. We can lie around on the beach all day and—"

"Oh my god, no, that sounds like death."

"Lying on a beach in the tropics sounds like death?"

"The lying around part. That's what we did on our honeym..." She paused in moving the sheets around, something gnawing at her brain about her ex-husband.

"Every vacation you and I have shared was spontaneous. You showing up on my doorstep in Napoli last summer, agreeing to come to Roma with me while we were sitting in your truck outside the airport, and then your business trip to Boston, which I crashed."

"I'm not a good planner sometimes." This was true. Samantha was about movement and action. Quick decisions. No doubt, her issue was that traveling together was a commitment. And it reminded her of traveling with Matt to wherever they'd gone on their honeymoon, before she realized marrying him had been the wrong choice.

"How about this? I'll show you the details she sent me. I expect there would be very little lying on the beach and doing nothing. They have scuba diving, hikes up the mountain and through jungle..."

She lowered the sheets and looked at me. "Really?"

"Maybe a couple of trips by helicopter to nearby islands, and lots of rock climbing and swimming. And did I mention enormous beds?"

"Of course they do." She laughed, shaking her head. "You're incorrigible."

"And a world-class spa."

She feigned a frown.

"Fine." I gestured toward the envelope in her lap before she could disappear into this little mystery. "I can go to the spa and you can fiddle with those papers that I know you have no intention of returning to my father before we leave."

She held them up again. "Focus. Fiori's going to call soon and you still have favors to call in."

"And you have an FBI agent to contact." I dialed the restaurant, identified myself, and was put on hold to speak with the owner.

CHAPTER 6

SAMANTHA

Charming people was Antonio's superpower. Some quick words, a few laughs, and the chef's table was ours, exactly as he said. What I wouldn't give to be able to deal with people so easily.

And then the jerk smirked at me.

"I know, I know..." I paired my phone with Antonio's car instead of smacking him. "Never doubt you."

"I was hoping for 'You're always right,' but I'll accept that," he said with a wink.

Elliot answered after a couple of rings. "Does this mean you're still speaking to me?"

Dad's letter and the secrets came back. Clandestine Service. Elliot had known all along. Mom hiding things from me.

Shake it off, Sam.

"Antonio's with me and we have news. Big news." I took in the handsome face next to me and the amazing man who continued to follow every crazy lead I went on. "I told him about the letter."

"That was what I expected when I reminded you to lean on him."

Antonio's big hand ran along my thigh, a mark of comfort and support.

"Now, what's your news?"

Antonio spoke up. "Pasquale Fiori reached out to me. He's in the area and wants to meet with Samantha and me."

"Antonio lined up drinks this evening at a restaurant in town—The Train Station—with a private dining room."

"What time and how private?"

"Nine o'clock," said Antonio. "The chef's table is separated from the dining room by a glass wall and overlooks the kitchen. It's private, but not hidden."

Elliot hummed aloud. "That doesn't give me many options, other than to get someone into the restaurant in case something clearly illegal happens. We can't set up surveillance—"

"Fiori doesn't have any warrants anywhere?" I asked.

"None."

I gripped Antonio's hand. There was something about the two of us being in close proximity that sent the world careening out of control. "Elliot, I have a feeling your team should be ready. Things are going to start happening."

"It's about time," said Elliot. "Stay safe, you two."

CHAPTER 7

SAMANTHA

As I reached for the car door to get out at my sister's house, Antonio gripped my upper arm.

"Un momento."

I settled back in my seat, but the look on his face wasn't the *Let me open your door* one. It was far more serious.

"What secrets do I have to keep in there?"

There was a hint of accusation to it, pointing out that I shouldn't hide so many things from my family. I'd spent my entire life squashing as many emotions as I could, focused on my goals and my future. Antonio brought out a different side of me. One that shared, despite the discomfort.

But that didn't change how little I could tell my family about the things Antonio and I had gotten mixed up in over the last year.

"Just the ones you probably expect. Don't say anything about Fiori, either here or in Naples. Nothing about Giovanni, Vincenzo, or the entire side trip to Rome. As far as most of them know, we spent two weeks in Naples after New Year's."

"It's a good thing that trip was such a good one. Lots of fodder for discussion."

"And nothing about Boston or the secret letter we found in your book."

He nodded. "So, we can speak of Napoli, and that's about it?"

I let out a sigh. "Except for Nathan."

Antonio's jaw tightened. It was slight, but I caught it. "You told *him* everything?"

He and Nathan had been at odds since before Antonio and I started dating. From the get go, my big brother stand-in saw Antonio as little more than a member of a dangerous family who was caught up in the smuggling ring investigation. We'd cleared that up and all I wanted was for them to find peace.

"Not exactly." I'd tried to keep him in the dark, along with everyone else, but failed miserably. "He's one of the prosecutors working with the FBI on the smuggling case, so he reads Elliot's reports. The write-up about the whole debacle at your uncle's in January mentioned two confidential informants Elliot had used before. Nathan figured out it was us."

"Why didn't you tell me this before?"

I shrugged.

"Bella." He ran his gentle fingers along my jaw, tilting my face so I looked at him. "I'm not jealous of your relationship with him. You know this, sì?"

Part of me did, part of me still expected the jealous rage that caused him to fly home in December. Sometimes it seemed like Antonio had always been in my life, but when the doubts crept in, it was like a sign reading 'You've only known him for ten months' started flashing over his head. "I know."

"But it can be difficult for me to think of you confiding about things we've done together with someone who dislikes me."

I'd been relieved when Nathan confronted me a month after my return from Italy. It meant I could talk to someone about what happened. But then he started in with the overprotective big brother act, which rapidly changed my mind. "Or you just can't handle anyone not liking you?"

He leaned in and pressed a soft kiss to my lips. "It's a rare person who can resist me."

I rolled my eyes intentionally and opened my door. "C'mon, we've got places to go."

"Hey, now!" he called, getting out from the driver's seat. No doubt there'd be hell to pay for opening my own door.

At least two dozen cars lined either side of the road in front of Cass and Kevin's house, three more in the semi-circular driveway of their two-story brick and white vinyl colonial. The porch stretched the full width of the house and was draped with balloons and streamers, as though they were celebrating my niece's or nephew's birthday.

Music poured out from the house and a pair of women sat on a bench on the porch.

I held the car door, closing it as he hurried around to my side. "I am fully capable of—"

"It's not about capability." He snatched my hand and yanked my body flush against his, holding me so close I had to lean my torso back to see him clearly. "It's about being a gentleman."

"A gentleman would walk me up to the house, rather than making a scene."

"This is not a scene," he said, the corner of his mouth climbing slowly, causing half the energy in my body to collect between my thighs.

"Don't you dare." I pushed against his chest as one of his hands slid from my waist to my hip, despite how much I wanted him to continue. "I *will* knee you."

"You'll do no such thing." He chuckled low in his throat and lifted his errant hand so it threaded into my hair. He closed the distance I'd made, bringing his lips to my ear. "You want me as badly as I want you. I can feel your heat."

I took in a sharp breath. Damn him. At least his face was hidden behind mine from any prying eyes. "We still need to see Fiori at nine."

His teeth raked across the shell of my earlobe. "How wet are you?"

"Sam!" called one woman from the porch. "Who's your friend?"

"See?" I squirmed against him, not about to admit he was right. "A total scene."

"I have a theory," he said as he straightened, releasing his grip and taking me by the hand. "That the more I do things like that, the more accustomed you'll become to public displays of affection, and then I'll be able to kiss you anywhere, anytime I choose."

"Or I'll just become numb to it." Semi-free, I waved to the women. One of them worked with Cass and the other was a friend of hers from college. I couldn't remember either of their names.

Antonio and I rounded to the trunk and he retrieved the bottle of Macallan he'd brought—the same one in the purple and gold box that had won over my brother-in-law at Christmas. "I doubt that very much, amore."

· · · · ● · ● · · ·

"Prince Annonio!" squealed Emma, as she tore down the curved staircase into the foyer before the door had shut behind us. My almost four-year-old niece wore a sparkly purple dress with a tulle skirt and the FBI vest I'd given her for her last birthday. She'd fallen in love with Antonio at Christmas, when he'd drawn coloring pages of various princesses for her. "Come push me on my swing!"

"Of course, principessa." Antonio handed me the scotch and knelt in front of Emma. "Where is the evil knight?"

"In his room. Yelling at video games." She was referring to her older brother, Logan. Eleven now, and deeply into tween angst.

"Alright," he stage-whispered over the din of voices. He took her hand and stood to give me a peck on the cheek. "We must be silent so he does not hear all the fun we're having."

Warmth pooled in my chest as I watched them head down the hallway and into the kitchen on their way to the back door. He was always charming little girls. And big girls. Cass's friends on the front porch had both given him obvious once-overs. Not that I could blame them. He should have been a model instead of an art conservator.

Although he was amazing at conservation, so he'd made the right choice. Plus—I sighed—I never would have met him if he'd gone into modeling. *Except for that time in college, when you turned him down.*

"Emma went through—"

I startled, turning to see my sister next to me.

"—three dresses choosing that one. She said she was picking it out for the prince." Cass wore a simple white blouse and black pants, her wavy brown hair in her new trademark super-short bob. She handed me a glass of red wine. "And she's hoping he'll draw more coloring pages for her."

"He'd like that." To the left of the entry, a crowd clogged the living room. Sitting, standing, laughing. I glanced into the dining room, which was much the same, but with food covering the table. At the back, the *Waterlilies*-inspired painting Antonio had given them. A couple stood in front of it, pointing vaguely at the flowers in the bottom right.

Cass and I walked to the bright white kitchen, where it was no quieter than the foyer. Three more people sat around the breakfast table next to the open kitchen, another two in stools on the other side of the peninsula. The music was loud enough people could talk, but not easily. A muffled cheer erupted, no doubt from the man cave downstairs, where Kevin must have had a game on the giant television.

My sister pointed out the window over the sink, to the swing set where Antonio was pushing the little princess. Emma would be four in July. One year younger than I was when my father left. Antonio would be a better father than that. He'd be devoted. He'd never leave.

Dad hadn't wanted to leave us, either.

Was that what I was doing every time I pulled Antonio into some crazy adventure? Was I forcing him into doing something dangerous that would cause me to lose him, too?

He'd been shot on one of those adventures. Let alone the other times he'd been shot *at*. I swallowed hard. I didn't want to lose him. I wanted that future that was right in front of me. Little kid on a swing, watching him or her grow up.

"Wow." Cass nudged me.

Right. *Focus, Sam, you're at a party.* I took a slow sip of my wine. "Wow, what?"

She pursed her lips and looked pointedly at my wineglass. No—not my glass. At my left hand. "No new jewelry yet?"

"Don't be ridiculous." I switched hands, cursing the skirt, which didn't have pockets to shove my free hand into. "He only got home an hour ago."

Cass returned her gaze out the back. "Did you completely freak out when he got home and you realized you're now living with a man?"

Yes to the freak-out. No to Antonio being the reason. "Why have we never talked about Dad?"

She spluttered, covering her mouth to hold her wine in. "I always knew you were the queen of subject changes, but I was expecting one more like asking what was for dinner."

I shrugged.

"You pregnant?"

"Speaking of subject changes."

She reached for a napkin on the counter and patted her lips. "I had Mom for Logan's pregnancy, but she was gone for Emma's. Going through that without her…" She took another sip, and I half expected her to point out that I'd been on the road and hadn't come home for the birth. "That pregnancy had me thinking about missing both of our parents. You know, wondering what kind of grandparents they would've been with a little girl."

At least I'd have Cass if I ever went through that. "I've just got a lot going on that's making me reconsider some things."

She raised her glass toward the backyard, where Antonio was catching Emma at the bottom of the tiny slide. "Dad used to leave for business trips—at least, that's what Mom used to call them—a week or two at a time. They seemed really happy together when he was home. I was twelve when he left for good, so I mostly thought they were gross, but it was a real shocker to me. Mom put on the brave face, like she always did, and said we'd manage."

My mother had been such a strong woman. Had that been a good thing? How would my life have turned out if she'd opened up?

"Plus, we had to focus on you, especially after you ran away."

I didn't remember it, but apparently I'd taken a flashlight and provisions, intending to track my father down and bring him home. I was five. What was going through my head?

"Mom said you were just like him—out to save the world."

My heart lurched. That was practically what Elliot had said.

She shrugged. "We never really talked about him after that."

"You got angry over it a couple of times when you were in high school."

"Yeah." She smiled and waved absently to a woman who sat at the breakfast table with the others, sharing laughs and hugs all around. "Mostly because Mom never showed any emotion about it. I mean, your husband just up and leaves out of nowhere, when you've got two small kids and there's no reaction?"

Her gaze rose to the ceiling and she blinked quickly. Exactly what I did when I didn't want to cry. What if I told her the truth? Would it fix it? Make it worse?

I placed my hand on her back. "Sorry for bringing you down on your big night."

Cass's lips drew into a forced smile and she looked at me. "Don't apologize for talking—"

"Where's the Italian?" Nathan came around the corner, sporting a smile far less fake than Cass's. He wore a blue dress shirt which lit up his bright blue eyes.

I inclined my head toward the window.

He joined us in front of the sink and kissed my cheek. He'd likely been part of the ruckus in the basement. "Sucking up to my niece, is he?"

I frowned at him. "You know you're not actually her uncle, right? She just calls you that because she's polite?"

Nathan pinched my arm that wasn't holding the wineglass and I instinctively smacked his shoulder. He was my brother-in-law's best friend, who I'd met when I was twelve and he was in college with Cass. He and Kevin had claimed me as their little sister right off the bat.

I'd grown up with Cass and Mom. No other siblings, cousins, aunts, uncles, or grandparents. It had struck me as odd that we didn't have anyone else around. Had my father's job been the reason for that?

So much for the party providing a distraction.

"I should mingle," said Cass.

"It *is* your party." I clinked my glass with hers. "Lucy's here somewhere, right?"

"Last I heard, she was upstairs with Logan, yelling at video games." Cass chuckled and headed toward the living room.

Nathan leaned his back against the counter. "You look stressed. Wasn't Antonio coming home supposed to fix that?"

I feigned a glower. "Shouldn't you be downstairs watching whatever Kevin has going on the big screen?"

"A couple of women came down to the bar to pour themselves a glass of something and they were talking about the hot guy with the sexy car they'd never met who just went outside with Emma." He shrugged. "I figured that meant you were here."

I snorted. It must have been the ones from the porch. "I don't even get a mention anymore?"

"Not from the women." He folded his arms, looking way too serious for a party. "Now spill. What's going on?"

I ran a hand over my cheek and stared into my wineglass. I didn't want to tell him, but he'd find out, eventually. "Fiori contacted us."

He pushed off the counter, eyes flying as wide as I'd expected. "He what? Did you call—"

"Shh!"

The couple at the counter only glanced at us, and the ones at the breakfast table must not have heard him over the music.

I stepped closer to him and lowered my voice. "We called Elliot right away. He advised us to go, but to be careful. Antonio arranged for a private table at The Train Station."

Nathan's body went rigid, his fists clenching and eyes narrowing to slits as he shifted his gaze out the window toward Antonio.

"It's not his fault. Fiori wants to see both of us."

"What's he doing here?" Nathan ground out.

"You read Elliot's report from January, right?" I hadn't and could only guess at what was in it, but I assumed anything I'd told Elliot was in there. "It must have included that Giovanni thought Fiori was going to come after me because I've impeded too many of his illegal activities?"

Nathan's death-glare subsided. "It did. It also included the theory that Fiori wants to recruit Antonio."

"We have to find out what he's up to. Why did he reach out? Why today, when Antonio just got home? It's either that or we wait for him to show up when we're not ready for him."

"You may have trained with the FBI, but you have no practical experience. You're playing right into his hands."

I could have hit him. "Maybe you need to revisit a few of Elliot's reports. You figured out Antonio and I were his CIs in January in Rome. Before that, it was December, right here in Brenton. September in Naples. And before that, I've worked on other cases with him and—"

"Calm down, Sam." Nathan put his hands up. "I didn't mean it like that."

The glass door by the breakfast table slid open.

Emma giggled as she pulled her prince behind her and her eyes lit up when she saw me. She ran over to tell me, "Auntie Sammy! Prince Annonio is going to do more drawings for me!"

I placed my wineglass on the counter and leaned down to her level, putting on the best Favorite Auntie smile I could. "You're a very lucky girl."

Antonio knelt next to her. "You go to your playroom with the drawing table and I'll be right there. I'd like to talk to your Uncle Nathan for a moment. I promise I won't be long."

She nodded and tore out of the kitchen, thundering up the stairs with enough force we heard it over the music and chatter.

Antonio stretched out a hand. "It's been too long, Nathan."

"Good to see you." Nathan shook with Antonio, but his jaw remained tight. "Listen, if you two are going to see that monster, you need to prepare. Review everything he would know about you, so you don't slip up and give him any more fodder."

"I see you told him about our little chat with our friend, bella?" Antonio's arm slid around my waist, either as a mark of support or an unspoken message for Nathan to back off.

Which he didn't do. "She did and I'm worried you're getting in over your heads."

Both my hands rose to cover my face, scrubbing up and down. Antonio's flight delays. The FBI case. Dad's letter. Fiori's call. I needed to get away. Get out. Get lost.

I needed my motorcycle. To go for a long drive all by myself. Or to a cliff to climb.

Another cheer erupted from the basement, everyone's attention snapping toward the hallway where the stairs were.

No tears, Sam.

Nathan's brows drew down and he squeezed my arm. "What's going on? You're getting way more upset than—"

"Nothing." I stepped away from them. I wanted to tell Nathan and Cass the truth about Dad. But I couldn't. I shouldn't have come to the party so soon after finding out.

"Lucy's here somewhere. I want to see how her movie experience was."

Nathan nodded.

"Sì, and I have drawings to do."

They were both trying to support me. The logical side of my brain knew that, but it was a near-silent voice in my head, with all the other things crowding it out.

I waved a hand and left the kitchen, unsure which direction to take. Upstairs to find out if Lucy was with Logan, then I could join them yelling at the games? Maybe to the basement where I'd be ignored while the sports fans cheered for whatever was on? The front door was the most tempting option, but the evening was about my sister, not me.

All I needed was to kill a couple of hours.

Then Antonio and I would leave to face Pasquale Fiori.

Chapter 8

Antonio

The maître d' led Samantha and me through the white neoclas-sical-themed dining room. White walls, white coffered ceiling soaring high above us, and white half-walls covered in greenery. All bracketed by smooth Doric columns.

"Someday, you and I shall have an actual date here," I said, squeezing Samantha's hand.

"That would be nice. But we need to focus."

"No, you need to relax. Did you see Lucy?"

The corners of her lips turned down. "You lead the conversa-tion, since he called you, and I'll probe for details, as appropri-ate."

This was not her relaxing. I gestured to a painting as we passed it, a modern take on figures from Greek red-figure vase painting. "These are stunning, are they not?"

"No mention of Vincenzo, the Casa di Marte fresco, or me being anything more than an insurance adjuster."

"And the double-drum chandeliers," I said, pointing above us. "Perhaps I should have one of those installed in our bed-room."

She took a deep breath as we approached the stairs—eight feet wide, carpeted in a cream shade, and open to the restaurant on one side. Her breath released in a shuddering exhale. "This isn't at all how I expected our first night to go."

I paused mid-step, and she came to an abrupt halt. Placing one hand against her glorious cheek, I pressed my lips to her opposite one. I held my lips there, inhaling her scent, forcing her to slow down. "At least we're together again, amore."

Her lids fluttered closed and she curled her face into my hand, kissing my palm. No words came, but her free hand pressed against mine on her face.

There was no telling which of the day's events were wearing on her the most. Perhaps it was all of them, but clearly I'd failed in my attempt to distract her.

"It's been so boring without you," I said.

She chuckled and pulled my hand away. "Tell me we've got this."

"You've got this, Samantha Caine. I'm just here for my looks."

She snorted, some of the stress finally melting away. "And the comedic relief."

"I do what I can." I gestured up the stairs to where the maître d' waited. "Andiamo. We have dessert to enjoy."

Enjoy would be a stretch, but it was the best option to keep her feet moving. Normally, she was the one hauling me behind her into a dangerous situation. What would she do if I insisted we go home? Perhaps that would get her moving even faster, and with less thought—never a good thing.

The tables upstairs were far more private, some looking over a balcony to see the diners on the main floor, others tucked away in quiet alcoves. The chef's room stood at the end, a glass wall separating it from the dining area, another glass wall on the other side to overlook the kitchen.

Flanking the door, there was something rarely seen here: Two dark-haired, olive-skinned behemoths in perfectly tailored black suits.

Samantha squeezed my hand. She must have recognized the same one I did. She'd called him Bodyguard Two at first, but we later knew him as Jason. He'd been on the boat that rescued us from the grotto where Samantha injured her ankle and had flown the helicopter which delivered us to the mainland after the doctor saw her.

She didn't know, however, that he was the one who secured Fiori's theft of the fresco from my worksite in Pompeii, nor that he was undercover for my Zio Giovanni.

Inside the room, Pasquale Fiori stood at the kitchen wall, observing the movements of those preparing meals.

The maître d' opened the door and Fiori spun to see us, spreading his arms wide. In his mid-60s with gray hair, he had a surprisingly kind face for such a dangerous man.

"My friends," he said, approaching Samantha to kiss the air at her cheeks. "You're looking much healthier than the last time I saw you."

Samantha smiled and stepped aside. "Not needing crutches is a significant improvement."

"And Antonio." He took my right hand to shake, and patted my upper arm, hard enough it stung the spot where I'd been shot at New Year's. Intentional? Or simply friendly? "Thank you for meeting me on such short notice."

The maître d' pulled out a chair and offered it to Samantha, who sat at the table large enough for six. A short vase of white roses and hydrangea topped the white tablecloth, with two empty glasses at each of our seats. Once Fiori and I sat, we received dessert menus.

Fiori inclined his head toward a bottle of white wine on the table. "I hope you don't mind, but I chose a moscato to enjoy with the food."

"Grazie, that sounds wonderful," I said. My uncle believed Fiori had poisoned him two years ago. At least this bottle had been closed when we arrived.

The maître d' opened the bottle and poured for each of us, then addressed Fiori. "How long would you like before your server arrives?"

"Fifteen minutes."

The man nodded and left, closing the glass door behind him. The bodyguards stepped closer to each other, making it clear the door was not an option for anyone inside or outside of the room. It was as though the room had shrunk significantly.

The private room was decorated like the rest of the restaurant, all white with neoclassical Greek influences and smaller versions of the paintings on the walls. One pendant light lit the table, while two candles flickered on either side of the roses.

This would have been an exceptionally romantic place to bring Samantha.

Movement from the kitchen below interrupted the quiet ambiance, but no doubt it would fade into the background the longer we sat. Sì, a nice, quiet meal alone together. Perhaps tomorrow.

"I was surprised to get your call, Signore Fiori."

He raised an eyebrow at me. "Come now, we talked about this. It's Pasquale. Friends don't use titles."

"Of course," I said, nodding. "But still, Brenton is quite a distance from Capri."

"How was your project in Pompeii?"

"Excellent. I only just returned today."

"Really?" Fiori's menu tipped down slightly. "I thought you said you would only be in Italy until Christmas?"

"Sometimes plans change."

"Indeed." He gave a half-chuckle—as though catching me in a lie—and raised his glass. "To changes in plans."

Samantha lifted her wineglass, smiling politely.

None of this felt right. His overly familiar greetings. His bodyguards blocking the door.

But it was the way he'd slapped my injured arm, like he knew what had happened, and was threatening me. There was an ulterior motive here.

"What's this now?" Fiori stopped raising his glass before it touched his lips, reaching for Samantha's hand. "You've married? Should I call for champagne?"

"No, it's only a promise ring," Samantha said, far too quickly. "I do hear that a lot." She glanced at me, then at the ring, a genuine smile peeking through the investigator's mask.

Did she know I had the engagement ring hidden in my bedside drawer since I was home at Christmas? I'd told her the entire condo was as much hers as it was mine, except that one drawer. When I visited for her birthday in March, she promised we could open it when I got home for good.

But did she know? And how could I ask her after such a horrible day?

"I apologize for being rude, Pasquale, but the jet lag is getting the better of me." I suppressed a fake yawn. "You were quite insistent you see us tonight. Was there something you wished to discuss?"

"This is why I always liked you, Antonio." He knocked twice on the table—a move eerily similar to my uncle's commandments.

Jason entered the room and the remaining guard shifted so he was directly in front of the door. "Yes?"

Samantha uncrossed her legs, planting both feet firmly, as though she were ready for an attack. It was subtle, a small reminder of how she liked to point out she could take care of herself.

"The case," said Fiori.

Jason moved the candles and flowers, glasses, and cutlery. He then retrieved an oversized black case from behind Fiori's seat and placed it in the space he'd made. It was hard-sided and perhaps three feet by four.

Fiori turned it to himself and worked the dial lock. "I have a damaged painting I'd like you to repair for me."

Samantha straightened at the word 'painting.'

"I can give you the address of our company here in town and you can have it delivered."

"That's very kind." He paused with the lock. "However, I must insist. This is a personal piece—very high value—and I don't want it going through your father's shop."

Fiori had been behind a stolen painting at my Zio Andrea's shop last summer. And had paid someone to steal a fresco from the site where I worked in Pompeii. Giovanni claimed it was to get back at him for getting out of the smuggling business. Was this work more of the same?

He opened the case and swiveled it around to Samantha and me. At first glance, I would have suggested it was seventeenth century Dutch. Slightly over two feet wide and slightly under that high. Its focus was a woman dressed in red velvet and white satin, playing a lute, with her instructor standing beside her.

Samantha's foot tapped mine. Did she recognize it as a stolen piece?

"It's *The Music Study* by Gerard ter Borch." Fiori smiled at the painting. "She takes your breath away, doesn't she?"

I stood, leaning over top of it for a better look. There was a line across the instructor's face. A scratch? A corrected tear?

"It's very pretty," said Samantha, playing as though she were little more than arm candy. "Did you contact your insurance company?"

"Ms. Caine..." Fiori folded his menu and placed it on the table, clasping his hands together. So much for friends not using titles. "Please."

"Yes, Pasquale?" She fluttered her eyelashes, pretending to be unaware of his obvious knowledge that she was more than she seemed.

As his gaze shifted to me, his irritation eased. "I had another conservator repair some damage, and he did a poor job. I don't want to run that risk again."

I ran my finger along the work. "They didn't use a fill-in medium when they repaired it, so the cut is still visible. The two sides of the cut meet, and it's fine from ten feet away, but as soon as you get close, it's obvious."

"Exactly." Fiori leaned back, bringing his clasped hands to his chest. "My artwork is to be enjoyed close-up, especially a piece with such detail. It looks like someone taped the back of it together and threw paint at it to cover it up."

Tilting my head, I took in the way the light played over the repair, a shadow casting across the surface. It went straight through the instructor's nose, making it appear to have been broken. And his eye? Terrible.

"I refused to pay the other conservator the balance of his invoice, I was so offended. But this is what I get for trying to rush the job, instead of sending it to a company as professional as Ferraro's."

I sat down, pulling my chair closer to Samantha's. "Papa should have time to look at it, I think."

"No." Fiori's word was a simple commandment, clear he was unaccustomed to people declining his requests. "I want *you* to take care of it."

There had to be something else going on. His insistence made no sense. "Assuming a professional did the work, no matter the quality of the execution, I should be able to remove the varnish and touch-ups, then redo them. What happened to it? Knowing that will help me with the project."

Fiori reached over and closed the lid. "My ship hit a swell and my wife tripped, breaking a glass that cut through it."

The cut looked too clean for that to explain it. Even so, I nodded.

"How long do you think the repair will take?"

Samantha asked, "How long are you in town?"

"That depends." He picked up his wineglass and took a sip, giving no hint of what it depended on.

"Mi dispiace, but Samantha and I are planning to travel in a few days. We'll be gone at least two weeks, so I won't be able to work on it right away."

Fiori shook his head slightly. "I don't enjoy repeating myself, so let me try this: You owe me. And I'm calling in the favor. I want the painting fixed this week."

Owed him what? After his kindness when Samantha hurt her ankle, we'd called it even because I had another of his paintings repaired by my Zio Andrea. I left nothing on the table—I made sure of that.

Nervous energy jostled around inside my chest. Did he mean what happened in January? Was he saying I owed him because Giovanni had the Pompeiian fresco stolen back from him? Or because Samantha ruined Fiori's intended theft of one of Giovanni's paintings?

Was there any other reason I might have owed him? Or was this more a threat than a request?

"Honey..." Samantha laid a gentle hand on my forearm. The only time she ever used that term was when we were investigating as a signal for me to pay attention. She'd already decided I was taking this job, no matter how I felt about it. "We haven't booked the tickets yet. I'm sure you can work on this piece."

So much for Papa's mysterious letter being the thing to hold her back from our vacation.

"I mean, Pasquale was so kind and helpful when I hurt my ankle last year. It's the least we can do." She turned the fluttering eyelashes on me.

All it did was increase the speed of the nerves crashing around inside me. "Of course, bella. You know I can't say no to you."

"It's settled then." Fiori took a napkin from his lap, dropped it to the table, and stood. "I'll call you tomorrow to check in."

I rose, and Samantha followed my lead. "It's Friday now. I'll work on it over the weekend. How about you call on Sunday evening? That should give me enough time to provide a more accurate estimate."

"Until Sunday, then." Fiori handed me a slip of paper with three numbers. "The combination for the case." He nodded to Samantha, then he and Jason left.

Once Fiori and both of his bodyguards were out of sight, Samantha's arms wrapped around me from behind, and she rested her head against my shoulder. "I don't feel up to dessert. Do you?"

I placed my hands over hers and craned my head back to kiss her hair. This entire miserable day was almost over. "I'll pay for the wine, then let's go home, bella."

Once we got there, I'd fix everything. I would make the evening as perfect as it should have been for my return.

Chapter 9

Samantha

Antonio carried the big black case with Fiori's damaged painting in one hand and ushered me through the condo door with the other. I held the bottle of wine from The Train Station. How did his first day home go so off track? How could we have wound up in such a romantic private room in the restaurant and not want to spend any time there together?

I dropped onto the bench by the door, setting the bottle next to me.

"What do you think, bella?" Antonio kicked off his shoes and placed the case at the end of the bench.

I pulled off one of my shoes and rubbed at my foot. Work boots, running shoes, or barefoot were my preference, but none of those went with the skirt. "I think there's no way this thing is on the up and up, if he's refusing to even send the painting through the company."

He chuckled and sat next to me. "I meant about us being home together. Shall we head straight to sleep?"

"Sleep? Who can sleep with that thing so close?" I gestured to the case with my second shoe.

He frowned, a sexy crease forming between his brows. "I don't believe broken glass damaged it."

"What do you mean?"

He dragged both hands through his hair, clearly as frustrated as I was with our evening. "The damage was covered but not well, so I could see the two sides of the cut butted up perfectly. Glass wouldn't have been so precise—there would have been a jag or frayed edges. I expect the perfect match is why an inexperienced conservator might not think to fill the tiny gap in."

"Do you want to go look at it now? Get a feeling for the work you need to do?"

His broad hand landed on my thigh and he rubbed up and down slowly, staring at it. "How are you feeling? You were quite upset when I got home and we haven't had a chance to talk about it."

Yeah, that was going to make my night better. Start *talking* about Dad's letter. "I'm good. So far, the evening's been one distraction after another. I've barely even thought about the fact that my mother lied to me and that Elliot knew about it the whole time."

He pinched my leg lightly and chuckled when I smacked the hand with my shoe. "So you're *fine*, as always?"

I dropped the shoe and stood, darting a few steps away from him. In case my actions weren't clear enough, I waggled my eyebrows. "It's possible I need another distraction."

His concerned look vanished, replaced by the way he'd looked at me outside of Cass's house. "How big a distraction?"

"How big have you got?" I backed my way through the great room, while he stalked after me, staying out of arm's reach.

"I have one bigger than you may be able to handle."

A tremendous pulse flashed between my legs, the empty ache that accompanied his absence reminding me he was here and about to satisfy my need. I fluttered my eyelashes at him. "Oh do you now, Dr. Ferraro?"

He matched my pace into the hallway to the bedroom, his gaze lazily tracing to my toes and back up again. "You said we could open my bedside drawer when I was home for good?"

My foot caught on the edge of the rug by the bed. That was *not* the distraction I was expecting. "Maybe?"

"You don't sound sure." Antonio sped up, as did I, to maintain the distance between us, until I ran into the bed. He grabbed me, effortlessly throwing me onto the mattress. "I do have another rather large distraction I expect you've missed quite a lot."

I pushed up on my elbows, staring at him, my heart racing. The bedside table drawer. The day I arrived home from our visit in January, he'd told me not to open it. That he wanted to see my face when I looked inside. It was too early for an engagement, but he kept teasing about a future together, about flying to Vegas for a quick wedding.

The need to open the drawer and find out what was inside had gradually faded over the four months since then, replaced with a desire to open it and accept the ring.

But what if that wasn't it? What if it was an old photo of his former fiancée and he didn't want me to see it because it would make me doubt him? What if he was hiding some big financial secret, like he got all his money from illegal activities? Or what if...

He held out a hand. "Let's go out to the patio upstairs. I want to watch the stars with you."

I didn't reach for his hand. "You want what?"

"To watch the stars." He put his hand out again, insistent.

"Not the distraction I thought you meant."

He winked at me and pursed his full lips. "Let's use the hot tub."

"I didn't have it filled. It's been empty since you left."

"Are you certain?" The tilt of his head made it clear my answer should be no. He had cleaners in and out of the condo, people who delivered his groceries for him, and maintenance workers who'd manage the place while he was gone.

"You had them fill it up without telling me?"

He laughed, full of mischief, and waved his hand before wandering off to the oversized closet. "I'll get the towels."

I pushed up from the bed and followed him. "I'll get my bathing—"

"No." Spinning on his heel, he put up a hand to stop me. "I'll get the towels, you go upstairs and turn it on."

Was he serious?

Of course, he was serious.

"I am *not* skinny dipping in the middle of town."

"It's dark out and this is the tallest building in Brenton. No one will see us."

I was not considering this as an option. I wasn't. No way.

He shooed me toward the door and continued his walk into the closet. "Think of what a perfect distraction all your worry about being caught naked on my patio will be?"

I huffed out "Fine" and traipsed off through the hallway, past the niche where he stored his alcohol, past the linen closet and laundry room, and into the kitchen. I climbed the circular metal staircase to the studio and slowed, taking in the studio area, the dozens of paintings stacked against the walls, the ridiculous painting that he'd bought for me in Naples hanging by the desk I normally used when I worked from home.

At the far end of the room, I pushed open the door set into the glass wall which led outside. The patio was fifty feet long and thirty wide, decorated with potted trees which had been covered through the winter, several seating areas, a couple of outdoor fireplaces, and a built-in grill. It was too dark to see most of it, but I'd been out to roam around a few times on days when the sun was out. I'd even done yoga to the sunrise a few times, trying to center my brain in the idea of living in this giant condo.

Large stone tiles covered most of the space, warmer on my feet than I'd expected, with raised planting beds for flowers. A strong floral scent wafted on the cool breeze—had the staff already planted something while I was at work? It was early May. Was that early or late to plant things? By the all-glass wall of his studio, a pergola covered in grapevines protected the hot tub from wind and kept it in shade while the sun was up.

I lifted one side of the hot tub cover but didn't bother to turn it on. The damn thing was still empty. The universe didn't seem to think today was a day for distractions.

Antonio would not be impressed when he found that out.

With a sigh, I turned around, prepared to head back to the studio. But my eyes had adjusted to the light of the moon, and I could see the space more clearly.

Things were not like they normally were. The patio heaters were on—that's why my feet hadn't been so cold. I hadn't done that. So who did?

And flowers.

A dozen bouquets of roses, lilies, and others I couldn't name, sitting on the patio table next to the hot tub, on the tiles, by the base of one of the heaters.

Music—soft and romantic—began streaming through tiny speakers hidden in rocks or furniture or somewhere. Then lights flicked on. Tiny fairy lights woven into the pergola and around the trees nearby.

I rotated slowly, taking it all in. None of this had been here the last time I was outside.

My heart melted in my chest, and a stinging sensation pricked at my eyes.

When I spotted Antonio walking through the studio, I couldn't help but laugh. He set all this up. For me. A romantic skinny dip and probably mind-blowing sex to follow.

When he came outside, I was still laughing.

"It would appear we can't catch a break today," I said. "The hot tub's empty."

"I know." His hands were in his pockets.

Shit. No towels. The stinging fled my eyes, dropping into my stomach to swirl around uneasily. "And you don't have any towels."

"Very perceptive, Ms. Caine." He closed the distance between us and held out his hand, which I took this time. "I changed my mind. I think I'd like to dance with you instead."

"I'd like that," I whispered.

He spun me lazily and pulled me against him, folding our joined hands to his chest. I slid my free hand to his neck and he wrapped his around my waist. "Maybe some quiet time will help quiet your brain."

"Quiet and you don't go together very well."

"Sometimes they do." He scrunched up his face and scanned the area, as though searching for ideas. "Come to think of it, perhaps they don't."

I squeezed his hand and let my head fall against his neck. "Maybe we can try. Just this once."

He kissed the side of my head, his gentle thumb sweeping over my knuckles. "Did you notice the flowers?"

"Only after the lights were on."

He inhaled deeply. "Seriously? The lilies are quite strong."

"I thought it was something you pumped into the air up here."

"You did not."

I pulled back to look at him, biting down on my lip to hold back my laugh. "It's the sort of thing you'd do."

"Someday, bella, you'll spot the romantic gesture before it smacks you in the face."

"Maybe." I ran my fingers into the short hair at the nape of his neck, as soft as velvet.

"Don't you dare say you'll become numb to it."

I shrugged. "Just oblivious."

His teasing smile faded. "Your investigator's eye spends too much time looking for deception and not enough looking for joy."

"That's what you're for, isn't it?" Whether that was to look for the joy for me or to provide my joy, it was hard to tell. Probably both.

"As long as you need me for something."

A new song started—"Perfect Symphony" by Ed Sheeran—its deep notes invading my chest. "It's our song."

Antonio remained silent through the opening lines, his thumb continuing to sweep over my knuckles. "Are you ready for your distraction yet?"

Since the day I landed on his doorstep in Naples at the end of August, there hadn't been a single day when we didn't talk or text for at least a half hour. We'd shared each other's beds, lives, and adventures. He knew me better than anyone in my life.

But the way he looked at me in that moment sent my heart skittering through my chest. It joined with a kaleidoscope of butterflies and all the crazy energy pinging inside me, swirling so quickly I was going to be sick.

I was as nervous as the first time I danced with him.

It was ridiculous. That was our first real date and we lived together now.

But we danced to this same song that night.

The flowers. The lights. The music. Was this it? Was I crazy or would he really propose to me after only ten months?

I sucked in a deep breath and let it out slowly. "I'm not entirely sure if I'm ready or not."

"We've been on quite the adventure, you and I. I wanted to come home and just be with you. No crimes, no thieves, no danger. And yet—"

"Is reminding me of who we were just visiting your idea of a distraction?"

He kissed my nose, continuing without answering my question. "And yet, this evening reminds me of who you truly are. Not a woman who craves a quiet life."

The sick feeling increased, then spread up my throat, spewing words out like an anxious little schoolgirl. "Good thing I'm with a man who talks so much. Not very quiet when you're around."

"True." His lip curled into a smirk, which he bit back. "And I need you to focus on my words alone right now. Block out all the other little voices that continue chattering in your head."

"I don't have voices chattering in my head." What I did have was pins and needles in my fingers. Every cell of my body demanded I rub those fingers together to get the blood flowing again, but he'd recognize the reaction. I couldn't let him think this had me panicking. I just had to try to stop talking.

"I know you're undecided about your career and whether you want to settle in Brenton for good, but—"

"Elliot says—"

He released my waist and put a finger to my mouth. "Stop talking, woman."

I nipped at his finger, so he moved it. "That's not what Elliot says."

Antonio rolled his eyes. "I'm sure he has. At least ten times."

A giggle burst out of me and I clenched my hand around his neck. *Calm down, Sam.* What if this was all there was tonight? Just a ridiculously romantic dance and time with the love of my life? That would be enough. That would be easy.

So much easier than everything else.

"As I was trying to say..." He paused, cocking an eyebrow. "No interruptions this time?"

I made a show of clamping my lips and shaking my head.

"I told you I'd follow you anywhere and that's as true today as when I said it at Christmas. So don't worry about leaving me because I'll always be there. For the rest of my life, I want to be by your side. Whether that's here, in Boston, Napoli, London, wherever in the world you want. I want to be there."

The stinging in my eyes came back with a vengeance. The butterflies must have been trying to escape.

He wanted forever. With me.

Memories flashed through my head. Me all in white. Staring at myself in the mirror and trying to convince myself I was happy. Walking down the aisle to meet Matt in a big church, surrounded by hundreds of people out to see the Foster heir hitched to the former FBI agent who'd abandoned her career to be with him. The fairytale wedding of the year.

The awkward silence on our flight to Aruba. The hours Matt wanted to lie on the beach instead of diving, parasailing, or horseback riding. The sex that was never quite right and definitely rare. The—

As the tiny lights all around us reflected in Antonio's eyes, a new image crowded my weary imagination: Meeting Antonio in front of an altar. Pledging the rest of my life to him. The energy dancing around inside me grew stronger, like it was trying to claw its way out. And claw it did, until a smile burst free from my chest.

That wasn't right. It was supposed to be panic. Terror. Fear of making promises to someone else who'd leave me at the first sign of trouble.

Every time you're in trouble, he runs toward you, Sam.

The music shifted again, to a faster paced song, light and welcoming. When the lyrics started, it still sounded like Ed Sheeran, but I didn't know musicians as well as Antonio did. The singer went on about beautiful nights, the sky, and making changes.

Antonio stopped our dance and took a deep breath.

Oh shit, this is really it.

He blinked a few times and moistened his lips. Shy Antonio was making the rare appearance. Shy and nervous.

Breathe, Sam, breathe.

"Samantha..." He took a half-step back and whispered, "I don't want to be your boyfriend anymore."

My heart, the butterflies, and all the energy stopped at once, dropping like a lead weight.

He said we were going to open the drawer when he got home for good. I was sure it was an engagement ring. I should have known better. Everyone leaves. Everyone always leaves.

Stop, Sam. This is Antonio. He won't leave.

But unlike himself, he wasn't talking. He just stopped. What did that mean?

Chapter 10

Antonio

I knew this moment would come from the night we met as adults. I'd joked and teased her about eloping to Vegas, talked about children with her, spent time with her friends and family. But now that it was happening, my mouth was drier than the superb wine I'd sampled at Cassandra's party.

A tremor shook my hand like the day I introduced myself to her in college. *Stop being so nervous, you fool.*

When I asked Faith this same question all those years ago, she'd been the one to bring it up, asking me when it would happen.

But this? This time, it was right. It was the right woman. The one I was meant to be with, and everything I'd planned to say flew from my brain.

What if she said no?

What if it was too much, too suddenly?

What if finding out about her father changed things?

Get out of your head, Tony.

Samantha took a shaky step backward, letting go of me and bringing her hands to her chest. She rubbed the fingers of one hand together, hidden behind the other hand—the sign her nerves and panic were taking over.

You just told her you didn't want to be her boyfriend. The start of this song and that line were supposed to force you to keep talking.

I reached into my pocket, fumbling with the blue leather box that must have weighed a thousand pounds. As I lowered to one knee in front of her, I clutched onto a decade of dreams about Samantha Caine. The knowledge deep inside me that she was the one I belonged with.

Words tumbled out of my mouth, none of which were the ones I'd rehearsed the entire way home from Napoli. "We don't need to set a date, choose invitations, a dress, a venue, anything."

Her eyes grew slowly wider, and her nervous fingers stopped moving.

I creaked open the lid of the tiny box and took her left hand.

She was silent. She was going to say the ring was too big.

I should've planned it better. Shouldn't be asking this my first night back, after she found out about her father or after visiting Fiori. Shouldn't have called the staff to decorate the patio.

Samantha remained still, not coming closer, not saying anything.

Marone, that was the worst proposal in the history of humanity. "All I ask is that you consider saying you'll marry me. Someday. Anyday."

Nothing.

An ache spread out from my heart. I didn't have a backup plan. Hadn't truly considered she'd say no. What if it scared her off? What if her fears were so strong she'd leave rather than risk her heart? I swallowed, trying to clear the lump in my throat, and my words came out weak. "And if you're not ready yet, I can put this ring away and—"

She let out a half-laugh and the barest hint of a smile appeared. "You talk too much sometimes, you know that?"

If I waved this off as another tease—claimed the ring was only crystal—would she believe it? "Am I distracting you yet?"

Her smile grew and she nodded several times. "Yes."

My stomach clenched at the word. It was the one I wanted, but it hadn't come after the right question. "Yes to me distracting you or... to the other?"

She bit down on her lip, the smile growing wider than I'd ever seen. She slipped off her promise ring and moved it to a finger on her right hand, then held out her left. Another giggle burst out of her—two in the space of an hour had to be a record for her. "Yes, I'll not be your girlfriend anymore."

"Yes?" I choked out, trembling as I withdrew the engagement ring from the box to place on her finger. "Really yes?"

She stretched her hand, shaking as much as I was. "Just don't ever do that to me again."

After I'd slid the ring onto her finger, I stood and threw my arms around her, squeezing my eyes shut and burying my face in her hair. "Maybe you've never noticed I mask my nerves with humor."

"Yeah..." She sniffled and pulled back to look at me, tears collecting against her lids. "I've noticed that."

I brushed away some loose strands of her hair, which had fallen across her face, tucking them behind her ear. "You have no idea how happy you've made me."

Her jaw flexed and she began worrying her lip, gaze roaming over my face. What was it now? Doubts? Worries? Memories overcoming her? Hopefully the silence was dreams of our future, plans for our wedding.

"And I'm serious, we don't need to set a—"

"Have I ever told you how handsome you are?" She brushed her hand across my cheek, then under my jaw.

"Will you still say that when I'm old and wrinkled?"

Her hand continued moving, into my hair, to the back of my neck, down my shoulder and against my heart. She nudged me backward, toward one of the patio sofas, until I sat. "Where did your father's gray start?"

Strange turn of conversation. "At his sideburns."

She nodded and lifted her skirt enough that she could kneel on the couch, straddling me. Both of her hands sank into my hair at the sides, her nails scratching lightly over my sideburns. "I want to watch your hair turn gray."

My hands ran across her bare knees, up her thighs under her skirt, until they found her strong ass and the surprisingly un-Samantha lacy underwear she'd chosen. "I want to watch your laugh lines grow."

One of her fingers traced my hairline and paused at my right temple. "You've let your hair grow a little longer, so there's more curl than in August. And you have a new scar by your chin. Here." She ran her touch over the spot.

"Minor incident at the Casa just after our trip to Boston."

She nodded, continuing to explore my face. "When we first met, you smirked all the time, but now you smile more."

"You used to scowl all the time."

She swatted my chest, mock-scowling at me. As her hand trailed down my right arm, she grew even more serious. "And you have a scar here." She gripped my bicep, and a single tear escaped her eye. "From where you risked your life to save mine."

'I was saving myself,' was the first thing that came into my brain to make her laugh. But I held it inside. That was hardly what the moment called for.

"I want to keep watching all these changes." She swiped a hand across her eyes. "I don't want to lose it because of a stupid job."

So much for the distraction. She was still thinking of her father's letter.

She sniffled and undid a button on my shirt, sliding her hand across the skin of my chest. "That was the secret in your bedside table?"

The knot twisting in my stomach re-tied itself. It had been fun and teasing when I tipped her off that it was there, and yet in this moment, I didn't want to confess I'd bought it so early in our relationship.

Why the doubts right now? She said yes. She looked happy.

"Sì, it was." I pushed my fingers under the edge of her panties. "That was my last secret."

"You really want to marry me." Her words came out in a whisper, like she was marveling over this, not asking for confirmation.

I shrugged one shoulder. "Well, I asked. And I gave you a ring."

Part of me hoped that an engagement would be enough that the staring and blinking would come to an end, but sadly, that hope fled as she stared down at me. Even after all her words about watching me age.

"Do you like the ring? It's not too big, is it?"

"Of course it's too big. But it wouldn't be your ring if it was smaller."

Time for the humor again. "I could return it for one that's bigger and make it even more me?"

Instead of responding with words, she lowered her mouth to mine and raked her fingers into my hair. Her chest swelled against me, a low moan emanating from deep inside her.

My hands dug into her hips as she ground against me. I moved her panties aside to find her sex. Her heat. Her wet need for me.

She broke from the kiss enough to whisper, "Tallest building in Brenton, right?"

"It is."

"No one can see us up here?" One of her hands left my hair and reached between us, undoing my belt.

Need, hot and urgent, flooded my groin and I hardened underneath her. My thumb stroked her clit while my fingers teased at her entrance. "Not unless you're right by the edge."

She undid the button on my pants. Squirmed against my hand as she slid my zipper down. Eased my underwear out of the way until she could wrap a hand around my shaft. "Today has been a wild ride."

I slipped one finger inside of her, reveling in her tightness. Of the sight of her eyes fluttering closed and her chest heaving as I explored inside her. "I think it's about to get much wilder."

"Don't say that." She stroked my cock, her stunning green eyes re-opening to lock on mine. "Tonight, I want quiet. I want us. Nothing else in the world."

I let out a low groan. This was more of what I'd hoped for on my return. It had only been three weeks since we'd last made love, but my body reacted like it had been months. "I need you."

She lifted on her knees and I withdrew my fingers from inside her, holding her lacy fabric out of the way. When she lowered herself down onto me, her walls stretching around me, my heart burst into pieces.

The small circles she made with her hips had me near to the edge in minutes. But more than that, it was the way her gaze stayed on mine. She didn't lean in to kiss me, didn't rip open my shirt, just watched me as she barely moved.

How lucky was I to have this incredible creature as mine? My fiancée. The woman I'd marry and grow old with. Have a family with. "I love you."

"You've changed everything, Antonio." She sucked in a quick breath and rose before descending slowly. So slowly. Excruciatingly slowly. "When I knew what was in Dad's letter, all I wanted was you."

My hips rose, needing more of her. Needing all of her. I slid her blouse out of her skirt, undoing buttons as she undid mine. Once it was open, I hauled her bra out of the way and took one nipple inside my mouth, sucking and lapping at it. She gasped, reaching for the back of the sofa with one hand, pressing my head against her chest with the other.

Our speed increased, her hips falling harder against me, and I looked up at her to watch her pleasure. She was magnificent, the way her small breasts bounced with each thrust, and the loose strands from her bun danced in the tiny lights.

I was about to explode. With a groan, I said, "I'm not sure how much of this I can take."

She stopped, breathing so hard and deep I could feel each one inside of her. Her hands clamped on the sides of my face, and she squeezed her eyes shut, wrinkling her nose. "I love you more than I've loved anyone else my entire life. You're everything to me. No matter what happens, never forget that."

There were too many thoughts still in her head. Too much thinking about her father, her parents, her past, and about Corsican smugglers. Time to fix that.

I wrapped my arm around her waist and pivoted us so quickly she yelped. We landed with her back on the sofa and me between her legs. "Enough words, chatterbox."

Her eyes flared open as I thrust inside her. Hard. Fast. Needing to consume every inch of her. Purging her brain of all her doubts and worries.

My climax built in the fiery heat, but I held back until her back bowed and she gasped my name.

"Antonio! Oh my god, Antonio!"

"Let go," I grunted, lowing my mouth to her ear to lick the edge, the way she liked.

"Oh god," she breathed. "Yes, please. Yes!"

I pumped furiously and she clutched at my shirt, pulling me closer as her hips lifted to meet me. I grabbed under her ass, angling her so I hit just the right spot and she bucked.

Her neck stretched and I pushed up on one arm to watch the orgasm wrack her body. All her muscles contracted, including the tiny ones surrounding my cock, and my release followed hers.

I poured myself into her, the greatest relief of my life. She wouldn't leave me. No. Instead, she would marry me and be by my side forever. I collapsed against her, putting some weight on my arm to not crush her.

We remained like that for what felt like an hour, still connected, simply breathing together. I let one hand fall to her chest, over her heart, which beat even faster than mine.

"Ooh, wow," she whispered after a few minutes had passed. "Engaged sex is pretty good."

I spluttered a laugh and pushed up to look at her. "Distracted yet?"

One of her arms had fallen across her eyes. "Pretty shitty distraction, if you keep reminding me of it."

"But if I do, perhaps you'll eventually deal with it."

"Don't wanna deal with it."

I lifted her arm to peek underneath.

"You knew I was going to say yes, didn't you?"

"Of course. Why would you ever say no to me?"

She snorted. "I'm pretty sure that's all I originally said to you."

"And now here we are, making love on our patio. Who would have thought that would ever happen?"

Her face tightened. "Promise me you'll never leave?"

I leaned in to press a kiss to her cheek. "I'm not your father. I'd chase you to the end of the earth if you ever left me."

More tears threatened at the corners of her eyes. "I'd do the same for you."

"Hopefully, it never comes to that."

Chapter 11

Samantha

The next morning, I sat on the floor in Antonio's studio, paintings and easels shoved against the walls, the standing safe open wide. Hundreds of sheets of paper surrounded me. Photos of paintings, of logbooks, of scribbled notes from Elliot's box of mysteries.

My priority was to review every painting recorded in the box. Study them. Learn the dimensions, the colors, the flow. Who was it by, if known? What style? Dates and names didn't imprint as soundly in my brain as the images, but I reviewed those, as well.

Behind me, the two items I wanted to focus on. I had a timer set on my watch for twenty-five minutes, and after staring at information from the pawnshop for that amount of time, I allowed myself five minutes with the mysterious onionskins sent to Ferrero's Fine Art Investigations. Five minutes of twisting sheets this way and that, holding them up to the light, trying to find an angle that made sense.

Then I'd go back to the pawnshop details, because the other item—my dad's letter—shouldn't have received any time. But it called to me from where I'd left it on the desk. Every time I turned around to look at the mysterious sheets, the looping code that Dad sent to Mom stared back at me.

I should have put it away somewhere secure and never looked at it again. I didn't even have Lucy's translation with me. What good was reading and re-reading it, now that I knew what the words were?

I'm sorry I have to leave again.

For twenty-six years, I thought he'd abandoned us. Thought Cass and I weren't enough to keep him around. The logical part of my brain recognized that belief caused most of my relationship fears—if my dad wouldn't stay around, why would I expect anyone else to? But that was ridiculous. Lots of people came from homes like that and turned out fine.

The fact was, I was different. I'd always been different.

I walked to the desk to pick up Dad's letter, smoothing my fingers over the old ink, which had barely faded after all these years. Being hidden inside the lining of the Shakespeare book must have protected it.

Mom had included the book in her will, insisting we never sell it. Did she plan to tell us about it someday? Was it supposed to be that same someday that she wanted Elliot to tell me the truth?

The day she—

I squeezed my eyes shut and drew in a deep breath. *It's okay, Sam. It's been eight years. You're alright.*

I opened my eyes and my new ring flashed in the bright studio lights, all the colors of the rainbow trapped inside the little—huge—piece of compressed carbon. It had to be at least two carats. A single round diamond on a platinum band channel-set with smaller diamonds. It was gigantic, yet somehow simple.

Fiancée.

Engaged.

Mrs. Samantha Ferraro? Caine-Ferraro? Stick with Caine?

For how many times he'd teased about marrying me, how many times I'd stared at his bedside table while he was gone, sure there was a ring inside, I hadn't decided. When I wasn't sure I wanted him to ask, I refrained from thinking about it because thinking would make it happen. And once I was sure I *did* want him to ask, thinking about it would jinx it and ensure it never did.

When I married Matt, I took Foster as my last name. Logistically, changing it and then changing it back to Caine a year later was a major hassle that I swore I'd never go through again. Maybe I could do it one more time, but I didn't want to more than that. Driver's license, insurance, passport, bills, voter registration, bank accounts...

All the energy drained out of me just thinking about it.

But when I married Matt, I knew it wasn't right before I brought it up. How many times had I told myself it was what I wanted, never believing myself?

There was something to be said for how much a stubborn person could accomplish when they set their mind to it. Whether it was the right choice or not.

A door closed downstairs, startling me. Antonio's deep voice carried up the staircase, singing some tune I didn't recognize, causing a smile so big I had to bite down on my bottom lip to contain it. My fiancé was home.

Fiancé.

"Come and get it!" After all the groceries he'd had delivered, it was silly that he'd gone out to get breakfast. Especially since we were supposed to be leaving town in a few days. He insisted it was another surprise, which meant he was probably headed to Russo's bakery, and there was no way I would turn that down.

"Bring it up here!" If we sat at the dining table to eat, he'd waggle his eyebrows at me, and we'd end up in bed. As appetizing as that sounded, I was getting into the zone and didn't want to pause the research yet.

Plus, Antonio needed to get to work on Fiori's painting. He joined me upstairs with a white box tied with a string.

"Is that a Russo's cornetto for me?"

His brow furrowed, that adorable crease deepening between his brows. "It looks like a crop circle."

I frowned at him, then at my work. "Except for the complete absence of crops."

"Sì, but paper circle does not have the same ring to it." He snatched my left hand and brought it to his lips. "Speaking of rings..."

"No, I haven't changed my mind."

He yanked me into his arms, beaming.

I narrowed my eyes playfully. "Yet."

"What is all this?" he asked, gesturing to the stacks.

"The stuff Elliot brought me. It has to stay in a secure location, so I'll have to lock it back up if we're going to leave. It was easier to spread it out here than lug it all downstairs, then lug it back up again."

He hummed in ascent as he let go of me to open the box and presented me with my choice of two sugar-dusted cornetti. "Lemon or chocolate hazelnut?"

"You have to ask?"

He grinned and pointed to one of them for me. "Can you tell me about the papers? I see paintings and invoices..."

I plucked my cornetto from the box and used it to point as I spoke. "The first stack is purchase orders, intake forms, sales slips, and inventories from pre-2010, then stacks in five-year increments as they got busier. The last two stacks are photos, in no particular order. That's where I'm focused right now."

"Best if you catalog them away in your remarkable brain first?"

I nudged him, heat climbing up my cheeks. My hair was in a messy bun, so I had nowhere to hide the blush I knew was there. "I know it's silly, but—"

"It's not in the least. It's astounding."

"Anyway..." I bit into the cornetto. There was more chocolate hazelnut filling than I expected, and I had to toss my head back to catch it before it dribbled down my shirt. I covered my mouth and continued. "If I commit them all to memory, it should speed up my review of the other paperwork and searching for links or connections."

"And this?" He pointed to the onionskin sheets. "You're looking into this for my father?"

"It's an interesting mystery. But I haven't gotten anywhere with it." I knelt to retrieve two thin papers, holding them up to the skylights.

"You know there's a light table over there?" He pointed to a table by the desk, with three stretched canvasses on top of it.

"How could I have missed it?" I swatted him with the sheets. "This place is a disaster."

He patted my ass as I walked toward the table. "You told me you loved it!"

"I do, except when it's hiding exactly the tool I need for my job."

"You'll have to give me more advanced warning the next time you plan on taking over the place when I'm not even living in the country."

My hands settled on my hips, the feigned irritation slipping as he moved each canvas to the stacks along the wall. All three paintings were of the night sky. One black with specks of stars crowding the canvas, another with the setting sun on the horizon as a dark sea swallowed it, and the third was all sharp edges and post-modern concepts in blacks and whites. "Good god, you are so talented."

He paused, staring at the paintings lining the walls. "I should probably do a purge sometime soon."

"What does *purge* mean in this instance? Please tell me you don't burn them?"

"No, no," he chuckled. "I give them away. Some as gifts, lots to the children's hospital—I have some fairy tale inspired ones in the back and maybe I'll give one or two to Emma—and others I donate to charities."

Warmth filled my belly. I knew he was a good man. Knew he and his father donated to the children's hospital but didn't know this.

My fiancé was a good man.

"You're staring, bella," he said, rolling his head toward me.

I swallowed hard. Maybe Mrs. Samantha Ferraro. "How do you turn this table on?"

He chuckled and returned to my side, flipping a switch that lit up the table. It was four feet by six with a simple, but sturdy-looking metal frame and two bins underneath. A white light lit the entire surface.

"What do you use this for?" I asked as I returned to pick up the rest of the onionskin sheets.

"Lots of things. Drafting, inspecting photos, sometimes I use it with a damaged canvas to help spot weaker areas that aren't ripped yet but may soon. I've even done some animation—flip books for Sofia's boys when they were little." He lined the eight sheets up, four per row. His elegant fingers with the black promise ring he still wore, the bespoke black matte watch Mario had surprised him with as a project-completion gift, the veins running up his forearms to where he'd pushed up the sleeves of his deep burgundy Henley.

Apparently, I didn't need to go downstairs for him to distract me. My thighs clenched just watching him organize pieces of paper.

I dropped the cornetto in the white box, licked the filling off my fingers and joined him, analyzing the set with fresh eyes. "The writing is slightly different colors."

"Mm-hmm."

"These marks here." I pointed at a group of four dots near the corner of one sheet. They were so pale, I hadn't seen them until they were on the light table. I rolled my shoulders and stretched my back. Leaning over piles of documents on the floor wasn't the wisest choice I'd made.

The desk was covered with a computer, two monitors, and other desk paraphernalia, so that hadn't been an option. Maybe I should have put the piles on the lab bench against the back wall. At least its equipment was stacked neatly on shelves.

Antonio stepped behind me and dug his powerful hands into my shoulders. "You're carrying so much stress in here."

"It's been a long four months."

"Only one day of work left before vacation. Then you'll have no choice but to relax."

Except we still had Fiori's painting to contend with. Plus, I wanted to work with the onionskins. My inner detective was doing so many cartwheels, I could barely focus on one.

"You know..." His hands loosened for a moment, hesitation coloring his voice. "We could always suggest to Papa that he hire you. You know, keep it in the..."

I stiffened and he stopped. Family. He was going to say family. If I had to be honest with myself—which I didn't like doing—it *had* hurt that Antonio didn't tell me about Dom's plans. Hurt they hadn't asked me to be some part of the hiring, at least.

But when Antonio said it out loud, it felt like more of a... a what? A commitment? Hell, I was engaged to the man. What more commitment to the Ferraro family could there be?

Would I enjoy working there? Was I qualified?

Should I keep Caine for professional services?

Who would I end up working for? At least if I was working with the FBI, I knew Elliot would be sure he was my contact for everything. I respected my co-workers at Foster, but I'd worked with enough jerks while I was on the road as an independent adjuster to know I wouldn't tolerate a bad boss.

Antonio pressed against me from the back, wrapping his arms around my waist. "You don't have to decide anything right now. Don't stress."

I sank against his hard body, his heart beating against my back, his warm breath on my neck, his overwhelming presence behind me. His hardening cock pressed against my ass. "You're making it very hard for me to focus."

He blew gently across my ear. "That may have been part of my plan."

"I can't leave the FBI files out." One of my hands crept behind me to caress the side of his hip. "I signed a confidentiality agreement."

"No one will come into the condo while we're here. Especially not if we're in bed." He slid one hand down between my legs.

"I'd almost forgotten what it was like to have you here in person."

"I suspect the last eight months have—"

Eight.

He kept talking, but I didn't hear any of it.

Holy shit.

Eight!

My hands landed on the light table, searching. The sheet at the bottom left had the dots near the middle—eight of them. The sheet at the top left had seven dots in its corner.

"It's like a die." I pointed at another. "Six." And another. "Five."

Antonio rounded to my side. "Seriously?"

"Yes! Seriously!" I shuffled the pages, lining the seven and eight sheets up so the die markers were on top of each other. Then I added the six and five. As the numbers got lower, it was harder to—

"No, I mean seriously? We were having a moment."

My head jerked in his direction. Shit.

"You always do this."

I needed to line them up. I'd figured out the code. It would put the pieces together. I glanced at the light table, then at Antonio, and back again.

What would I do if I lined them up and figured out the mysterious letter? Would it tell me everything I needed to know? Or would there be more research? More digging?

Antonio folded his arms. He was clearly doing his best not to lecture me or complain. But he was right—I did always do this.

The spike of adrenaline coursing through me tiptoed sheepishly back into my brain. Why was a random person's mysterious letter more important than my fiancé?

Be honest, Sam. And calm the fuck down.

It wasn't.

"That shirt looks really nice on you," I said.

His face scrunched up. "Scusi?"

"For better or for worse, Antonio, this is me. I'm not sure it's something I can change."

"I'm not following."

"In case you haven't noticed, I relate better to puzzles and frauds and artwork than I do to people." I placed a hand on his forearm, all corded and muscular and clenched tight. "It may seem like it, but it doesn't actually mean I love you any less."

He tilted his head, scrutinizing me. "What you're saying is... if I'd approached it this way—"

Before I could ask what he was talking about, he grabbed my face and his mouth crashed into mine, his hot tongue sliding into my mouth. He moaned and stepped closer, wrapping an arm around my waist to draw me against that still-hard cock.

Everything in the world vanished other than his hard body and the heat crashing around inside of me. My fingers drove under his shirt, the ridiculous diamond catching briefly against the hem. I'd missed him—his body, his scent, his lust for me—so much.

He stopped suddenly, pulling back and wiping at the corners of his mouth. "Then it would have worked better?"

"Huh?" I reached for his neck, wanting little more than to calm the thundering pulse between my legs.

"I'll take that as a yes." He winked and knelt next to the table. When he stood, he displayed a roll of tape. "We can secure the ones you're sure of to the table and work out the rest."

I accepted the offered tape. "I was hoping for more of that kiss."

"Bella, get your brain out of the gutter." He pointed at the table. "We have work to do."

With each investigation I charged headlong into, Antonio's resistance grew weaker. It had started with *That's not your job* and had evolved into *Let me help*. I placed my left hand against his chest, admiring the flash from my engagement ring. "Thanks."

We worked together to identify the positions of five of the sheets, a wild array of alignments. None of them lay properly together. The sheet with four dots only overlapped eight dots by two inches. Whoever had created it worked hard to ensure it could be recreated easily, but only by someone who knew how.

I twisted one sheet to find the right alignment with the stack of five, while Antonio searched for a way to match the final two. Once we had them all lined up and taped to the table, we stepped back to absorb it.

At the center, a rectangle with what looked like a pastoral scene in it. A gentle hill, a few trees, and cattle. It must have been a painting. Off to the side, a shape that resembled a hand. Opposite that, wavy lines that evoked a symbol for water. Underneath the painting, the author had written 'Stolen' and '13 Fell' beneath that.

Antonio draped an arm over my shoulder. "Does it mean anything to you?"

"The 'Stolen' part is pretty clear, but what does '13 Fell' mean?" Maybe it was an address? But why hide it like that? And what were the water and the hand supposed to mean? And whose was it? Hell, what was the painting? "I need to mull this over."

"Now? Or...?"

Where did I leave my phone? I needed a map. The envelope came from New York. Maybe 13 Fell was an address somewhere in New York? Fell Street? Fell Avenue? And was the painting stolen *from* 13 Fell or was it being kept *at* 13 Fell?

"I enjoy working with you, bella. It's when you shut me out that bothers me."

"It's never intentional." I sighed, staring at my phone over on the desk, too far away to sneak off to. "Just poke me or something and tell me to share."

"Poke you?" he said, a hint of mischief in his voice. "I believe that's what I was trying to do."

Laughing, I shot him a coy glance from the corner of my eye. "I'm not doing anything now."

"On the desk again?"

I spluttered another laugh and covered my face. "We broke the monitor last time we did that."

"Sì, that was a poor choice. To the bedroom, then?"

"Only if..." I smacked his ass and twisted out of his reach, darting to the stairs. "You can catch me!"

CHAPTER 12

SAMANTHA

I collapsed from my hands and knees, smothering my face in the feather pillow. That *was* better than lining up sheets of paper.

Antonio crashed to the bed next to me with a groan of satisfaction. "I must say, shared orgasms are infinitely better in person."

With what little energy I had left, I rolled over to nestle my head on his chest, plucking damp strands of hair from my face.

He wrapped his powerful arms around me and kissed the top of my head. "Can you believe this is the first time we've made love without a ticking clock?"

"Ticking clock?"

"Well, I suppose last night was—" He yawned, releasing me to stretch one arm, then pulled me closer. "But the ticking clock? Neither of us is leaving in two weeks."

Our first time together in Naples had set a poor precedent for our relationship. I'd been there for ten days. When he visited at Christmas, it was also two weeks—followed immediately by two weeks in Italy. "Technically, we're both leaving in less than two weeks."

"But we're both leaving and then coming back—" He yawned again, either the orgasms or the jet lag draining him.

"Together?"

"I love this word. Together," he sighed, his arms growing heavy. "I need a nap before we head back to work."

I stroked my fingers over his chest, glistening with beads of sweat. "You haven't done any work yet today."

He squeezed tighter. "I'm fairly certain I just did some very important work."

"Incorrigible."

"Sì, this is true."

My phone pinged from the bedside table, a special sound for the building's security app. Antonio's did the same from somewhere on the floor where his clothes had landed.

"Crap." I rolled over to see what the front desk wanted, whether it was important mail, more groceries, or a change in the cleaning schedule. Part of me wanted to complain about being waited on, but that was why I'd lived in a hotel for more than half of last year—room service and housekeeping.

"Ignore it." Antonio patted the empty space next to him, not even opening his eyes.

The app said we had a visitor, and when I switched to the lobby's security camera, I bolted up from the bed. "Fuck."

Antonio's eyes shot open. "What?"

"It's Janelle."

He shook his head and closed his eyes again. "Tell her to come back later. We have other priorities."

"She's in uniform. This isn't a social call." I snagged Antonio's pants from the floor and threw them at him, then hit the button to have her sent up. "Get dressed."

"Che cazzo. Why's she here?"

"I don't know!" I hauled my pants on, grabbed my shirt, and hurried into the bathroom. I had to clean up. No time for a shower. Fix my messy bun, which had turned into a disaster. Get dressed. "We've only talked about business, always at the police station."

Antonio headed into the massive closet, which adjoined both the bedroom and the bathroom. "You two are still dancing around each other?"

Officer Janelle Williams and I had grown up as best friends and had a complete falling out in college. We hadn't spoken until last summer, when we worked together on a fraud case. The same one I met Antonio working. Fraud was apparently good to me.

"Hey now!" I poked my head into the closet, ready to blast him for not understanding how difficult making up was for me, but was struck by how good he looked in his jeans and black T-shirt with its tiny DG logo.

"Too casual?" he said with a smirk.

"Honestly? Mouth-watering." I shook my head to regain some focus. My jeans and bra look would not cut it, so I nipped into the bathroom and hauled on my shirt. "I screwed up with her big time, even though it was an accident."

"You've never told me the details."

With my shirt on, I undid my bun and retied my long hair into a low ponytail. "And now's not really the time. She's on her way up."

"You could leave the hair down, you know." Antonio leaned against the door frame between the bathroom and the closet.

"I could, but it's a pain in the ass while I'm working." I separated my ponytail in two, wrapping the halves around each other instead of braiding it. "Maybe I should cut it all off and wear it short like Cass's."

"I'll take the ring back."

I paused in wrapping the pony around its base, unable to contain my laughter. "No, you wouldn't."

How was it suddenly so easy? Was the rapid fire progression of our relationship really a given, like he'd said it was?

"Do you mind making some coffee while I finish up here?"

"Certainly." He came into the room and kissed my cheek before leaving.

Janelle and I had chatted at the police station several times since the shooting at New Year's. Our old schoolmate and friend, Officer Jimmy Slater, had come clean in the wee hours of the year about everything he'd been doing—working for someone at the pawnshop in Detroit, sneaking property into fire scenes as part of a fraud scam, planting evidence. He got involved with a plot by David and Olivia Scott to kidnap me and get money from Antonio. And then he killed them and nearly killed Antonio and me.

Life would have been very different if Janelle and I had stayed friends. Our plan growing up was to join the FBI together. If we'd graduated in the same class, she wouldn't have let me leave when Mom died. I wouldn't have married—

Oh shit. What if something happened to Cass? What if she was here with—*No, don't go there, Sam. Everything's going well. Everything's going to continue going well. Life can be good.*

"Bella!" hollered Antonio. "She's here!"

I ran out of the bedroom, down the hall, past Antonio in the kitchen, through the great room to the foyer, just as she knocked.

Don't be bad news. Don't be bad news.

One deep breath, a failed attempt to settle myself, and I swung the door open.

Janelle was a hair taller than me, with skin as dark as ebony. Sometime between college and last year, she'd shaved off the hair she used to wear in Bantu Knots or curls, giving herself an even more intimidating look than she possessed naturally. The extra bulk of her duty belt and vest added to the effect.

"Sam." She took her cap off and nodded curtly.

"Come in." I closed the door behind her, a shake in my voice. "Antonio's making coffee, if you'd like some?"

"I thought he was still in Italy?"

"Good morning, Officer Williams," said Antonio from the kitchen. "Milk, sugar, alternatives, or black?"

She waved to him as we made our way to the dining table by the kitchen. The dark wood table was decorated with a white runner and squat glass candleholders. Six chairs surrounded it. "Black is good, thanks."

"Is everything alright?" I offered her a chair and sat at the head of the table, clutching my hands together in my lap. *Don't be Cass, Kevin, or the kids.*

"I have news about Jimmy."

All the air rushed out of me and I leaned on the table. "Thank god."

Antonio placed a mug in front of Janelle and touched my shoulder. "Are *you* alright, bella?"

Janelle put her cap on the table. "I should have called. Unexpected visits from the police aren't usually greeted with smiles."

"Is his court date finally set?" I asked.

She fiddled with the hat, turning it around, tapping the crest on the front, running her fingers over the peak. "There was an incident."

My hand launched up to grab Antonio's. "Incident? That doesn't sound good."

"It's not." She moved the hat aside and pulled the mug closer, gripping it with both hands and staring at it. "Between the FBI wanting to question him about a case related to your abduction and the concerns about his safety, they moved him from Clinton County to Wayne County in March."

I kept my eyes glued to her. She was normally the most commanding presence in a room, but something was different. This was going to be bad. "He didn't escape, did he?"

She shook her head.

"Bail? Out on leave?"

Janelle stood and paced toward the foyer, her thick-soled boots thumping against the hardwood. She gripped her head, rubbing her hands over her buzz-cut hair. "Rumor had it he was starting to discuss a plea deal with the FBI."

"Starting to?" I looked up at Antonio, who was as rapt as I was.

She cut off, looked up, then spun on her heel to face us. "They're calling it a suicide."

A shiver shot through me, and my gaze fell to Janelle's police cap. Jimmy and I were friends from college, too, where all three of us had studied Criminal Justice.

She said, "There's no way he could have avoided jail time, but a plea could have made the time he'd be serving easier."

Dead. How did I even feel about that? Awful because one of my friends had died? Relieved because I wouldn't have to testify against him in court?

Janelle stomped over to us and knelt to look me in the eyes, fury twisting her face. "Don't you fucking feel sorry for him. He made his choices and nothing could have washed that stain on the department clean."

He'd shot Antonio. Could have killed him. Would have killed me, too.

"He seemed genuinely upset about everything he'd done," said Antonio.

Janelle turned her glower on him but didn't say anything.

"It hardly absolves him, but it's surprisingly easy to get caught up in things like he did." Antonio spoke from experience. He'd fallen in with his uncle's smuggling business and gotten himself shot for that nine years ago.

But Jimmy hadn't been the only one caught up in the crazy web. He'd covered for Parker Johnson, who'd tried to kill Antonio and me more than once at Christmas.

"What about Parker?" I asked.

Her nostrils flared. "Also in Wayne County."

"Is he working on a plea agreement, too?"

"No, he's awaiting trial, but I hear he's living the good life. Just got a new lawyer, too."

Antonio let go of me and headed around the counter into the kitchen. "Can I get you anything to eat? I picked up some pastries this morning or I can prepare breakfast?"

Janelle shook her head at him, stood, and dropped back into the chair.

"New lawyer?" I asked. "I thought he had a public defender?"

She blew some steam off the coffee and took a sip. "This is fantastic."

"Grazie." Antonio nodded and busied himself with something on the counter, hidden by the breakfast bar.

"About the same time they moved Jimmy, some high-priced guy from Detroit waltzed in and took over Parker's case. I wouldn't have thought Parker had the money for that."

"His girlfriend just sold her house." Although that had taken months until the FBI cleared it after their investigation into Parker's smuggling efforts. He'd hidden several paintings behind secret walls in the house, and the search for more couldn't have helped her sale price.

"I'm pretty sure she's out of the picture now."

"His ex-wife, maybe? She works at Mason's Gallery. Or his son, Cam-ron?" The last I'd seen him, Cam-ron was still living with his mother and rolling out of bed without a shower by noon. He wasn't likely paying for any lawyer.

Janelle shook her head. "As far as I know, they haven't been in contact. Cam-ron didn't end up charged with anything—it was clear he had nothing to do with Parker's attempts on your lives or the stolen paintings. He did work for his father occasionally, which is how he got roped into the original Chagall fraud, but his involvement was legitimate on that one."

I leaned my elbows on the table. Something was off. Janelle was obviously upset, but there was something she wasn't telling me. "What's up?"

She sucked in one cheek, chewing on it. Yup. Definitely holding something back.

"You said they're *calling it* a suicide." I inched closer. "You don't think it was, do you?"

"No." She pushed back her chair again to pace. "Why did the FBI want Jimmy? Was he involved in something with Parker?"

"Yeah."

Jimmy's arrest had been a mess. The Brenton Police Department wanted to take him in, but Elliot had been on scene and took over, saying the local police would have to wait until the FBI finished with him. I didn't know the full details, but Jimmy had been involved *somehow* with the smuggling ring we suspected Fiori was behind. He confessed to Antonio and me that he'd done things for the people at the pawnshop. But that was all he'd said about it.

"So the two of them get moved to Wayne County at the same time. The one who keeps his mouth shut gets a new lawyer." Janelle stopped, balling her fists on her duty belt.

"And the one who talks gets dead," I said. Could Fiori have been behind that, too?

"I had a feeling you'd come to that conclusion."

"Great minds," said Antonio, who was busy cutting something behind the breakfast bar. "Are you sure you don't want anything to eat? I thought I'd make some French toast."

"Thank you, but no." She returned to the table and retrieved her cap. "I'm still on duty and need to get back to work. I thought it would be best if you heard it from me before it made the news."

I escorted her to the door. "This can't be easy on you."

She put on her cap and gripped my arm, more than professional courtesy swimming in her eyes. "Or you."

"Listen..." I was better at stuffing my emotions down deep than expressing them, but how was I supposed to win back my former best friend if I didn't go out on a limb now and then? "Antonio and I are heading out of town in a couple of days, but when we get back, would you like to go out for coffee?"

"I'd like that." She pursed her lips and smiled. "It's been long enough."

I wanted to hug her but refrained. Antonio's easy-going manner was rubbing off on me.

Once she was in the elevator, I closed the door and stopped behind the breakfast bar. "What about the cornetti you bought?"

"I worked up some extra appetite." He shrugged, whisking eggs in a shallow dish. "Would you like anything else?"

"There's a lot I'd like, Antonio." I gripped the back of one of the chairs, bile churning in my stomach. All I could see was Antonio's flashlight flipping end over end in a dark house and the flash from Jimmy's gun. Blood covering my hands as Antonio slipped from consciousness. He tried to kill Antonio, so why was I so shaken up about his death?

"I'm going upstairs." The pawnshop was the link between Jimmy and Parker. I needed to get back to the evidence Elliot had brought me. "There's something in those files and I'm going to find it."

CHAPTER 13

ANTONIO

"Wait, bella." I set the knife and bread aside. We had to discuss this. I couldn't leave her investigating the pawnshop files without getting any of the news about Jimmy out of her system.

"Why?"

"Jimmy was your friend."

"I've done a relatively good job for the last four months of suppressing everything, so I don't have to think about what he did. Him being dead doesn't change that I don't want to talk about it."

I wanted to round the bar and take her in my arms. Tell her everything would be alright. But there were some things she needed that for—like the letter from her father—and others she didn't. "What if *I* want to talk about it?" I was the one he'd shot, after all.

She raised those blasted hands and rubbed them over her face. Always with the walls, this one. "Do you really? Or have you already talked it over with more than a dozen people and you're using that to get me to open up?"

"That's true, but I'd like to talk to *you* about it."

"I can't."

"Please tell me there's a *yet* coming for the end of that sentence."

"Yet." She dragged her hands down, pulling at her cheeks, emphasizing her exhausted features. "For right now, I need to feel useful, Antonio. There's no way I'm going to weasel information about Jimmy's death out of anyone in the know, so this is all I've got."

I picked up the knife and placed it against the top of the loaf. Was I hungry or was this stress eating? Perhaps I was avoiding working on Fiori's painting. I should have been starting that work so I'd be prepared when he called tomorrow night. "Maybe I'll go down to the gym. Want to join—"

Our phones pinged with another notification from the front desk.

"Marone. What now?"

"Delivery." Samantha flashed her phone in my direction. "For you."

"Allowing you to escape my overly active emotions?" I hadn't ordered anything, so was unsure what it was.

She gave me a tight smile, already halfway up the stairs. "Maybe."

I left the meal prep on the counter, reconsidering my gym idea. Two long days of travel, plus Cassandra's party, and the evening with Fiori—not to mention getting engaged and several rounds of lovemaking—had me exhausted. It was likely I'd injure myself in the gym.

Instead, I did breathwork on the way down the elevator. Deep inhale, hold it, slow exhale, hold again.

She's more open than she used to be. Take that as a win.

Building a life with her was a marathon, not a sprint.

Deep breath in.

The building manager stood behind the concierge desk in the stunning three-story lobby. In his sixties with gray hair, Marcus's sharp eyes missed little. Pink and purple flowers decorated the desk today, the scent of lilies and cedar in the air. Soft music hummed from speakers mounted on the walls. "Dr. Ferraro, I didn't get to see you yesterday. Welcome home."

"Grazie mille, Marcus. You texted I had package delivered?"

He signaled to a young dark-haired woman down the counter, and she slipped into the back office. "Private delivery. No return address."

Fantastico.

The woman returned and handed me a plain box, less than a foot square. Not only was there no return address, there was no actual address, either. Only my name.

And I had a good feeling who sent it.

On the way up the elevator, I turned the box over, hearing the gentle thud of a light item inside. What now? Why was my cousin sending me another burner phone?

All I wanted was to enjoy my time with Samantha in peace.

Entering the great room, I felt her presence and stopped.

She stood at the top of the stairs. "What is it?"

"I think Cristian wants to talk." I crossed to the kitchen and grabbed a knife. Part of me wanted to slam it into the box and make it go away, but I sliced the tape gingerly instead. Sure enough, it was a clamshell phone with a sticky note inside which read *Dial 1*. "Sì, this would be my cousin."

"You look as unsettled as I feel." She took one tentative step down. "Should I be here for this?"

"No. You go upstairs and feel useful. I'll grab you if there's something I think you should hear, but otherwise I'll tell you after we're done. Is that all right with you?"

"It's sort of has to be, doesn't it?" She didn't move. If I knew her, she was likely replaying the scene from our time in Napoli when I'd hidden one of Cristian's phones from her, and she thought I was cheating on her.

"I won't hide anything from you. I promise."

"I know." She gave a weak smile and climbed the stairs to the studio.

My chest swelled at her words. She trusted me. It had taken us a lot of work to get to that point, and it was all I needed to support me through this call. I headed down the hall by the foyer, in the opposite direction from our bedroom. Past the den, to the library, where I closed the door.

After speaking with Samantha that morning, I saw the library in a whole new light. It was spacious, with bookshelves lining three walls, a propane fireplace, and a desk off to one corner. There was also a piano, but I could move that somewhere else. Maybe reconfigure the great room or change one of the three spare bedrooms into a music room.

Then this would make a splendid office for her.

I pulled out my phone and texted a friend with a few logistical questions. Samantha would have all the floor space she needed for her crop circles.

Two well-cushioned wing chairs sat by the piano, with a reading table between them. I sat, flipped open the phone, and dialed eight, as I'd been taught all those years ago—if I'd dialed one as the note instructed, it would have been a sign someone had intercepted the phone or I'd been compromised.

Two rings and Cristian's voice greeted me. "Cugino!"

"What news, Cristian?" Four months ago, he and his father, Giovanni, had been the pariahs of the Ferraro family. But they'd come to my aid more than once, and I was working hard to see them as something other than antiquities smugglers, which they weren't anymore.

Or so they continued to insist.

"First, the pleasantries. Did you know your father called Papa yesterday?"

"Really?" My Zio Giovanni had asked me to help bridge the distance between the two brothers, and after he began cooperating with Interpol and the Italian Carabinieri, I put in a few good words. Frankly, for how long it had been since they'd spoken, it surprised me that so little had meant so much to my father.

"It lasted all of five minutes, but it's the most they've spoken to each other without yelling in, what, fifteen years?"

"Then I suppose that's progress."

"And second, I'm calling with a favor."

Here we go. What now?

"Cesca has been talking about visiting you this summer."

Cristian's youngest sister was a promising artist who'd won Samantha over during our time with them in January.

"Mamma looked at some summer programs available in your area, and there are some student programs at the universities. She was hoping you might have room for her?"

This was not at all the type of favor I would have expected. It was almost… familial rather than manipulative or self-serving. However, adding a fourteen-year-old into the mix when my relationship with Samantha was still so new would hardly be a wise plan. "I'll talk to Sofia. She has three boys, so that might be too much for Cesca. But Sofia might enjoy it."

"Perfect. Let us know."

I stood from the chair and paced across the room to the desk. "I know neither of these things required a burner phone, so what's the third item?"

And please don't let there be a fourth, fifth, and sixth.

"I understand you had a visit from our mutual friend?"

"Fiori?" It shouldn't have surprised me Cristian would know that. As he liked to say, knowing things was one of his talents.

He grunted in the affirmative.

"It was a strange visit." I sat in the leather office chair and pulled open a drawer absently. "No references to you or Zio Gio. Nothing about Vincenzo or anything that happened in January. Not even a word about the fresco or the press conference when we returned it. Nothing."

"I understand he gave you a painting he wants repaired?"

I riffled through pens and pencils in the drawer, paper clips and a stapler. This desk had once belonged to my grandfather and he'd left it to me in his will. It had moved with me from my parents' house to my two different apartments in Delaware, and finally here. I preferred the space upstairs for working, with all the skylights. "He did. Said I owed him."

"Porca puttana."

"When we were on his yacht in September, he said the debt for taking care of Samantha was paid in full by arranging for Zio Andrea to repair one of his damaged paintings." I hit on the item I'd been looking for. An old photograph of Nonno with Papa and his two brothers, along with the rest of us kids. I was five and Lorenzo was just a baby. It was our first Christmas after moving to Roma. So many changes since then. "It was strange, Christian. He said things… things that sounded like accusations, but nothing came out."

And the way he smacked my injured arm made it clear there were unspoken threats floating around the room.

"And I also understand you took it?"

I rocked back in the chair to stare at the ceiling. Cristian couldn't tell an honest story if he was reading it from a sheet of paper. There was always subtext, just like with Fiori. "Why call if you already know everything?"

"Jason's worried—he's asking to come out. Fiori knows there are leaks in his organization and is looking to plug them."

"What do you think these leaks mean for any of us?"

"Until Fiori leaves your area, I told Jason to stay with him. I can't risk him doing something to our family."

My gaze shot to the door. Was Samantha still in danger because of my family? She couldn't be. "No, he didn't do anything after Zio Gio took the fresco. Why would he be acting now if it's revenge?"

"This is the long game, Antonio. An empire the size of his isn't built overnight, nor does it crumble overnight. The man has patience."

"Should we send the painting back?"

Nonno and Nonna smiled back at me from the photograph. Had he ever had problems like this? Of course he had. He ran the business through the Second World War. His problems were far greater than ours.

It was little consolation, though, as I knew he'd survived his trials. It was my own I was not so sure about.

"You know," mused Cristian. "This could be related to the rumors he's trying to recruit you."

"I don't know why he'd think I'd work for him."

Cristian had his arm around me in the photo. Two years older and a few inches taller, his smile was as full of cunning as ever. "Is Samantha involved?"

"Of course." *Tell him we're engaged or not?* I hadn't told my parents or siblings yet—Cristian should not be the first to hear it. "We're living together now."

"That's good to hear." His voice softened for a moment, quite unlike him under normal circumstances. "She seems a good match for you."

"She is." Ten years after the photo, my grandfather died. He'd been running the studio in Brenton since before I was born, and in his absence, my Zio Andrea was supposed to take it over. But Papa had such a falling out with Zio Giovanni that he whisked us out of Italia. How different would my life have been had I stayed there? "I don't like this, Cristian. I'm worried."

He grunted his agreement. "Don't destroy the phone. I'll call if I find out anything. I may send some more people your way. And..." Even more unlike him, he paused.

"And what, Cristian?"

"Memorize my personal number. If something happens so you don't have the burner and you can't count on the authorities, call me anyway."

I nearly dropped the phone. That was a risk he'd never taken, as far as I knew. He was even more worried than I was.

"Now that Papa is cooperating, even if it's not as fully as the Carabinieri want, I'd rather risk they hear something from you than risk your safety."

Elliot had told us he expected as much, and I'd hinted to my father it was a done deal, but to hear Cristian admit it was a surprise.

"He's cooperating?"

"Two months now. It's slow-going, because they want more than he'll give, but we're trying to work it out. It's difficult to figure out what information can be passed over that will implicate Fiori and none of his other associates." He made a spitting noise. "We should have had the Reynolds team take photos when they snuck onboard his yacht."

"Thank you, Cristian. For everything."

"Let me know what Sofia says about Cesca."

"I will. Talk to you later."

I stood with the photo and returned to the wing chair. The last four months had been quiet. My team in Pompeii worked hard and nothing disappeared. I flew to the States twice for brief visits with Samantha, and my world was at peace. Now here I was, my future ready to begin, and the peace had vanished.

Had Giovanni been involved in the smuggling trade the year the photo was taken? Did he truly work for the International

Monetary Fund back then, as I'd been told? Or was there a hard truth hidden behind all the smiles that Christmas?

Did my Zio Gio ever worry about what he was getting his family into?

Samantha gravitated toward criminals. But not in the way I had, when I threw myself into their world for the blink of an eye. No, she wanted to set the world right.

How much would we have to pay for that desire?

There was a quiet knock at the door.

"Come in, bella."

She poked her head in, surveying the room. When her eyes reached the desk where the burner lay, she opened the door and came in. "And?"

And there was so much to tell her. "You remember Jason? Fiori's helicopter pilot and the one who opened the painting case for us last night?"

"How could I forget?" She approached me, taking a seat on the chair's arm.

"He's Cristian's man inside Fiori's organization."

Her eyes widened and one of her hands covered her mouth. "Sì, he—"

"Jason was in the hotel where Umberto and his girlfriend were staying, just before I went to talk to her. He's the one who took the fresco, isn't he?"

"Sì, and—"

"Shit." She swatted my shoulder, her brain's gears grinding so loudly I could practically hear them. "He's the one who saved my life in Naples, isn't he?"

I nodded, rather than getting cut off again. That mad dash through the city to find her had been one of the worst moments of my life. If Cristian had done nothing else for me, having his man save her life was enough to earn my eternal gratitude.

"Does Cristian talk to him often? Does he know what Fiori's up to?"

Foolishly, I'd expected more of an emotional reaction, rather than business mode. But business mode was what Samantha Caine did best. The more facts and figures she could cram into her brain, the less she had to feel.

"He heard about our meeting at The Train Station, but does not know what Fiori's up to. Apparently, he's rooting out moles and Jason wants out."

"Can't blame him."

"And on the family front, Cesca wants to come and visit for the summer, plus my father called his father."

She chuckled and kissed the top of my head. "That's the worst job of changing the subject you've ever done."

"I think Cristian is worried that Zio Giovanni is sacrificing too much to heal the rift between him and the rest of my family. He's talking with the Carabinieri, giving them information about Fiori's business, but..."

"But Fiori might come for those of us who are less protected?"

"It's possible." Or there was another explanation. A simpler one. "How many people reviewed the paintings at the auction last August? How many Carabinieri officers tried to figure out where that fresco went before Fiori got it? Who stopped Parker? Who ensured Fiori didn't get that painting at New Year's?"

She slid off the chair's arm and into my lap.

"Samantha, you're a thorn in Fiori's side. You're his kryptonite." The way he'd looked at her at the restaurant... Laughing with me one second, then glaring at her. Stating that friends don't use titles, then refusing to call her by her first name. I pulled her left hand to my lips and kissed the finger where she wore my engagement ring. "We need to sit down with Elliot on this."

She pulled back, cocking her head, more surprise and confusion clouding her face than from my revelation about Jason. "You're not going to tell me to hand it over to him and be done with it?"

I wrapped my arms around her and buried my face against her neck, breathing in her scent. Warm Mediterranean breezes with a hint of citrus. Fresh and calm, despite the chaos that swirled in her wake. That was my Samantha.

How fortunate was I to have found her again after all these years.

"Bella, I want to move forward with my chosen family." I wanted my own photo. My parents, my brother and sister, my nieces, and nephews—and my wife and our children. "But if Fiori won't let us do that, then we're going to make him."

"In that case..." She squirmed out of my tight grip and stood. "Let's get upstairs and figure out what's going on with his painting."

CHAPTER 14

ANTONIO

After speaking with Cristian, the rest of the evening was quiet. Samantha spent some time searching for 13 Fell, coming up empty. After storming up and down the stairs several times and a glass of wine, she returned to reviewing her files from the pawnshop while I began testing Fiori's painting to ensure the repairs had been done with materials I could easily reverse. Luckily for me, the repair was sloppy, but executed with reversible conservation paints and varnishes.

I made a spectacular dinner, we made love, and we slept in each other's arms. After a big breakfast and shared shower, we were both working in the studio, with the mid-morning sun streaming in through the skylights.

Working alongside my fiancée was paradise, despite the worries still twisting in my stomach. Fiancée. How different did that word feel with Samantha than it had with Faith?

Samantha stood at the lab bench, with her back to me, studying piles of photographs. Hair tied back in a messy bun, wearing an oversized sweater and leggings. Focused. Brilliant. Analyzing and memorizing everything she saw.

Yet, if I called her over to see what I was working on, she'd leave it in a moment. Faith would have come over only if I'd begged, and even so, she wouldn't have been curious or interested in the least.

Samantha? She'd listen, consider my words, ask intelligent questions.

And she'd smell better than the adhesive I was breaking up. Its fish-gelatin base evoked memories of Italian markets and Christmas Eve afternoons with Nonna, preparing the branzino for dinner. After eight months of not working with it on a daily basis, it stank.

I slid my scalpel underneath the silk organza the conservator had used to protect the tear. Bridging with linen would have been more stable. I only would have chosen silk if the canvas had been far thinner. More evidence that whoever did the work had the right tools and knew *how* to execute the work but lacked guidance from someone more experienced in what work to do.

"What?" Samantha's voice startled me. At some point, she'd turned on the microscope and was inspecting an image more closely.

"Scusi?"

She flicked the microscope's light off and turned to face me. "You made a noise like you found something."

"Did I?"

"Geez, and you say I get focused." She joined me at the conservation table, one of her hands trailing its way up my back. Sì, far more interested than Faith ever was.

"You see this?" I leaned closer and pointed at the tear with my blade. "Look closely. It's a perfect slice, even finer than I'd thought from the front. No loose fibers, no ragged edges, it's just perfectly straight on either side."

"Definitely not glass?"

"Not a chance."

"Why would Fiori say that if it wasn't true?"

"He could simply be a pathological liar."

"Or it's linked to whatever reason he had for insisting you do the work."

We remained huddled over the back of the painting, ideas churning in my brain.

Samantha ran her finger over the cut. "You said they didn't use fill-in medium. Would it need that, considering how perfect the join is?"

"Sì, otherwise there's a line showing on the front."

"I bet your scalpel would make a perfect cut like that."

"Or a knife?" I stiffened, unsure I wanted to have this conversation. One of Fiori's bodyguards had shot at me in January and we were dancing around the discussion with Janelle that he was behind Jimmy's death—even if Janelle didn't realize we knew who was behind things. "Could something have happened on his boat and he's covering it up? Perhaps that's why he insisted on secrecy and on calling in a favor to a man he knew would honor it?"

"If Fiori knows about your past with Giovanni, he'd assume you won't talk."

"Could I be contaminating evidence?"

"Let's assume for a moment there was a crime." Samantha twisted her head, moving closer to the painting to inspect the back. "Another conservator's already worked on it. They would have cleaned it first, right?"

"The work was amateur. Maybe they didn't clean it properly. What if there's blood under the paint? In the cut?"

"That's not it," she muttered. "Think clearly. Logically. If it were involved in some sort of crime that left blood splatters on it, he wouldn't have someone repair it, and *then* bring it to you. He would have the first conservator test to be sure it was clean. Otherwise, it's too much of a risk you'd do an ultraviolet test—which would be completely normal—and find it. Fraud or theft, he might trust you to ignore. Then if you went to the authorities, he could easily claim ignorance. But not murder or anything like that."

"True."

She straightened, tapping her fingers against her lips. "Did Christian ever figure out what Parker was talking about when he said Fiori wanted to recruit you?"

"No, but he suggested this might be related."

A smile gradually spread across her face, and her eyes lit up. She was on to something.

"What is it?"

"What if it's nothing more than a test?"

I walked over to my second worktable, which was covered in photographs and notes I'd taken last night. "Meaning he or one of his men cut it intentionally?"

"Meaning... You said when we were visiting Giovanni that he could use his new conservation studio to facilitate his smuggling."

I stowed the scalpel in its holder and scanned the ultraviolet photos, finding only the expected patterns of retouching. No blood splatters. "I don't think he is, though."

"Not my point." Her speech hit a sharp staccato as her excitement grew. "I mean, what if Fiori is doing exactly that? He tries stealing the fresco from you in Pompeii, and the piece is eventually re-stolen and returned, so he fails in his attempt to hurt Giovanni by stealing from you. What if his new approach to hurting Giovanni is recruiting you? What if this is a simple job, so you work together under completely legal conditions?"

"I don't think that's it, bella." If that were true, he wouldn't have insisted I do the work myself before we leave. Like Cristian said, Fiori was patient. He could have sent it to the company and still requested I do the work. That would have accomplished the same thing. He wouldn't have played the secrecy game. "I think this is about everything I said earlier. This is about you."

Her body deflated, clearly not prepared for this theory yet. Or perhaps disappointed I'd not jumped onto her first idea.

"Think about it." I returned to the table with the painting and flipped it over to look at the front. "He insists *I* work on it, but not at the studio. Here. Because who will be here with me?"

"Me." She stood next to me, but didn't touch me, too busy thinking. "Because what will I do? Ask questions."

"Ask away."

She placed her hands flat on the table, on either side of the painting. "If you're right, my first step would be to assume it's either stolen or a forgery. That means I need to find out where it was stolen from or what it's a forgery of."

"That settles it. I'll continue my work, in case we're wrong. You work your magic."

• • • • ● • ● • • • •

"Well, shit." Samantha laughed to herself, hidden from my view behind one of the giant monitors on the office desk.

"Find something?" I stretched my arms over my head, twisting at the waist. After eight months of working in Pompeii on vertical surfaces, my back was not ready to resume working over horizontal ones for so long. It had been over an hour, and we'd both been so engrossed in our tasks, we'd not spoken.

"This painting is actually called *The Music Lesson*—not *The Music Study* like he said, although I could almost chalk that up to a translation issue. But the interesting part? It's apparently owned by the Getty in Los Angeles."

"And missing?"

"Nope." She beckoned me with a finger, and I obliged. On her screen, she displayed an email message with a photo of the painting hanging on a wall. "I've done some work with the Getty—called in by their insurers for consults—and have a few contacts down there. When I tracked down where the painting was supposed to be, I emailed one of them, and she informed me it's still on the wall."

"That means Fiori's painting is either a copy or a forgery?"

She cupped her chin in one hand and chuckled at her screen. "Or the one in the museum is."

"Can your friend send us any documentation? Provenance? Imaging?"

She nudged me with her shoulder, not even looking up. "I love it when you talk conservation to me."

We were discussing potential crimes, but I couldn't help the flood of joy rushing through me. Every ounce of my body wanted to pick her up and swing her around to celebrate working on something like this together.

"And, yes, I already asked her."

As though called simply by our desire to access the information, Samantha's email inbox updated with another message from the Getty.

"How many galleries and museums do you have contacts at like this?"

"Dunno." She opened the first attachment, a close-up of the tutor's face. "If we kept it to major museums, over a dozen, but when you throw in smaller ones and galleries, I'd have to spend some time figuring that out."

"It matches. I'd like to say perfectly, but that would require comparing them side by side." I stepped closer to the monitor, examining the area where Fiori's version of the painting had been cut. "Do they have..." I took control of the mouse and switched between attachments. Stretcher. Stains on the back of the canvas. Provenance.

She eased out of my way, first with her shoulders, then her entire chair. "Feels like déjà vu."

The last time we'd done this, she was wearing a tank top and her motorcycle pants, which hugged her luscious ass in a way that made my heart cry for joy. "Can you imagine if I'd done this that day?" I kissed the side of her head. In fact, that day, I'd tried to kiss her, but she rejected me yet again.

"Probably not this." She snaked her arm between me and her chair to pinch my ass.

I tsked, which elicited a laugh from her, and I resumed inspecting the documentation. Once I found a black-and-white infrared image of the original, I nodded. "I think I'll start with this. It's simple. I can compare any underdrawings, and I have a camera specially fitted for that here."

"Geez, you barely ever need to leave this place. All the equipment to do your job, an awesome gym downstairs, people who deliver your groceries—"

"Not to mention the giant bed, the sexy girlfriend—"

"Sexy fiancée, I think you mean?" She flashed her left hand, wiggling her ring.

"Even better." An image of designing our dream home flitted through my brain. I could build a studio in the backyard with all the equipment I needed. Perhaps if Samantha needed to move for work, I'd do it then. Open my own little shop and take what work I wanted. *That* would be even better, still.

"I texted Elliot yesterday about the meeting with Fiori, but I'll call him. With this potential link to the Getty, he may want to drop by."

CHAPTER 15

SAMANTHA

"Thanks for calling me." Elliot followed me into the condo from the foyer. "How are you feeling?"

That was not happening. We were not about to discuss my father or his letter. "Antonio's upstairs."

"Sam—"

I put up a hand.

"Bella!" Antonio appeared at the top of the round staircase for a fraction of a breath and vanished into the studio. "Andiamo!"

"He found something?"

"Yeah." I gestured for Elliot to go up the stairs first. "The painting Fiori gave us had been cut. Antonio's certain it was too straight and sharp to be an accident. So that got us to thinking, what if it's a test? I was only planning on discussing that much with you, and maybe get someone at Art Crime to track down whether the painting at the Getty was a fake, but Antonio discovered something."

"Thank you for coming." Antonio met us at the top of the stairs and shook Elliott's hand vigorously. He was expressing all the excitement I'd had before Elliot showed up.

But as soon as I saw Elliot's face, it was Friday all over again. He was telling me about my father. My mother's lies were fresh again.

Elliot scanned the room, gaze lingering on the rows of paintings and the ones covering the walls. "This is fantastic."

"Grazie." Antonio gestured to the painting on his worktable.

I said, "Our first thought was about Parker and Cristian telling us that Fiori wanted to recruit Antonio. Probably to hurt Giovanni. It was still possible he was after me, like Cristian also warned us in January."

Elliot stood over the supposed Dutch masterpiece and folded his arms. "Why now?"

"Fiori called us the very day Antonio came home. That strengthened our belief it was about Antonio."

Antonio retrieved a few printed sheets from his second table and held them against his chest. "Or I was simply his way to get to Samantha."

Elliot canted his head to glance at me. "Or maybe he's after you for the same reason I am. A human stolen art database would be valuable for somebody who's dealing in stolen art."

"A what?" I asked.

"Imagine—he's going into a sale and needs someone to authenticate the work. With your eye and critical brain..." His gaze shifted to Antonio. "And your skills—the two of you could ensure he's never fooled again."

That made too much sense and hadn't been something we'd even considered. "So not just recruiting Antonio, but..."

"Listen, Sam, I know I've mentioned before that you two are a good team and I meant it. But if I could have anything I wanted, it would be both of you working for me."

Antonio's brows furrowed. Was it a look of surprise, revulsion at the idea of working with the FBI, or complete confusion? "You must be kidding."

"I've never really thought of it that way," I said.

But how amazing would that be? Antonio kept saying he'd move anywhere in the world, so I could take the work I wanted, but what if he worked with me? Or would that be stifling? Always having him right there? We hadn't spent more than a month and a half together since we met. At least, not on the same continent.

"I suppose that puts a different perspective on my father's new business, doesn't it, bella?"

Elliot said, "New business?"

"Sì, he's launching a fine art investigations company as a side business. There's enough going on around my family, given my Zio Giovanni and something that happened with my Zio Andrea, that he's decided he wants to make a difference in the world."

"Don't tell me you Ferraros are going to steal Sam from me." Elliot shifted to look at me again. "After I almost had you convinced to leave the insurance industry?"

I never said I was going to leave the insurance industry. Might have thought about it every single day, especially now that I had a desk job, but I didn't tell him that. "Anyway, here's what we found. Fiori's painting is a forgery."

"How certain are you?"

Antonio handed his first sheet to Elliot, which was covered in his notes. "I started paint tests, checking for chemicals which wouldn't be appropriate to the age of this painting, such as synthetic pigments. Once I got past the recent conservation work, everything appeared as it should. Paint like this will normally stay not quite wet but... I don't how to explain it, but wet."

"Until the polymers become cross-linked?"

Antonio and I looked at each other, surprised by Elliot.

Elliot chuckled. "You don't spend a decade with the Art Crime Team and learn nothing."

"Of course. But these paints were dry. And with the correct pigments, my next option was texture. It had the crackles I expected, the aged coloring inside each valley. Everything on the surface looked right."

Elliot nodded. "No doubt they said the same about Han van Meegeren's forgeries."

A Dutch art dealer and forger of the early twentieth century, Van Meegeren was practically the grandfather of modern forgery techniques. Thanks to a high-profile trial in the 1940s, the legitimate art world learned a great deal about the process.

"I have a friend who works at the Getty, and she sent me photos of the original. Even the frame and the canvas are right, including stains on the stretcher and the gallery tags."

"You're telling me we're dealing with a master forger?"

"Not quite." Antonio handed the other sheet to Elliot. "When I looked at it under infrared, I discovered this."

Elliot held the sheet up, pulled it in close, straightened his arm, absorbing every detail.

I clasped my hands behind my back so Elliot couldn't see how much they were fidgeting. He was taking too long. He had to see it. Otherwise, it could have just been Antonio and me hoping to see what we saw.

"There's not much detail to it. The composition of the three characters reminds me of..." Elliot placed the sheet on the table and pulled out his phone. He typed and scrolled until he finally put the phone down next to the painting. It showed a photo of exactly what Antonio and I had seen.

I cracked before Antonio did, unable to sustain the silence. "Exactly! It's a rough sketch of the composition of *The Concert*!"

Elliot folded one arm and stroked his short goatee. "A mistake on the forger's part?"

"Fiori handed this painting off to me, asking that I repair a poor conservation job. He didn't ask for detailed analysis like this or for authentication."

"How much would he know about the time you two spent in Rome in January with Giovanni?"

One of my sneaky hands landed on my face. If Antonio had been standing next to me, he would've grabbed it before I could put up the shield. As wonderful as our time in Naples had been in January, the week that preceded it had been a chaotic mix of heaven and hell. "I'm sure Vincenzo didn't figure out I'd been in the FBI, so he wouldn't have passed that information on to Fiori. But he could have told him about my wanting to join. For all I know, Fiori has the resources to find out the truth."

Antonio stepped around Elliot and took my hand, intertwining his fingers with mine. His soft smile was likely meant to convey support, maybe even a *You don't have to hide your past with Vincenzo from me or protect me from it*. So long as it wasn't followed up with *We should let Elliot deal with this*, I was all good.

Except this wasn't the time for handholding.

I withdrew my hand from Antonio's and shoved it into my pocket. "Part of me wants to hop on a plane and never look back, but the bigger part of me wants to—"

"Jump in headfirst and figure out the details later?" chuckled Elliot.

Antonio gave a halfhearted laugh, his normally unflappable self not inspiring any confidence. "You know her too well."

Better than I'd thought he did. He'd worked with my father, who I wouldn't recognize if he walked straight up to me and introduced himself. *Push it aside, Sam, this is work*. "What do you think we should do?"

Elliot scratched the goatee. "As a senior agent with the Art Crime Team, I want the pair of you as assets. I want you to set up another meeting with Fiori and see if we can get information out of him."

I rubbed my fingers together inside my pockets, a vain attempt to discharge some of the energy zipping around inside me. Seeing Elliot always did that, but this time, it was different. Normally, I was fighting back my desire to work for him, but this time I was fighting back my desire to kick him out, while still wanting to work with him. "I feel like there's a but in there."

Elliot flicked his gaze toward Antonio deliberately. "This differs from the cases or the manner I wanted to work with you. I wanted you researching, maybe even undercover, but in a tightly controlled situation. I'm not happy about this, but I suspect it will push the smuggling case to the next level. We've been dancing around the outside of the smuggling ring, picking off minor players, until we got to Giovanni Ferraro. He's cooperating, but hasn't given us nearly as much intel as I'd hoped for."

Antonio took in a slow breath, grazing his hand down my forearm until it was almost in my pocket. Maybe holding my hand wasn't about me. Maybe it was about him, and him borrowing some of my resolve.

No, that was silly.

Antonio Ferraro didn't need something like that.

"Fiori said he'd call me tomorrow, after I've had some time with the painting. Should I tell him what I found? Or do the repair and pretend nothing happened?"

I took Antonio's hand, more as a show of appreciation than anything. Normally, I was the one leading the charge, but since he talked to Cristian—had something else happened on that call he hadn't told me?

"What do you think, Sam?" asked Elliot.

That I wanted to take down the smuggling ring and protect those I cared about. I turned to Antonio, looking up into his big brown eyes. What I really wanted was to get lost in them and have a few days of nothing but us. "Did you ever talk about Fiori in front of Vincenzo?"

Antonio shook his head. "I couldn't say for sure. But after Zio Giovanni presented us with the fresco, it's possible he said where it came from in front of his men. Or during the planning of the recovery, I suppose?"

"Then I think we approach this like we did Friday night. Pretend we don't know what he does and make it look like we think someone cheated him with this painting. If Fiori calls us on it and says anything about Giovanni saying Fiori was behind the fresco theft, we say we didn't believe him. We fought with Giovanni enough that Vincenzo probably passed that along."

Elliot nodded as I spoke, while Antonio's jaw grew progressively tighter.

"If we work on the assumption Fiori's looking to recruit the pair of us as authenticity experts, and that he doesn't know my link to the FBI, I think we should tell him what we found, but dance around it. Say we're regretful and pretend we don't suspect it was a test." I squeezed Antonio's hand. "And maybe you offer to continue with the repair if he wants, but that you recognized the painting from the Getty and suspect it's a forgery."

"I already alerted my task force that Fiori is in the area and reached out to you," said Elliot. "Where do your vacation plans stand?"

"Up in the air, from the sounds of things." Antonio's voice betrayed the conflict inside him. He'd committed to finishing this, but obviously didn't want to get as deep as we were getting.

"I'll be at the Foster Mutual office tomorrow morning for a meeting," I said. "Can we set something up for there, rather than having the FBI waltzing in and out of our home?"

"Wise choice." Elliot gestured toward the stairs. "I'll see you tomorrow."

CHAPTER 16

ANTONIO

"You're pacing," said Samantha.

I was not. I was simply looking out the glass wall to the patio and then returning to glower at Fiori's forged painting. That was not pacing. Not even when I'd done it ten times.

"Why don't we go to bed?" She sat in the office chair behind the desk, having closed her files for the evening. Apparently, her brain possessed a limit, after all.

"I'm not tired."

"You're exhausted."

I halted in my innocent trek from the worktable to the door and dragged both hands through my hair. Our engagement was the only thing which had gone right since I arrived home. Everything else was a disaster. But I had to keep her safe and the only way to do that was to tackle this problem head-on. "You go ahead. I don't think I could sleep if I tried."

In the reflection from the glass wall, I watched her stand and come over to me. Her arms snaked around my waist from behind, finding their way to my chest. "Who said anything about sleep?"

I pressed her hands over my heart, admiring the two rings she wore. The diamond solitaire and the trinity ring. "No, bella, I need to be prepared."

She twisted around me, nudging my arms up so I held her. "You're a smart man and you've dealt with his type before. The only preparation you need at this point is to relax."

A laugh burst free from deep inside me, and she smiled. "Who would have ever thought—"

"That *I* would be the one telling *you* to relax? I'm guessing no one."

I ran my hands over her head, wanting to comb them through her hair, but she'd tied it back in a braid. "You're right, you know."

"I know." She winked, clearly taking too many of my habits. "But it never hurts to hear."

"It's past ten already. What's taking him so long?"

"Maybe he's not calling until tomorrow?"

"No." I released her and returned to the worktable, staring at my lifeless phone. "He's exerting control over the situation. It shows we're on *his* schedule alone. I guarantee he'll call tonight."

"See?" She nudged my arm, suddenly standing beside me. "You know what you're—"

The phone sprang to life, the screen and ringer startling me so much I snatched it on the first ring. *Not the way to wrestle for control, Tony.* "This is Antonio Ferraro?" *Sounding like it's a question is even worse.*

"Antonio, it's Pasquale. I apologize for my lateness, but I just finished the most stunning dinner. How's my painting doing?"

Don't let him set the tone. "I wish you'd given me your number, so I could have called you yesterday."

"Is there something wrong?"

"I'm going to put you on speaker." *That's more like it.* "Samantha will be joining us for the conversation."

"Of course, of course."

I switched the output and put the phone on the table, next to the sheets of paper and pencils we'd prepared in case we needed to communicate separately.

"Good evening, Pasquale," she said.

"And to you, Ms. Caine." There it was again—not using her first name. "Now tell me, Antonio, what is it you wanted to speak with me about yesterday?"

My gaze drifted to the tutor's face on the painting. I'd cleaned the paint away from the original repair, making the tear obvious from the front. "I'm not sure how to say this, but the painting you gave me—"

"It's the damage, isn't it?" His voice was hesitant, despite him leaping in to cut me off.

Samantha's nose wrinkled and she mouthed, *What the?*

"I've felt bad ever since I gave it to you. I wasn't completely honest about what happened." Was he acknowledging that it hadn't been glass to cut it? Or that he knew it was a fake?

Don't suggest either. Play the innocent. "The repair was actually quite good, other than the lack of fill-in medium."

"Come now," Fiori drawled. "You and I both know my wife didn't break a glass and puncture the painting."

I remained silent. Samantha's mouth opened and I shook my head. I didn't know what she was about to say, but I wanted Fiori to continue talking.

"I'd intended to have it cleaned, so one of my staff took it down from the wall. They had packing materials, including a sharp knife for the tape, but they dropped the knife onto the painting."

"That would have been helpful to know." And unfortunately, a reasonable explanation for how straight the cut was.

"I'm sorry for not telling you."

Samantha wrote on her sheet, *Why hide that?*

I shrugged and wrote back, *Part of the test?*

"Do you have an estimate for the repair? I know you were talking about traveling, but I do so want her back on my yacht. We're leaving the area soon and I'd hate to ship her off somewhere, leaving her in a wooden box, apart from those who love her."

Creepy, wrote Samantha.

I nodded, a vision of a coffin swimming in my head. And the way he referred to the painting as *her*, despite there being two people, made my skin crawl. "I cleaned the paint that the other conservator used and removed the patch in the back to apply a proper one. This is where the problem comes."

"Problem?"

"The cut is exact, which allowed me to see slivers of other colors under the top layer that didn't seem right to me. I hope you don't mind, but I did some additional tests to get a closer look at it, including some infrared photos."

"Ah ha!" Fiori's voice grew excited. "That pride in your work, the intellectual curiosity—this is why your family is so well-known. I knew sending her to you was the right choice."

His reaction didn't match my expectations.

Samantha tapped the line I'd written about it being part of the test.

"I'm dreadfully curious about what you found."

I pulled the infrared photo closer to myself. "Original sketches underneath. Very loose. Shapes and outlines only."

"Fascinating. Is this something you could send to me? It would be a wonderful addition to my provenance library."

"Honestly, Pasquale, I don't think it would be." I paused for effect, still working to take control of the conversation. "The sketches were for a different painting."

Fiori gasped. "What does that mean?"

Samantha's face grew hard and she wrote, *Such a liar*.

Was there any chance he was being honest and didn't know? My family was one of the best in the business, so it made sense to call us. Could Samantha and I be leaping to wild conclusions about this? I trusted my uncle and cousin when they said Fiori was in the smuggling trade, because they used to work with him. But what if this single piece was part of a legal collection?

However, the way he spoke to Samantha meant I wouldn't give him the benefit of the doubt.

"You see," I said. "It's not out of the realm of possibility for an artist to sketch one piece and then paint something different. Or even to paint one thing and then repaint over it. In fact, this sort of thing is fairly common."

"Yes," he mused. "I heard about a Van Gogh recently, where they discovered one of his self-portraits on the reverse of another painting."

"You showed me that news report." Samantha's voice held a tone of innocence, rather than her normal sharpness. This was her own test for Fiori, continuing the ruse she'd presented at the restaurant. "Didn't they say it's one of his earliest self-portraits?"

"Sì, bella, I'm surprised you remember that."

Fiori made a noise, perhaps a doubting laugh—either that or I was coloring his response with my own suspicions. "If it's so common, why do you need to tell me about it?"

I said, "I researched the painting and discovered it was created around 1668, by Ter Borch, as you mentioned. However, the sketch underneath is for a painting done roughly four years prior to that."

"What are you saying?" The accusation was thick in his voice. Not that he had done anything wrong, but that I had. So much for admiring my curiosity.

With a tremendous smile, Samantha drew a checkmark on the page.

"Mi dispiace, signore, but it's not just that. We spoke with—"

Samantha nudged my arm and pointed her pencil at me.

"*I* spoke with a friend at the Getty Museum in LA, who insists they have the original, along with all the provenance and paperwork."

He was slow to respond, but eventually did, with no malice or ill-intent. Unexpected. "What do we do now, then?"

"It's up to you, Pasquale. I can continue the repair and you can hang it on your wall to admire for the beautiful piece it is. But you'll also know it's not the authentic Ter Borch."

"That sounds rather deceptive, you think?" he said.

No kidding. "Or I can simply return it to you."

"Or we can report it to the authorities." Samantha waved her hand over my sheet of paper before I could ask what she was thinking. "Maybe they can help get your money back from the dealer who sold it to you?"

Stop, I wrote.

She scratched my word out and jotted underneath it, *He knows I'm not clueless.*

It was a calculated risk, but likely the right one. Every time she pretended not to know anything, he'd scoffed at it.

"That's of no use. I bought it ten years ago and can barely even remember who I purchased it from."

Poor provenance library? I wrote, eliciting a nod from Samantha. "I feel bad having to break this news to you. It's rare but happens occasionally."

"Did you tell anyone you took this job for me?"

Samantha grinned, like she knew what was coming next. The truth.

"You asked me not to."

He hummed in question. "That doesn't actually answer the question."

"Pasquale, I'm bound by a code of ethics, which includes working in the best interest of my client and the artwork. If it was particularly complex, I might have discussed it with my father, but it was not."

"In that case, I have another job for you."

Samantha added another checkmark to her sheet.

"I have a painting I'm intending to sell. The sale is proving difficult as the provenance is... somewhat murky. I'd like for you to authenticate it."

Samantha shook her fists, exaggerating her excitement, as though I could have missed the twinkle in her eyes or the way she practically danced from one foot to the other.

"If I have it delivered to you, could I be assured of your discretion? No discussions with anyone. Other than Ms. Caine, of course. I wouldn't expect the two of you to separate for this job."

"I can look at it," I said, not wanting to, but recognizing it was the right choice. "Depending on how much work is required, it may have to wait until we get back from our vacation. And I may need to take it to the Ferraro's office."

"I understand, so long as you only take it to the office after hours. Again, discretion is required—I'm sure you're accustomed to that?" He must have been referring to my prior work for my uncle. How much had Vincenzo learned?

"Sì, and what about *The Music Lesson*?"

"Give me your address. One of my men will deliver the new painting and bring the other home, so we can burn that piece of trash. I'm not hanging a fake on my walls."

Samantha wrote, *Here?*

My gaze rose to meet hers. I didn't want one of his men here. Didn't want them to know where we lived or to be inside our walls. This was too dangerous. This was a step beyond what I was willing to do. Fiori was still controlling the exchange. He knew what Samantha did. He intimated he knew about my work with my uncle.

He knew too much.

Enough of this silly game. "Prior to Friday, the last time I saw one of your bodyguards, he tried to kill me. I'm not interested in anyone from your organization coming to my home. I don't mind doing the work. It will cost you, but I'll do it."

Samantha's eyes widened and she mouthed, *What are you doing?*

Perhaps some of it was my temper peeking through or my desire to keep my fiancée safe. But I was not playing the fool in front of this man.

"I was wondering how long you'd continue this dance." Fiori chuckled and I could have thrown my phone against the wall. "I like you, Antonio. We have a great deal in common, you know?"

Samantha frowned and folded her arms, continuing to telegraph very clear emotions to me.

"You flatter me, Pasquale."

"I tell you what—I can send a familiar face, if that would make you feel better?"

Samantha practically dropped her pencil before scrawling, *NO!*

Red, hot rage bubbled in my stomach. "If you mean Vincenzo, you can cancel the entire deal. I will not have him anywhere near my woman."

"So she told you the truth, did she?" Fiori sounded almost surprised. What had Vincenzo said about his relationship with Samantha? Did he genuinely believe she was in love with him and not me?

"Of course she did," I snapped. *Calm down, Tony. He's baiting you.*

"No need to worry." Fiori's voice was almost a purr, the tone of a man who knew he'd won the night. "Vincenzo's elsewhere right now. Do you recall my pilot, Jason? He flew you both back to the mainland after my doctor took care of Ms. Caine's ankle? He was also at the restaurant on Friday night. This piece is precious to me and I'd like one of my most trusted men watching over it."

That sounded like a longer-term commitment than a simple delivery.

Samantha mouthed, *Watching over?*

"He can be at your place tonight."

"No," I said. There were plans to make. Discussions to have with the FBI. If it were anyone other than Jason coming, I would have argued further. But there was little point. "I'll need to go by the studio and pick up additional equipment. Plus, it's late and I'm tired."

"Tomorrow afternoon, then. Jason will arrive at three o'clock." He cleared his throat, no doubt intending the next as a threat. "Be sure you're there. I look forward to this new arrangement."

After I provided our address, I disconnected the call and stared at the phone. "Marone, bella. What have I gotten us into?"

Chapter 17

Samantha

A conference table large enough for twenty dominated the Oaks boardroom at Foster Mutual Insurance. Windows along one end overlooked the building's front lawn, parking lot, and the trees dotting the roadside.

Elliot and another Special Agent took seats across from me, withdrawing laptops from their bags.

We'd agreed to meet at my office since I had to be here anyway, and the stream of people coming in and out of the building would mask the two FBI agents' attendance. I'd told the front desk I had some policyholders in to discuss a large claim and left it at that.

Elliot—in a dark suit with a white shirt, as usual—gestured to the similarly dressed female agent with him. "This is Kelsey Bernard. She's been working with me on the smuggling case for the last year."

Kelsey's white-blond hair was styled in a pixie cut. Between that, her dark suit, and her bright red glasses, she reminded me of a younger version of Rhonda Wells, the owner of Mason's Gallery in town. "I have paperwork for you to sign, consenting to surveillance, and I want to go over some ground rules with you."

"Of course. Do we want to get started?" My schedule for the morning was tight. "I've only got a half hour before I'm meeting with my boss."

Kelsey tapped a few keys on her keyboard. "Once Dr. Ferraro and our prosecutor arrive."

"Antonio won't be joining us today."

Elliot cocked an eyebrow at me. "No?"

"Unfortunately, things are moving too fast. He had prep work to finish at home before heading to his office to pick up additional equipment. With the painting arriving this afternoon, we need to be sure he's ready." Not that we knew what *ready* meant. It was possible Fiori was being honest about the second painting and it wouldn't be a stolen piece or a forgery. We could wind up researching a fifteenth century da Vinci or a 1980s Basquiat. "I can go over everything with you and I'll fill him in. If it's paperwork, we can figure something out."

Elliot nodded. "We reviewed the notes you sent about your conversation with Fiori last night. Are you maintaining the theory that it was a test and that he wants you both working for him?"

"It still makes sense, but we'll have to wait and see how everything plays out."

Kelsey looked up from her screen. "Can we trust Dr. Ferraro? It was a reckless move to bring up his uncle during the conversation."

"I felt the same way." I glanced at my watch. Twenty-five minutes before my meeting with SIU and Matt. "But we talked about it afterward. Antonio said the goal was to sound emotional, which would make Fiori think he was sharing more than he'd intended—making him think he still had the upper hand."

Elliot smiled, that same smile that usually went with *When are you coming to work for me?* After his comment yesterday about wanting both Antonio and me working for him, that look took on a whole new meaning. Antonio Ferraro and Sam Caine—partners.

My phone buzzed and I glanced at the screen. "That's Nathan. He's at the front desk. Let me sign him in."

Before the door fully shut behind me, Kelsey whispered, "I thought we were getting a federal prosecutor to replace him?"

Elliot responded, just as quietly, "Not with her in play."

Kelsey said something else to him, but the closed door muffled it. Did she object to Nathan because she knew he and I were close? Or was there some other issue?

The Oaks boardroom was at the front of the building, down a long hallway from the entrance. High cubicle walls on one side, smaller boardrooms dotting the other. Nathan waved at me from the large reception desk down the hall. I raised a hand to return the gesture and a flash of dazzling light hit my eyes.

Shit.

The ring.

I tucked my hands behind my back and smiled as I hauled off the engagement ring, placed the promise ring back on its original finger, and slipped the giant diamond into my pants pocket. I hadn't called Cass with the news and would get in so much trouble with her if Nathan found out first.

"Sorry I'm late." Nathan placed a hand on my arm and kissed my cheek.

"No problem." I talked with the receptionist, a pretty woman with dark hair whose gaze lingered too long on my big brother stand-in. Getting the visitor's badge should have taken thirty seconds, since I'd advised her there would be a third visitor for my meeting. But it must have taken five minutes.

Unphased by the attention, Nathan accompanied me down the hallway. "I got stuck in another meeting that went over. How are you holding up?"

"I'm fine."

He lowered his voice. "You know I'm not happy about this, right?"

Reason number fifty-three why I'd encouraged Antonio to take all the time he needed at home and not join me for this meeting. "This is about taking down an art smuggler, not about your happiness."

Outside the Oaks, I reached for the door handle, but Nathan stopped me.

"I'm not the enemy here, Sam. I don't know what was going on with you Friday night, but you know I care about you and I'm looking out for you."

"I know." And most of me appreciated it, but I wasn't about to confess everything.

"There were rumblings one of the federal prosecutors on the task force was going to take over for me on this case, but I insisted. I don't trust anyone else to have your best interests at heart."

That must have been what Kelsey and Elliot had been talking about. "You don't think there's some conflict of interest going on here?"

"Don't get me wrong, Sam. I'll still do my job. But you're not just a cooperating witness or a confidential informant if I'm involved."

Or with Elliot involved. No, with Elliot, I was his mentor's daughter.

A wave of nausea flew through my stomach.

No thinking about your father now. This is work, Sam.

"I know," I repeated, and opened the door before he could say anything else.

Nathan started talking before he'd even pulled out a chair. "Goals, boundaries, and how far we'll let this go. That's what I'm looking for."

Kelsey frowned at him.

Nathan was smart, and although I'd never seen the professional side of him, I knew he was good at it his job. But it was more intense than I'd expected from the goofy guy who used to pick me up and spin me around every time he said hello. He placed a leather messenger bag on the table and pulled out a laptop as he sat.

"Good to see you, Nathan." Elliot grinned. "Now that you're here, let's get going before Sam has to leave us. We're assuming the next painting Fiori delivers will be a stolen one, given his comments about a murky provenance. The priority is to identify it, meet with Fiori and record him admitting he knows it's stolen and that he's intending to sell it. Our goal isn't for him to admit he's the head of our smuggling ring, but that would be helpful."

None of this was news, but hearing him say it in such a formal setting caused a tiny pain in my chest. What were the odds we'd be able to accomplish all that and still get away for vacation? Antonio would not be happy.

Kelsey pulled a small black box from her bag and pushed it across the table to me. "I understand you drive a Ford F-150. Fortunately, those are common enough around here, so we had a recording device ready to go."

I opened the box, which contained a key fob resembling the one for my truck.

"Lock button to record, unlock to stop the recording. It can store days of conversation, so don't worry that you're recording too much."

"Does it have to be out in the open?"

"That would be best, but so long as it only has a thin layer of fabric over it, like in a pocket, you should be fine."

I turned the device over in my hand and pressed the Lock button. A small red light flashed. Clicking Unlock, two flashes. "Recording indicators?"

Elliot nodded. "Kelsey will give you her number. The second you make any plans to meet Fiori, you call me and if you can't reach me, call her. You've been in danger too many times over the last year, and I don't want to take any risks right now."

"None of us do," said Nathan.

From the moment I'd met Pasquale Fiori, I'd felt there was something off with him. The bodyguards, the superyacht, the way he'd originally said Antonio would owe him a favor for helping me. But him being involved with the smuggling ring Nathan had been talking about since August hadn't occurred to me that beautiful summer day. That he was involved in some sort of illegal activities, sure, but not that.

"Wait." I tapped my fingers against my forehead. Memories flashed through my brain as pieces of a puzzle I didn't know I had to solve were falling into place. Nathan telling me about the smuggling ring. Adjusting a claim at Nathan's house, where he had reference books about the Gardner Museum Heist. Elliot telling me there were whispers about Johannes Vermeer's *The Concert*, which was stolen during that heist.

Holy shit. Goosebumps exploded up and down my arms. "You think he's bringing us *The Concert*, don't you?"

Nathan's guilty glance toward Elliot told me everything I needed to know.

"You think that's why he brought us the fake Ter Borch?" I raised fingers as I hit the big three reasons. "Same country. Same period. Same size. It was a test because it's so similar?"

Elliot shrugged, but I'd known him long enough to spot the tiny twitch of his lips. "No one knows where it went after the heist, except the people who took it. How many hands did it change since then?"

"But the Ter Borch was a forgery. With a sketch of *The Concert* underneath. What if the actual test was to find out how good his forger is?"

"In the end," said Elliot. "These are the things we're hoping you'll find out."

"Do you suspect Fiori's at the top of the smuggling ring? Is he the one you've been going after this whole time?"

"That's none of your business." Kelsey stood and retrieved the empty box the key fob had been in. "You're an informant, not a member of the—"

"We're still not sure." Elliot's disapproving gaze fell on Kelsey, making it clear who was in charge. "At a minimum, he's a buyer who most of the pieces go to. A massive collector. We've located houses in Corsica, Miami, and Hong Kong, plus a warehouse in Brazil. His holdings, businesses, everything we and Interpol have been able to get their hands on is a maze. We have a team of analysts combing through details, but he's either legitimate or Fiori's team is better than mine."

Nathan sat forward, swiveling his chair toward me. "We originally suspected Antonio's uncle was a major player. I still think he originally was, before his efforts to get out of the smuggling business."

Elliot scratched his goatee. "There are other parties we're watching closely—a museum director from Amsterdam and a couple of antiquities dealers in Brasília—but the only person we've got reliable details from so far is a former chef of Giovanni's."

"Wait." My hands shot up to stop him. "The chef who poisoned Giovanni?"

Antonio told me Giovanni *got rid of* the chef. We'd thought that meant he was dead.

Kelsey's lips had tightened so much they should have turned blue. "Elliot, this isn't appropriate."

Elliot rounded on her uncharacteristically. "This is my case, not yours. I decide what's appropriate for *my* resources." Or maybe it *was* characteristic, and I'd simply never seen it before?

"Samantha has proven herself repeatedly, so she's getting the information she's earned."

"Earned?" Kelsey snapped back. "No. Intel about what she's about to face, sure, but not this. She doesn't get this kind of clearance."

She'd said doesn't *get*, not doesn't *have*. Was Kelsey one of the people preventing Elliot from obtaining my security access?

Nathan said, matter-of-factly, "Kelsey's right."

Elliot took one slow breath and returned to his normal pulling-all-the-strings self. Knowing he'd started with the Clandestine Service put a different spin on how well he normally controlled his emotions. "This case has been a challenge, but I have a feeling if we can take down Fiori and remove his money from the equation, the landscape will change dramatically."

And once again, it was on my shoulders. Well, mine and Antonio's. For the first time, he was all-in with me. Maybe Samantha Ferraro. "Is it all art and antiquities?"

There was a knock on the door and Harry Bell, one of my SIU co-workers, stuck his head in. "Sorry to interrupt, but—Special Agent Skinner, I wasn't expecting to see you here."

Kelsey flipped her laptop shut. "This is a closed-door meeting."

I was officially late. I didn't do late. "I'll be right there, Harry."

Harry didn't pay me any attention, instead smiling at Elliot, who rounded the table to shake Harry's hand. "Are you here for Roger's case? Our fraudulent claims? Or maybe about the Scotts?"

"I'm poaching," Elliot said.

Harry stood as tall as Elliot, with graying brown hair and as commanding an aura. He'd retired from a career in the Brenton Police Department and came to work at the insurance company's Special Investigations Unit. "She's on leave for the next three weeks. So as long as your poaching doesn't last longer than that—"

"And if it did?"

I stood, no intention of allowing this conversation to continue. I hadn't discussed my hopes to consult for the FBI with anyone at Foster Mutual—including my brother-in-law, who worked in the IT department—and didn't plan on starting that conversation now. "I said I'll be right there, Harry."

Harry's keen eyes stayed on Elliot for a beat before he turned to me. "Don't forget, the president of the company is waiting for you."

I flipped over my watch. Ten minutes late. I had the key fob, knew what was required, and only had the paperwork left. The rest was nothing more than curiosity. "I'll be upstairs in two minutes, Harry."

CHAPTER 18

SAMANTHA

No matter what I wanted, Kelsey was right. For this case, for this moment, I had a job. Receive the painting from Jason, help Antonio figure out the truth, and then meet with Fiori. But the way she'd reacted... If she was behind the delays in my security access with the FBI, maybe performing well in this operation would change her mind. Maybe she was the key to unlocking my future as a consultant.

I scanned the door in front of me, barely able to look at the nameplate with my ex-husband's name on it. How many twists and turns would my life continue to take? Leaving the FBI due to grief over my mother's death, running into a sham marriage with Matt to cover it up, and floating around the United States for six years after the divorce.

Fate kept bringing me back to where I'd began. Meeting with the FBI. Meeting with Matt.

I was stuck in a never-ending cycle, my goals still out of reach.

Not all your goals, Sam. I switched my promise ring to my right hand and put on the engagement ring. Marrying Antonio would be the right choice. I could do that. Right?

The door swung inward and I startled.

Matt stood there, close-cropped brown hair and beard, his perpetually furrowed brow just as furrowed as always. "Were you coming in? Or were you inspecting the door frame? You're not going to tell me there's some structural issue with it, are you?"

I waved the sarcasm off and walked in, carrying my laptop under my arm. The recording device weighed heavily in my pocket. Fiori was smart—that was clear from Elliot's comments that they hadn't been able to tie him to anything concrete yet. It wouldn't be easy to get a confession out of him. This wasn't a low-level criminal we were dealing with.

Last month, Matt had redecorated the office. It used to house his father's giant mahogany desk, which was designed for intimidation. It suited Roger. Matt had chosen a paler wood, much smaller, and a casual meeting area with a low table and couches instead of office chairs. This suited him.

Matt and I sat on the couch next to each other, opposite Harry and Quinn. Quinn was the other member of our SIU team, and in some ways was a female version of Harry. Same age, same graying brown hair, same brown eyes. But despite the two of them talking as though they shared the same brain—picking up when the other slowed in speech—he was calm while she was emotion.

"Mother of Pearl, Samantha!" Quinn said when I sat my computer on the table. "That ring is gorgeous! And new! Spill the details."

So much for keeping it under wraps. I should've left the ring in my pocket.

Or at home.

"No real details to share. Antonio got home Friday and popped the question."

Quinn smirked at me. "Those are facts, not details."

As usual, when Quinn started prying, Harry came to my rescue. "Quinn."

"Oh please, you old stick in the mud. The girl just got engaged."

"The woman doesn't want to talk about it," said Harry.

Undeterred, Quinn leaned forward and gave me a mock whisper. "Just tell me it was intensely romantic?"

Heat flushed through my cheeks. The lights, the flowers, the music. The dance. The sex on his patio. A different heat flooded through my body.

Quinn sat back on her coach. "Enough said."

Matt cleared his throat. "Can we get down to business?"

How did he feel about this? He was the one who asked for the divorce. He was the one who'd fallen in love with someone else. Hell, after I found out he got remarried, I jumped out of a plane five times. Once for every year between the divorce and then.

Not that it mattered.

"I'm more interested in the meeting she was holding in the Oaks." Harry hadn't appeared bothered when he interrupted us, but his tone made it clear he was. "You actually going on vacation, or is this a cover?"

Shit.

Quinn didn't slip out of the sly mode. "I thought I saw that Special Agent here. Elliot Skinner, right?"

Matt sat up straighter and turned to me. "Is this about my father's trial? Should I know what's going on in my family's company?"

As far as I knew, Elliot hadn't taken on Roger's case, except where Olivia Scott had been involved. "Yes, I'm going on vacation with Antonio. Yes, the FBI had some questions for me about the Scotts because they're still working that case. Yes, I met with them in the Oaks boardroom so I wouldn't be late for this meeting. And no, Quinn, before you ask, I don't know when the wedding is going to be."

The depth of the lines on Matt's forehead could have competed with the Grand Canyon.

"Matt, I swear. It had nothing to do with your father." Our current meeting, on the other hand, had plenty to do with him. "I met with IT last week, and the last of the safeguards I'd proposed have been implemented. No one should be able to override any of the fraud flags in the system without at least one other person authorizing it. Not even Matt or one of the software architects should be able to."

Matt got that same look as he did every time we discussed his father—who'd defrauded the company by manipulating a loophole in the software system—like someone had pinned him down and forced him to eat pineapple on his pizza.

"I wanted to finish reviewing the claims I suspect Jimmy filed fraudulent police reports for, but I have one more for when I get back."

Taking advantage of the change in subject, Matt pointed to Quinn. "You take that claim."

She nodded, scribbling in her notebook. "Most of the claims Sam flagged for Jimmy's case turned out to be fraud. I expect it's just a matter of going through paperwork?"

"I'll review my progress with you before I leave. But the focus of that investigation has shifted." I'd been pulling more than double-duty on those cases, searching for signs of fraud both for Foster Mutual and for the cases against Jimmy, Parker, and possibly the people behind the pawnshop. "Jimmy died, so that part of the—"

"When? How?" Harry dropped his notepad on the couch and pulled out his phone. He maintained close contacts inside the Brenton Police Department, which he put to frequent use during our SIU investigations. News like this rarely surprised him, and the scowl on his face made it clear he wasn't happy.

"I heard about it Saturday. They're calling it—"

Matt stood from the couch and we all watched him stroll the length of the bookcase lining the wall beyond the couches.

This company had been in his family for generations. Roger hadn't been a good father-in-law, nor a very good father. Matt never said anything about it, but given some things Roger said to me after Matt and I got divorced, I couldn't imagine what he said to his son.

Now every time we had this meeting, when I updated him on the status of repairing the company after his father almost destroyed it, at some point he sank into this mood. Hearing about Jimmy couldn't help, considering he was also awaiting trial.

Who knew what was going to come up in court, but my instincts told me that Jimmy was going to factor into Roger's case.

Harry's phone pinged and he returned his focus to it. Someone must've had news about Jimmy.

Quinn looked pointedly at me and inclined her head toward Matt. *Go say something to him*, that look said.

Feelings. Yeah, that was what I was good at.

I got up and crossed the twenty feet until I stood next to Matt. "Do you know when your dad—"

"I haven't talked to him since January. I wanted to assure him that the company was in good hands and that I'd negotiated a deal with the reinsurers." He pulled a framed photograph from one of the shelves. His grandfather and the Board of Directors when he took over. "But when I told him you were the one the board insisted on, he lost it."

They'd chosen me because I was the one who figured everything out. If Cass hadn't gotten sick, and I hadn't come home and taken a job at Foster Mutual, and I hadn't taken on Olivia Scott's burned Chagall claim, Roger could've kept doing what he was doing.

One more thing for Roger to blame on me.

"All he cares about is himself." Matt put the photo back on the shelf but didn't take his hand off of it. "He even started in on me about Ty again. As though *I* was the colossal disappointment because I married the man I... Sorry, Sam."

I put my hand on his back and lowered my voice to keep my words as private as I could when there were two other people in the room. "Don't hold back to spare my feelings. I'm engaged to an amazing man now. If you and I had stayed married, neither of us would be with the partners we belong with."

"You were always a good friend. I've missed that."

Better friend than a wife. At least for Matt. "But an even better investigator."

"So good, we almost don't need you anymore," said Harry.

Before I could turn around and ask what he meant, I heard a smack. Quinn must've been expressing her displeasure with his comment.

"Seriously." Harry placed his phone face down on the table and picked up his notepad. "With the software upgrades you specified, the workflow changes in both underwriting and claims departments, and the awareness you've brought to the entire team about how even our little company is susceptible to fraud—"

"We barely have anything to do," Quinn finished for him. "I know we talked about it already, but this really is the perfect time for your vacation. Give us a chance to test and see if the reduction in bogus claims is because of the changes, or because you're so busy hanging over everybody's shoulders."

"I don't hang over people's shoulders."

Harry and Quinn's gazes slowly met. They shook their heads and looked back at me.

"Okay, maybe sometimes." But I'd been asked to do a job and I was going to do it right. As an insurance adjuster, it often made people's lives easier if I could meet them in the evenings, so I was used to working around the clock. Plus, it distracted me from Antonio's absence for the last three and a half months.

"If you really want, when you get back..." Harry paused.

Harry never paused. At least he never paused without Quinn immediately picking up for him. Without looking away from me, he nudged her. They had something prepared. Something she didn't want.

Matt finally tore his eyes away from the photo. "I'm meeting with the Board just before you get back. Harry, Quinn, and I all agree that my report will recommend we implement a transition strategy. Reducing the SIU staff from three back to two."

Was one of them retiring?

"Hon, I know your original plan when you moved to Brenton was to only stay until spring. Working in the office is obviously driving you crazy." Quinn was right, but when she said it that way, I wasn't sure how to take it. "Cliff wants you back adjusting claims. I want you with us."

But what did I want?

I wanted to work with Elliot.

At least, I had until Friday. Had too much changed on Friday?

"Is that what you want me to tell them?" asked Matt.

This meeting was not going in the right direction. It was supposed to be about Jimmy. About Roger. About the claims. About the changes.

None of it was supposed to be about me.

I flipped over my watch. Noon. Antonio was expecting me. "I apologize for cutting this short, but I think we've already covered everything. Quinn, you and I need to review the claim I have left linked to Jimmy, and I need to be out of here in ten minutes."

No one argued. Undoubtedly, everyone wanted out of the meeting.

"Matt, I'll let you know. I need to think."

Five months ago, he'd told me he needed me in this SIU role if the company was going to survive. I'd met that challenge head-on, and now what? Why wasn't my chest bursting with pride? No one expected I'd be able to do so much in so little time.

It had to be everything else weighing on me.

I had to get going. *The Concert*—a painting I'd dreamed about finding for over a decade—might be headed to my doorstep.

So why wasn't I excited?

CHAPTER 19

ANTONIO

I pulled my SUV into my spot behind the Ferraro's office. Matt Bellamy of Muse wailed from the stereo about pressure and the expectations of everyone around him. "I feel you, my friend."

The music stopped as I opened the door, the guitar riffs running through my brain as I walked to the building. Everything was ready at home—including a special surprise for Samantha—so my goals were simple: get in, tell Sofia about Cesca's desire to visit, and get the portable x-ray machine loaded into my vehicle.

Most importantly, don't lose your cool. Every time I replayed the conversation with Fiori, the fire in my stomach grew hotter. Hidden motives. Veiled threats. And the ever-present knowledge, deep in my gut, that Fiori was trying to pull me into his organization.

Samantha would arrive at any minute, so the two of us could go for lunch and hopefully forget everything that was going to happen. At least for the few hours we had left before Jason would arrive at my condo.

When my feet hit the concrete floor, a little of the weight sitting on my chest released. This office was almost as much home as my parents' house. From the time we moved to the States when I was fifteen, so long as I lived in Brenton, I worked here at least part-time. Cleaning brushes, sweeping floors, calibrating equipment. Before that, I did the same things at the studio in Roma.

As much as my father encouraged me to follow my passion with architecture restoration, it had always seemed a given I would work for the family company.

"Antonio!" My cousin Frank waved a hand in greeting from his worktable near the front of the room. The last time I'd seen him—my throat tightened—the last time I'd seen him, he was still in the hospital. Memories of his blood on my shirt flooded over me. Of the fear which had clutched my heart while I waited to find out if Samantha had survived the shooting.

I ground my teeth together, holding back the emotions. How dare Parker Johnson have a new lawyer? He deserved to rot in prison for what he did to Frank, Samantha's friend at the climbing gym, and what he tried to do to the two of us.

We're all fine and he's in jail. Remember that.

I walked over to his table and gave him a hug.

Alice, his girlfriend and one of our other conservators, dropped a swab to the side of her work and came for her own hug. "Where's Sam?"

"She'll be here soon. We're heading out for lunch."

The clacking of stilettos against the floor reminded me how foolish I was to think I'd be able to get in and out quickly. My sister paused in the open space between the lobby and the studio, crossing her arms. "What exactly are you doing here today?"

"I'm here for the portable x-ray machine."

"Why? I thought you two were leaving for three weeks? Because if you're staying, then I can speed up a few projects." Office manager, bookkeeper, professional pain in the ass.

I squeezed Frank's arm, intentionally not looking at how he'd changed the part in his hair to hide the scar, and approached Sofia. Folding my arms right back at her, I frowned. "You know that letter you gave her on Friday?"

Sofia's mock disapproval of everything I did faltered. "Yes?"

I dropped my act, as well, and pulled her close to kiss her cheek. Lying was not something I wanted to do, but there was no way I could tell her what was truly going on with Fiori. "Samantha figured out how to line up the onionskin sheets and she wants to do a little digging. I think she's using it as a delay tactic."

"Why would she delay going on vacation?"

I shrugged. "Sometimes, I don't think I'll ever understand that woman."

"Good for her." Sofia smacked my chest faster than I could get out of the way. "You need a woman who'll keep you on your toes." She patted the spot she'd hit. "In a good way, of course."

Sofia had adored Samantha from the moment they met. My big sister had always advised me on how to handle women, rarely giving me advice I wanted to hear, but it was almost always right. Had it not been for Sofia's meddling, Samantha and I never would've gotten together.

I wanted to confess about the engagement. The nervous energy consuming me since the first call from Fiori on Friday night battled with a new energy. An excited one from being this close to my sister and so close to telling her I was getting married.

As though the woman could read my mind, Sofia's eyes narrowed. "You're hiding something."

"Never." Fortunately, I had something to cover my deceit. "Cristian called me."

Sofia threw her arms in the air and stomped back to her desk. "That son of a pig. What does he want now?"

Apparently, Papa agreeing to give Zio Giovanni a chance didn't extend to my sister.

"You know they're trying to change things? And they're helping the authorities?"

"You mean they're telling you they are?"

No, I mean the FBI has told me they are. More lies and secrets. "He said Cesca wants to enroll in a program here this summer, and I was thinking you might have room?"

Sofia's eyes lit up, and all of her anger, whether real or exaggerated, vanished.

"I was not sure if it would work out with the boys and a teenage girl, but I know she's normally surrounded by men every day, so maybe—"

"I always wanted a girl." She leaned a hip against her immense desk and finally smiled. "There's too much testosterone in my house. I'll talk to Pietro about it." Her smile turned wicked. "It'll be worth it just to take her out of that miserable house with our uncle."

No argument from me on that point.

"Speaking of too much testosterone." She waved a hand toward the street, visible through the glass wall. A sleek black Audi coupe parallel parked in front of the building, a petite passenger with dark hair in the front seat.

Lorenzo, my younger brother, got out of the driver's seat and came around to open the passenger's door. He was casual, despite it being working hours, in jeans with a quarter-zip navy sweater.

"I could smack that boy," said Sofia.

"Why?" I stood transfixed as—as Lucy got out of the car.

Talking a mile a minute Lucy. Always popping gum bubbles Lucy. Samantha's best friend Lucy. Why was she with—and why was she wearing a Wharton T-shirt under her black jacket? That was Lorenzo's alma mater.

Wait.

When Samantha and I arrived at my cousin Mario's home in January, Samantha mentioned Lucy had texted her many times about Lorenzo. That was the last time she'd told me about it. My brother was not as open about his personal life as I was, but surely Samantha would have told me about this? "What's going on with them?"

"Nothing!" She threw her hands in the air as she made her way to the door. "You see how he looks at her? You need to talk some sense into him."

Lucy entered first, gave Sofia a quick kiss on the cheek, and rushed to my side, throwing her arms around me. "Antonio! It's been too long!"

"Sì, it has." I kissed the air by her cheeks and stepped back. "How are—"

"We're just here for a few minutes. Lorenzo needs to talk to your dad about some business stuff, and then we're going out to—"

"Do you want to see the offices upstairs?" Sofia slipped her arm around Lucy's waist. "It's almost finished."

"Ooh, yes!" Lucy patted my arm as she left. "Good to have you home again."

Lorenzo's gaze lingered on the spot where the women disappeared around the reception wall, Lucy's voice trailing off as they got further away. He came to my side, lips tightening. "Good flight home?"

"What are you doing here?"

"I see the charismatic brother is just as charming as always." Strange comment, considering he flirted as much as I used to.

"No. I mean, shouldn't you be working?"

He shrugged. "Lucy's commencement is this weekend and she needed to get some new shoes."

"You're dating Lucy?" This felt like information I should have had.

"Lucy?" He scoffed. What did that mean? "We're just friends."

Sofia might have been right about him.

"You took the day off work to help a friend buy shoes? A friend who owns her own car?"

"I told you, we're just friends." He put his hands up, as if in surrender. "I know the rules."

This conversation made less sense the longer it went on. "What rules?"

"She's yours. Flirt, but don't touch. You've been very clear about that in the past."

"No... *Samantha* is mine. Don't flirt with *her. D*on't touch *her.*"

"Whatever." Lorenzo rolled his eyes dramatically, like the youngest born he was. He walked past me, toward the studio. "I need to see Papa about his investment portfolio."

I grabbed his arm, turning him to see me. "Not whatever."

He yanked his arm free and straightened his sweater. "No dating your girlfriend's best friend."

"My relationship with Samantha has nothing—"

"Like that friend of Faith's I hooked up with?"

"Friend? It was her little sister!" The memory of Lorenzo coming out of her hotel room during our trip to Jamaica made my stomach squirm. Faith had been furious and insisted I do something about it.

"We were both twenty-two." He pointed at his nose, then swiped the hand through the air, as though to hit me, but thinking better of it. "You broke my nose for that one."

That had been one more sign about Faith I'd ignored. "But Lucy—"

"Lorenzo!" bellowed Papa as he entered the room. "I was starting to think you weren't coming. But then I saw the lovely young Lucy with your sister, and I knew you wouldn't be far behind."

"They're just friends, apparently," I muttered.

"And Antonio? What brings you here today?"

Again, why I thought I could sneak in and out of this place was beyond me. "Samantha and I decided to stay in town for a few more days, and I have a project I want to work on at home."

"It must be wonderful to be here with her again." My father clasped his hands over his heart dramatically, like the true romantic he was. So romantic I could almost forget he was the one who forced me to Italia for eight and a half months.

"It is." Although it would be far better if we were on a remote island somewhere without cell phones, emails, and paintings.

"This project of yours—Sofia didn't mention having you on the schedule this week. Is it a personal project? Found something interesting underneath one of your own paintings?"

"No, Papa, it's just—"

"You know, my boy, you can bring it here to work on instead of lugging all the equipment home. I'd love to have you in the studio."

"I'd rather spend the time at home with Samantha."

"Of course." Papa waved over my shoulder and I turned to look out the front glass. "Speak of the angel."

The universe slowed, and my heart gave a tremendous single beat before continuing with its familiar rhythm. Samantha's smile built slowly—the stress of the last few days showed on her face, no doubt compounded by meeting with her ex-husband—but the longer our eyes locked, the larger it grew. She'd chosen a stunning black suit with skinny pants and a pale pink blouse for her meetings with Elliot and her SIU team. Her poor hair was confined in a too-professional bun.

The moment we arrived home, I'd have to untie it, comb my fingers through it, and encourage her to relax for what few moments we had before Jason's arrival.

I hurried to open the door for her, bowing my head as I did.

"So cheesy," she whispered.

"My love!" Papa made a beeline for her, to kiss her cheeks, as he always did.

But I inserted myself between them and snatched her left hand to cover the ring before he could see our surprise. "Can I tell them?"

"Tell them what?" asked Lucy, as she and Sofia appeared from the studio.

Samantha squeezed my hand, sending a wave of joy through me.

"I wanted to let you all know…" I kissed her hand and lifted it to show them all the ring. "Samantha has agreed to—"

The squeals from Lucy and Sofia drowned out the rest of my words. They ran at Samantha, nearly toppling me over in the process. Sofia assaulted her with a barrage of questions: how long was the engagement to be, where did she want to get married, who would she ask to stand up for her? Lucy spoke over my sister, talking about average engagement lengths, average wedding sizes, and a tradition she witnessed somewhere in Portugal while traveling with her family.

Papa clapped me on the back, his ever-present smile even broader. "Congratulations. Should we call your mother?"

I'd secretly talked to Mamma about this a few times. She even helped with some ideas on how to ask. The fairy lights were her idea. But I hadn't called to tell her the result. "We'll come by tomorrow or Wednesday and share the news."

Lorenzo had remained silent since our argument about Lucy, lurking behind Sofia's desk. His gaze remained on Lucy, his mood appearing to lift a bit every time Lucy laughed.

Sofia was right. He *did* look at Lucy *that way*.

I approached him. "Lorenzo—"

"Congratulations," he said, barely looking at me. "Papa, we should get our meeting done."

"Of course." Papa braved the fray of women and they parted so he could give Samantha a hug. "Congratulations, my love. I'll be proud to have you in the family."

"Thank you." Samantha's face had turned several shades of crimson, her discomfort at being the center of attention clear. With the opportunity to change the subject, she looked over his shoulder at me. "Did you get your things yet?"

"I've not had a chance. Can you give me twenty minutes?"

"Take your time." She checked her watch, inspiring me to do the same. We had two hours before Jason would arrive. "I brought those onionskin sheets with me in case I had some downtime."

"More wonderful news!" Papa waved his hand in the vague direction of the office upstairs. "Why don't you use the investigator's space? You *are* doing an investigation for Ferraro's, aren't you?"

"Need a hand with anything?" asked Lucy. "I was just going to hang out and wait until Lorenzo's done, anyway."

Samantha grinned at her best friend. "I don't suppose you have your computer handy?"

"Of course!" Lucy walked to the desk and held her hand out in front of Lorenzo.

Without a word between the two of them, he dropped his keys into her hand and she darted out the front door.

Samantha watched Lucy go, then frowned at Lorenzo. That look told me she knew more than she'd told me.

Sofia smacked the back of Lorenzo's head as he left with Papa, ensuring our father didn't see it. "Come on, Antonio. Let's find whatever it is you need."

"Remember, we have to get lunch and be home in two hours." I kissed my fiancée on the cheek. There was a fifty-fifty chance she'd become so absorbed in her research she wouldn't want to leave.

CHAPTER 20

SAMANTHA

Lucy placed her backpack on a desk upstairs, once the two of us were alone. "Did you ask Elliot if he was the guy in the letter from your mom's book?"

My brain stuttered. I couldn't escape Dad's last message. "I've got something else that's higher priority."

"Ooh!" She rubbed her hands together. "What are we looking at?"

I handed her the envelope the sheets had arrived in and made my way to the big windows at the front of the office. Not as tall as the ones downstairs, but they were roughly eight feet, starting at thigh height. Between the light streaming in through the front, plus the open space overlooking the studio and the light coming in from the skylights, this would be an amazing office to work in.

Classical music filtered through the air from recessed speakers in the ceiling and walls. It shifted to a rock bass line, and Sofia broke the calm, yelling, "Antonio!"

Lucy laughed again. "They're as bad as when we worked on the Scott case last summer."

"Always." I hung the onionskin sheets on the window with some bookbinder tape I'd grabbed on my way upstairs. Antonio and I had already secured them in the correct orientation before moving them from his light table. Next to them, I taped a scanned printout we'd done, after digitally enhancing the drawings. "These sheets arrived at Ferraro's on Friday, in that envelope, addressed to Ferraro's FAI."

"FAI?"

"Fine Art Investigations." I pointed to the sign leaning against the wall separating the stairs from the office. "It's a new initiative Dom's launching. Given some of the cases Antonio and I have been involved in, as well as some stuff that happened to Dom's brother Andrea—"

"The brother who runs the Rome branch of the company?"

"That's the one." *Should I ask about how much she and Lorenzo discuss his family? Or why she's waiting around here while he's in a meeting? No.* "Dom's passionate about combating art crimes, so he's doing something about it."

"Hold up, now." Lucy raised her hands, craning her neck to look at the Investigations sign and back to me. "You're marrying into this family. Is *this* what you're leaving Foster Mutual for? Not the FBI?"

"I never said I was leaving."

"You said you weren't sure."

I dragged a hand over my forehead. *Focus, Sam.* "I only found out about this place on Friday."

"Antonio didn't tell you?" She unwrapped a piece of gum and tossed it into her mouth, the scent of classic Hubba Bubba wafting off it.

"He didn't know, either." I tapped the printout. "So, these sheets were loose inside the envelope."

Lucy turned the envelope over. "No return address?"

"Just the stamp cancel telling us it's from New York."

"Old stamp, too. Not something you get at the post office these days." She held the envelope against the window with the other papers. "And not a regular envelope, either?"

It was a non-standard size and shape, with crisp edges and an almost handmade feel to it.

Lucy put a finger to a seam and popped the back open. "Not held together tightly."

As she unfolded it against the window, we drew closer. There was a lighter section near the middle, in the shape of an x.

"Is that a—" I started.

"Watermark? Yeah." She popped a bubble so big it almost hit the paper.

I turned my head slowly, cocking one eyebrow.

She swallowed, but not the gum, and twisted the sheet so it was upside down. "Two crossed paintbrushes."

Something skittered through my brain. A memory. I knew this symbol from somewhere. I closed my eyes and tried to stop thinking about it—tried to let it come to me. "It's an art supply store's logo."

"From New York?" She handed the unfolded envelope to me and pulled out her phone, typing away.

"Maybe?" I'd spent a lot of time in New York, almost as much as California. Working storms, gallery and museum consults, and general claims adjusting. "Could it be related to the words written on the onionskins?"

Lucy held her phone out in front of me. "Indigo Lake Art Supply in SoHo."

"What's their address? Any chance it's 13 Fell Avenue or something?"

"Lemme check." She scrolled and tapped, navigating her way around their site. "Pretty high-end products, from the looks of it. Conservation materials, antique paints for period reproductions, and a wide selection of handmade papers from around the world. But nothing about 13 Fell."

I paced away from the window, toward the railing to look over the edge. The conservators were practically statues, each of them working small pieces in front of themselves. I headed to the nearest desk. To the sign. "Maybe the people at Indigo Lake know something about it?"

"You think the watermark's another clue?" Lucy took the envelope from me and sat at the desk, pulling out her laptop. "They go to all these lengths to conceal the actual images and words. Why not spell everything out clearly once the whole thing was together? Why bother with the mystery?"

"If 13 Fell isn't an address—the only one I could find was in California and the envelope came from New York—what else could it mean?"

"Maybe the address in California is where a stolen thing is going to? Or where it came from? Maybe it's a..." Her keyboard clacked as she typed, no doubt searching for each thing she rattled off. "Brand name of a color, like Blue Number Thirteen or something? Maybe it's about thirteen things falling?"

"Depending on who you ask, thirteen's either a lucky or an unlucky number." I closed my eyes, running through religious meanings, mathematical significance, television, and sport. How did any of them relate to falling? "Thirteen people at the Last Supper, just before you could say Jesus fell."

"It's a prime. A Fibonacci number." Lucy popped a bubble. "Atomic number for Aluminum."

"Twelve gods in the Greek pantheon, plus Zeus as the thirteenth."

"Speaking of which, did I tell you I'm going to Greece in a couple of weeks?" Lucy's fingers continued moving across her keyboard as she talked, chatter being the sign she was getting close, but not quite there yet. "My parents are doing a tour of the Greek islands for the summer, and I haven't gone anywhere with them since I started at MSU, so I figured, what with graduating and all, I'd join them. You know, make videos, eat food, meet people."

A little pit opened in my stomach and I lost focus on the scanned sheet. She was leaving?

Her fingers paused. "I need to clear my head and get back to my roots."

"Your roots aren't in Greece." They were as firmly in Brenton as mine were growing.

Lucy was of Chinese descent and her travel-vlogging parents had adopted her as a baby. Despite being a numbers and data whiz, she was also a free spirit. "I'd been traveling with my parents for as long as I can remember. Living out of a suitcase *is* my roots."

That made some sense. Still, she'd weaseled her way into my life and the thought of her not being there was... was... not good.

Everyone leaves, Sam. No, they don't. "We should focus on this mystery letter."

The hum of her keystrokes resumed. "I like working with you, Sam."

Same.

"Never the same thing twice, you know?"

Hold on. What if it *was* the same thing? What if it was from Fiori and had something to do with the painting Jason was bringing us? I strode to the window to stare at the sheets. This was the same as Dad's letter. The more I stared, the more I got lost in the trees instead of seeing the forest. I ran a finger over the scan—we'd obviously picked up some dust when we made it, as there were additional markings that didn't fit with the rest.

Lucy's bubbles popped over and over. Voices floated up from downstairs. The music returned to classical.

And still I stared.

Was it dust?

I shifted to the onionskins, closing in so tight the lines blurred. The stray marks were almost visible. Untaping the top sheet, I flipped it up to look at the next one, and the next, and the next. Each of them had extra dashes and dots near the word Fell. "I think whoever made this messed up. The sheets got out of alignment as they were finishing it."

Fell was only part of the last word.

I spun to discuss it with Lucy, but she was chewing furiously and put up a finger for me to pause before her fingers increased in speed on her keyboard. "One sec. Chatting."

Antonio's voice came from the main floor, "Frank, can you help? It's heavier than I expected."

Something lurched inside my stomach, like the moment when Antonio got down on one knee. Not the nerves or anxiety I usually felt. Not the numb fingertips. It was more like the first time I found a foothold on El Capitan. I was all of two feet off the ground, but the overwhelming surge of excitement and wonder for what I was about to do overcame me.

I loved a good puzzle, especially a good art puzzle. Usually that meant insurance claims, but over the last year, the puzzles also brought a ridiculous amount of danger.

But no one was in danger now. In this moment, with Antonio downstairs and Lucy working by my side, everything felt... what?

"Indigo Lake's website—" Lucy's words snapped me back to the moment.

What had just happened?

"They've got a chat function and someone in the store responded right away. No one working there today knows about the letter, although they've all heard of Ferraro's." She hit several more keys. "The conservators, not the investigators. No one's heard of them."

I took the scanned version off the window and twisted it ninety degrees. "I tried a visual search on a few art databases based on the sketch in the letter, but it wasn't complete enough for any hits. The squiggles have to be water, but what does the hand mean?"

"Pointing to something?"

"No. It's just open like it's holding something."

"They're asking if they can forward one of their clients to Ferraro's." Lucy giggled at her laptop, apparently still engrossed in her online chat.

Was the hand dropping the water? Is that why they were on either side of the painting? Or was it a sketch showing placement?

"They have an old painting they suspect might be a looted piece from World War II."

"There are databases for things like that." Hell, the hand could be an Egyptian hieroglyph, for all I knew. But the way it was cut off, with the bent wrist, maybe it was a stand or a display for something? Maybe it was another painting?

"I guess this client was saying—"

"Lucy, one mystery at a time."

"Sure, boss. I'll give them the address."

My head rolled forward and I fought to hold in the sigh. Dom hadn't hired anyone to work here yet. Sending more investigations his way wouldn't help.

"Related note: they called their boss, who also didn't know about the onionskins. Except that they sell onionskin sheets, of course." She was suddenly at my side, took a photo of the painting, and returned to her desk. "I'm going to send this to them. Maybe they'll recognize it."

I sat on the windowsill, the cool glass at my back. "If it's not the staff, it must have come from one of their customers. I expect there's too many of those to check with all of them."

With a flourish, she hit one key—likely to send the photo—and looked up at me. "What next, then?"

"Look for that stamp. Maybe there's a clue to who the letter came from?"

She nodded and popped a bubble, hunkering down in front of the laptop once more.

Stolen 13 Fell-something.

Fell-something. I pulled out my phone and did some searches for words starting with Fell. Fellah. Fellow. Felling. Fellsmere, Florida? Fellatio? No.

Unless the misaligned letters were another word, not a continuation of Fell. Stolen 13 Fell Off? Fell Away? Fell Down?

None of it made any more sense than the original.

All I had was Stolen 13 Fell.

I stood and taped the sheet to the window again.

Unless... prickles ran up and down my arms.

There were thirteen items stolen during the Gardner Museum heist. Could there be a link to Fiori and the FBI's expectation he was bringing us *The Concert*?

But the painting on the onionskins wasn't a Vermeer and it wasn't one of those taken during the heist. And even if it was, what did Fell mean?

"Boom!" announced Lucy.

I spun to see her hands launch into the air.

"I. Am."

"A genius, I know." I walked to her side and looked at her screen.

"I found completed auctions on eBay, Sotheby's, and another little auction house where those stamps have been sold within the last couple of years. I ruled out eighty percent of them, which had already been canceled by the Postal Service before

1900. A complete tangent, but interesting: The face value may be two dollars on each of those stamps, but an unmarked one is valued at $5,000."

I peered at the unfolded envelope next to Lucy. "That's a bit more than was needed."

"Maybe our mysterious author didn't know?"

"How do you forget paying that much for a stamp and accidentally put it on an envelope?"

"Eccentric billionaire? Amnesia? Alzheimer's?"

Two of those would explain the letter, not just the stamp. "Do you think this is a wild goose chase? Someone's playing with us?"

She shrugged, browser windows flashing across her screen as she continued working. "Not like I've got anything better to do."

I lowered my voice, in case it carried over the railing and Lorenzo wasn't sequestered in Dom's office. "Why are you here with him?"

"I'm going to see if I can find anything out about the buyer." Not wanting to talk about it was a change for Lucy. Not wanting to talk about *everything* was a change for Lucy.

"Did something happen?"

"One mystery at a time, right?" She blew a tremendous bubble, which she let die and deflate. "I wouldn't bother with the big sites, but this little one might yield something. How much time do we have?"·

"I'm serious, Lorenzo." Antonio's voice and footfalls carried up the stairwell.

"Sounds like we're out of time, Luce." I gestured to her laptop. "Do you mind digging into this a little more? Antonio and I have another project to work on, and—"

"I'm all over it." She closed the lid and stood to stuff it into her backpack.

Antonio and Lorenzo arrived, neither of them smiling. "Ready?" they said in unison, then frowned at each other.

"Good luck with the shoes," I said to Lucy, as she and Lorenzo left.

Antonio joined me at the front window, where I was peeling off the tape which held the sheets in place. "Any discoveries?"

"Lucy's got a lead she's going to track down. I don't know if it'll amount to anything, but it's worth a try."

Antonio's arm wound around my waist, and he kissed my temple. "Do you mind if we head straight home so I can get the x-ray ready in case we need it?"

"Good idea." The more prepared we were, the faster the process would go, and the sooner Fiori would be out of our lives again. And hopefully the sooner *The Concert* would go back to Boston and the Gardner Museum. And the sooner I could win over Special Agent Kelsey Bernard—assuming she was blocking my security clearance—and get that consulting spot with the FBI.

I folded the sheets and turned toward the office. Whoever Dom hired would be lucky. Maybe until then, I'd pick up some of their jobs. That potentially looted piece from Indigo Lake's customer might be interesting. Lots of research to do there. I could bang that out quickly.

"Bella?" Antonio was holding my hand, urging me forward. "We were leaving? Remember?"

"Yeah. I just need to let your dad know about another investigation being sent from New York. I'll meet you at home."

Chapter 21

Antonio

I monitored the security feed from my phone, watching as Samantha exited the elevator. Her conversation with Papa must have taken longer than expected. Perfetto. It had been just enough time to finish my surprise. "She's almost here."

"Perfect timing." Claude, one of the security contractors my family dealt with regularly, closed the door to the library behind him. "It'll only take a few minutes to initialize the system and she'll be as secure as the safe upstairs."

Marcus had let him in while Samantha and I were away to install a special lock on the library door. It should meet Elliot's requirements, allowing her to spread her crop circles all over the floor and not have to worry about hiding them away every time she left.

I hurried to meet her at the door, opening it with a flourish.

"Are you going to keep doing that all day?" she chuckled.

"If it keeps you smiling."

"Sorry it took so long. Your father likes to talk." She slid out of her shoes, dropping two inches. "And Sofia cornered me with wedding venue ideas."

"Sounds like her." I grimaced for Samantha's benefit, but it was for the best that someone else was nudging her along the decision path. "Good thing you escaped. I have a surprise for you."

Her shoulders drooped. "Please tell me it's a good one."

"You'll love it." I grabbed her hand and hauled her behind me.

Her grip tensed when we arrived in the hallway. "Claude?"

The last time she'd seen him was the day of the shooting at Ferraro's. Claude had been our detail that day, and Parker nearly ran him over.

"How are you do—" Samantha's gaze fell to the panel next to the door, and she cut short.

"I was thinking." I pulled her closer, so the three of us huddled in the hallway around the closed door. "You need a space to call your own, which you don't have to tidy whenever you're distracted."

Claude tapped something into the tablet he carried and a yellow light at the side of the panel began flashing. "Whoever wants to start can press their finger on the panel."

Samantha didn't budge, just blinked in a rhythm which almost matched the security panel light.

"Bella, this is your office now. We can limit access to you, if that's what you need, or—"

She ripped her hand from mine and flung her arms around my neck. "You're kidding? You're giving me an office?"

Claude, no doubt accustomed in his role as a security consultant to being in the background of people's lives, averted his eyes.

"Bella." I laughed, hugging her back. "I can only give it to you if you set up your fingerprint."

She leaned back, took my face in her hands, and planted a tight-lipped kiss against my mouth. Something Samantha Caine did *not* do in public. "This is seriously the best present anyone's ever given me."

Claude was fighting back a smile. "If you can apply your finger to the panel?"

Samantha released me, nodding her head rapidly. "Of course."

"I didn't know if you needed biometric or key or what, so I had him install the best system he had."

She and Claude went through several fingers and her thumbs, processing them from every angle. The lock clicked and whirred. They opened and closed the door. He explained how to manage the system, how to add me, if it became appropriate. Once they finished and we'd walked Claude out, she held me tight once more.

"I'm serious, that was the most thoughtful—oh my god!"

"We can move the piano to one of the other rooms, maybe move some of the books elsewhere, as I expect you'll need shelves for your reference library."

"I'm going to get the pawnshop box right now!" She darted out of my arms and up the stairs, two at a time, even more excited than I'd expected.

While she was upstairs, a phone rang from the direction of the bedroom. Cristian's burner phone. It was almost three o'clock and Jason would arrive soon. Did Cristian have a warning to pass along?

I dashed into the bedroom, to where I'd left the phone on my bedside table and flipped it open. "Ciao?"

"What news with the painting?" Cristian's voice was sharp, fast, lacking the control and command it usually possessed. He must have expected me to call with the details.

"It was a fake."

"And Fiori?"

"Took it better than expected." I walked to the great room when I heard Samantha coming down the stairs. "He asked me to authenticate another piece."

Cristian muttered a curse under his breath. "Of course he did."

She paused on the bottom step when she saw me and mouthed, *Cristian?*

I nodded and waved her to continue. The box of papers and photos was heavy—I'd stored it away in the morning—so the last thing I wanted was her lingering around while carrying it. "Jason didn't tell you?"

Samantha's excitement over her new office had already faded with this call. And perhaps with the crushing reality that Jason was almost there with the mysterious painting.

"No. He normally only checks in every month or two, but I expected more frequent, considering Fiori was messing with you."

I leaned on the back of one of the dining chairs where I had a clear line of sight down the hallway. My body wanted to pace, but that wouldn't inspire the calm I needed. "Jason's bringing this new painting to us and Fiori said something about him watching over it."

Cristian was silent.

"We *can* trust him, sì?" If Fiori truly meant for him to remain in the condo until I was done, I needed to know. Were we safer with him than any other of Fiori's bodyguards? "There's no question of his loyalty?"

Samantha came out of her new office, closed the door, used her fingerprint to unlock it, opened it again, and closed it. For all the stress and worries, she was still excited about this small thing.

"I trust him with my life," said Cristian. "And with yours, otherwise I wouldn't have demanded he stay in place."

Samantha's fingers drifted to her neck, where she clasped the diamond necklace I'd given her for Christmas. Then she opened and closed the door one more time. She was playing with the lock.

"Alright." My smartphone buzzed in my pocket, with an alert from the front desk.

Samantha pulled hers out and typed something into it before turning in my direction. "Jason's here."

"Cristian, I need to go."

"Keep me up-to-date, if you can. And remember what I said about my phone number?"

"I will." I clicked off and met Samantha at the front door. "You told them to let him up?"

"Yeah." She gripped my hand. "Are you ready for this?"

"Bella…" I gave her my most debonair smirk, hopefully exuding more confidence than I felt. "I was born ready."

She shook her head and opened the door. The elevator numbers climbed to ten, and the door opened.

Jason stepped out, wearing black cargo pants and matching T-shirt, with a backpack slung over one shoulder, and a hard-sided case. It was a similar size to the first one he'd provided, which was propped against my worktable upstairs, waiting for him to take it away. He stopped before entering, and spoke in English, "Dr. Ferraro. Ms. Caine. In case you don't remember me, my name is Jason."

"Of course." I waved him in and let the door close once he was inside.

"So we are clear, my job is to ensure nothing happens to this painting." Jason pointed deliberately at his ear. "I'm not leaving without it."

I couldn't see a hearing device, but that must have meant someone was listening. Was it in his ear? His watch? The case? My doubts about Jason calmed for a moment. Surely, this warning meant he was loyal to the Ferraro family. Unless it was designed to throw us off and there was more than one listening device?

Several rooms in my condo had glass walls, but they were all reflective, so no one could watch us, at least.

"Antonio's studio is upstairs." Samantha walked out of the foyer and into the great room. "If you'll follow me? He has all the tools we suspect he'll need up there."

"Suspect?" asked Jason as he climbed the stairs.

"Until I see the painting and run some tests, I won't know exactly what I need. Pasquale didn't provide any details on artist or period, which makes it difficult to anticipate." I guided him to the worktable near the back, by the wall of windows and the patio.

Jason placed the case on the table. "Signore Fiori asked me to remind you that he's looking for proof the piece is authentic. However, if there are any repairs you think are absolutely necessary, he will entertain those as well. No matter what, there is to be absolutely no risk to the integrity of the painting."

"Sì, of course. That's standard for any art conservator. The art comes first. Always."

He slid aside a panel by the top handle, revealing a keypad and scanner. "Before I open it, I'll have to ask that you don't take any photographs or tell anyone about this project."

"I'll have to take some as part of the conservation effort. Infrared and x-ray images, if nothing else."

Samantha stood on Jason's other side from me, her breathing becoming more obvious with every passing second. She flexed her fingers, drummed them against her thighs.

Jason was quiet, raising a finger to his ear. It *was* an earpiece and it was two-way, not just one. He nodded slowly. "So long as they're not sent to anyone and you destroy them after, that is acceptable."

Samantha shoved a hand into her pocket. I had to stop looking at her or the anxious energy would rub off on me.

Jason punched in a code and placed his thumb next to the keypad. The case clicked, and he unlatched the lock, opening it to reveal my fate.

I drew in a sharp breath and tried in vain to slow the beating of my heart. Nestled in a foam lining cut perfectly for its ornate wooden frame lay one of the most sought-after pieces of art in the world. *The Concert*, by Johannes Vermeer. Barely more than two feet by two. Stolen over thirty years ago.

Samantha's gaze was glued to it, her mouth and eyes wide. Its theft was the one she was supposed to investigate for the FBI when she joined all those years ago. She breathed, "It's beautiful."

"Dio santo," I whispered. "I could have made a thousand guesses about what you were bringing me, but this would never have been one of them. It's gorgeous."

A woman in yellow and white sat at a harpsichord, a male lute-player sat next to her, and another woman stood while singing. The black-and-white floor pulled me in, then it was the way the light hit the white skirt of the seated woman, the paintings in the background, the lush decoration of the harpsichord's lid. I wanted to soak it in for hours.

If it was the real thing.

What were our next steps if it was? There hadn't been time to review strategies or tactics with Samantha, or even to discuss her meeting with Elliot. What were we supposed to do? The first step would be to verify if it was genuine. Then what? Hand it over to the FBI? If Jason brought it to us, was that enough of a link to Fiori?

Jason swung his backpack onto the table and withdrew a manila envelope. "And in case your word isn't as good as Signore Fiori believes it is…" He slid out two large photos and my heart seized.

The top photo was of Cassandra and little Emma, playing in their front yard. Samantha lunged forward and grabbed it. "What's this supposed to be?"

The second was Sofia with her youngest son, Nico. Che cazzo, no.

Jason had not cracked a smile or a grimace, nor given any hint of emotion since he'd arrived. "There's a substantial reward for information leading to the recovery of this painting. I trust you don't need the money, but all the same, we don't want it to go missing."

Samantha leaned against the worktable, as though her legs were about to surrender. She'd lost so many people in her life. There was no way I'd risk doing that to her, nor to my own family.

"I'll let you get to work." Jason zipped the backpack and walked over to my desk, peering around the setup. "I expect you're feeling inspired and want to get to work. I'll be downstairs and will check in every thirty minutes."

I wrapped an arm around Samantha. "Don't worry, bella."

Jason waved us over to the desk, where he'd grabbed a pencil and paper. He wrote, 'The earpiece microphone is good, but it shouldn't pick up things you say when I'm downstairs. Watch your volume anyway.'

One of the fifty knots crowding my stomach loosened. He *was* on our side. That was something.

Finger pressed to his mouth, Jason headed to the stairs.

Once he was gone, Samantha snatched my hand and dragged me out to the patio. She kept her voice down. "We need to call Elliot."

"Are you mad?" I flung my hand toward the worktable. "That's exactly what this threat is about. We can't call them."

"The FBI can protect them."

I could barely form words. Was she serious? "The way they protected Jimmy?"

Her hands landed on her face, and for once, I let her leave them there.

"And even if they could... If Fiori can't get to Sofia and Cassandra, who next? Lorenzo? My parents? Lucy? My cousins? Mario?" I was already too deep in this, and I hadn't even touched the painting. "Samantha, there are no charges pending against Fiori. These are just random photographs. You wouldn't even be able to arrange for any protection."

"Then we tell them to get out of town."

"For how long?"

She dragged the hands down to her cheeks, determination glistening in her eyes. "Until Fiori's behind bars."

I grasped her hands and held them against my chest. "Bella, how long have they been after him already? Elliot just said yesterday the case is not progressing fast enough."

"Fuck." She tried pulling her hands back, but I held them steady. "We have to do this, don't we?"

"If we believe Fiori was behind the attempt on Zio Giovanni's life two—"

"Elliot confirmed he was."

I sucked in a breath. Marone, how far did this go? "If we also believe he was behind Jimmy's death, there is no reason to think those photos are an empty threat. I need to go back in there and do exactly what he's asking. And as much as I hate to say this—you need to keep it quiet."

CHAPTER 22

SAMANTHA

Abstract impressionism. Primary colors red and blue. Ground of white. Thin streaks of yellow and gold, almost like marbling. My gaze followed the paint strokes and the splatters, absorbing the flow and the abrupt halts in the painting. Fifty inches by eighty-four. Big piece. Stretched canvas, no frame. Stretcher had two gallery tags and a stain near the bottom left.

The box Elliot had given me was full of photos and documentation of paintings and other artwork from the pawnshop's hard drive. Most of them were long gone by the time the FBI shut the place down, and they weren't sure how many had been bought and sold legally.

The working theory was that the pawnshop was involved with the smuggling ring Elliot's team was investigating. Antonio and I had found a stash at Parker's girlfriend's that was headed *to* there, another at an auction which had come *from* there, and the FBI had also found several other stolen pieces in their inventory.

I closed my eyes and placed a finger on the bottom left of the photo I was reviewing. Tracing my memory of one yellow thread, around a blob of blue, into an explosion of red. I re-opened my eyes with my finger in the right spot.

This painting was committed to memory. I moved it to the pile on my right and pulled one from the stack in front of me.

I sat on the floor in Antonio's library—now my office—with my crop circle all around me. My office. Antonio couldn't even get in without my say-so.

How had I wound up with a man who understood me like that? Who knew what I wanted and needed without having to ask? How lucky was I?

Cass's face flashed through my brain over and over. She and Emma at the party on Saturday. Family dinners every Sunday while Antonio was away. Birthday parties.

Focus on the paintings.

I should have known tangling with Fiori was a mistake. We had to put an end to this. And it wasn't by going along quietly and doing his bidding. That painting upstairs had to be a fake. The universe couldn't allow someone like him to own the real thing. It just couldn't.

The next photo was another covered in splatters. My brain refused to let it in, so I tossed it onto the stack it had come from. Twisting at my waist to release some of the strain on my back, I found the Impressionism folder behind me and pulled that one closer. Maybe I needed to shuffle the art movements.

How was Antonio doing upstairs? Was he having the same problem focusing? I'd offered to work with him, but he wanted privacy. Quiet. So I'd changed into some jeans with a sweater and sat on the floor of my new office. By myself.

That was normally how I preferred things.

Not now. Not today.

Impressionism is your favorite style. It will distract you.

I flipped open the folder and slid the top photo toward me.

But—holy shit—I knew the one underneath it. I got up on my hands and knees to get closer. A bundle of energy ripped through my chest.

Holy shit.

It was the painting from the onionskins.

I was sure of it!

Where did I leave them? They were in my purse when I went to Ferraro's. Did I take them out? I launched to my feet. Whoever sent the letter to Ferraro's either had that painting right now or had it at some point. Which one made more sense? And why send the coded letter?

It was real. The painting was real. It wasn't a game by some eccentric billionaire.

I had to get the onionskins to be sure it was a match.

Slow down. I knelt to look at the notes with the painting. Many of the others had a record of who'd brought them to the shop and when they'd sold, but not this one. No notes at all, except its name: *Grainfield at Midday*. But it... I scanned the documentation. It wasn't in the pawnshop when the FBI got there.

Had it been sold illegally? Maybe moved to the next leg in the smuggling line? Or it could have been a victim of data loss from the recovered hard drive.

If the letter came from whoever had it now, that might point us to another step in the ring.

My phone buzzed from the desk and I jumped. I was off work, so I wasn't answering for them. I couldn't talk to Elliot, not with Jason there. And I definitely couldn't talk to Cass, because she'd know something was wrong. Who else would be calling me?

It wasn't important, so I ignored it. There was a mystery to be solved, right in my hands, and I couldn't leave it.

The phone went still, then began buzzing again. I crossed to the desk. It was Lucy. What if she'd discovered something from her search?

"Luce! What's up?"

"Okay, so I can't tell you who won that auction." She popped a gum bubble. Was that on purpose? She knew it grated on my nerves.

"Why are you calling, then?"

"Because I got into a directory listing with some hashed values in it and the same value as on that stamp is on a few other pieces."

"Hashed?"

"Encrypted. I told you all about that three months ago." She paused, slurped a drink, and continued. "Database admins hash critical data, like social security numbers and stuff like that. So if we assume the most important piece of data an auction house is keeping would be the buyer's identity—because there's also no field showing that information—then I can filter the listing down to only those with the same hashed value as the stamp."

"And?"

She'd obviously found something, but this was what I had to endure to get information from her. The more clever her solutions were, the longer the explanations took. "Theoretically, that means I have a list of everything that buyer ever purchased from the auction site."

"Which means...?"

"One of the things purchased from that auction site was a giant sculpture of a hand, with a wrist bent at ninety degrees."

I punched one fist into the air but kept my tone as neutral as possible. The last thing I needed was Lucy's head to get bigger. "Excellent. But how do we find out who that buyer is?"

"Check. Your. Email."

I woke my laptop, which was sitting on the desk. "Is this where I'm going to call you a genius again?"

"I'll just wait in silence for a moment."

"Doubt that."

She giggled. "Okay, maybe not. Do you have it yet?"

"One sec." I opened my email program and the message from Lucy dropped into my inbox. It included a link to an article from an architectural magazine that included the hand statue as a yard installation. "How did you find that?"

"Insta. Found an influencer who posted a photo of herself with the statue—it was a lot bigger than I was expecting, about twice her height—and a comment referenced the article, and I found it. I contacted her, but from the sounds of it, she totally edited the photo."

I skimmed the article. A reclusive art collector, known only as Mr. X, let the magazine reps into his house, a 23-acre haven for art in the heart of Long Island. They took photos of several rooms, immaculately curated. "This is perfect, Luce. Do you think you could dig a bit more into who this guy is?"

"You bet! This is kinda fun."

"Thanks. Call me when you have more." I hung up and almost tapped on Elliot's number. In all the excitement, my brain had pushed aside the worries about Cass and Sofia. What if Jason and his earpiece overheard me talking to an FBI agent? Even if it wasn't about *The Concert*, it would risk our families.

No, the best option was to support Antonio in any way he needed with the painting, then cut all our ties with Fiori. Maybe I could get the recording the FBI wanted, maybe I couldn't. But I'd worry about that when we got close to him.

Maybe this *Grainfield* painting was the key. It was at the pawnshop with no details in the inventory. What if... what if the painting Antonio and I found at the auction was in their inventory somewhere? Maybe the way they'd recorded it would be similar enough to *Grainfield* and then we could find a trend for the stolen artwork.

I scanned the piles littering the floor. Which folder or stack would it be in?

There was a loud knock at the door. "Ms. Caine, it's time to check on Dr. Ferraro's progress."

"No thanks. You go ahead," I called, hoping he'd leave it at that. I couldn't let him see all this paperwork, in case it got back to Fiori what I was doing.

Jason knocked again. "I'm afraid I insist."

"Fine," I muttered to myself.

My office was one of the few rooms in the condo that didn't have windows, and I used that to my advantage. I flicked on a lamp on the desk and shut the other lights off, then opened the door. A cursory glance inside the dark room would likely only reveal the desk, with my laptop, or the piano. Hopefully, the dark lumps all over the floor would go unnoticed. I swung the door open, stepped out, and closed it behind me. The lock clicked.

"Why so much security on this room?"

"Insurance company business. It's mandatory for anyone working from home with client information." I waved a hand and started down the hallway, as though I were as innocent as I was attempting to sound. "You know, addresses, house values, inventories. I handle a lot of data that could be used for identity theft."

"And you're abiding by our agreement? I don't have to send anyone to visit your sister?"

My stomach clenched and I bit back the bile climbing its way up my throat. "Of course I'm abiding by the agreement. You were very persuasive."

Oh my god, we needed to finish this job. And soon.

CHAPTER 23

ANTONIO

Samantha had stayed upstairs with me until Jason's first half-hourly check-in. As desperately as I wanted her with me, her presence was one more reminder of what we were risking by doing this, so I asked her to go downstairs. There was too much at stake for my focus to wander. I had to finish and do it quickly.

After she left, my first test was obvious. The infrared of the forged Ter Borch painting showed a sketch which shouldn't have been there. When I ran the same test on *The Concert*, I'd found a sketch of the right painting, at least.

But a little voice chirped at me from the back of my brain. I was certain Vermeer sketched with paint, not with charcoal. And the latter was what I'd found. I could have researched it further, but Samantha was faster at that, and stopping to sit at the computer would just let my brain remind me of the photo of Sofia and Nico.

Another voice told me to call Cristian. But what could he do? All the arguments I gave Samantha would still stand. How long could he keep them safe? And how many people were in line right behind them needing protection?

I stared more intently through the microscope on my lab bench, studying a minute sample of paint. The painting and its case remained on the worktable at the other end of the room, far enough away I could almost convince myself I was working on a personal project like I'd told my father.

"Hey, honey," called Samantha in a singsong voice.

Jason climbed the stairs behind her. "Done yet?"

I straightened, rolling my neck. "This project will more likely take days than hours."

"How's it coming?" Samantha walked around to my back and dug her fingers into my shoulders.

"I'm still doing preliminary tests in case I can find something quickly." I gestured to the microscope and she leaned in to look. "Charcoal black shows up as opaque, with splintery or fibrous particles. Imagine it's a piece of wood you took out of a fire. You can almost recognize that structure."

"Yeah, I see it." She resumed kneading my shoulders. "Jason, did you want to see what it looks like?"

He shook his head, moving over to the worktable. "So long as you're making progress."

"Sometimes artists used bone black, but its particles are rounder, with a brown cast and sometimes transparent. I need to get my hands on some chemical analysis of Vermeer's works to find out which he used." It was all true, but part of my goal was to bore Jason with technical discussions, so I could ask Samantha about the sketches. "I have a friend who works with the National Gallery of Art. They recently did a survey of four Vermeers, so they may be able to help."

Jason grunted. "You can call this friend, so long as I'm present and you aren't revealing your reason."

I patted one of Samantha's hands, grateful for the work she'd done with my stress knots.

Instead of releasing my shoulders, as I'd expected her to do, she said, "Didn't you tell me about some study on Vermeer's paints by a German guy in the '60s or something, honey?"

There it was again. The codeword. She knew exactly the data I needed but didn't want to give herself away. "Sì, I'm surprised you remember that. And you're right, that might have the information I need."

"I can help. I'd like to feel useful." She sat at the computer desk and woke my laptop. "What should I search for?"

Good question. "Try the keywords German... Vermeer..."

As I rattled off various names and terms she could use, she typed her own search: Hermann Kühn pigments study Vermeer 1968.

When the results came back, she asked, "Do any of these look right?"

I could have kissed her. The first article looked like exactly what she'd been pointing me to. "Sì, try the first one."

With a few more clicks of her mouse, she had a copy of the document available for us. "Isn't that interesting? They studied thirty of his paintings. Is that statistically significant?"

"Depending on who you ask, only thirty-four of his paintings survive."

"Very significant, then."

"Stop." Jason strolled in our direction, rounding the desk to look at the monitor. "Let me see what you're doing."

Samantha scrolled to the top of the document, showing the title matched what we'd said we were looking at.

"It looks alright." He paused, pointing at the earpiece—signaling someone had ordered him to check? With a nod, he headed for the stairs. "I'll be back in thirty minutes."

The moment we heard him sit on the sofa across the great room, Samantha and I both exhaled.

I cupped the back of her neck. "Marone, but you're brilliant."

"No, just have some experience with Vermeer." She placed her hand over mine. "It's been several years since I read this, but I think there are some elements that will help. If that fails, tell Jason you need to call that friend at the National Gallery of Art."

"First, look at what I found." I crossed to the far end of the room, to the wall next to the worktable where the painting lay. I'd taken down a few of my paintings to hang my notes and tests on the wall. "The infrared showed the same sketch as the Ter Borch painting."

Samantha stepped closer, taking in the printout. "I'm pretty sure he blocked with paint."

"That's what I thought."

"The folks at the National Gallery would know?"

"They'd know about the four they worked on. What about the thirty others?" I ran a hand through my hair, letting it rest against the back of my head. "We can't say it's a fake based solely on that."

"Fair." She crossed her arms and returned to the computer. "But I'm betting they have some videos online that might inspire us, so we don't have to get Jason back upstairs."

I knelt next to her once she'd sat and lowered my voice. "Did you notice the sketch was exactly the same as the first painting Fiori gave us?"

She nodded, searching for a Vermeer video on YouTube.

"Do you think, maybe Fiori has a forger who started *The Concert* on that canvas, but switched to *The Music Lesson*? And then they started again with this canvas?"

She stopped searching and played the first Vermeer video on her screen. It must have been to cover our discussion, because it had nothing useful in it. "You think he's intentionally feeding you forgeries?"

I waved my hands in front of myself, like I could grasp an answer out of the air. "Perhaps? Or perhaps this one is the real thing and the first one was going to be a copy of it?"

"So the forger uses the original and starts by duplicating the under sketch, then changes to a different forgery?"

My head fell forward to her arm and she ran her fingers through my hair. Thank all the goodness in the universe I had her by my side. "I don't want to call anyone for advice unless I have to."

"Stubborn man going it alone?"

I lifted my head to gaze up into her stunning green eyes. Green with hints of blue in the right light or when she wore the right shirt. Pale, like the waters off Capri. "I refuse to risk our families for this."

She looked away from me for a moment, and a sinking sensation spread deep in my gut.

"Tell me you didn't call Elliot?"

"Shh." She tapped a finger against her lips and leaned next to my ear. "They gave me a recording device for when we see Fiori."

I shot back. There was no way. "You wouldn't."

The first video ended, and a new one started automatically. At the sound of Lucy's voice, Samantha turned to the screen. It was one of her travel vlogging family videos from the Rijksmuseum in Amsterdam, six years ago. She was discussing the use of ultramarine in Vermeer's paintings.

Samantha gave a tiny laugh. "I guess we just needed to ask Lucy."

"Bella," I hissed, bringing her back to the discussion. "Promise me you won't do this."

"They'll never know. It's hidden inside a key fob. We need to finish this work and set up a meeting with him. I'll record him, we leave, and the FBI can take care of everything after that. If I don't get what they need, that's where it ends."

She didn't understand men like this. I'd worked with them and I knew how dangerous they were. Fiori would just as easily swat a fly as give the order to kill Emma. "You can't do that, bella."

She slid off the chair and knelt in front of me. "I've been running from all the shit in my past for too long. My future..." Her voice broke and she swallowed hard. "It's right in front of me. And I refuse to run anymore."

CHAPTER 24

ANTONIO

I pulled around the circular driveway to the Morning Star Yacht Club. It was a long white stucco building in the Spanish Revival style with tall windows, a rich wood balcony running its length, and a terracotta roof. The yacht club lay on a narrow slip of land in the middle of the Detroit River, boasting a lauded restaurant.

This was the spot Fiori had chosen to discuss my findings.

Jason drove in a separate vehicle behind us, both paintings in his possession. Despite my insistence it would take days to discover the truth, it had only taken six hours. It was Tuesday morning and we still had plenty of time to pick a vacation destination.

Samantha pulled her key fob from her small tan handbag, fidgeting with it as she surveyed the building next to us. She wore navy slacks with a white and blue pinstriped blouse and ballet flats. She'd pushed her aviator sunglasses on her head, like a headband. The sun glinted off the glorious caramel highlights in her light brown hair.

"You're so beautiful."

She grimaced, not looking at me.

I slowed in line behind another vehicle, heading for the valet. "Everything will be alright, bella. We'll give him the news and we'll leave. I won't take any more work from him, and everyone will—"

No. The key fob.

"The one for your truck is shaped differently. It doesn't have a key that folds out of it."

She stared into her lap, clutching the tiny piece of black plastic. "We need evidence."

"We need to get out of his sphere of influence. Not further into it." I placed a hand on her forearm. "We talked about this last night."

The set of her jaw was all I needed. She wouldn't concede this point.

I pulled my sunglasses down my nose to make myself clearer to her. "What if they wand us?"

"It's a key fob. If this one triggers the wand, so would yours." She held it up to me. "It says Ford on it, has all the right buttons, and a little light that flashes when you press one of them. My truck is nowhere near here, so it's not like they can come to the parking lot and start clicking it to test."

I inched the car forward. One car remained ahead of us in line.

She was right. It was well concealed. "It's risky, I know. That's why I didn't tell the FBI we were coming."

"So we're on our own?" Releasing her arm, my hand shifted to her thigh, squeezing gently. "I almost brought Cristian's burner with me."

"Not as easy to hide."

It had been tempting, but I memorized his number instead, as he'd recommended. "You're the one with the training, bella. You talked to the FBI agents. I trust you to make the right decision."

She took my hand, interlacing our fingers. "The biggest risk is leading the conversation. Elliot would want to hear Fiori admit he knows *The Concert* is stolen and that he's planning on selling it. But since we're calling its authenticity into doubt, I think we're looking for a confession of *anything* illegal. Elliot doesn't expect details about the smuggling ring, but he said that would be nice."

"And a tremendous risk."

"Exactly." She jutted her chin forward, and I moved the car to the valet position. "Stick to the basics. I want him in jail, but I'm not willing to probe too far."

"A compromise, then?" I shifted into park.

"Of my morals, yeah." She leaned over to kiss my cheek as the valet approached her door. "And it's really pissing me off."

I cupped her chin in my hand and held her lovely face in front of mine. "Try to keep that to yourself, sì?"

"Not sure if you've noticed, but I'm pretty good at concealing my feelings."

"A little too good sometimes." I gave her a quick peck on the lips and winked at her. "Now sit still in that seat, my love. We have a performance to give."

I pushed open my door and dropped the keys into the valet's waiting hand. Before the other valet could open Samantha's door, I waved him off in time to see her press a button on her fob.

She was live.

A staff member showed us through the two-story lobby, past potted plants and scale replicas of tall ships with complete rigging. Through the framed glass wall at the back of the lobby, double doors granted us access to a vast stonework patio with three dozen tables set up for diners. The patio led to the docks, where over a hundred ships and boats moored, waiting for their owners.

To the right of the patio, an open green space provided room for running and squealing children. A row of trees separated it from the houses next to the yacht club.

Fiori's table stood out, as no one sat at the tables next to it, and it was the only one with two bodyguards hovering next to it.

Samantha walked close to me, wrapped her arm around mine, and leaned in to kiss my cheek—and whisper in my ear. "There are two more goons by the building."

I kissed her temple, using it as a cover to spot them. It took no time, but what concerned me more was what I didn't see. "Where's Jason?"

"Didn't he follow us the whole way?"

I pulled my arm tight against my body, pressing hers to me. "How are those hairs on the back of your neck doing?"

"Standing at attention." She cleared her throat. "I see Pasquale has two guards at his table, another two by the building, and another man seated with him." How good was the microphone on the recorder? She'd hidden it in her handbag, which had an open top, so hopefully it would pick up any conversation without having to make a show of it.

Fiori raised a hand in greeting and stood as we got closer. "Beautiful morning, is it not?"

"It is." I took his offered hand with a smile, then Samantha did the same.

"This is my son, Baptiste." He gestured to the man sitting next to him.

Baptiste barely lifted his chin in greeting and remained sitting. He was in his early twenties, if that, with eyes duller than Fiori's and the same strong nose, olive complexion, and thick dark hair.

Fiori smacked his shoulder. "Get up and greet our guests."

"Good to meet you." Baptiste spoke so quietly I barely heard him over the gulls circling the docks, the water, and the conversations around us.

"And you," said Samantha. "Pasquale, I don't see your boat anywhere? I can't imagine it's hiding behind any of the others?"

"She's too big for many of the marinas around here, so we left her anchored downriver, where there's more space." His superyacht had been one of the most luxurious I'd ever had the pleasure of boarding. The beautiful black and white vessel was reminiscent of a military destroyer, complete with rib boats and a helicopter, softened with teak decks and an impressive art collection.

As we all sat, Fiori spread his arms wide. "It's only been four days, but I can't help but notice there's a new piece of jewelry at the table. This is no longer a promise ring, I'm sure this time. Congratulations are in order?"

Samantha turned to smile at me and my heart warmed. How did she have this power over me, even under these circumstances? "Yes, that would be congratulations. He surprised me with it after we saw you Friday night."

Fiori clasped his hands over his heart. "Ahh, young love. And to think I was part of that glorious evening. Not there, of course, but that I was the last person to see the two of you before you made this commitment to each other." He smacked Baptiste again. "Offer them your congratulations."

His son, no more impressed than when we first arrived, nodded. "Congratulations."

"Let me order some champagne this time." Fiori looked in the distance, as though to signal a server, but his gaze drew back to me. "Or should I wait for after the news you've brought me?"

Samantha placed her bag on the table. An innocent move, but it caused a spasm in my chest. She wanted the recorder closer to them. "We seem to have lost Jason, though. He has both *The Music Lesson* and—"

Fiori's hand shot up to stop her. "We will not speak of that piece of trash. I paid for that painting under the assumption it was genuine. I assure you, it will be burned."

"Of course." She leaned back in her white metal chair and crossed her legs. "You said you're planning on selling *The Concert*, though?"

"Ms. Caine." Fiori eased back, matching Samantha's easy posture. "I was hoping for an update from your fiancé, if you don't mind?"

She handled the dismissal far better than I would have expected. This must have been FBI Samantha, unflinching in the face of veiled insults. "Sorry. Honey?"

I'd handled negotiations and discussed less than legal matters with many people for my Zio Giovanni. Having Samantha next to me both soothed my soul and made me far more nervous. I was not just risking myself, but her. And, marone, our families. "I have to be completely honest. There are indicators that your copy of *The Concert* is inauthentic."

Fiori's face was a mask. Just like Samantha, he gave no emotional reaction to the news. "What indicators?"

"There's a sketch underneath that feels wrong to me."

"That's the same thing you said about my first painting."

"I know." I leaned forward and lowered my voice, almost directly above the recorder. "Unlike that painting, you know this is not a copy of one at a museum, sì?"

Fiori nodded, saying nothing.

Baptiste's gaze meandered across the other tables. Clearly, our conversation held no interest to him.

"And because that painting has not been seen in public for over thirty years, there are few tests we can do to prove it's *The Concert* that was hanging in the Gardner Museum."

Fiori nodded again, gesturing with his hand for me to continue.

"But I discovered something else concerning. Vermeer was known for many things, and one of them was his stunning work with blue shades. He used ultramarine predominantly in his paintings, but this one uses indigo and smalt to a degree I wouldn't expect from a genuine Vermeer."

Fiori scratched at his temple. "You're certain?"

"If I had more time and resources, I could be certain that—"

"No." His lips tightened and he looked at Baptiste, whose gaze had fallen on Samantha's legs. "I meant, are you certain this is the advice you want to give me?"

"I'm not sure." I folded my arms on the table, suddenly conscious that I was the only one sitting forward. It was a position of less calm than the others, but I was there, so I had to remain. "There are other people who are far more experienced with Vermeer's paintings and may have gathered evidence to dispute—"

He let out a long sigh and sat forward, matching my posture. "You know, I've had other people look at it, and I was told it's fine. Why do you think that is?"

"As I said, I'm not an expert in this."

"Do you think it's simply because they're telling me what I want to hear?" He seemed genuine, as though asking for my guidance. "Maybe they're afraid of what would happen if they displeased me?"

No, he was not looking for my guidance.

"The truth is, Antonio, I don't want to put this painting up for sale and be made a fool of. If it's a fake, that destroys my reputation." He held out a hand, palm up, as though wanting me to take it or put something in it. "And was the lovely Ms. Caine involved in your analysis?"

I spoke before she could start asking him questions again. "She was. She has a great deal of experience with art claims. You may not remember this from September, but she's an insurance adjuster."

"I think you mean she's in special investigations?" How did he know that?

"Sì, overseeing the work of the adjusters and underwriters at the insurance company where she works."

"And fraud?" He shifted his focus to her. "Isn't that right, Ms. Caine?"

She pulled her chair closer to the table. "Please, call me Samantha. And yes, my role shifted a few months ago, so I work primarily ensuring no one defrauds the insurance company. Some people exaggerate injuries or car accidents."

"You see?" His focused zoomed in on her, leaning further forward and dropping his voice. "That's exactly what I mean. If I've been defrauded on this painting, I should find out, shouldn't I? And I certainly shouldn't defraud anyone else? Just like *The Music Lesson*. I wouldn't hang it in my house and tell someone it was the real thing when it's not. A man is only as good as his word, and if every word out of his mouth is a lie, how much is that man worth?" He smiled at her. "Or, of course, how much is that woman worth?"

Samantha moved closer still, as though we were having an old chat among friends, rather than one that sounded like threats and insinuations. "Did you buy it from someone you trust?"

I unfolded one of my arms and touched her hand. "I don't think that's an appropriate question."

Fiori continued. "What I find most interesting is that the others couldn't prove it was a fake, so they told me it was real. You, on the other hand, Antonio..." He placed the open palm down on the table. "You can't prove it's real, so you tell me it might be a fake. Does that make you the glass half empty person?"

"I think it makes me cautious."

"An admirable quality."

"And speaking of admiration and appreciation..." I looked at Samantha, wanting little more than to hop on one of the boats with her and never look back. "I've done this work for you. What about our families?"

Baptiste raised two fingers over his shoulder and a bodyguard shifted to listen to his whispers.

Fiori said, "Who would punish one person for the sins of another?"

The bodyguard nodded, straightened, and turned his head while stepping back into his original place. His lips moved, but I couldn't make anything out.

Fiori's eyes narrowed. "Particularly a niece or nephew for the actions of their uncle or aunt?"

Che cazzo. The moisture in my mouth dried up. Was he talking about my uncle? He'd threatened my nephew and Samantha's niece. He was planning to punish me for Zio Giovanni's actions?

Samantha pushed her chair back, scraping its metal feet against the stone underneath us. "So, we're done?"

I felt, more than saw, figures approach me.

"No, Ms. Caine." A corner of Fiori's mouth twitched. "We're not done."

Another bodyguard hovered too close to Samantha, preventing her from moving her chair any further. The two behind Fiori and Baptiste moved closer to them, flanking the Corsican men.

"I have more jobs for you." Fiori lifted one finger, and the man behind him withdrew a thick envelope from his pocket and placed it in front of me. "I know we didn't discuss the actual terms of payment, but I'm sure you'll find I'm very generous. And I need the same input on four other pieces."

I couldn't let him pull me in further. That would be the end of me. "I'm sorry, Pasquale, but I have a job."

"Didn't you say you were heading on vacation? I'm sure it won't take you more than a couple of weeks." This was the same tone my uncle used all the time. It sounded like kind words, but it was a commandment.

"What if I say no? You'll have your men hurt me?"

"Hurt you? I thought we were friends, Antonio." He acted as though my words injured him. "No, I would simply look for a way to convince you to say yes."

I twisted my head toward Samantha, who'd planted her feet firmly. She was ready to run or fight, whichever was needed. Cristian's words from January came back to me. *She's a liability. It's clear you'd do anything if someone took her.*

Instead of keeping her safe, I'd marched her into the viper's den, thinking they wanted her brain. When all they wanted was her as leverage.

Without taking my eyes off her, I said, "If you promise you'll leave my family alone, I'll do these jobs for you."

"Antonio." Samantha began to stand, but the man pressed down on her shoulder.

Was there even a job? Or was it only revenge against Zio Gio? "Leave her out of this."

Fiori's hand landed on my crossed forearms. "Honesty is a rare commodity these days. Antonio Ferraro, you're the only one who's told me the truth, regardless of whether you thought I'd be happy with it or not."

"Samantha and I have not lied—"

He squeezed. Not threateningly, but as though it were a mark of support. "Don't start lying to me now."

Baptiste's gaze left us, rising over my shoulder and the building, to the sky in the distance. Then I heard helicopter blades slicing through the air. Not uncommon in this area, where many tours ran out over the river.

Fiori nodded to someone past Samantha and a fifth man appeared, carrying a black wand, only a foot long. He ran it along her side.

"This is how you treat friends, Pasquale?" She inched forward on her seat, making it look as though she were squirming under the one who held her in place.

The helicopter grew louder and my eyes cast about the restaurant patrons. Some looked at us as the bodyguards closed in, while others pointed toward where Baptiste watched.

"Enough, Pasquale." I sat up straighter, fighting the urge to ram a shoulder into the man who'd touched Samantha.

"Try the purse," said Baptiste.

Samantha lunged forward and grabbed her bag. "I've had enough of your hospit—"

The guard snatched her bag and emptied its contents onto the table, her wallet, phone, and key fob spilling out along with lip gloss and some scraps of paper.

As I attempted to stand, a giant hand landed on my shoulder. I grabbed the wrist, twisted at my waist, and pulled his balance forward. My body turned from Samantha and I heard something smash on the table.

"That's not a key, Ms. Caine," whispered Fiori.

No, no, no.

They knew.

Fiori's guard was next to me, his knee connecting with my shoulder, and I recoiled into the guard who'd been behind me.

Another smash—this time on the ground near Samantha—and she grunted.

"Leave her—"

One man grabbed my right bicep, exactly where the bullet had punctured the muscle four months ago. I swallowed a cry, shifting my balance enough to drop from the chair and out of his grip, but the other followed behind, wrenching my arm against my back and punching my bad shoulder.

"Don't hurt him," snapped Fiori. "Let's go."

They'd twisted me enough that I caught sight of Samantha. Her phone lay in pieces on the ground, the key fob shattered. She'd downed the man who'd been behind Baptiste, but the other grabbed a fistful of her hair.

"Hey!" yelled a man at a table nearby.

Screams erupted from the crowd. What was going on? I couldn't move to see anyone else.

Samantha's hands flew to her head, and she latched onto the wrist of the man holding her. It wasn't enough, though.

A dark blue helicopter landed in the green space. Fiori and Baptiste were already on their way. It must have been the one he kept on his yacht.

The man holding Samantha ripped something from a pocket, put it to his mouth, and jabbed it against her neck.

She shrieked, sending ice splintering through my veins.

A jolt of power surged through me, and I threw my head back, connecting with the nose of the man behind me. He let go.

Samantha's legs gave out underneath her, and the man released her hair, throwing her over his shoulder before she hit the ground. He dashed toward the helicopter and I scrambled to my feet, trying to catch them.

Two of them ran with handguns. That must have been what scared everyone else away from helping.

Blood pounded through my body, my injured bicep, through my back and shoulder where they'd hit me. Pain streaked through my head, but I pushed forward. "Samantha!"

Fiori climbed into the helicopter. Baptiste followed him. One guard, two, three, and the one carrying Samantha threw her in before climbing in himself.

Ten feet. I was almost there.

And the two guns turned on me.

I stopped. Getting killed wouldn't save her. "Take me with you!"

Fiori yelled over the sound of the rotors spinning above him. "You'll do the work for me?"

"I will. I swear!" Anything for her.

He patted one of the gunman, who holstered the weapon and held a hand to me, hoisting me inside.

I collected Samantha's limp body, practically falling into a seat as the helicopter took off. The interior held two facing rows of four abreast, with another two in front. The bodyguard next to me fastened my seatbelt, while the one with the broken nose scowled from the seat opposite me.

Jason—of course—was the pilot.

That's why he hadn't been behind us. So much for Cristian's assurances Jason would keep us safe.

I cradled Samantha against my chest, staring out as we lifted off.

The guard who'd gone after Samantha first was trying to sit up by the table we'd been at, while a thin man and a woman with shocking white-blond hair ran toward him, guns out. Navy windbreakers. They separated to surround him, and the yellow letters 'FBI' on their backs were a kick to my gut. Had they followed us? Or had there been a tracker in the key fob, as well as the recorder?

I pressed my lips to her head.

If we'd held them off for five more minutes, it wouldn't have been too late.

Instead, I held my unconscious fiancée in my arms. Her lungs expanded slowly, far shallower than when she slept. *She's going to be fine. You have her. She's not alone.*

The FBI would get information from the man they had. They'd find us.

They had to.

Chapter 25

Samantha

Darkness.

A gentle sway.

Antiseptic.

Memories. Antonio. A man's hand. My neck.

I cracked one eye open, the light driving through my skull like a knife straight into my brain.

My head.

"Here. Sip this." A soft male voice.

Something touched my lips. A straw. My spiked champagne on New Year's Eve. I couldn't drink anything. "No."

The straw followed my mouth as I shifted my head, sending the world tumbling end over end. I was going to be sick.

"It's only water."

The voice didn't belong to David Scott. And it wasn't New Year's Eve. I wasn't duct-taped to a chair. I was lying down. In a... a bed or on something soft.

All I could manage was a single rasped word. "Where?"

Metal wheels rolled across the floor. One click. Then another. "I shut most of the lights off. Try opening your eyes again."

My eyes fluttered open, tentative. In the dim light, a man in a white jacket sat next to a hospital bed. My hospital bed. Not a hospital. Too small. A clinic.

The sway churned in my stomach again. We were on the water.

Fuck.

I was in the sick bay on Fiori's yacht. The same place I'd landed in September after twisting my ankle. I forced my gaze around the room until it landed on the man holding a cup with a straw—dark blond hair and hazel eyes that seemed full of more regret than kindness. "Dr. Ivan Hayle."

"Samantha." He held the cup in my direction. "I want you to drink. It'll help your throat."

"Where's Antonio?" I tried keeping my eyes open, but they closed. So tired. Had Antonio gotten away? The two goons were on him before... what did they do? Smashing my cell phone was obvious, but how did they know about the key fob?

Think, Sam, think. The detector the meathead used.

Antonio was right. I should have left it at home.

They caught us. Shit! I bolted upright. Cass, Emma, Sofia, Nico. Everything spun around me so quickly I fell back, grabbing my head to stop it from moving. And to stop it from exploding. So much pain.

A tug on my arm. A pinch. A... an IV?

"What's going on?" I groaned.

"The nausea and vertigo will pass soon. The headache you likely have, not so much. I have a lot of things here I can give you for that, but—"

"No drugs." Whatever the goon had injected me with had acted quickly. One second I was two steps into getting free of him, the next, the sting in my neck and everything went hazy.

Ivan's chair rolled across the floor. He opened a door and then a pill bottle. "How about you drink the water and I give you some acetaminophen? It'll take the edge off."

Helpless was not my preferred role. But until I could sit up without wanting to vomit, I had little choice. I held out a hand and he placed a pill on it.

"Water first."

The straw touched my lips and I sipped, popped the pill in my mouth, and swallowed it all down. "Last time I saw you, you were talking about coming to Detroit to visit your family."

He placed the cup on the counter and took my wrist, checking my pulse.

Keeping every muscle as still as possible, I eased one eye open. "I apologize if my kidnapping got in the way of that."

Ivan settled his hands on the bed next to me. "It's been about nine hours. They brought you in here as soon as the helicopter landed."

"Helicopter?"

"Antonio came willingly, but they confined him to his stateroom."

"Willingly, my ass. How badly hurt was he?" I'd seen him go down, two men on him, but I'd been too busy trying to save myself to watch everything.

"Bruises only. I checked him once I had you set up."

The IV was in the crook of my left elbow, the same side he sat on. I couldn't have screwed this up more if I'd been trying.

Please let Cass and Emma be okay. "You don't know about my family, do you?"

I should have told Antonio to say no. To the first job, maybe. Definitely to the second job. *Tell the girls I love them.* At least someone at the yacht club must have taken a video and told the police what happened. Someone would—oh, shit. If my colossal screw-up hadn't gotten my family killed, the attention it brought to Fiori probably did.

"Signore Fiori asked me to let you know they're safe for now. And he's hoping you'll be more careful about their safety going forward."

Thank god. Now stay calm and think. All you've got right now is your brain. Get the information you can. "Where are we?"

"On the St. Lawrence."

"Going where?"

"I don't know." He leaned forward, pressing the back of his fingers against my forehead. "How are you feeling now? Your color's coming back."

The headache was easing and I risked looking around the room again. My world only swayed a little more than the ship, rather than spinning out of control. "The vertigo's fading. I want to see Antonio."

"Soon. One of the men will come for you when I let them know you're ready."

Bile rose in my throat. "Ready for what?"

He stood from his rolling chair and collected the cup. As he walked to the sink at the far end of the room, his shoulders fell. "I'm sorry, Samantha. But I don't know."

CHAPTER 26

ANTONIO

I finished my circuit of the stateroom and slammed my palm against the door. I'd lost count somewhere around fifty-eight times. They hadn't locked me in, but every time I opened it, there were at least two guards stationed there. Not technically a prisoner, but what other word was there for it?

They refused to let me see Samantha. The moment the helicopter touched down—only a half hour or so from the marina—one man took her to the sick bay to be monitored. Fiori swore she would get the best attention from Dr. Ivan.

He also said I should be happy they found Samantha's recording device. Since they recovered the small drive inside of it, our sisters and their children were safe. For now.

I paused at the thick windows, looking over the water. When we'd arrived, the sun was visible through the window. How many hours had passed? They'd brought me lunch, a snack, and offered me wine.

The room was nothing more than a gilded prison. A large bed I'd sat on, laid on, threw the pillows off in a rage. A bathroom complete with a tub and a disgustingly beautiful tiled shower.

Closet space. Writing desk. Large television on the wall I'd nearly thrown a chair into.

I dropped into a seat in the sitting area. How long would they keep me from her? Was she alright? Was she conscious? Were they hurting her?

A knock came at the door and I launched from the chair to swing the door open.

Jason stood there, as calm as when he'd been in my home. Writing secret messages to make me believe he was on my side. "Signore Fiori would like to speak with you now."

"Che cazzo, it's about time." I followed him out of the room, glowering at the guards standing on either side of my door.

Jason held up a hand to them. "Dr. Ferraro is our guest and he won't try anything. Isn't that right, Dr. Ferraro?" He rolled his head slowly toward me. "We wouldn't want anything to happen to Samantha, would we?"

"Where is she?" My voice came out a low growl, which inspired only grins from the bodyguards.

"You'll see her soon enough. Can we trust you for now?"

An ironic question coming from Jason. I balled my sore hands into fists—slamming them into the door had not been a wise choice. "You can trust me."

The hallway was barely wide enough for us to walk two abreast, and Jason led us through sliding doors, down a set of stairs to an area without carpets and luxury, along another hallway, and up another flight. Either the ship was far larger on the inside than I'd expected or he was intentionally delaying our progress. He slowed his pace and whispered, just loud enough to hear over the hum of the engine. "She's fine. I checked on her ten minutes before I got you. Dr. Ivan thought she'd be awake soon. Once she's steady enough, I'll bring her to you."

I scanned the side of his head. "No earpiece?"

His gaze remained fixed on the length of the hallway. "Security's much higher on the ship since the new year. A party snuck onboard and stole something, so there are more locks and sensors. We primarily focus the cameras outward, so they don't disturb the signore and his family."

"I don't trust you."

"I don't care. Trust me or not, but I'm the best friend you have on this ship, other than your fiancée." His jaw clenched and he whispered, "The only reason I'm still here is because of you. So try not to piss me off too much, or I'll just leave, like I wanted to."

Either this was an elaborate ruse by Fiori and Jason, or he was telling the truth. My gut told me to trust him, and it was rarely wrong when I was evaluating people.

After a few more twists and turns and a narrow metal staircase, we came to the dining and lounge area where Fiori and I had enjoyed scotch and a lovely view last September. How times had changed.

One more set of stairs took us to a sun deck with seating area and hot tub, surrounded by brass railings and five teak steps up to the tub. Fiori sat at the back, arms stretched wide on the ledge, while two women and one man dressed in the light blue shirt and navy pants of his staff stood ready for any command. The water was lit from underneath, brilliant blue with tiny white lights all around the area surrounding the loungers.

The sun was approaching the horizon, maybe an hour or two before sunset. Rays of golden sunshine burst through the clouds.

How dare he have such a beautiful life?

"Antonio, my friend. Why don't you join me?" Fiori gestured to his male staffer. "We keep spare trunks for guests. Baptiste will be up in ten or fifteen minutes."

"I want to see Samantha."

"Of course you do." He stood, water streaming off of him. The evening was cool enough that steam surrounded him.

The man grabbed a plush robe and rushed over to present it to Fiori, so he didn't have to even stutter in his stride.

He climbed out of the hot tub, wrapped the robe around himself, and walked down two of the steps to the main deck. It kept him taller than Jason and me by a few inches. "Did you know your fiancée was in the FBI?"

Oh, marone, no. "Scusi?"

"Seven and a half years ago." Instead of continuing down the stairs or joining us, he walked the length of them, ending near the curved railing. "All I could find out was it lasted two weeks. After that, there are some inconsistencies in her files. And I can't figure out what that means."

"It means she's an insurance adjuster."

Fiori held out an absent hand, and his staff member placed a towel in it. He draped it over his head, drying off his short hair. "Special Investigations Unit, not adjuster. That's a big difference, Antonio."

"I know, but—"

He turned, leaving the towel around his shoulders. "Here's where it gets even more interesting. Her mother was a state prosecutor, after several years in private practice. And I can't find anything about her father. Who he was or what he did."

How much power did Fiori have to figure this much out? Were FBI employment files that easy to obtain?

"That means we have one state prosecutor, one mystery man, and one daughter whose file says she resigned from the FBI after two weeks." He smiled, a predatory look, and gripped either end of the towel. "But all the details about why are classified or off the books. I'm dreadfully curious about what this means."

I knew about the two weeks. She'd confessed that she left after her mother's death. But the rest of it? Why would any of her files be classified? She hadn't been hiding more things from me, had she? *Don't be ridiculous. He's manipulating you.* It was likely something to do with her father or possibly Elliot's instructions.

Fiori spread his arms wide, a pained look coming over him. "And then I try to have a polite brunch with the two of you, and she has a listening device in her key fob. I don't like that. It's not honest."

"You have her mistaken, signore. She's—"

"Caused me more trouble than I care to think of." He removed the towel and threw it toward his staff man, who scrambled to catch it. "As have you."

If I'd learned anything from my Zio Giovanni, it was that calm preceded the worst of things. When he would speak plainly about a betrayal, that meant he was calculating. A strike out of anger was vicious, but one borne out of controlled rage was horror-inducing.

Fiori had gone to great lengths to work with us and bring us aboard his ship. If he'd been planning to eliminate us, there had been plenty of opportunities—a carefully planted drink at The Train Station could have been poison, Jason could have done anything last night while we slept, or the injection they'd given Samantha could have been fatal.

If I was certain of nothing else, it was that Fiori wanted us alive. "What's it to be, then? Out to sea and throw us over?"

"No." He descended the stairs and held out an arm to encourage me to walk with him, while Jason remained close behind.

Around the far side of the stairs was an outdoor dining area and bar, with sliding glass walls which were half-open to the cool evening air. The white and black painting my Zio Andrea had repaired was hanging on the wall by the bar, rather than in the lounge where it had hung the first time I visited.

"Your uncle does good work," he said. "Andrea, that is."

Another staff member joined us, placing a tray with antipasti on the bar. "Can I make you anything?"

I shook my head.

Fiori waved the man away and picked up a small bowl of olives, strolling to a long white couch decorated with blue and white throw pillows. "I was being honest at the yacht club, Antonio. I have some projects I want your help with, and that's all."

If that was all, his bodyguards wouldn't have attacked us and they wouldn't have had an injection ready. "So why the first two paintings?"

He popped an olive into his mouth, chewing a moment. Still controlling the conversation. "The first one was a test for you. I wanted to know what you'd do."

"You wanted to know if we'd turn you in?"

"And you didn't. At least not for that painting." He smiled, placing the bowl on a low table in front of him, with a lipped edge to hold things while at sea. "But what bothered me was when I made a simple request for a second painting, what did I see? Two FBI agents entering Samantha's place of work, just after she arrived. They left before she did, but what could that mean?"

Had he been following her? Or both of us? How long had he known about her past? "I'm afraid you've lost me."

"I was clear with you that I was going to destroy the forgery. You didn't even know what the second one was, and yet your fiancée is meeting with the FBI? What did she think I was going to have? Why would she suspect anything?"

I folded my arms, feeling at once in control and out of it. "You play the innocent, but then you threaten our families?"

"And if I hadn't, you would have the FBI onboard my ship already, wouldn't you? Even though I've done nothing illegal."

"We were afraid it was related to Giovanni."

"That son of a..." His act dropped and the genuine man shone through for a moment. "I want my painting back."

Did he mean the one with the yellow flowers Samantha rescued in January? "It belongs to you?"

He stood, raising a finger at me. "I've been chasing that painting down for five years. Your uncle promised to get it for me, and when he finally had a lead, he got out of the business and refused to tell me where it was. It doesn't work that way. He gave me his word that it was mine."

Zio Giovanni had decided to leave that business two years ago. Could he have been working on getting that painting for so long? "How does all of this have anything to do with you forcing Samantha and me to work for you?"

"Everything." His eyes sparkled with excitement. "*The Concert* also belongs to me."

"I still believe it was a forgery."

"Not that one." A grin spread across his face. "I don't know where the real one is, but it's mine. And you are going to help me get it."

I was what?

CHAPTER 27

SAMANTHA

I slid my legs over the edge of the bed, and Dr. Ivan helped me stand. The IV remained in my arm, but the headache and nausea had finally passed.

"How do you feel?"

"Like I don't want to be here."

"Mm-hmm. I think we can take the IV out now." He remained close while I eased myself back on the bed. Pretending he cared if I needed help. Ivan had been kind and chatty the last time I was onboard. It hadn't felt like an act, but it had to be.

I should have met Antonio in Chicago and surprised him by hopping on the first plane that left the airport after the storm.

Ivan walked to the sink and washed his hands. Dried them. Returned to his chair and sat. All in silence.

"Did you give the meathead the syringe? Show him how to use it on a struggling woman?" I couldn't stop myself. It could have been some side effect of whatever drug they'd given me, but with my head clearing, the rage was building in my stomach. Was my sister already dead? My niece? Sofia? Nico? A wave of cold shot through me and the world went into a spin again. I fell back onto the bed. Fiori wanted me to know they were alright, so they had to be. "Where the fuck is Antonio?"

Ivan pulled on a pair of gloves and retrieved my hand. "You'll see him soon."

"I liked you better the last time I was here."

"So did I." He pulled up the tape holding the needle.

"Why do you work for him?"

"Would it be too predictable if I said gambling debts?"

He'd told me the last time that the goons working for Fiori were good guys after you lost a few rounds of cards to them. Maybe there was a shred of truth in his words. It was eerily similar to the line Johann had used as his cover for winding up working for Giovanni. I chuckled, a weak sound. "Any chance you're an undercover Interpol agent?"

"Sadly, no." He pulled out the needle and pressed a cotton ball to the inside of my elbow. "Just a man who made a lot of bad choices."

Exactly what Jimmy had said. One bad choice led to another and another until he was stuck working for... who? It had to be part of Fiori's organization.

"And you can't get out?"

He checked under the cotton ball and reapplied the pressure. "Considering my options, this is as good a place as any."

Everything in life came down to choices. Good ones and bad ones. But more importantly, it came down to how you reacted after you'd made that choice. Make a good one, keep making them. That's what Antonio used to tell me—enough times I started believing I could good-choice my way out of a life that wasn't as perfect as I'd let on. But if you made a bad one, follow it up with something better.

Ivan checked the needle site one last time and covered it with a bandage. "Good as new."

His kind eyes weren't those of someone who belonged here.

"There are options, Ivan. I can help—"

A knock came at the door and Jason peeked his head in. "Is she ready to see the signore?"

"Should be." Ivan stood from his wheeled chair and moved it away from my bed. He held out a hand to me. "How do you feel? Well enough to make your way upstairs?"

I'd pretended to be weak—physically and intellectually—around these men to hide my position of strength. Considering they went after me as fast as they went after Antonio, they'd seen right through it. Unfortunately, all I felt was weakness. Sluggish reaction time. Nausea bubbling in my stomach when I turned too fast. No way was I letting them know. "Yeah, I'm fine."

Jason escorted me through a few short hallways and staircases. I peppered him with questions the whole way. Where were we? How was Antonio? Where were we going? Why did they drug me? But he did little more than grunt.

I kept my eyes on the floor ahead of me, fingers trailing along the walls when I needed the support. The more I moved, the better I felt. Sitting still had never been my forte.

We climbed one final staircase leading to an upper deck and a hot tub. The salty air and cool evening breeze were a relief after being cooped up all day.

"Bella!"

I spun to see Antonio on the other side of the stairs and raced around the railing to grab him. By the time I reached him, the world was spinning again, so I held on tighter. *You're supposed to be showing strength, Sam*. Fuck it. He was okay. I pulled back, scanning every visible inch of skin, not finding any of the bruises Ivan mentioned. They must have been under his clothes. "You're alright?"

"You're—" He cut off and pulled me against his chest. "I was so worried."

"Ms. Caine." Fiori stood next to the bar. "So happy to see you standing again."

I swallowed hard, an acidic burn creeping up my throat. I pivoted, so I had one arm around Antonio's waist and he maintained his around my shoulders. We were always stronger together.

Focus.

Baptiste lounged on a couch nearby, popping olives into his mouth, looking like he wanted to be in that room even less than he'd wanted to be at the yacht club. The man I recognized as Bodyguard One—who'd worked with Jason our first time on the yacht and who'd been the one Vincenzo escaped with in January after trying to kill Antonio—stood just outside the track where the sliding walls were open. Another bodyguard with him, two more on the other side of the ship, along with two women in staff uniforms holding water pitchers and a man next to Baptiste, holding a tray for olive pits.

None of them had been at the yacht club. How many staff did Fiori have with him on the boat?

Jason remained by the stairs, chatting quietly with a young man in the staff uniform.

"That's two times I've come aboard your vessel under someone else's control." The last time, it was Antonio carrying me since I couldn't put any weight on my ankle.

"You don't strike me as a woman who likes that." Fiori crossed through the room, stepped over the track, to the railing where Bodyguard One and his fellow goon shifted so they flanked him.

"So long as I'm leaving under my own steam, that's what matters."

He waved us over to join him at the railing.

Antonio's arm tightened around my shoulders the closer we got. "The view is spectacular, Pasquale. I've not sailed the St. Lawrence at night in many years."

Moonlight glinted off the water, a million shards flickering as the boat cut through the wide river. We were far enough out I couldn't see a shoreline or any city lights, other than a haze in the distance that might have been a city.

I was a strong swimmer, but if I wanted to escape, jumping wasn't an option. How many twists and turns would I need to follow in the maze of hallways to find a rib boat? "How far along are we? Is that Buffalo out there?"

"Cleveland," called Baptiste from behind us. "We're sailing slowly."

Fiori turned, eyes narrowing at his son. "No one asked you."

"She asked if—" Under his father's glare, Baptiste raised his hands in apology and returned to his olives. From what little I'd seen of them together, the son seemed to be the opposite of the father. Relaxed and bored with the world, rather than possessing a drive to control it.

"I think I've been very reasonable." Fiori leaned his arms on the railing. "But you bring a recording device to the yacht club, hoping to get... what? What was your goal with that, Ms. Caine?"

Antonio held me even tighter. "Pasquale, we—"

"I was talking to her."

Shit.

Bodyguard One moved closer, as did the man on our other side. They were too close.

Double shit.

One of the women with the water took a half-step forward, but the moment one of the guards looked at her, she resumed her position.

I stepped in front of Antonio, bringing his arm around my upper chest and pulling the other around my waist. We'd be more difficult to tip over the edge as two people locked against each other, and we'd have more of a chance to make it to shore together than apart. One could float while the other swam, then switch. It would be cold, but it least it was May, not March. But how strong was his bad arm? "They forced me."

Fiori remained calm, not looking at us. "Did they also force you to meet them at your insurance office?"

Antonio cut in. "Pasquale, if you want my help, you'll—"

Fiori ignored him, not budging or raising his voice. "You're wondering whether you can make it to shore if we throw you over, aren't you?"

It was like he was reading my mind. He knew every step before I'd thought of it.

"From the looks of you, I expect you're both capable swimmers. I'd say maybe we should do it, then place some bets, but we're already underway. We'll be long gone before you either reach the shore, grow too tired and sink, or maybe—if you get really lucky—another boat shows up and rescues you. Although in the dark, those odds go down."

I needed an excuse. Something to go with the line that they forced me. What did I have? "I covered up a bunch of fraud cases my ex-husband was involved in. They found out and I—"

Antonio's body jerked. "You what?" He hadn't been at the meetings with Foster Mutual or the FBI, so maybe he believed it. Maybe he trusted me and was going along with it.

"I'm sorry, Antonio. I couldn't let Matt go to jail like his father."

He spun me to face him. "Why didn't you tell me?"

"Because I knew you'd react like this."

Baptiste's low chuckle almost had me break character, but this was too important.

Antonio leaned in to glare into my eyes, his words coming out with a slow rasp. "You let me play the fool."

My heart could have sung. It was a line from *The Merchant of Venice*. He was telling me he understood.

"I'm mortified, Antonio," I said, hoping I'd picked the right word from later in Gratiano's line in the play.

"As you should be." He straightened but pulled me against him again.

Fiori pushed off the railing. "To save your own skin, you'd risk not just your life, but your fiancé's life, your sister's, your little niece?"

Antonio said, "And my sister and nephew."

"Selfish," muttered Fiori. "Not to mention dishonest."

"It won't happen again."

"I knew you were going to be the wildcard in all of this, but I didn't realize quite how much." Fiori shook his head, returning to the room. The bodyguards resumed their positions next to the railing, away from us. "Let's get to business, shall we? I have a proposition for the two of you."

The two of us? Elliot must have been right.

Fiori gestured for us to follow him to the bar, where one of his staff opened a bottle of red wine. "As I was telling Antonio earlier, I have people working for me who aren't doing their jobs properly. The challenge is in determining whether it's incompetence or if they're sabotaging my business. How good would you say the first two forgeries were?"

"Excellent." Antonio kept his pace even with mine as we approached the bar. No more than an inch separated us at any second.

"Ms. Caine? Your opinion?"

"I don't know, I'm just a—"

Antonio touched my arm. "He knows about your past with the FBI, bella."

But how much? "Alright, they were very good."

Fiori handed Antonio and me each a glass of the wine. "I have four more paintings that I've been told are authentic, but I want to be sure. I no longer trust many of my employees to provide me with the correct information."

I stared into the glass, debating whether it was safe.

"Don't worry," Fiori chuckled. "If I wanted you unconscious, Dr. Ivan would have seen to that. And if I wanted you dead, well... we could have easily arranged that, as well."

"Why us?" Antonio inspected his glass. "And why not simply sign a contract?"

Baptiste held out a hand and the bartender poured another glass. "You don't believe in verbal contracts?"

Fiori frowned in his son's direction. "I'd like to put all that in the past. Time to look to the future and our new agreement."

"I'm not interested in a new agreement. You said two paintings—"

"The scales have shifted, young Dr. Ferraro. Your debt to me *was* paid. But now? Now you are deep, deep in debt. Authenticating four paintings will get you out of it. That, your lives, or four other lives."

I placed the glass on the bar without having drank any. "What if we agree to do this for you? Are we to believe that we can just leave afterward, after everything you've done today?"

"Of course. I'm a man of my word." Fiori placed one hand over his heart. "I swear I will only ask you to authenticate four paintings, then we'll be done with each other. So long as you keep this work secret until your grave, then I won't have to collect any other price."

"And if we decline?" asked Antonio, clutching his glass.

Why bother asking? There was no chance Fiori was letting us go so easily, after how much he'd risked bringing us here. The brazen kidnapping was one more show of his power. No doubt we were on the Canadian side of the lake already, to make it harder for the American authorities to pursue him. Add to that any delay from state forces having to coordinate—now that we were out of Michigan—and throw in the FBI angle.

Fiori was too smart. Too calculating. He'd have an army of lawyers that could tie up any warrant.

No, the only option for us was to go along with him and survive. Maybe I could figure out some way to collect the evidence we needed while keeping everyone safe.

Fiori grinned, like a man who knew he'd won. "You won't decline."

"Scusi?"

"Ms. Caine wants to know what I have and her curiosity is too great for her to choose to leave." He inclined his head toward me. "I admire a woman with that kind of drive, despite the circumstances."

"You want me to be honest, Pasquale?" I clutched my hands in front of me, letting them tremble so he could see. "Part of me didn't believe you'd hurt any of us. It was little more than a game I thought I could win with the recording, but you proved me wrong. I don't want to go along with what you're asking, but I will."

Antonio looked down at me, the corners of his eyes pinched. Did he understand what I was doing?

Fiori knew I'd been lying all along, and he would continue escalating until he broke me. My only option was to appear broken. Not clueless about art, not arm candy. Smart, but broken. Defeated.

"Where are the paintings?" I slipped an arm around Antonio's waist to pretend I was hiding the tremble.

Baptiste stood with a yawn. "Finally. Can I go eat now?"

"Sit down and learn something, boy," Fiori snapped. He turned to Antonio and took a slow breath. "Is your father proud of you?"

Antonio's brow furrowed. "Sì."

"Keep it that way." He sipped his wine, closing his eyes as he swirled it in his mouth before swallowing.

Two uniformed men appeared from a staircase at the back. "Dinner is ready to be served, signore."

"I'll take it up here." Fiori beckoned to Bodyguard One, who lumbered toward us. "See them to their room. I'll have some food sent down."

The bodyguard nodded and gestured toward the stairs.

Fiori called over his shoulder as he and Baptiste walked toward a table at the back of the room. "The paintings are in one of my homes, where I have all the tools you could possibly need. Jason will fly us there tomorrow morning."

Chapter 28

Antonio

Samantha marched into the room ahead of me—the surprisingly clean and orderly room, which must have had staff go through it—steam practically rising off her head. Before she reached the bed, she spun to face me. "Tell me the truth. How's your arm doing?"

"It's perfect."

"Liar." She blew out a sharp breath. "If we jumped overboard, would you be able to swim to shore?"

I couldn't have heard that right. "Miscusi, but do you mean could I reach the shore, which is miles away, while outpacing their rib boats and possibly gunfire? Are you seriously asking me that?"

She turned again and continued stomping toward the window, tracing the same pattern I'd followed for hours. "That's only if they knew we'd gone over. And he seemed fine with the idea of *throwing* us over without going after us, so maybe they wouldn't care."

I grabbed her by the arms and turned her to face me. "Bella, that was a threat, not him being alright with us jumping."

"Fine." She clenched her fists and teeth. "Maybe that's not the best plan I've ever had."

"I thought your plan was for us to go along with him and wait for our opportunity?"

"We should sabotage the engine."

"Or poison the food?" I chuckled.

She smacked my chest and barged past me. "I'm being serious."

"As am I." My strides were longer than hers and I caught her, pulling her back against my chest. "I can't keep doing this. Watching that man with the needle. And the way you collapsed."

"What does he want?" Unlike usual, she didn't soften when I held her. She was too wound up.

"*The Concert*. He says it belongs to him."

"What does that mean?"

"I don't know, bella." I began sliding my arms around her, but she moved again, escaping me. "I'm sure half the words coming out of his mouth are lies, half-truths, or manipulations."

"And yet he keeps going on about honesty."

"Ironic, is it not?"

Honesty and trust were the two characteristics Samantha declared were most important in a relationship. And here was Pasquale Fiori, using those words as though he had some idea what they meant.

"It's pathetic, that's what it is." She halted at the door, smacked a hand against it, and turned to continue her pace, but with a lower voice this time. Her brain was overcoming her rage. "Why are you so sure we should go along with him?"

"As he said, if he wanted us dead, we would be. He could have drugged me at the marina and left you behind." I shrugged and dropped onto the edge of the bed. The comforter was plush, the mattress soft. It was late and the day had left me exhausted.

"And why did they have that needle ready to go?"

"He knew you met with the FBI. He must have suspected—"

"So he just keeps getting what he wants?"

I caught her arm as she attempted to pass and pulled her to me. "Until the FBI and every other police force around the world stop him, sì, I suspect he will."

She gave a half-hearted tug, then stepped between my legs. "You should call Cristian. Get some advice."

"I tried while you were still out. Several times." I dropped my forehead to her chest. "I couldn't get a signal, so I don't know if we're too far from land, in Canadian waters, or if they have some sort of jammer onboard."

Her fingers combed through the hair over my ears.

"You should take Papa's job." I sighed. The onionskin letter didn't get her into any trouble or danger.

"I'm not an art conservator."

"I mean the investigator's position." Wrapping my arms around her waist, I pulled her closer. "You've been so focused on the FBI since our experience in Napoli last September, I assumed that was what you wanted."

Her fingers continued exploring my scalp, to my neck, to my back. The FBI *was* what she wanted. I knew it was.

"But the way you took that letter from Papa and ran with it. The light in your eyes when you figured out how to match the sheets up. Marone, it was beautiful."

She made a noise of assent. "Your dad needed a hand."

"But what if…" I pushed her back so I could see her. "Bear with me here, but what if we could work together? You'd be upstairs, I'd be downstairs—"

"The opposite of our offices at home." She laughed it off, like it was a silly suggestion.

"You'd have travel opportunities. Think about it. Working on the provenance for some pieces would require you to visit archives in other states or in other countries."

She cocked her head as though the idea were news.

I had an in! "We could do some of those trips together. If we had to authenticate a real Chagall, we could travel to France together. Take some vacation days before or after the business, sample the wine, the food, everything."

Her fingers brushed down my jawline. "That might be fun."

I was getting ahead of myself. Papa and I hadn't discussed any of the hiring plans for his investigative branch, but I could make it work. She was as qualified as anyone else we could find—likely more so. "And who knows? When Elliot has a case he needs you on, your staff could handle things for you."

"My staff," she chuckled.

"Is that not how things have wound up at Foster Mutual? You're calling the shots for SIU?"

"I'm just a member of the team."

I grabbed her hands so she couldn't distract herself—or me—with them. "A member of the team who inspects the other members' work? Who redesigned the workflows? Specified the software changes? This is not how a *member* works."

"Huh." Her gaze rose to the ceiling in thought. "I hadn't really thought of it like that."

"Everyone wins this way!" I pulled her onto my lap, the excitement overwhelming me. "My father gets an excellent staff he can rely on. You get an art investigation job, just like you've always wanted. You'd have the freedom to choose cases—within reason, of course—just like we choose which artwork we take on."

"Slow down," she laughed.

"We'd be together every day." I narrowed my eyes before she could complain. "But not completely together, so you'd still have your space. And you wouldn't be heading off on dangerous missions for the FBI, leaving me at home wondering when you'd—"

Her face pinched and the excitement fled as fast as it had come over her.

"I'm sorry, bella. I shouldn't have—"

"No." She pushed up from my lap and resumed a slow pace toward the window. It was too close to what happened with her parents. "Never apologize for your excitement."

I got up and followed her. "Would it bother you to have your life so tied to mine? Working with Elliot, you have a great deal of autonomy, but working for Papa would mean I was involved. I know we say no secrets, but if you worked for Elliot, they'd be common. Like those crop circles I'm not supposed to see."

"Even if I wind up staying on with Foster Mutual, I'd like to work small files here and there with Elliot. It feels like I'm contributing to something bigger."

"You don't want to stay at Foster, do you?"

She shrugged, staring out the large, thick window at the inky darkness. "I don't know what I want, Antonio. When I moved back to Brenton, I didn't have any choices I wanted. Now, it's almost like I've got too many."

"I hope there's at least one thing you know for sure?"

"Yeah." She stepped backward, pressed against my chest, and pulled my arms to wrap around her. "At least I've got one sure thing."

"I promised I wouldn't leave you."

"Now you're stuck on this crazy man's boat with me."

I kissed the side of her head, grateful she'd woken up and was safe. "When we arrived onboard, they took you from me, and you were still unconscious."

Her breath shuddered, along with the rest of her. "The worst was the headache and nausea when I woke up. Plus, not knowing where you were really sucked."

I laughed quietly at her attempt to be intentionally vulnerable. "I know you insist you don't need a man to protect you, but it was like watching my future evaporate in front of my eyes and I couldn't stay behind."

"I put up a good fight, though."

"You did." I walked backward, not letting go of her. When my legs touched the bed, I picked her up and sat with her on my lap. "The one you knocked out didn't recover until the helicopter was already in the air."

"Good." She snuggled closer. "None of the people at the restaurant did anything?"

"It was hard to tell, but there were screams and I heard tables and chairs flying. When I reached the helicopter, two of the bodyguards had their guns out, so they must have pulled them on the crowd."

"What a mess."

"Two FBI agents came running out and surrounded the guard. I'm assuming they arrested him."

Her head jutted back. "How'd you know they were FBI?"

"The windbreakers. Giant yellow letters."

She twisted in my grasp so she straddled me, looking at me straight on. "I didn't call them. I thought it was too risky."

"It wasn't Elliot or anyone else I recognized. Although I had to do a double-take—one of them looked just like Rhonda Wells."

"Wait, what?" She pulled back further. "Short white-blond hair and red glasses? Black suit?"

"Under the blue jacket, sì."

Samantha pushed against me, like she thought I was about to let her resume her pacing. "That's got to be Special Agent Bernard. She's the one who gave me the key fob."

"Do you think they hid a tracker inside it?"

"Dammit!" Her muscles tightened. "Of course they did! I bet that's how the guy with the wand found it. If they'd told me, I would have left it at home."

I shifted further back on the bed, keeping her on top of me.

"What are you doing?"

"Four days ago, I promised you a distraction. I've failed miserably at that."

"No." She pushed me onto the bed and crawled over me, her long hair draped over one shoulder. "More like you've been so successful, I don't remember what you were trying to distract me from in the first place."

I tossed her to the side and rolled on top of her, settling my hips between her legs. Two hours ago, I was pacing this room. Now here she was with me. "I think it's all a manipulation."

"Exactly. He's pulling so many strings I don't know which ones to try cutting." Her brain was on Fiori.

Mine was rapidly descending from my head to my groin. I leaned in to kiss the tip of her nose. "I mean you're trying to distract me from going on vacation."

She rolled her eyes playfully. "Yeah, I got us kidnapped so we wouldn't have to leave home."

I undid the top button of her striped blouse. "Have I mentioned how beautiful you look in this shirt?"

"You seriously want to have sex right now?"

"What do you think?" I pressed my hips against her so she could feel how hard I was.

She pointed toward the door. "I think there's at least two guards standing right outside that door."

"And?" I popped another button. "We've made love under these conditions before."

Her eyes widened. "Not when someone's just threatened to throw us into Lake Erie."

"Do you remember our conversation when I drove you home from the charity gala last August?"

"The fourteen hours to live part?"

"After that." I stroked a hand down her cheek, taking in her lovely face. "I asked what you'd do if you only had two hours to live. Do you remember what I said?"

"No." Her leg crept up my hips to settle at the small of my back.

"I said I'd spend the time with those I love, so there were no regrets. No words left unsaid. Because life is about love, Samantha. Without it, there's no value to life."

She blinked several times at me, her leg tightening. "That was pretty deep."

"I don't know what tomorrow will bring or how long we'll have to work for Fiori to keep everyone safe. But I know this much." I leaned down on one elbow, allowing much of my weight to settle on her, sinking her deeper into the delicious bed. "My only regret would be not making love to you one more time. Not showing you how much I care for you. How much you mean to me."

She gripped my sides, her free leg running along mine. "That's an even better answer."

I closed my eyes and handed the world over to sensation. Dipping my head to kiss her, my tongue found hers and she moaned into my mouth. I progressed down her body. Kissed the exposed skin where I'd undone her shirt. Finished with the buttons, and pulled it open, so I could trace circles around her belly button. "I adore this body."

While I explored her chest, she undid the button and zipper on her pants.

"Is that an invitation?" I moved further along her and eased her pants down so I could ghost my lips across her silky panties.

"Yes, please." She hooked her thumbs around the waistband of her underwear, and I stopped her.

"You relax. Let me distract you from absolutely everything in the world."

She smiled and nodded, letting her head fall back against a pillow. "Just promise me they'll be safe."

"They'll be safe," I whispered as I slid her pants and underwear down, trailing kisses the length of her leg. Over her knee. Along her shin. Across the top of her foot.

"Promise me you'll be safe." Her hands scrubbed up and down her face. We were losing this battle already.

I made my way up her leg, stopping to lick the side of her thigh, which had fallen off of me during my journey. "I'll be safe."

"Okay."

I blew across her sex, and her hips lifted to meet me. "And I promise you'll be safe, as well, bella."

Whether that meant I kept her safe or by some miracle she didn't jump into the fray the next time something dangerous popped up. Whatever it took, she would make it out of this alive.

"Because I swear upon all that is holy..." My tongue ran around the edge of her opening, teasing at her folds, encouraging her to forget about the men outside and focus on me. "You're going to marry me, woman."

She chuckled behind her hands, and her tense arms fell to the bed. While she'd not completely relaxed, she was making progress. "That sounds like a threat."

"It is." I stroked her clit with a finger and lapped at her opening, savoring the flavor that was intimately her and no one else. I'd missed this—her taste, her scent, everything about Samantha Caine—so much.

"I love you," she groaned.

Tonight, my job was to take care of her. Her heart, her soul, her body. The same job I wanted for the rest of my life.

To do that, I had to hide my greatest fear: That when Fiori said he'd be done with us after four paintings—it was because we'd be dead. The hardest part would be sacrificing myself for her before she could do the same for me.

CHAPTER 29

SAMANTHA

After a fitful night's sleep, Antonio and I cleaned up, dressed in the same clothes we'd worn yesterday. Two bodyguards escorted us through the hallways and sliding doors. Unlike last night, when the boat had been quiet, I caught glimpses of staff disappearing around corners and slipping quietly through doors.

Dr. Ivan had checked on us and ran a few tests on my pupils and reaction speed. He declared I was ready to travel and escaped before Antonio wrung his neck for being part of everything.

We climbed two sets of stairs in the ship's heart, coming out into a grand dining room which smelled of fresh bread and ham. A woman had delivered breakfast to our room, but I'd barely been able to touch it. My body had recovered from yesterday, but my mind hadn't. Antonio may have distracted me last night, but this morning, I was back to the battle between protecting our families and preventing Pasquale Fiori from getting away with everything he'd done.

At the front of the dining room, the guard slid open a glass door so we could step out into the morning sunshine. From higher than our stateroom, I took in more details of our surroundings. The ship pointed straight at the shore and, given the tankers and cargo ships near us, that likely meant it was the canal system leading to Lake Ontario.

We wouldn't see any of it, other than from high above. Sitting on the ship's bow, on its huge yellow 'H' symbol, the helicopter's rotors had already started. Fiori climbed in, followed by Baptiste and two other bodyguards. Jason sat at the controls.

I grabbed Antonio's hand, gave it a squeeze, and focused on mentally sending him *We've got this*.

Our escort backed away once we were inside and settled with headsets on.

"The headsets are a courtesy," said Fiori. "As much as I paid for this helicopter, it gets loud. Your communications will be off for the duration of our flight."

"Where are we going?" Antonio sat across from me, the bodyguards in the middle, while Fiori and his son sat opposite each other by the other door.

"To work." Fiori stared out the window, nudging Baptiste's foot and pointing at something.

"How long will we be in the air?" A fully fueled helicopter of this size could fly three hundred miles in any direction. If we were near Buffalo and the canal system, he could even circle back and fly us to Detroit, let alone into Ontario, Quebec, or any half dozen states. "Sometimes I get airsick."

"You were fine on the last trip. And the one before that, when Jason flew you two to Sorrento." Fiori waved vaguely in our direction. "It will only be a couple of hours."

That didn't narrow down the options at all. One of the bodyguards reached under his seat and tossed wadded up black fabric at Antonio and me. Hoods.

Antonio's lip curled. "Don't be ridiculous. We've already given you our word."

"Trust is earned, my friend, not simply promised. As I said, Ms. Caine tipped your scales in the wrong direction, and you need to balance them out again."

He will not throw you out of the helicopter, Sam. Just put it on. I stretched my legs and Antonio did the same, so we were in contact before placing the hoods over our headsets. The fabric was thick enough that barely any light penetrated. Pins and needles shot up my fingers and through my hands as the helicopter lifted off, going to who knew where.

The only positive was that the headset microphone held the hood several inches from my face.

Deep breaths. Calm. Find your center. I mentally flipped through the paintings in Elliot's box. I'd memorized fifty of them but had barely made a dent. Colors swirled through my brain while I rubbed my panicky fingers together. Two hours of darkness and random airborne movement was just the opportunity I needed to review the *Grainfield* painting and let my mind figure out what *Stolen 13 Fell* on the onionskins meant.

In that moment, working for Dom sounded like a good idea. My need to be with Antonio every passing second was still strong. How long until that faded and I craved solitude? How much of that solitude would he tolerate without frustration? Or what if he felt stifled by my presence?

His foot flexed and straightened, rubbing my ankle. It kept me centered, so I could focus on the paintings in my head, rather than the panic of where we were headed, whether anyone would ever see us again, and what would happen to my family.

A few minutes after takeoff, Antonio hummed a quiet song which carried over the headset. It cut off with two grunts and his feet jostled against mine. One of the bodyguards must have shoved him.

"Shut off their communications now," said Fiori.

My headset switched from noise reduction to active noise canceling, and I popped my ears, searching for a comfortable pressure. This was going to be a long flight.

CHAPTER 30

SAMANTHA

It could have been an hour or it could have been five. However long it took before the helicopter descended was too fucking long. My muscles ached. Brain was wired. And the pins and needles had come and gone the entire flight.

We touched down, and my headset switched back to receiving.

"You can take the hoods off now," said Fiori.

I shaded my eyes with a hand, the sunshine far too bright after hours of darkness.

Antonio's hood was still on, his arms crossed and feet stretched out next to mine. Head lolled to the side. He was asleep. I'd spent the entire trip worrying, researching photos in my head, and imagining the joy of throwing Fiori out of the helicopter door.

I nudged his leg at the same time the guard next to him nudged him.

He shot awake, hands going to rip the hood off his head, but he stopped. Even coming out of his nap, he was aware of our situation.

"We've arrived," said Fiori. "Take it off."

Antonio pulled the hood off, smoothed his hands over the sides of his hair, and winked at me. "How do I look?"

Always trying to make me laugh. I loved that about him.

"Do I have to listen to them?" Baptiste stretched and pulled off his headset when Fiori removed his own.

The door on their side opened, and I surveyed the scene beyond them. No clues about where we'd gone. A vast green lawn stretched all around us, framed by trees. A two-story mansion covered in gray and pink brick, with white windows, three chimney stacks, and several gardens dominated the yard. Pockets of trees and bushes dotted the lawn, but it was mostly open, not providing many hiding places.

I twisted to look out my window. A long dock ending with a gazebo, running into either a lake or a river. Whatever body of water it was, it was wide enough I could barely make out a sliver of land in the distance.

Where were we? So long as they weren't jamming his phone, Antonio would be able to find out if we found some privacy.

The ring of trees blocked out the view of any other houses. The sun was overhead, but without knowing how long the flight had taken, it was impossible to tell which direction we'd gone. A speedboat came into view, then a jet ski. Wherever we were, it wasn't completely isolated.

Antonio tapped me. He sat forward, with his headset off, and I removed mine. "It's good to see your face again."

"Did you seriously fall asleep?"

He shrugged. "I was busy last night and didn't get enough rest."

The engine shut down and the rotors slowed, ceasing their overwhelming noise.

"Welcome to your new home!" Fiori slid out of the helicopter with the help of a middle-aged man in the blue uniform. At least it wasn't another bodyguard.

Baptiste and the two guards followed, and they all waited for us, ringed by five male staff members.

I hopped out, trying to gain my bearings. There had to be a clue somewhere about where we were. Probably inside, but it was unlikely we'd have the run of the place to find out. "What are the rules?"

"Don't go beyond the tree line, don't call anyone, and be respectful of other people's things."

Respectful? Really?

Antonio joined me and brushed off his navy blazer. "We'll need resources to do our work."

"Within reason and with all your promises in place." Fiori lifted a hand, inviting us to walk with him. "You'll have your own room and I've supplied clothes which should fit. There are tennis courts, a basketball court, and a gym. The weather's not optimal, but we also have a heated outdoor pool and one indoors."

Baptiste, the guards, and the staff followed as we approached the house.

Fiori pointed to the left. "There's also a pond with a small rowboat, a media room, and a well-stocked bar and kitchen."

It sounded more like a luxury hotel than the prison it was.

We passed onto a sprawling terrace at the back of the house, with five-foot-long rectangular stone slabs floating on a layer of pea gravel. Two fountains, a post-modern sculpture of a tree sprouting from someone's head, and two separate stone tables surrounded by metal chairs.

A staffer opened the door for us into a garden room with white wicker furniture, a travertine floor, and a twenty-foot arched ceiling. More sculptures decorated the room; a red inverted V, a bronze woman in a flowing gown, three Greek water carriers.

Through paned glass doors, he walked us into a carpeted room with the same high ceilings. More sculptures, small pieces on end tables, and two metallic acrobats hung from the ceiling. The walls showcased stunning post-modern pieces, including a graffiti-inspired black and neon piece that must have been a Basquiat—which tickled the back of my brain—over a marble fireplace.

Antonio walked next to me, his hand resting at the small of my back. Now and then, it urged me forward when I stopped too long to admire something.

Elliot had said Fiori was a massive collector. How did he have the time to smuggle anything when he was showcasing so much art around his house? And why was I so transfixed by it all?

"Do you like my collection?" Fiori led us down a wallpapered hallway, past a bathroom and another closed door, to an open staircase next to twenty-foot tall windows. More paintings. Another sculpture—this time of random shapes reminding me of a wave crowned by bull's horns—rose ten feet at the center of the curved staircase.

"It reminds me of the Gardner." I climbed the stairs behind Fiori, Antonio still next to me. "Like a living museum."

Fiori stopped short and turned to face me from four stairs up. "Exactly my goal. Thank you."

Giovanni's estate had felt claustrophobic. Eyes everywhere, thick stone walls, tiny balconies. But Fiori's home was expansive and light. White walls decorated with explosions of colors and plants in every window.

He resumed the climb. "Antonio, what would you like to see first? The room where you'll be working or the one where you'll be staying?"

"Will it be just the two of us?"

"No, no. I have two other restorers working here. Neither is your caliber, although one is a second generation." He crested the top of the stairs and stopped. "Not as good as third, like you, though?"

"I'd like to shower and change, to be honest." Antonio had tried to convince me to share the shower in the morning, but our stateroom bathroom was far too small to fit both of us. "You said you have things for us to wear?"

Fiori nodded and pointed to one of the goons behind us. "Show them to their room, then bring them to the conservation lab in an hour."

The guard would probably also hover in front of our door for the hour, like they did on the yacht.

The ceilings on the second floor were ten-feet high, with chandeliers reminiscent of lanterns holding candles. The walls were pale peach, with rows of small paintings between the doors. At the far end of the hall, there appeared to be another staircase, more utilitarian than the sweeping central one. Likely for staff.

"I'll be back in an hour," said the guard, after he'd stopped at a door. Back? He was leaving us?

Antonio opened the door and ushered me in. "Your palace awaits."

Palace it was. The room was larger than ours at home—which was oversized, like the rest of Antonio's condo. Our condo. A king-sized bed in sage green sheets with a matching canopy nestled against one wall, while a seating area with love seats and a wing chair clustered around a fireplace. Two sets of bay windows with plush seating looked over the front yard. More sculptures on the chests, on the mantle, and standing near the door.

"I hate this place," I muttered, wandering to a door which led to an opulent bathroom. "How dare he have so much fucking money?"

Antonio paused by the bed, where stacks of blue clothing lay. He picked one shirt up and held it in front of himself. "They're soft, if nothing else."

Simple white sneakers sat next to the bed. "Staff uniforms. Awesome."

"Care to join me in the shower? We have an hour, you know."

I made my way to the door and whipped it open. But no one was there. I closed it and locked it behind me. "How is this even possible? Your own uncle wouldn't leave us be, but Fiori does? The one we could legitimately call the police on for kidnapping us, let alone anything else?"

Antonio shook his head slowly. "Because he knows we won't. He holds too many cards."

"How are you so calm about this?" I marched to the closest bay window and studied the geography. Driveway. Garage with five doors.

"We have a job to do here. And getting angry will only delay our progress." The air grew thick behind me, his scent faint after not being able to put his cologne on this morning. He smelled more like the floral shampoo from the yacht, which was all wrong for him. "In this world—the smuggling world—they don't sign formal agreements or contracts. A man is only as good as his word. And Fiori's given us his."

"You said he was a manipulator."

"This is about promises, not about conversations. My Zio Giovanni is the same way. He'll say anything to convince you to do his bidding, but if he swears on something, that's different."

The driveway wound through the woods, preventing me from seeing how long it was or where a road might be. The trees were too tall to see any other houses. I continued sweeping left when I saw—

Shit.

I jabbed my finger at the window. "Look at that!"

"At what?"

"The hand!" A sculpture stood on the lawn, at the center of a round rose garden. A hand. Bent at ninety degrees, cut off at the wrist. "From the onionskin sheets!"

"You're kidding?" Antonio leaned around me, peering outside.

"This is Mr. X's house!"

"Mr. X?"

I spun in his grip. "Lucy sent me a magazine about an art collector called Mr. X and his amazing house on Long Island!" We were in New York! "And it included that sculpture!"

Antonio's head tilted. He was missing some facts to help put it all together.

"Mr. X bought the strange stamp on the letter that went to your father's office and the hand statue. Fiori is Mr. X. But here's the best part: the painting on the onionskins was in the files Elliot gave me from the pawnshop."

"So..." He made shapes while he talked, circling to collect his thoughts. "The onionskin letter came from here, with the note *Stolen 13 Fell*. The water symbol must mean the water at the back and the hand was that statue. The person who wrote it was clearly giving us a location, so the address must be 13 Fell."

"Fell-something. I think they screwed up with the layers."

"Let me check." He pulled out his phone and turned it on.

"Leave it off, save the battery until we can find a charger." Our location wasn't as important as the rest of it. "But if the painting was at the center of the letter, that means—"

"It must be between the hand and the water at 13 Fell."

"So, somewhere inside this house is *Grainfield at Midday* from the pawnshop. That's a link, Antonio. A concrete link between Fiori and the pawnshop."

"Evidence." He took my face in his hands, a darkness creeping over him, pushing back the light he was trying to share with me. "Evidence that gets us or our families killed. You remember that part, sì?"

"I do." But there had to be a way to make this work. "If we take him down, do you think someone else would carry through on the threat?"

"I don't know. But by the time we find out, it might be too late."

CHAPTER 31

SAMANTHA

An hour later, Bodyguard Three led Antonio and me down the hallway, around a corner, and into a long room with a half dozen tall windows. I held my head high, despite the light blue shirt and dark blue pants—no matter how comfortable or well-fitting they were—proclaiming I was under Fiori's control.

The conservation studio was a surprise inside the mansion. Large worktables on caster wheels, bins of equipment, a fridge that no doubt held perishable materials. Empty frames hung from the walls, while an open rack of shelves seemed to hold paintings. Two easels sat against the far wall, with louvered spotlights pointing at them.

It reminded me of a small-scale version of the conservation lab at the Metropolitan Museum. All professional, without the warm and cozy feeling of the Ferraro's studio in Brenton.

Antonio strolled through the room. "This is impressive."

Why did he have this in his home? Although Elliot had mentioned three homes in other countries, so maybe that was simply what he did with *this* home.

"Blue suits you, Ms. Caine." Fiori entered the room with one bodyguard, Baptiste and the man who'd opened the helicopter door for him. Fiori pointed to the open shelves. "The storage racks are over there. The four pieces you'll be working on are marked with red tape."

Antonio knelt next to a worktable, rummaging through the shelves and drawers underneath. "I confess, Pasquale, I doubted you'd have what I'd need, but I think you're right."

"Do you do conservation in all of your homes?" I asked.

"I like this inquisitive side of you." Fiori's chin raised and his chest puffed, his superiority complex on full display. "I'm a serious collector. Rather than having to rotate my pieces and ship them off to conservators around the world, I found it easier to hire in-house. So, not in all of them, but a few."

Antonio continued his exploration. "Raman spectrometer, x-ray fluorescence spectrometer... do you have a gas chromatograph? And a charger for my phone?"

Fiori turned to Bodyguard Three. "Show the others in."

The big man walked to the end of the long room and opened a door, calling through it for someone to join them. He returned, followed by two men.

The first walked with a swagger, chin just as high as Fiori's. Tall and thin with light brown hair and too much pomade, his hawkish nose held up thick black glasses.

"This is Zane," said Fiori. "He's our chief conservator here."

A second man appeared from behind Zane, moving much slower.

I froze.

Short, dirty blond hair and a goatee. It couldn't be. Tired, almost unfocused eyes, and a forced smile which grew when he saw me.

"This is..." Fiori's speech slowed. "I suppose I don't have to introduce Cam-ron Parker, do I? He's our second generation conservator. You know his father, don't you?"

Cam-ron was a conservator? Not just a painter? And he was *here*?

"Yes." My brain whirred with questions. "Brenton's a small town."

Cam-ron held out a hand to shake, as strong as wilted celery, just like the first time. "Good to see you again, Samantha. It's been a long time."

I'd gone on a blind date with him last summer. It went so poorly, I got up and left, but I met Antonio because of that. Without that night, I never would have ended up at the auction to find the stolen painting, in Naples to find the stolen fresco, and Rhonda wouldn't have called me to investigate the paintings Parker was helping to smuggle.

It may have been the worst date ever, but it set my life on the path to amazing things. Maybe our fates were intertwined.

"It's a pleasure to meet you, Cam-ron." Antonio came to my side and shook Cam-ron's hand. "Samantha never mentioned you were a conservator."

His head fell. "I did restoration work for my dad from time to time. I'm more of a painter than anything else, but I..."

Zane's lip curled and he shouldered his way past Cam-ron. "I trained at the Courtauld and have worked at the Louvre Abu Dhabi and the Met."

Antonio shook Zane's hand. "They hardly need me here with that pedigree."

Were one of these two responsible for telling Fiori *The Music Lesson* and *The Concert* were authentic? With all this equipment and Zane's attitude, I would have expected better work.

"Samantha, your workstation is over here." Fiori waved me to a desk in the corner with two monitors and a laptop. "I've provided an email program which will allow you to communicate with any of your or Antonio's sources. I trust you'll be discreet."

Memories flashed through my brain. Tucking Cass into bed after chemo. Antonio pushing Emma on the swing. Sofia pressing me for wedding details. Nico's face when he opened his Christmas Eve present last year. My gaze settled on Antonio, in conversation with the two conservators. The terror after Parker shot into the Ferraro's studio and I didn't know if Antonio was dead or alive.

"We're not experts." My voice sounded weak even to my ears. "True authentication work requires study that can't be done from a single room."

Fiori placed his hand on the small of my back, his velvet cologne wafting over me. "You're resourceful. I'm sure you'll figure things out."

Zane piped up, apparently listening more to my conversation than Antonio's. "You'd be surprised what you can do here. I authenticated a remarkable seventeenth century Dutch masterpiece just the other week."

So he was the one who'd authenticated at least one of the forgeries.

Fiori's dangerous smile turned on Zane. "And that's why they're here."

"What do you mean, signore?"

"Because you said *The Concert* was the real thing. And it's not."

Zane's chin dipped. "What? Did they tell you it's not?"

"It had indigo in it, Zane." Fiori turned to me. "That was it, right? Indigo was the wrong blue?"

I nodded.

Zane scoffed at me, no doubt happy to have somewhere to direct his derision. "Indigo has been used since the Greeks and the Romans."

"Pasquale, we're also playing the odds." Antonio shrugged. Arguing against our findings wasn't the safest idea, but hopefully it helped increase Fiori's trust in us. "There was a study done in the 60s which covered most of the known Vermeers and only one used indigo. It's possible it was present in more, but the study simply didn't sample those sections."

"And the sketch underneath?" Fiori seemed to argue in our favor now.

Before I could say anything else, Zane rolled his eyes. "I'm going to take a second look. These two don't seem sure of anything."

"You will do no such thing," snapped Fiori. "You will continue the work you've been assigned. If they ask you to do something, you do it."

Antonio spread his hands wide in conciliation. "We're all professionals, right? I'm sure we can get along."

"I know I can." Cam-ron smiled up at Antonio.

The physical difference between the two of them struck me. How did I wind up with this tall, gorgeous, brilliant Italian art conservator? How was I wearing his engagement ring on my finger? And how the hell was I going to get out of this place so I could marry him someday?

"Perfect." Fiori crossed to the open shelves. "Would you like to see what you'll be working on?"

Antonio, Cam-ron, Zane, and I gathered around the shelves.

Fiori pulled out the first one and my stomach twisted in knots.

Nineteenth-century painting of a man in a dress coat and top hat, sitting at a desk by a window, writing on a sheet of paper. There was a glass of pale wine next to him. It was *Chez Tortoni*, by Manet. Less than a foot tall and just over a foot wide.

Stolen in the Gardner Heist.

"You recognize this?" Fiori's words snapped me back to the moment.

I nodded.

He placed it on the floor, propped against the lower shelves. He pulled out another piece. Just under two feet high and over two feet wide. Dark clouds hanging over a gnarled old tree, a small building, bridge, and an obelisk to the left.

I sucked in a breath, goosebumps spreading over my body. "*Landscape with Obelisk*."

Fiori nodded. "By Flinck."

Also stolen in the Gardner Heist.

"Don't tell me the two large paintings you're about to pull out are the Rembrandts?" Since I was a kid, I'd dreamed about joining the FBI to solve that case. No one knew where the thirteen works of art had gone, but if someone were going to own them, a billionaire art collector who was the head of a smuggling ring sounded like a valid candidate.

A wicked grin spread across Fiori's face. "What did you do after you resigned from the FBI? I know you were in Boston for the Gardner case, but nobody leaves the FBI that quickly after making it through Quantico. Tell me the truth."

My mother's words the morning of my graduation—the morning she died in a car accident—flowed through my brain. 'Next time I see you, I'll be calling you Special Agent Caine.' And every time someone called me that, it was like losing her all over again. "I got married and became an insurance adjuster."

"No. An insurance adjuster doesn't do what you do. Doesn't calmly walk into a meeting with me, with a recording device. You should have been terrified to be there. You should have been terrified when Jason was in your house. For that matter, you should have been terrified when you were helping Vincenzo Romano recover my painting."

Should have been? I was.

"Mi dispiace, signore." Antonio's soft voice pulled me from the memories. "I love my Samantha dearly, but she's not an emotional woman. Terror looks the same as love looks the same as happiness."

I tried glowering at him, but he was right.

Fiori chuckled. "People are my currency. I like knowing what makes them tick. And it's clear from the look on your face that these paintings are dear to you."

I nodded, no reason to hide it. "I want to see the rest."

Fiori grinned and stepped back, gesturing for Antonio to pull the next one out. "Baptiste, come and see how a true art lover reacts to these masterpieces."

The younger Fiori approached. Their obviously strained relationship was a fact that might come in handy in our investigation, but at that moment, all I cared about was the treasure in front of me.

As I expected, it was a seventeenth-century portrait of a man and woman in black. Three and a half feet wide by four feet high, the seated woman wore a huge white ruff and brocaded front panel down her gown. The man stood with a hand on his hip under a thigh-length cape, in an almost confrontational pose. *A Lady and Gentleman in Black*.

Antonio placed it next to the others and pulled out the last piece, the largest.

I held my breath as it slid out of its slot, knowing which masterpiece was left. Over four feet wide and five feet high, he carefully withdrew it and leaned it against the shelves beside the other paintings.

Zane, who'd been quiet through this display, pressed his hands to his heart. "Isn't it beautiful?"

I soaked in the details. The dark and stormy sea. The boat at the center, crewed by Jesus and his disciples. It fought against the waves, with its bow swept up to an almost forty-five degree angle by the tempest. The men at the bow manned the sails, buffeted by wind and water, in a state of near-panic. In the stern, one man leaned over as though about to vomit, while Jesus sat between several of them, radiating calm.

I stepped closer and knelt to inspect it. There he was. One of the disciples at the side held onto a line, hand on his hat, looking straight out at me. Rembrandt's face hidden in the painting.

"They were taken before I was born. I never saw the real things." How many times had I visited that museum and stared at the empty frames where these pieces were destined to hang again someday?

Antonio joined me in front of *Christ in the Storm on the Sea of Galilee.* "If they're the real things."

Zane groaned. "They are. I've already confirmed them."

I peered up at him, his swagger having returned after the earlier lecture. "We'll see."

Chapter 32

Antonio

I'd finished taking inventory of the equipment and completed a cursory review of the four paintings. "I need to take a walk and plan my next steps. Which tests to run first? Which painting to start with?"

Zane worked at an easel, touching up some damage to a stunning flower by Georgia O'Keeffe. "I started with the Manet when I reviewed them."

"Why's that?"

He pushed his glasses onto his head as he zeroed in on his work. "It's the smallest."

That was a silly reason to start with the Manet. This was an authentication, not a restoration. Surface area hardly mattered. There were x-rays to be done, infrared photos to take, paint patterns and chemical samples to test. "Grazie, I'll take that under consideration. Either way, I need to take a walk to clear my head. Bella? Would you like to join me?"

She'd sat behind the computer for the last hour, muttering now and then, but not speaking to anyone. Her gaze drifted to me and then away each time I caught her eyes. "I'm going to stay here, if you don't mind."

I walked over to her and pressed a kiss to the top of her head, whispering, "I don't think separating is a good idea."

She flexed her fingers over the keyboard and took my hand. "If you need to think, me being there probably won't help. I've got a lot of contacts who could give me everything we need, but if I reach out to any of them—"

"Too many questions?"

"Yeah. I'm rusty on a lot of this stuff."

"Remember, you studied art history. You studied provenance. You worked at museums." I leaned close and spoke directly into her ear. "And you've studied fakes and forgeries. You trained for this."

She cupped the back of my head, pulling my cheek to hers. "Thanks. I may need to remind myself of that a few times."

I kissed her cheek and straightened. "Last chance to join me?"

"Go. Use that brain of yours and stop distracting me." She gave me a weary smile and waved me on my way.

I walked to the main double doors to the hallway and found Jason and the man Samantha had dubbed Bodyguard Three waiting outside.

Jason asked, "Can I get you something, Dr. Ferraro?"

"I was hoping to take a short walk before I get started. Would you mind showing me around? I noticed from our window there are several sculptures in the yard and I thought that might help my brain get going."

He checked with Bodyguard Three, who nodded. "Certainly."

We walked together down the long hallway to the curved staircase at the center of the house.

"I expect there's no discussing your job, is there?" I asked.

"No."

"Last year, when we met in Capri, Pasquale mentioned his wife. She was onboard then and he invited us to dinner with her. Was she not on the ship this time?"

Jason's eyes remained straight ahead as we descended the stairs. "You won't be seeing the family during this visit, other than Baptiste."

If we were free to roam the house and grounds, not running into them must have meant they weren't there. "Will we take meals with Pasquale? Or the other conservators?"

"I don't know." Jason was not a talkative man. Whether that was due to his training and role as a bodyguard or perhaps he took the job because it was his natural tendency. Or perhaps it was because we were inside the house where other ears could hear us?

He led me through a sitting room, into the foyer with its geometric tiled floor and giant paintings, around a stone table easily eight feet across, with an urn holding white roses tipped in red, which could have come from the garden we'd seen around the hand statue.

We crossed the circular driveway where two gardeners pruned globe hedges and headed along a stonework path edged with ivy.

The fresh air cleared my head but being there with Jason was even more of a distraction than Samantha would have been. "Can we talk yet?"

His face remained impassive. "That depends on what you want to talk about."

I kept my voice low, despite there not being another soul visible, save one guard at a door hundreds of feet away. "Would Fiori actually kill our families?"

"They wouldn't be the first."

"What if he was out of the picture?"

Jason's jaw clenched, a rare sign of emotion from the big man. He whispered, "He's leaving everything to Baptiste, who's little more than a child. Fiori's been trying to train him for the last year, but I suspect everything will crumble when Fiori dies."

Dies. An important word. "But not if he goes to prison?"

Jason followed the pathway, taking a turn before we got close to the trees. "For a man like him, prison is little more than an inconvenience. Something that slows his communications but doesn't limit his power."

I nodded. "Officer Jimmy Slater? Do you know if he—"

"Just walls, Antonio. His power doesn't stop on one side or the other."

Marone. If Fiori was behind Jimmy's death, there was little hope for our own families. As Samantha and Janelle said, the man who kept quiet got the lawyer while the man who talked died.

"Do you think you can do what he's asking you to? Prove the paintings are real?"

"I'm not sure. Something feels wrong. He's already given me two paintings, and both were fakes. Are they all just tests?"

"I don't know."

"What do Cam-ron and Zane do here?"

"Take care of his paintings from here, on the ship, and from his residences in the Americas. European works go to his home in Corsica." He took another turn, and we headed along the path toward the pond. "Cam-ron's only been here a month. I don't know how long he's going to last."

Last as in work or last as in live? "What do you mean?"

"You know who he is?"

"Parker Johnson's son." Son of the man who tried to kill Samantha and me twice. Of the man who Jimmy had been working with.

Jason knelt and picked up a chunk of rock from the path. "His father cut a deal with the signore. Parker said Cam-ron would work for him, taking Parker's place in the organization until he got out of jail."

"Pasquale paid for Parker's new lawyer, didn't he?"

Jason nodded and stopped on the bank of the pond, which was a few hundred feet across, large enough for the small row-boat to float around. Trees gathered around its far edge. We were on Long Island, but this place felt removed from the world. The faint sounds of cars carried on the wind, proving we were not.

"Cristian told me they were cutting ties with Parker."

Jason tossed the pebble into the water, sending ripples across its width. "I guess a conservator with his morals is a valuable commodity."

"It sounds like Zane is much the same."

Jason folded his arms. "Plus, I think Fiori appreciated Parker's initiative, going after you and Samantha."

"He what?"

He rolled his head in my direction. "He hates your family. I still don't fully understand why he wants you so badly."

"You haven't asked him about that?"

"Asking questions is not my job. Listening is." That was exactly what Cristian would say. Men like Jason were how he knew so much. "But I'm sure it's some combination of respect for what you've accomplished against him without even trying, combined with his hope that it will piss Giovanni off if you're working for him."

"It's only one job. It's a one-off, and then we go home."

He chuckled and picked up another rock. "That's what most of his employees say."

A male voice behind us said, "I got tickets to the Rays at Yankees game tonight."

"Don't turn around," whispered Jason.

"How are your seats?" answered another male voice. It was faint, but at least two of the other guards were too close for us to continue.

Jason raised his voice to a normal level. "Have you cleared your head yet?"

Our conversation was done. I'd learned everything I needed from him, anyway. "I'd like to walk a little longer. I'm alright as long as I don't go past the trees?"

Jason nodded and turned back to the house.

I left the pond and climbed down a set of wide stone stairs, discovering access to the tennis court. What if I got something wrong? What if I displeased Fiori?

What if Samantha ended up like Jimmy?

Part of me had expected the ship to be boarded through the night. Expected? More like hoped. But the way the special agents came running out of the yacht club, they were not prepared to follow a helicopter. Could they have contacted air traffic control? It would be logical that Fiori would be on his yacht. Could they know where Fiori's boat was? Marone, and then they'd have to have known that the helicopter left the yacht this morning. Could they be after the yacht right now, hours behind us?

What if these four additional paintings were also fakes? He sounded displeased with Zane's error in claiming *The Concert* was genuine, but at least Zane was still breathing and didn't look any worse for wear. Perhaps Fiori was more forgiving than I expected.

Keeping it close to my body, I turned on my phone, hiding it from the view of anyone at the house.

I sent a quick text to Cristian's regular number. *Fiori's taken us. He's threatened our families. I need you to get something ready to protect them in case we need to move. Don't let any of it be suspicious and make sure you avoid the authorities. Don't text me back.*

As an extra measure, I deleted the conversation, turned the phone off again, and slid it into my pocket. Hopefully, my next text to him would be *Never mind*.

CHAPTER 33

SAMANTHA

I needed a walk as much as Antonio did. But he had to focus on the job and not on me. So I paced. I took in all the details, scanning the walls and ceilings, under the desks, around the windows, and found nothing. No cameras. No microphones. At least, none that I could see.

How could this place be so similar to Giovanni's and yet so different? Giovanni had obvious cameras all over the place. But here? They had to be somewhere.

Or Fiori had enough experience making threats people didn't disobey.

I dropped into the desk chair, resuming my research. There was nothing new. I'd already read everything worth reading about the Gardner Heist and the paintings. Whenever an article came out, I read it as soon as I saw it.

Elliot would have access to plenty of documentation we could compare against, but I couldn't call him.

Vermeer was easy to research, since he had so few paintings, and the Kühn paper was perfection. But Rembrandt? He'd produced hundreds. How could we make conclusions about these paintings without access to more information? The Gardner

Museum wouldn't share anything about the stolen paintings with me. I couldn't call in an expert.

Antonio had said if I worked for his father, we'd take trips when we needed this sort of information. That sounded perfect. Fly to Amsterdam, go to the Rembrandt House Museum, talk to their curators. Bring the paintings if need be.

I scrubbed my hands over my face. There was a solution somewhere. I just had to find it.

Cam-ron stood over *Christ in the Storm on the Sea of Galilee*, while Zane lectured. He talked about brushstrokes, comparing it to the couple in black, talked about Rembrandt's vision and how he painted himself into the sailor's face. He'd been with Fiori for two years, made a ton of money, and was grateful for the opportunity to work on such beautiful pieces.

Any true conservator wouldn't have been so proud of working on stolen artwork.

Cam-ron glanced at me several times during the conversation.

I did my best to ignore him, but he kept doing it. I swiveled one monitor to block him.

What next? News reports, investigative journals, documentaries, and conspiracy theory sites. Everyone had a guess about where the Gardner artwork had gone, but the chance of finding them together was low. Was Fiori amassing a collection of forgeries? What were the odds he would find at least one authentic piece among them?

He'd taken the news about *The Concert* being a fake too well. He pushed back when Antonio told him it was a fake, not on the fact that it *was* a fake. Did he know all along, like he had with *The Music Lesson*?

I sat back to watch Zane and Cam-ron. Were they the forgers? What if Zane's disgust over us questioning the authenticity of *The Concert* wasn't about his ability to authenticate it himself, but about the quality of his forgery?

When Antonio's Uncle Giovanni showed us the plans for a new branch of the Ferraro's office near his home, Antonio hadn't believed it was real at first. We'd talked about how a restorer could just as easily paint over a stolen painting to ship it safely or break down a statue to be put back together on the other end. Was that what was really going on here?

Cam-ron's eyes met mine, and he left Zane in the middle of a sentence, although he kept talking.

"He knows his Rembrandt," I said.

Cam-ron leaned closer and whispered, "I'm super happy you're here—that you figured it out."

I pointed at all my open browser windows and documents. "I haven't figured anything out yet."

"We need to talk." His eyes flicked to the side, like he was referring to Zane, then he returned to the shelving.

"As I was saying." It was as though Zane talked to hear himself speak. "There are nearly eighty self-portraits. These men loved to paint themselves. Take a look at—"

Cam-ron coughed, catching my attention, as he slid a painting out of its slot.

Holy shit! *Grainfield at Midday*. I shot out of my chair. "Zane!"

He startled and finally shut up.

"I need a bottle of water. Can you get one for me?"

He straightened his glasses. "I'm in the middle of a discussion right now."

"Pasquale told you to take care of whatever Antonio and I need." I put my hands on my hips, ensuring I looked as intimidating in the blue uniform we all wore as I could. "And what I need right now is a bottle of water. Cold."

What I *needed* was to talk to Cam-ron.

"Alright. But you can explain to the signore why Cam-ron is not receiving his instruction." Zane lifted his chin and spun on his heel, marching out.

As soon as the door closed, I raced over to *Grainfield*. "You sent the letter?"

Cam-ron sagged, nearly dropping the painting. "I'm so glad you understood. How are you getting me out of here?"

If only I knew how I was going to get *me and Antonio* out. "You're not here because you want to be?"

He slid the painting back onto the shelf. "The choice was I work here or my dad dies."

"Oh my god, Cam-ron." I sighed. What could I do now? "Same thing for us, but our sisters and their kids."

His big doe eyes closed and opened, like he couldn't process my words. "You're not here for me?"

"I'm working on it." I was the same age as him, but every time we'd run into each other, it felt like I had a decade of life experience on him. "Why did you send it?"

"Before my dad... you know..." He looked at the floor, talking to it instead of me. "He told me about all these paintings he was going to be working on as a special project. Said he was going to need my help with some of them. I assumed it was legitimate work and he was getting his company going again after the FBI investigation last summer."

"But it wasn't?"

"The police arrested him before I could find out. Then all those paintings they found at his girlfriend's house?" He smoothed a hand over his scruffy hair. "Mr. Fiori's people came to see me last month and said my father recommended me for a job. When I got here, it started out with cleaning a painting and re-varnishing it. I did a few pieces, they were happy, then they had me do some more cleaning and a few minor repairs."

How much time did we have? Not enough for a long story. "Zane's going to be back any second."

"Zane had me clean a piece so much the entire top layer of paint came off." He looked up at me, brows drawn tight together. "I remembered all that stuff you told me about fraud and jail time and—and I freaked. I was going to tell the police, and that's when they threatened my dad."

Like everyone else, he made one bad choice, followed by another, and then he was stuck. Just like me. But if he was cleaning stolen paintings... I pulled another out of the shelf. I didn't recognize it. Pushed it in, grabbed another, and my heart leaped. I recognized it from the pawnshop files. As Cam-ron continued, I pulled out one after another, finding four more. This was it. This was what we needed.

"It took me a bit to figure out, but Zane's job is restoration, but he also covers up stolen pieces. Someone somewhere else is doing the same thing, so my job is to strip that cover off."

There was a noise outside, deep voices. Cam-ron's eyes flew wide with panic. I stopped checking paintings. But no one came in. Maybe a shift change?

"Quickly now—why send the letter to Ferraro's?"

"There was another guy here when I started. He heard them threaten my dad and said he was going to the police if I couldn't." He lifted one shoulder. "I never saw him again and Zane said he was probably dead. So I knew the police weren't the right ones to contact. And Mr. Fiori was yelling one day a few weeks ago about Dominico Ferraro starting an investigation company. He was so angry, yelling stuff about those damn Ferraros."

Like Dom said, he'd told a *lot* of people about his plans. One of them must have told Fiori.

"I figured Brenton's small enough. It's only got one ZIP code and I knew the street name, so I hoped someone would get the letter to them."

"And 13 Fell? Is that related to the Gardner?"

"No." His head flinched back slightly. "It's this address on Fellsmere Court."

Dammit. I had the wrong Fellsmere.

A tiny smile appeared, and he hunched his shoulders like a mischievous kid. "I stole the stamps from the library down the hall and slipped my guard long enough to make the envelope at an art supply company."

I'd always thought Cam-ron was out of touch with reality. A grown man who relied too heavily on his mother to run his business and his life. He didn't seem to understand people or the world around him. He had talent, considering what a good job he did faking the original Chagall and based on some of his paintings I'd seen at Mason's Gallery. But the ingenuity to get that letter to Ferraro's wasn't something I would have expected from him.

The door swung open, and Zane appeared, brandishing the bottle of water. "It's cold. Princess."

"Thank you." I smiled politely, despite wanting to throw the bottle at his miserable, cocky face. "And Cam-ron, thanks for showing me the other paintings. You're doing great work."

He nodded and attempted to return to his worktable, but Zane caught him to continue the lesson.

CHAPTER 34

SAMANTHA

I couldn't let Cam-ron rot here. He was out of his depths.

One more life on my hands.

But I knew where *Grainfield at Midday* was, along with at least four paintings from Elliot's files. We had a link between Fiori and the pawnshop. Better yet, we had someone who'd been working in his smuggling operation and wanted out.

We had evidence. And we had a star witness. I covered my cheeks, feeling a warm flush coming over them. Even if that star witness was Cam-ron Parker, we had one.

And—oh fuck—a dead conservator. Maybe not dead. Maybe working with the police? No, if he was working with the police, Elliot would have known.

I had to do something. Had to tell Elliot. But how?

Where was Antonio? We needed to talk about this. Needed a plan of action.

Antonio. My eyes darted to the door where he'd left. What if he gave Fiori bad news? What if Antonio was wrong and Fiori wasn't a man of his word? Hell, he'd had me drugged and carried off to a helicopter in the middle of the day at a yacht club. That wasn't a man who gave two shits about other people or his word.

I scanned the open browser windows on the computer and clicked on YouTube, navigated to the video of Lucy at the museum where she was talking about indigo. *Help me out, Lucy. Give me an idea*. She'd worked through so many mysteries and puzzles with me, and she always gave me the answer.

The video switched to her parents, strolling through the museum. Her mother said, "The Baroque period began in the sixteenth century and made its way to Holland in—"

My inner detective jumped. That was it. Sixteenth century Baroque. It was a running joke between me, Lucy, and Alice at the Ferraro's office. I could email her a coded a message. Get the FBI here.

I pushed back from the desk and stood. This was a stupid idea. It was too risky. Fiori may not have had cameras all over this place, but there was no way he didn't monitor the communications.

Although a YouTube comment might go unnoticed, especially if I could write it in a way that looked like I was asking for help. The video was about the Rijksmuseum in Amsterdam, which had an extensive Rembrandt collection. I could ask them a simple question. Easily explain it away if I got caught.

"What are you doing?" Zane's glasses were up on his head again, his face inches from *Storm on the Sea*.

"Work." I shook my head and sat, pausing the video, electricity and fear surging through every cell of my body. I didn't want to die. I didn't want to be my father, leaving for one more job and never coming home. My sister didn't even know where I was. Had the kidnapping made the news? Were people looking for us?

Wait—I had an Internet connection. I could find the answer to that easily.

All the major news and news-ish sites had covered it, showing the same phone video over and over. It started after I was unconscious. Someone running had taken a shaky video from hundreds of feet away, so we were little more than blobs on the screen. It ended as the FBI agents arrived.

My heart wrenched watching the bodyguard run with me over his shoulder. Two gunmen, people running and screaming, and then Antonio. He scrambled to catch me. No one would have recognized us from the blurry video, but I recognized Antonio. He faced the guns, demanding he go with them. And he picked me up from where the guy had tossed me.

That was it. That was the moment.

Not only would he never leave me, he *would* always come after me.

Mrs. Samantha Ferraro, dammit.

There was no way Fiori and his crew of goons would take that away from me.

I flipped back to Lucy's video. Fortunately, Zane's account was logged in, so I typed my comment:

Found a 16th Century. Baroque painting at auction. I was hoping you could help with it?

Do you know how. A painting. Named. Girl with a Pearl. Earring was prepared? Rough sketches or blocking?

Comment below. Or. Not. Do you know any. Others who could help?

Many thanks, an art lover in a polyalpha space.

The sixteen century Baroque would tell her it was me. She'd figured out my dad's letter was a polyalphabetic code and she'd identified the space first, so she'd know there was a code hidden inside. And the first letter after every piece of punctuation spelled out FBI DANGER CONDO.

It was dangerous. But what other choice did I have?

My hand rested on the mouse, finger ready to click. The message was a reasonable request based on their video. I could explain it away if they challenged me.

If it worked, Lucy would call Elliot. They'd go to the condo to find out the danger. The photos of Cass and Sofia were still there, as well as Antonio's notes all over the wall. They'd get our families to safety.

Then what? They didn't know where we were.

If I included an address in the comment, there'd be no explaining that.

This is a stupid plan, Sam. Just use Antonio's phone to call Elliot.

"Samantha!" hollered Zane, startling me so much I jumped.

My stomach dropped. I'd hit the mouse button.

I had to delete it.

"I was asking you if—" Zane kept talking.

Adrenaline spiked through my body, but I figured out how to delete the comment. There was no proof I'd sent it. If they were tracking it, had I acted fast enough?

Zane marched over to the desk. "Are you listening to me?"

"No, Zane, I'm not." I shoved the chair back and stood. "I have to go to the bathroom."

To vomit.

CHAPTER 35

ANTONIO

I made my way through another garden, full of shoots rising from the dirt, surrounding a stone fountain topped with a reclining woman pouring water. Birds flitted about the garden, a particular robin whistling at me so much there must have been a nest nearby.

Walking the grounds—and knowing Cristian was preparing—had given me the inspiration to move on.

The two Rembrandts would come first. Same painter, similar timeframe, so the first step would be to compare and contrast. I'd also compiled a mental list of resources who could help. Conservators, researchers, and possibly Samantha's other old intern boss, Thomas Grange at the British Museum. He'd worked for me in Pompeii and we'd become good friends over that time.

Rembrandt had done enough work that I could spread the questions out without raising suspicion and I could mull over the Manet and the Flinck as I worked.

Part of me hoped they were all authentic and that Samantha would have the knowledge in her soul that they'd survived since the heist. The other part of me hoped for obvious signs they were fake, so we could leave sooner rather than later. We had just shy of three weeks before people would expect us back at work.

I knelt by a rosebush, inhaling the perfume of the early blooms. Sì, I'd recovered my center and was prepared for the task ahead.

A black sedan pulled up the driveway, passing the low stone wall which surrounded the courtyard. A thin man in a gray suit exited the passenger side and waited as the driver got out.

It was a woman with short, white-blond hair. They were the FBI agents from the yacht club. What were they doing here? Did they find us so quickly?

A lead weight settled in my stomach.

Would Fiori be setting my sister's death in motion right now?

I sprang to my feet and dashed to a side door. Intercept the FBI agents? Tell Samantha? Assure Fiori we didn't contact them?

A guard paused in his slow pace around the end of the house. "Slow down."

"Sì, will do!" I tore the door open and dashed down the hall, coming to an abrupt halt when Fiori descended the last step of the grand central staircase.

"Antonio, perfect timing. We have some guests I suspect would like to speak with you."

Bodyguard One glowered at me from behind Fiori. Baptiste was nowhere to be seen. If the FBI were involved, that didn't surprise me.

"I didn't call them. I swear it."

Fiori approached me and clapped a hand on my upper arm. "I know you wouldn't. I trust you." He came closer, lowering his voice. "But I also trust you remember your fiancée is upstairs. We don't want any accidents, do we?"

"No, signore."

He patted my arm. "Come now. It's Pasquale. We're friends."

We walked into the foyer and toward the adjoining library. Why were they here? What was I going to say? *Calm yourself, Tony. You know how to handle this.*

Fiori entered the room first.

Jason stood just inside the door to the library, where the agents sat on a yellow antique couch, surrounded by a show of the smuggler's wealth. Rows of shelves crammed with leather-bound books, decorated with crystal statuettes, and a huge floor model globe which sparkled like the countries were designed in granite. A rolling library ladder rested in one corner, as though anyone actually used the books on the top shelves.

The agents stood and introduced themselves, Special Agents Kelsey Bernard and Ben Abbott, while the two bodyguards took their places by the door.

Fiori invited me to sit on a sofa opposite the agents and he sat next to me.

Special Agent Bernard leaned her elbows on her knees, a mark of open discourse. "I don't want to take up too much of your time, Mr. Fiori, but we're investigating a kidnapping which occurred yesterday in Detroit."

"Detroit?" Fiori pursed his lips. "But this is New York?"

She nodded. "There's a video that's been circulating on the Internet showing what appears to be your helicopter taking a woman aboard it. Several witnesses claim she fought with your men before being rendered unconscious and was carried to the helicopter."

Fiori looked at me and gestured to the agents. "Would you like to explain what happened, Dr. Ferraro?"

The weight in my stomach grew. They'd produced no warrants, didn't mention any evidence, and there were only two of them.

"Sì, my fiancée and I were meeting with Pasquale yesterday morning about some work I'm doing for him. I'm afraid what you saw was..." I sighed, leaning into the role I was playing. "She drinks sometimes and can become agitated. We're working through it together, but I can't always control her."

Agent Abbott leaned forward next. "And carrying her to the helicopter with guns drawn?"

"I don't recall any guns." I squared my shoulders and lifted my head, as though battling Samantha's shame. "But she passed out. That's all that happened. She had too much to drink."

Agent Bernard smiled and nodded, turning to Fiori. "If you don't mind, we'd like to speak with—Dr. Ferraro, is it?—in private."

Fiori straightened. "Should I be asking if you have a warrant?"

"No need. I just want a few words with him."

"Are you alright with that?" Fiori cocked an eyebrow at me, as clear as he had to be about the threat. "I know you have a lot of work to do."

"Sì, I can spare ten or fifteen minutes." I addressed the agents. "Do you need more than that?"

Agent Bernard shook her head and everyone stood. Before the door had closed behind Fiori and his bodyguards, she whispered to her partner, "Wait outside and keep the bodyguards busy. Make sure they aren't listening."

She shifted to sit next to me, keeping her voice low. "Is everything alright? I saw them destroy the key fob, but they took the recorder."

"How did you find us at the yacht club?"

"There was a tracker inside the fob."

"Samantha didn't know that."

"I told her it was there." Agent Bernard frowned. "Have you learned anything?"

Telling her the truth was not an option. I didn't even have to convince her. I simply needed to not provide her with any justification to stay. "Samantha and I are here as guests with an old friend. You mistook what happened."

"I saw the fight."

"You think that's what you saw, or perhaps you want to believe you saw it?"

"What about the smuggling ring? Do you have any evidence?"

Marone, not about the smuggling ring itself, but possibly about the Gardner Heist. "There's nothing here. Pasquale was duped by two art dealers who sold him fakes. He asked Samantha and me to verify the authenticity of a few other pieces from the same seller, but we only just got here and haven't had enough time yet."

Agent Bernard inched closer on the sofa, curling one leg up to face me. "You're sure? Nothing I can report back?"

Every fiber in my body wanted to tell her what we knew, wanted to rescue Samantha. But this was not the way, with only two agents and no warrant. "Niente. I'm sorry. Now, if you don't mind, I was just out for a walk and need to get back to work."

"Samantha gave you my number?"

"She did." I stood, her cue to leave.

She cast about the room, eyes darting from one work of art to another. "I was really hoping this was going to be a break in our case."

"I understand, but I think you're pursuing the wrong man." Not the wrong man at all. The man responsible for an attempt on my Zio Giovanni's life and who tried to take my Samantha from me.

"I understand." She stood and shook my hand. "Can I speak with Samantha?"

"She's sleeping off a tremendous hangover." I'd done my job as best I could, shut her down and gave her no fodder to pursue this. The FBI was back to where they'd been before we received *The Music Lesson* on Friday. So be it.

I saw her out of the library and into the foyer, where her partner, Fiori, and his two guards waited. "I'm going back upstairs."

Jason joined us. "Signore, you called?"

"See Antonio upstairs while I say goodbye to our friends from the FBI."

We walked in silence through the hallway to the grand staircase. Every step taking me deeper into the awareness that I'd shut down the authorities. With every investigation Samantha launched into, it was the first thing I told her to do—call Elliot. Call the police. Call someone else. She always found some reason to say no until this case. And now our roles had reversed. She wanted to bring them in and I said no.

At the top of the stairs, Jason stopped and yanked me close enough to speak directly into my ear. "Did you tell her anything?"

"Of course not."

"I've seen her meeting with him before. I think she works for him."

I jolted and took a half-step back, the weight in my gut settling deeper. Too many questions. Had I said anything that gave us away? Was there truly a tracker on the key fob? Was everything we told Elliot going straight to her and back to Fiori? Had they even detected her recorder? Would it have mattered if she'd turned it on or not, because they knew?

"Jason!" hollered Fiori from downstairs.

We walked to the railing and looked down to see him climbing up to meet us, One and Three with him.

Once he reached the top, he dismissed the guards, who took up positions further down the hall. "What did she want?"

"To know what happened in Detroit."

"And what did you tell her?"

It was all another test. She asked me questions, no doubt reported back to him, and he verified. "I told her exactly what you wanted me to. I continued the ruse that Samantha was sleeping off a hangover and that we're here for work. We promised to keep your silence and we will."

"Good," he drawled.

"I'll take care of your paintings, but I need to know something for certain first. I'm asking for the same honesty you request from me. Did you believe *The Concert* was authentic?"

He slid his hands into his pockets and rocked on his heels, tilting his head back. Was that question a step too far? "I do like you, you know?"

"Grazie." But that was hardly an answer to my question.

"The four I showed you earlier—I'm not sure. *The Concert* is the one I truly want."

"Did you think the one you sent to me was the real thing?"

A sly grin emerged, and he eased his eyebrows up. "No. Zane made that one, but I told him to say he'd authenticated it if anyone asked."

That explained why the cocky conservator was so offended when we called it a fake. It was true, but it meant he'd failed in under six hours. "Why go through all this to convince us you thought it was real?"

"It's the great prize, is it not? The most valuable piece of stolen art in the world. It's a legend. Every cheap art thief claims to have it." He shifted closer to me. "But if a man like me says the same thing and has at least one of the other originals, what do you think happens?"

Other than the FBI beating down his door? "I don't know."

"Someone is going to crawl out of the woodwork and proclaim mine is a fake because they have the real one."

"And then you'll know who to go after for it?"

He inclined his head toward me. "And that is how you're going to help me."

"What if the other four are all fakes?"

He shrugged, as though it hardly mattered to him. "Then I suppose I'll need a new plan, won't I?"

But did that mean Samantha and I would still be free?

"Jason." Fiori turned away from me and began in the opposite direction from the conservation studio. "With the FBI snooping around, I want you with me. The other two can protect my artwork."

CHAPTER 36

ANTONIO

An hour passed, with Bodyguards One and Three loitering in the conservation studio. Samantha had seemed nervous when I returned, but perhaps that reflected how I felt. My nerves were a jumble with Jason's revelations that Fiori had Jimmy killed and Special Agent Bernard on his payroll.

The two supposed Rembrandts lay side by side on my table. Had I done anything other than stare at them for an hour? It had been such a long day, starting with the helicopter ride here, my brain was beginning to protest the work.

Zane came to my side. "I'd start with chemical analysis."

I craned my neck slowly to glower at him. "I was thinking about starting with an infrared comparison, given how the first two paintings Pasquale asked me to confirm both had incorrect sketches underneath."

His lip curled. Good. Calling out his easy failures had been my goal.

"Now leave me to my work."

He skulked back to his easel.

"Antonio." Samantha beckoned me to her desk. "I reached out to a photographer friend of mine in Boston about *Storm on the Sea*. He's working on a project to digitize his father's professional photos from the Gardner in the '80s and says he'll—"

The door blew open and Fiori stormed in, Jason behind him. The other two bodyguards snapped to attention.

"You!" He pointed at Samantha, and my world stopped. "Did you really think you were that clever?"

She eased out of her chair, like a deer attempting to blend into the background. "I—"

"These are seventeenth century Baroque. And you've already dealt with the Vermeer, so *Girl with a Pearl Earring* has no relation to this investigation."

I darted in front of her, hands out and voice soft. "What's going on Pasquale?"

"Get out of the way, Ferraro," he growled. "You swore both of you'd abide by my rules. And yet she sent out a message."

Marone, Samantha, seriously?

"I wasn't going to, I swear." The desperation in Samantha's voice told me it was true. She'd been caught and she knew it.

"I'm tired of the lies. What is it you Americans say, Ms. Caine? That's strike number two?" Fiori tore a handgun out of Bodyguard One's holster and began unscrewing the thread protector from the end. That meant a suppressor was coming.

Samantha's body moved behind me and I danced into her way. When we faced off with Jimmy on New Year's Eve, she stood to my side, dividing his focus. But tonight, she was the only target. I had to stay between her and that gun.

"I deleted it, Pasquale. Yes, I wrote it, but I decided not to send it."

Baptiste came barreling into the room. "I'm here. What's up?"

His father ignored him. "And yet still, my men tell me you sent it."

Samantha's hands curled around my arm, but she didn't try to get around me again. "Zane startled me and I accidentally hit the button. But I deleted right away."

"You make it sound so innocent. Even using Zane's account, so I wouldn't suspect you. The problem is—he's not smart enough for that!"

Zane moved, coming out of his hiding place behind his easel, his ego obviously stronger than his sense of self-preservation. "I studied at the—"

"Shut up!" Fiori put out a hand and Bodyguard One put a suppressor in it. "What is it, Ms. Caine? You think you can get away with all the same things here as you got away with in Cittavera? Giovanni and his minions may have fallen for your lies—Vincenzo may have fallen for you—but that won't work here."

"She's telling the truth." Cam-ron came around from the back of his easel, nervous hands fidgeting in front of his stomach. "Zane was yelling at her because she was working too hard. She jumped and got really stressed out."

"And then I deleted it. Have your men—your IT staff or whoever—check. I was too fast for anyone to see it, I'm sure."

The sound of metal gliding over metal as he screwed the suppressor onto the gun had never made me so sick. "She knows what's at stake here."

"I *did* check with them." Fiori gave the suppressor one final twist and held the gun up just to my side. "And fortunately for you, you're right. However, I feel you need to understand that I will not tolerate a third strike."

Zane's cocky chin jut out, an even more obvious act that earlier. "I can do this job. You don't need them."

Fiori's nostrils flared and he swiveled.

One shot. Straight into Zane's forehead. The conservator went limp and fell.

Samantha shuddered behind me and I grabbed her hand.

Cam-ron screeched.

"It was the wrong blue, you useless piece of garbage!" Fiori shouted at the body before slamming the gun into his bodyguard's hands. He balled his fist at me. "Four paintings is not that much to ask."

I stood still, barely breathing, while Fiori and Bodyguard One left. We had to find a way out.

Jason frowned. "I'll call the cleaners."

"I've got the kid." Bodyguard Three nodded to Baptiste, who'd turned green. "C'mon Bap, time to go."

"Is that what he called me here for?" murmured Baptiste.

The bodyguard steered Fiori's son out of the room. "I don't think that was his plan."

I spun to wrap Samantha in my arms, but she was gone before I could, at Zane's side to feel for a pulse.

Cam-ron had collapsed, tears streaming down his face.

Jason helped him up. "I'll take him to his room. You two should go to yours until the signore calms down. Don't leave your room until I come and get you."

I knelt by Samantha, who sat next to the body, a pool of blood slowly creeping across the floor.

"This is my fault," she whispered.

"No." I cupped her chin and forced her to look at me instead of the body. "It's no different than with Jimmy. He paid for his poor choices, and so did Zane."

She clamped her eyes shut, as though unable to look at me. "I swear, Antonio, I wasn't going to send it. I typed it and realized it was the wrong choice right away."

Even if that were true, it existed long enough for Fiori's men to see it. Did that mean it reached her intended recipient? Had the message got to Kelsey Bernard, and that's why she was there, probing for answers?

"Bella, you need to come with me." I gripped her upper arm and eased her to standing.

"It's all over a few pieces of fucking art. All these deaths." She buried her face against my neck and held tight. No tears this time, though. She was all cried out. "Why?"

"You can keep asking yourself that for the rest of your life, and you'll never understand."

"I don't want to."

"Let's go." I pulled back, running a gentle hand over her cheek.

She'd made a huge mistake and we got lucky Zane was here and had failed Fiori more than once. His death was the price for our survival and that of the people we loved.

But there were no more Zanes here.

The next mistake would fall to us.

CHAPTER 37

SAMANTHA

I'd tried to delete it. It was my fault. One more mistake to throw on the pile of shit that was my life.

Antonio settled on the love seat next to me, arm draped over the back, brushing his fingers across my shoulders. "I need my Samantha back. Snap out of it."

"But Zane. He—"

"No Zane. No Jimmy. No David and Olivia. None of them. We need to focus."

Death surrounded me. I was responsible for it. People who got involved with me died. Antonio couldn't—

"I saw Kelsey Bernard."

The veil lifted a little. "You what?"

"On my way in. That's why the bodyguards were in the studio instead of in the hall. She and another FBI agent came to question me about what happened at the yacht club."

That made no sense. "Why would she travel here when someone from the New York office could do that?"

He pulled one of my hands into his lap. "Jason told me he's seen her several times before."

That *did* make sense. "She works for him?"

"Put the pieces together, bella."

I stood, looking down at him, at his serious face. "That's how they tracked us to the yacht club."

He nodded. "She said she told you there was a tracker in the fob."

"No, she didn't. I'd remember that." My brain was clearing, facts falling into place. "That's how they knew to smash it. She told them. They knew exactly what was going to happen—that you'd identify it as a fake, they'd use the fob as a diversion, they'd take me, and you'd follow."

"Sì, exactly."

I took a few slow steps, working to push the shock of Zane's death aside. "Zane was covering up stolen paintings to be shipped and Cam-ron's job is cleaning ones sent from somewhere else."

"Zane painted both the forgeries Fiori gave us."

Three strikes. "Zane created two poor forgeries and was responsible for me sending that message. That was his third strike."

"With the added benefit of ensuring we obey."

"Fuck." I swatted a hand at Antonio's shoulder. "Cam-ron told me there was a third conservator when he started. That guy said he was going to the police and then Cam-ron never saw him again."

Antonio's eyes widened. He'd been egging me on, but this was a revelation. "Four conservators. Two dead and two alive."

"We need to get out of here. We can't wait around for an opportunity." I crashed onto the love seat next to him and grabbed both of his hands. "We need to call Elliot. We're witnesses to murder and Cam-ron's a witness to a lot of the smuggling operation. There are at least five paintings from the pawnshop files in the studio. There's more than enough evidence in here to put him away."

"Jason doesn't think prison is enough to protect us."

"Antonio." I let go of his hands and grabbed his face. That handsome face with the chiseled jaw and the beautiful brown eyes. I was *not* losing him. "We can't sacrifice ourselves for Jason's doubts. We have to try."

He nodded.

I jumped up and dashed over to the bay window. The sun had set ten or fifteen minutes ago, but the area around the house was as bright as day.

"There are too many lights," he said, joining me.

"What about the pond?" I pointed off to the side, where a sliver of the water was visible. "Late night stroll and a row across the water? We could say it's a romantic evening?"

"And then a mad dash through the trees?"

"How big do you think his property is?"

Antonio pulled his phone out and turned it on, the seconds it took to power up extending into hours. He opened an app with a satellite view. "Roughly six hundred feet to the first houses in a subdivision."

"How do those uniform sneakers fit?"

He tucked his phone into his pocket and chuckled. "Better shoes for running in than the Oxfords I wore to the yacht club."

"Better than my ballet flats, too." One more reason I hated Pasquale Fiori. His uniforms were really comfortable.

Antonio wrapped his arms around me. Every time he did that, my brain short-circuited. That was why I usually escaped him when I needed to think.

"Let me call Cristian. His people can act faster than Elliot's."

There was a knock at our door and both of us spun.

"Fiori?" he asked.

I shook my head and picked up a twenty-pound crystal sculpture and headed for the door. I raised my eyebrows at Antonio.

"Who is it?" he asked.

"Jason."

I hefted the sculpture over my head, just in case it was someone else, while Antonio creaked the door open.

Jason shoved his way through, swinging the door shut behind him. "I'm getting you two out of here."

"We were just talking about that." I placed the sculpture on the nearest table. "Do you have a plan?"

Jason handed me his phone. "Contact your family and tell them to get out of town."

"Cristian's already setting something up." Antonio looked at me. "Contact Cassandra and Sofia and tell them someone will pick them up. Go with them, no questions."

I wanted to call my sister, but if I did that, there'd be too many questions. We didn't have time. Instead, I texted her: *This is Sam. I can't talk right now. I'm in trouble and so are you. There's someone coming to your house to take you to safety. Pack an overnight bag only for you, Kevin, and the kids.*

She responded right away, *Who is this?*

Of course, she wouldn't believe an unknown number. I added, *Friday night, you asked about Antonio and me getting married and we talked about Mom and Dad. And about your pregnancy with Emma. I really can't talk. The people work for Antonio's family. Trust them.*

Antonio spoke into his phone and we passed information back and forth. I gave him Cass's address; he gave me Sofia's phone number.

While I texted with Sofia, Cass sent me several more messages. What should she pack? What would the man's name be? Would there be a code word?

"What about Lucy? Or the rest of your family?"

Antonio repeated the question into the phone, then told me, "If they can get to Cassandra's or Sofia's within the next five minutes, do it, otherwise tell them to get out of town."

I nodded and sent another message to Cass asking her to call Lucy and Nathan; Sofia was to call Lorenzo and their parents. We were really doing this. We were coordinating an escape plan from an international smuggler and murderer. By telling our families to hide out with another international smuggler instead of the FBI or the police. What had my life become?

Antonio hung up as I finished. "Cristian has teams heading to both houses. When I was out earlier, I asked him to be prepared, and he was."

"Where are they going?"

"I didn't ask. It's better we don't know, in case we get caught."

Jason held out his hand and I returned his phone. "Speed is more important than details right now."

"One sec." I took Antonio's phone. "I need to call Elliot."

"Be quick, bella."

Fortunately, Elliot was in Antonio's contacts, so I didn't have to go through a field office to get the number. He answered on the first ring. "Antonio?"

"It's Sam. I don't have much time."

"We've been trying to find you since Fiori took you. I've already been to your condo and I'm on my way to the airport right now," said Elliot. "Where am I going?"

But I deleted the message? "Long Island. Thirteen Fellsmere Court."

"Okay. I just got off the phone with Kelsey who's going to coordinate the protection detail for your families."

"No!" My whole body shuddered and I clamped a hand over my mouth. That was too loud. "She's on Fiori's payroll!"

Antonio grabbed me, fear covering his face.

Elliot swore under his breath. "Call them. Tell them to get—"

"Already done. There are people on their way." *Cristian's men will be there in less than five minutes. They're safe. Now focus, Sam.* "Listen, Elliot. I've got to be quick. Fiori kidnapped us. We're at his house, but he's just killed one of his conservators and we're afraid we're next. I've found at least five paintings from the pawnshop here, and we have a conservator who's been involved in the smuggling trade."

"Can you get out?"

Antonio mouthed a quick *I love you*.

"We're going to try. All the evidence is in this house, Elliot, but you need to get a team with a lot of firepower in here and fast." I waved my hand at Jason, who was listening at the door, and held the phone out so Elliot could hear. "How many bodyguards work here and how many are loyal to Fiori?"

"Three bodyguards, another eight security, twenty staff. But loyal enough to be an issue? Maybe two of the bodyguards."

"Did you get that?" I asked.

"I did."

"Elliot..." I turned away from the others, needing to keep this quiet. "If I don't make it, thanks for everything. Absolutely everything."

"Don't say that. I couldn't bring your dad home, but I'm sure as hell bringing you home."

"Okay. See you soon."

I hung up and handed the phone to Antonio.

"Here's the plan." Jason guided us to the bay window. "Quiet as possible inside the house. There's a side door that lets out facing the pond. One guard mans the door, plus a security camera."

"We can't just go for a walk and disappear into the woods?" I asked. "That was our original plan."

Jason frowned at me. "Signore Fiori just murdered someone in front of a group of people, which includes you. You're not *just* going anywhere."

Good thing Jason had arrived.

"There's another guard coming on duty in fifteen minutes. I'll intercept him, disable him, then take his position during the shift change. Then you can come through that door and we make a run for the pond. There's a ten-foot high security fence surrounding the property, but if we go in a straight line from that door, past the left of the pond, through the woods, I dug a hole under it this afternoon we can fit through. It's about two hundred metres to a neighborhood and we can call the police."

Antonio pulled out his phone. "I can call the police now."

Jason turned the frown on him. "That's how the last conservator died. If the police are called to this residence, your chances of survival go down. If they're called anywhere else, your chances go up."

Two dead conservators. What would happen to Cam-ron if we left him? "We need to get Cam-ron out of here."

"No." Jason started for the door. "You two are my job, not him."

"I'm not leaving without him." I looked at Antonio. "If we leave, he's next. I can't let that happen. Not only because he's the most valuable witness we'll have against Fiori, but it's—"

"The right thing to do." Antonio stroked a hand down my back. "I'm with her. If your job is to get us out of here, it has to include him."

Jason placed his hand on the door handle. "If we end up dead, it's going to be his fault."

CHAPTER 38

ANTONIO

Samantha and I crept along the hallway behind Jason toward the center of the house, rather than to the smaller staircase at the end. Cam-ron's room was in the wrong direction for us, but it was the only choice.

It was eight in the evening, but the house was eerily quiet. It should have been bustling with staff preparing beds, late dinners and drinks, or movies. Cards. Entertainment. There should have been laughter in a house this beautiful.

Jason stopped to knock quietly on a door.

No response.

Had they already come back for him? Were we too late?

Jason knocked louder and Samantha's head swung about, looking for other people.

A quiet voice came from behind the door. "Who is it?"

Samantha wedged herself between Jason and the door. "It's Sam. Are you alright?"

Cam-ron cracked the door open, but his eyes flew up to see Jason and he backed away, attempting to slam it shut.

Jason intervened, pushing effortlessly above Samantha's head, gaining us entry.

Cam-ron stumbled back, hands in front of his face, to fend off an impending attack. "Please, no! I didn't—I mean I won't—"

"We're here to get you out," hissed Samantha. "Calm down."

"No, no, no!" He rocked his head violently. Tears streaked his face. His shoulders rolled in and he blinked repeatedly, unable or unwilling to rip his eyes off of Jason. "They'll kill me if I leave."

Jason stood guard by the door, with an ear pressed against it. "We don't have time for this."

Samantha widened her eyes at me, inclining her head and hands toward Cam-ron. What did she want me to do? Pick him up? Force him?

No. My job was to talk. Convince him. "I know you're scared, Cam-ron. We all are. But we need to go. Fiori's not getting what he wants out of our arrangements. The forgeries weren't good enough. The paintings he thinks are authentic likely aren't. And with the Zane dead—"

Cam-ron let out a sob and sagged to his knees. "He just shot him. Right there, in front of all of us. It's all I can see. The blood."

Samantha, in an uncharacteristically soft voice—when dealing with anyone other than me—whispered, "I know what you're going through. The same thing happened to me on New Year's."

"The people my dad worked with?"

"Yeah. But Jason's going to help us escape. If you stay here, you'll wind up dead, too." So much for the softness.

I grabbed Cam-ron under his arms and pulled him up. "Time's running out."

"But what about my dad? If I leave, Fiori's going to have him killed. I can't..."

There was nothing we could do for Parker. And the only part of me that cared was the part that was trying to convince Cam-ron to come with us. "If he kills you, like he killed the other two conservators, why would he keep your father alive?"

His knees went weak and he nearly crumpled again.

Marone, boy. "If you stay, maybe you and your father live until Fiori is taken down."

"Please tell me someone's going to do that?"

"That's what we're trying to do." Samantha's razor-thin patience had already run out. "But we can't do it from in here. You and your mother did the right thing last summer when you told me about Olivia Scott and her fake Chagall. If we can get you out and into the FBI's hands, based on the work you've done here, they'll make you a star witness. They'll be able to protect you and your mother and probably your father."

Cam-ron nodded. "I can do that. I'm sure I can do that. Maybe. Just let me pack my things."

Jason checked his watch. "We're out of time."

"Leave your things." I yanked him toward the door.

He resisted, squirming out of my grip. "My lucky paintbrush is in the studio. That's all I need."

I worked hard to look less stunned than I was. "It's not very lucky if you wound up here with it."

Samantha touched my arm. "We have to go."

The door opened behind me, and Samantha left with Jason.

"Come with us?"

Cam-ron wrung his hands, looking around the room. Samantha was right. My priority was her safety, not his.

I hurried out the door.

Jason pointed down the hall. "You go to the staircase at the end. I'll go down the main stairs to the security control room. The other guy will be down there putting on his radio. I'll intercept him."

Samantha held up her watch. "You'll be at the door in...?"

Jason lifted his. "Seven minutes."

She was in her element, working with him. No doubts, no time to think, just muscle memory and action. In this head-space, she could take on any danger. "We'll slip into the stairwell and meet you down there in seven."

Jason nodded and headed back to the main staircase, gradually shifting from sneaking to walking like one of Fiori's trusted guards.

Our pace remained slow, ensuring we made as little noise as possible. We passed a room where a television blared, the first noise I'd heard outside of discussions in our rooms. Did the staff live here? Or were the rooms exclusively for guests?

Using the noise as a cover, I pulled closer to Samantha and spoke against her ear. "If I haven't told you this already, I love you. And if we don't get out of here, I'm—"

She placed her hand over my mouth. "Don't talk like that. Run through everything in your head. Scenarios where everything goes perfectly. Scenarios where everything goes wrong. Plan how you'll deal with each of them, so you're not left deciding instead of acting."

That was why this was her element. "All I'm thinking right now is that I want you in that tiny white bikini on a beach in Tahiti."

Her shoulders bounced twice and she shook her head.

The reaction soothed the overwhelming presence of dread, which threatened to prevent me from breathing. If I was to be in mortal danger again, at least I was with her.

"I'm coming!" Rapid footfalls thundered behind us and we both spun as Cam-ron hurried to catch up.

Samantha and I both slammed our fingers against our mouths in a warning to be silent.

He froze, mouth gaping. "Oh yeah. Sorry."

Perhaps Jason was right about the added risk of bringing him along.

Samantha muttered under her breath. "Now go over all of those plans in your head again, with *that* variable."

CHAPTER 39

ANTONIO

At the end of the hallway, the landing opened to the left, where a U shaped staircase led to the ground floor. Samantha gave a sign to stop and Cam-ron jostled into me. He was a tremendous variable.

Samantha peered through the large window in front of us and snapped back, pointing downward.

I looked, spotting the security guard, and pointed to the stairs.

She nodded and we gathered at the top step. It kept us out of sight of the hallway and the guard, but we also knelt, making ourselves as small as possible.

Cam-ron asked, "What now?"

Samantha mouthed, *Hold steady. Be quiet.*

"What?"

She placed a finger over her mouth, eyes beginning to roll, but she pulled them back down.

I held up my watch to her, tapped it, and she responded by holding up two fingers.

Jason would be there in two minutes. All we needed was to stay quiet, wait for him, and hope his plan worked.

A male voice spoke from down the hall. "What about the Jays?"

My eyes flew wide and met Samantha's. Jason hadn't mentioned other patrols.

"I'm telling you, Astros are going to repeat." There were at least two of them. Possibly the two who'd interrupted my conversation with Jason by the pond. More likely security or other guards, rather than staff, but I didn't recognize the voices, so they weren't Bodyguards One or Three.

Cam-ron's lips opened and Samantha clamped her hand over it, her gaze boring into his skull so strongly that he made a sign like turning a key over his mouth.

I tapped her, pointed to myself, and then to the window. I crept up to the landing, remaining in the stairwell, and eased myself along the wall until I could spot their reflections in the window.

Two men walked down the hall, wearing the dark cargo pants and shirts like the other security guards. The saving grace was their conversation, which masked most noise we might make. They passed the last doors in the hall and didn't turn around. How close would they come? Would they turn at the window? Would they come down the stairs?

I inched back to Samantha and spoke as quietly as I could without risking misinterpretation. "Two guards on patrol."

"Jason's late. He should have been here three minutes ago."

Cam-ron waved his hands in front of himself, color draining from his face.

I jabbed my finger toward the stair he was crouched on, and he sat. I eased his head down between his legs. The last thing we needed was him passing out.

The baseball discussion grew louder. They were not turning.

Samantha leaned against me. "If we go further downstairs, and they hear us, that's us against three of them until Jason shows up. Not good odds, and those two would have the advantage of being behind us with the high ground on the stairs."

"I can't take two out at once."

Samantha pulled back to mock-glower at me, her standard line of *I can take care of myself* clear, then resumed her close position. "I'll take the big one."

No, she wouldn't, but there was no time to argue. "The bigger one is on the far side. You can have him."

"It'll make a lot of noise. May bring attention to us. But it's at the end of the hall, so maybe not." She ran a hand over my hair and clutched the back of my head. No matter how calm she seemed, she was scared. "They're all carrying guns, stun guns, batons, and zip ties. Watch out for weapons. We tie them and leave them gagged."

We climbed to the top step. The lights outside helped ensure the window was less a mirror than if it were dark, but all the same, we moved slowly enough to not catch their attention in the reflection. So long as they didn't hear my heart crashing around inside my chest, everything would be fine.

I did as she'd said, planning my route around the corner, to the man on the closer side, who was at least four inches taller than the other. Samantha would be angry I lied about which one was bigger, but I'd deal with that once we were done. I'd surprise him. Fist to the nose. Kick to the knee. Disarm him, get rid of his radio, tie him up.

And pray it worked.

Samantha put up three fingers.

Three.

Two.

As she reached one, an urgent voice came over the radio. "I need help in the locker room."

I grabbed her waist before she could move, and in the window's reflection, we watched the guards tear back down the hallway toward the center of the house.

"Cazzo Madre di Dio," I breathed, closing my eyes and resting my back against the wall, with Samantha's body tight to mine. "That was close."

The pounding of their footsteps faded in the distance, while the door below us opened. Samantha's body went rigid and I didn't dare move. Was the guard down there leaving his post to help?

Voices filled the air from the guard's radio. The call for help came again, followed by questions of protocol. Was there an attack? Did they need to call in backup?

Cam-ron, still sitting on the step with his head down, let out a whimper.

"Who's up there?" asked the guard at the same moment the door closed and I heard the pop of the gun drawing from his holster. Until he'd climbed at least two steps, he wouldn't see us huddled against the wall.

Which one of us should respond? Who'd be the least likely to arouse any suspicion? Unfortunately, that would be Cam-ron, but there was no way he was up to the task.

Samantha poured every ounce of innocence she could muster into her voice. "Me! Samantha Caine! I'm a guest!"

"Come down where I can see you!"

"Um, yes, sir." She slipped out of my grasp, sliding her fingers down my arm as she stepped gingerly around Cam-ron. "I heard a ruckus and got scared."

The guard's voice rose. "I said get down here!"

When she rounded the landing, her hands shot up over her head, and she froze. "Oh god. Is something going on?"

"Here! Down here!"

"Oh—Okay." She added a shake to her hands, which may have been genuine, but not likely. She was in control, eyes flicking between the step to the guard. "Two guys just went running past my—"

Jason's voice cut her off. "What are you doing?"

The guard said, "There's someone—"

Samantha ran down the rest of the stairs and grunts replaced words. I bolted off the wall to the railing, running down the stairs, past Cam-ron with my eyes on the three people. Samantha had the gun, blood streamed from the guard's nose, and Jason had him in a headlock.

He was late, but he was there, and just in time.

"What happened?" I asked.

Jason released the guard's head, switching to hold him under the arms, and dragged him into the stairwell. "I thought I had the other guy out cold, but apparently not. He saw me coming, so we're out of time."

"Get Cam-ron." Samantha pulled back the gun's slide and released the magazine to check it, then tucked it into the back of her pants.

I hurried up the stairs, where Cam-ron still had his head down. "Come on."

He looked up at me, clutching the sides of his face. "Maybe I should go get that lucky paint brush after all?"

I grabbed one of his arms and forced him up. "I'll buy you a new one when we get out of this."

"I'm not ready to die."

"None of us are. Believe you'll make it, so you can fight as hard as you need to." I hauled him down the stairs.

"It's off." Samantha tossed a black shape at me. The guard's stun gun in a belt-clip holster.

For once, I didn't decline the weapon and attached it to my waistband.

Jason pointed through the glass in the door toward the row-boat by the pond. "Straight past there until we get to the fence. Antonio first—"

"No, Samantha first."

"Shut up, Ferraro." Jason's jaw clenched. "You take the lead, then Samantha and Cam-ron, then me."

Another voice came over Jason's radio. "It was Jason. Where is he?"

"Alright, everyone." Jason pushed open the door. "Now run."

CHAPTER 40

SAMANTHA

We sprinted across the lawn, toward the pond, voices shouting in the distance. No one had seen us yet, other than the guard at the end door Jason subdued. I kept my eyes on Antonio's back, thirty feet ahead of me and getting further away.

We were outside the reach of the house lights, illuminated by the pale moon. Once we got to the trees, another hundred feet ahead, we'd be under total cover and safer. We'd also have to slow down and watch out for roots.

I put a hand on Cam-ron's back, trying to help him move faster. He was already sucking wind. "Move your ass."

"I." He gasped. "Am!"

We passed the small rowboat, and a high-pitched whistling noise blew past me.

Fuck.

The first bullet. They'd spotted us.

There was no gunfire, but I heard a dull thunk in the ground ahead of us. They had suppressors on their guns.

"Faster!" said Jason, only feet behind me. He grunted and was no longer there.

I did a quick shoulder check.

He was on the ground, holding his leg.

I cut short and spun back to him, keeping my head down. A popping noise came from the little dock next to the rowboat, splinters flying into the air.

"Don't stop!" Jason ground out through gritted teeth. "I'll distract them. You three get to safety."

"No." I grabbed his arm to pull him up, but he was ridiculously heavy. "We wouldn't leave Cam-ron and we won't leave—"

He shoved my hand away as another bullet whizzed past us. "They'll have spotlights on any second and they won't be firing into the dark. You're too big a target."

"And you aren't?"

Jason grabbed the collar of my shirt in his fist. "I've protected the Ferraro family for over a decade. I'm not about to slink back to Italy and tell Cristian I failed him now. You and that man up there are my job."

I understood that too well. The sense of duty. Putting yourself in harm's way. I kept telling Antonio all these crazy investigations were my job, but none of them really were. It was something important inside of me. Like it was inside my father. But in this case, Jason was right. This *was* his job. "I can't leave you here to die."

"Don't underestimate me." He released me and his grimace shifted into a near-smirk. "Pasquale's been doing that for far too long already. Now go."

I knelt back on my haunches. Another bullet hit the ground, close enough to us that dirt hit me.

"If nothing else, maybe the police will react to gunfire." He pulled out his gun and turned to aim at the house. His first shot echoed through the night and took out the light over the door. "I'll buy you a couple of minutes this way."

Two more lights went out, the sounds of gunfire no doubt traveling for miles along the water, let alone through the neighborhoods surrounding Fiori's property.

"Samantha!" called Antonio.

"Coming!" If I didn't hurry, he'd run back to grab me, putting himself in the line of fire. I wanted to pat Jason's arm, but he was aiming again.

Antonio and Cam-ron stood behind a nearby tree waiting for me. When I caught up, I saw enough of Antonio's angular face in the moonlight to know he wanted to lecture me. But we had more important things to do.

"Let's go!" I swatted his shoulder and the three of us ran in the dark until faint lights appeared in the distance. House lights. Neighbors! "Look!"

"My ankle!" Cam-ron howled and grabbed me, taking me to the ground as he fell.

I clamped a hand over his mouth. "Swallow it, or you'll tell them exactly where we are."

He mewled, obviously in a lot of pain. "You two go. I'll get their attention."

"Goddammit." I smacked his shoulder harder than I should have. "We've already had one martyr. I refuse to lose another."

"I don't think I can make it." He let his head fall back onto the ground.

Antonio landed next to us. "What happened?"

"He twisted his ankle." I grabbed Cam-ron's stupid blue uniform and jerked him back up so he couldn't avoid looking at me. "Listen to me. The only way this ends for any of us is if Fiori is behind bars. *You* are going to be the star witness in that trial. Not us. You need to get to safety."

Antonio's deep voice was an excellent good cop to my bad. "I can see house lights from here. We're almost out. Do you see them?"

He craned his neck to look past me. "I think so."

I pulled his face back to me. "If they catch us, Antonio and I will make sure you get away. And then you're going to call the FBI and ask to talk to Elliot Skinner. You got that?"

"Elliott Skinner, Elliot Skinner."

"Exactly. He's from the Detroit office and he'll take care of everything."

Antonio and I helped him stand, but he was unsteady on the bad ankle.

"Elliot Skinner," he repeated quietly to himself. "Elliot Skinner."

How did my sister ever think he was a good match for me? I ran a hand over my cheek. I needed to talk to Elliot and find out how long his team would be. If I did that in front of Cam-ron, it would panic him more. It would have to wait.

Cam-ron swung his arm over my shoulder and we made far slower progress. "I meant it, you know. About how you turned my life around?"

He'd told me that at the police station in December, after he and Parker had been taken in for the shooting at Ferraro's.

"It was like one of those shows where they take kids into jail and scare them straight. You know?" He hobbled a few steps, then hopped, and returned to hobbling. "I always listened to my dad, but nothing was ever good enough. After the whole thing with the Chagall, I went back to school to prove I was more than what he said."

"You're a better man than he is." A week ago, I would have said he was a better man than my own father, too. I was either luckier than Cam-ron because my dad had left to do good things or I was unluckier because I didn't have him there. Although from the sounds of it, Parker probably screwed Cam-ron up even more.

"He always called me a loser."

"That's bullshit. You came here, risking your own life, to save his. That makes you a hero."

He sniffled. Maybe it was the pain, maybe it was the moment. We didn't have time to deal with either of those.

Antonio—who'd scouted ahead—took Cam-ron's other arm. "We're almost at the fence."

Another thwack against a tree. They were firing aimlessly into the woods. I twisted to check behind us, but there were very few lights on. Was Jason still alive? I hadn't heard his gunfire in a few minutes. "Antonio, give me your phone. Let me call Elliot again."

He reached for his pocket. Then the other pocket. "Che cazzo."

Shit. "Lost it?"

He craned his neck to search the way we'd come. It was out there somewhere. "This is the most foolish thing we've ever done, you know that?"

I sighed. I should have driven to Chicago and left for a vacation with Antonio as soon as he'd landed. "I thought that was getting mixed up with you?"

Antonio laughed ruefully as we continued our awkward pace with Cam-ron slung between us. "No, Bella, that was the best decision you've ever made."

Cam-ron whispered, "You two are kind of extra, you know that?"

"Shut up, Cam-ron." I glanced at Antonio, wanting to kiss the man, but this wasn't the time. "Move faster."

He grunted as we picked up speed. "Okay, but yeah. Wow."

"Extra. I feel like that suits me."

I rolled my eyes, even though no one could see it. "One of many words."

"Dashingly handsome?"

Cam-ron chuckled.

"Keep your volume down, you two."

Antonio used humor for almost everything. To flirt, to entertain, to convince, to express boredom. Sometimes to deal with fear. We were going to survive this. We were almost at the—

"I see it! The fence!" It was tall, vertical bars in powdered black with some shapes along the top. I ducked out from under Cam-ron's arm. Jason would have mentioned if it was electrical, but I reached for it slowly, just in case. Nothing but cool metal. I tried to shake it, but it was sturdy.

Antonio said, "That's awfully tall."

"Ten feet." I knelt to check the bottom, where the bars met the ground. There was no hole. No goddamn hole! Every cell in my body wanted to scream.

"We must have veered off the straight line." Antonio was far too calm. Maybe he could make another joke about it.

"Do we climb or look for the hole?"

Cam-ron continued staring at the top.

If I climbed it, Antonio could lift Cam-ron and I could help him the rest of the way. But Antonio? I couldn't pull him up. "If I boost you, could you climb over?"

The light was dim with the partial moon hidden behind the tree leaves, but my eyes had adjusted enough to make out the tense look on Antonio's face.

"Your arm isn't fully healed, is it?"

"No."

My heart sank. I was *not* leaving him. "Alright, we can go left toward the water or right toward the front gate. The hole's got to be here somewhere."

Antonio said, "If we assume we don't find the hole, the water's our better chance. The fence will end and we can go around it to get to a house."

I scanned the bottom of the fence to the right until it vanished in the darkness. "I'll explore ahead. You two follow behind, and I'll circle back when I find it."

CHAPTER 41

ANTONIO

Cam-ron and I moved at an excruciatingly slow pace. Voices carried on the wind. Joyous ones from the neighborhood on the other side of the fence—apparently gunshots didn't impact their moods—and frantic ones from the direction of the house. They were still far enough away I didn't fear being caught yet, but we walked in silence, all the same.

Samantha had been gone too long. How many men could Fiori have looking for us? How had they not found us?

Marone, what if they already found her?

Ice splintered through my veins.

What if they'd already caught her and were waiting for me to arrive? The earlier gunshots had been suppressed, so if all the guards did that, she could already be dead. Surely if she was, I'd feel it. Just like when she came back into my life, I felt something change in the air. The axis of my entire universe shifted. If she was dead, I would have felt it shift back, putting me out of balance.

Cam-ron groaned quietly.

"Let's stop for a moment." I leaned him against a tree and knelt as he slid to the ground. "Does that help?

He nodded. "It hurts a lot."

"You're going to have to fight through it. Take some deep breaths and calm down."

"I heard a saying once, that fear is just excitement without the breath."

I spluttered a laugh. It would appear I was not the only one coming up with cheesy lines to avoid my feelings. "Sì, I've heard this, as well. Perhaps if you breathe enough, you'll get excited?"

Cam-ron made a half-hearted attempt at laughter. "Did you know Samantha and I went on a date once?"

"As a matter of fact, I do know that."

"We weren't very well suited for each other.

"It takes a while to find the right woman."

He let out a small grunt. "She got up and left."

"Fate is a strange mistress, my friend." I patted his shoulder. "Did you know that was the night she and I met?"

He cocked his head.

"She took her bruschetta and wine to the bar, and when my date left me—"

"Your date left you?"

"Long story." I waved my hand in the air to dismiss the memory. What a disaster. "But when she walked out on me, I also went to the bar."

Cam-ron sighed. "And then the rest is history?"

"You could say that."

"And then you two found the painting my dad tried smuggling into that auction, plus the ones he'd hidden at his girlfriend's house. Then he tried to kill you." He looked down, a greater darkness than the evening settling over him. "I wonder how things would have turned out if I'd been a better date?"

I couldn't hold back my chuckle. "For one, we wouldn't all be running for our lives."

"We should probably get back to that."

"Sì, we should."

Cam-ron took my hand and I helped him up. "Samantha's taking longer than she should, isn't she?"

I'd expected she would move fast and return to us regularly. Perhaps we should have gone right instead of left. "She is."

"We need to catch up to her." He threw his arm over my shoulders.

"Do you think you can?"

"Yeah, I—"

"Antonio?" Samantha's hurried whisper sent a wave of warmth and relief through me.

"We're here, bella."

She appeared further along the fence. "I found the spot Jason dug. It's only two hundred feet away."

"And it's big enough for us to fit through?"

"We need to hurry." Shadows hid her face from me, but there was something wrong in her tone. This would not be as easy as we'd hoped.

An owl hooted nearby and something skittered through the leaves which remained on the ground from last fall. Voices, closer than before, joined the night sounds.

We all turned, looking behind us.

Cam-ron whispered, "They're getting closer."

"Dogs are barking on the other side of the fence further up. We'll make more noise if we move faster, but I think that's the smart choice."

I gripped Cam-ron's waist tighter with my good arm, held his hand around my shoulders with the bad. Pain was screaming up and down my bicep with each movement. If I'd been fully healed—if I hadn't played stubborn at New Year's and saw a doctor in Roma while we were at Giovanni's, maybe I'd be better. Maybe I could do more. Sling Cam-ron over my shoulder and run with him.

Why don't you, Tony? I was asking Cam-ron to battle through the pain of his bad ankle, but I couldn't suffer through my own? "I'm done."

Samantha whipped around to me. "What?"

"Sorry, Cam-ron." I leaned over, put my shoulder into his waist, and picked him up.

"Antonio—that's dangerous out here. Your balance will be off and if you—"

"Does my balance matter if I'm dead? If he is? Or you?" I charged forward, not interested in the debate. Two hundred feet, she'd said. I could do that.

Samantha dashed ahead of me.

Fire licked through my arm with every movement. I couldn't keep up with Samantha but moved infinitely faster than if I'd continued walking with Cam-ron.

She skidded to the ground, barely visible under the tree cover. "Here!"

There was no hole. She was sitting on the ground, digging with her hands. I set Cam-ron down and looked behind us. "Flashlights."

"This is the spot. Someone must have filled his hole in, but it's loose. You both need to help."

Cam-ron and I dropped next to her and joined the effort. It was fast progress, but with every second we were digging instead of escaping, the flashlights got closer.

The mound of dirt grew larger and larger until I stopped. "Cam-ron, it's big enough. Go now. On your back."

"Okay."

As he went through, squirming and inching his way under, Samantha looked at me. She knew what I knew. It was a tight fit for him. She'd fit. But there was no way I would.

"Bella, you're next."

"No." She resumed digging. "It's not big enough for you yet. Jason would have dug a hole that would fit him, so enough has to be loose for—"

I grasped her hands and pulled them away. "You see the flashlights behind me? There's not enough time for this. We'll both get caught."

"No." She struggled against me. "I can't lose you."

"Bella." I reached for her feet and put them into the hole under the fence. "If any of us are going to make it out of this whole thing alive, you know it's me. He needs me. But more than that, I'm Giovanni's nephew. If Fiori kills me, he's signed his own death warrant. You're just the woman who's ruined every one of his plans."

"Are you guys coming or not?" asked Cam-ron.

Samantha whispered, "I love you, you stubborn fool."

She tucked her feet into the hole and sank down, legs squeezing under the bottom bar.

I tried always being honest with Samantha, but there were moments that called for lies. Fiori would likely kill me. But at least Samantha would live. When we'd met, she'd cut herself off from the world. She didn't want more friends. Didn't want a lover. Didn't want to open her heart to anything. All she wanted was to do her time in Brenton and leave.

She held the metal rungs, twisting to find a better grip, like the rock climber she was.

Hopefully, the friends she'd found over the last year would change that. She'd learned much about herself and gotten past many of the scars that held her back. Her heart was finally open. And with my dying breath, I would cling to that. Not just that her body was alive, but that her heart was.

Samantha moved backwards out of the hole. Finding a better angle? Was she going on her stomach instead?

She pressed her face to the bars and pointed past Cam-ron. "I need you to listen to me. Do you see that tree over there?"

He nodded.

What was she doing?

"Bella, the flashlights. The voices." They were getting louder.

"You hightail it over to that tree and then you sit on the other side of it and don't make a fucking noise. Do you hear me?"

"Yeah. No noises."

"It's going to get loud here very soon, and I need you to stay behind that tree—no matter what happens—until it's quiet.

And once you can't hear anything, not even a squirrel rustling a branch, you count to five hundred. You got me?"

"Five hundred."

"Then you run to those houses with the lights over there. Forget the ankle. Don't you dare hobble. You fucking run."

No. No. No. All the hairs on my body stood up. She was not doing this. "Bella, no!"

Her focus remained on Cam-ron. "What's the FBI agent's name?"

"Elliot Skinner."

"Repeat that over and over until it's quiet. And when you talk to him, start by telling him that Fiori has us and he's about to kill us."

I knelt behind her, trying in vain to push her through the opening. "Don't do this, you fool woman."

"And no matter what happens in the end, you tell them everything. Absolutely everything." She sucked in a breath, her words coming too fast. "You are not the loser your father said you were. You're a goddamn hero, and I need you to promise me you're going to do all of this."

I gripped her shoulders, pulling them away from the bars, trying to get her horizontal so I could shove her through.

She was too strong and had too much leverage. "Go! Now!"

"They're almost here!" I kept my voice as quiet as I could, but what was the point now? The security team was too close.

As Cam-ron limped to the tree, Samantha stood.

"I change my earlier answer. *This* is the stupidest thing you've ever done."

"Maybe." She brushed the dirt off herself and pulled the gun out of her waistband. "They won't stop. This isn't about saving a piece of art. It's about ensuring these men don't come for you—"

"Or you."

"I know." She blew out a sharp breath and shook her head to regain her focus. "It's about us and our future. We won't have one if we're looking over our shoulders for Fiori the rest of our lives. He won't settle for continuing to play his little games. He wants your uncle—and me—to pay, and our lives are the cost."

"You know I won't let you go alone?"

"I wish I could convince you differently, but I understand. I did just screw up my escape so you wouldn't be alone."

I tapped her chest. "And we're going to that resort when we're done."

She let out a weak laugh. "It's a deal."

"Good answer. Now what's your plan? Other than running into the bad guys' arms, being held against our will, and possibly getting killed?"

"We run." She pointed in the direction we'd been headed. "Make it to the water at the end of the fence. So long as they're chasing us, they aren't going after our families."

Chapter 42

Samantha

Antonio and I tore off through the woods along the fence. The water had to appear sometime. We'd have a clear path. None of Fiori's men would be there. They were all behind us.

He and I were athletes in our own ways. We'd done three-and five-mile runs together, but never at a complete sprint. The sound of voices behind us gave way to rough breaths and the sounds of our feet hitting the soil. It was late enough in spring that the trees were almost fully in leaf, which provided plenty of cover. Good for hiding, shitty for running.

The weight of the Glock in my hand was a comfort, almost as good as the presence of the man next to me. If we got out of this, I was done. Risking my own life or my own future was one thing, but this adventure has snowballed out of my control.

Screw being out of control.

Part of my brain wanted to turn around and open fire on the men pursuing us. I even slowed for a moment and prepared myself for the eventuality I was going to kill someone. But as my speed slowed, Antonio slowed next to me, his head turning to look over his shoulder.

He focused on the men behind us, but a pair of flashlights lit up to our left. To the right, the fence. Straight ahead, somewhere in the darkness, was the water and our salvation. Unless Fiori's men were already there.

Antonio panted, "You should have been safe back there with Cam—"

"Shh!" If any of them were close enough to hear us, I'd rather they kept searching for Cam-ron, rather than knowing we'd gotten him out of the property.

Was he counting to five hundred already? Was he still listening? Did he remember Elliot's name?

In what world was my fate in the hands of Cam-ron Parker?

A blinding light appeared from the top of the fence, so bright we had to cover our eyes. I stumbled to a halt, rather than running into a tree. The lights lined the entire fence, as far as I could see. We weren't anywhere near the water yet.

"Into the woods." Antonio nudged me to our left, in between trees and into shadows, avoiding the flashlights.

"I see them!" shouted one man from the direction of the water.

"Over there!" yelled another.

My lungs ached and feet were killing me. The shoes were good, but not made for trail running.

Antonio's hand found my free one and we raced together, searching for a way through the net that was closing around us.

Two more flashlights appeared ahead of us.

"Enough!" This time, it was Fiori's voice. "You've lost."

We stopped and I raised the gun in his direction. "Not yet, we haven't."

A high-pitched whistle blew past me, followed by a thwap against a tree and the sound of bark clattering to the ground.

Fiori said, "I'd suggest you drop that."

Three more dull thuds in the ground directly in front of us.

I closed my eyes, heart still pounding from the run through the woods. *His name is Elliot Skinner, Cam-ron. Make sure you're counting.* I pulled my finger off the trigger and held my hands out as I knelt to place the gun on the ground. "I'm so sorry, Antonio."

"Don't apologize, amore." He took my hand again. "This has been the most amazing ten months of my life. I wouldn't trade a moment with you for all the—"

Pain screamed through every ounce of my existence, and I crumpled to the ground. My muscles clenched so hard I would have screamed if I had control of them.

Antonio crashed next to me, convulsing.

Stun guns.

Please, Elliot. Please hurry.

CHAPTER 43

ANTONIO

Samantha and I were each tied to white wicker chairs in the garden room. The first room we'd entered of Fiori's magnificent home. The travertine floor would be far easier for them to clean than the hardwood upstairs. *Stop thinking that way. Make a plan.*

But what plan was there? We were surrounded by Bodyguards One and Three, the security guard Jason had choked out, and three other burly men I recognized from either the yacht or the house. There was no sign of the FBI, no sign of Jason, and the zip ties were too tight to break.

My body ached from the stun gun. That was an experience I was happy to never have again.

"So…" I said, "are we sleeping here tonight?"

Bodyguard One, who'd shot at me at my Zio Gio's place in January, stepped forward. The glower in his eye suggested he was about to punch me, but one of the guards stopped him.

Fiori entered, with Baptiste on his heels.

"Is this necessary?" asked Baptiste.

Fiori spun on his heel and raised a finger to his son's face. "This is how you run an organization. If you don't learn, I'll have to replace *you* with someone else."

Baptiste grimaced, his gaze roaming about the room. What was going through the poor man's head? What did *replace* mean to his father, perhaps?

"Ms. Caine." Fiori came to stand in front of her, rolling his neck. "There are those whose loyalty comes easily." He waved his hands toward the men surrounding him. "In my experience, for people who choose not to give that loyalty to me, threatening their loved ones is the most effective way to ensure they don't betray me. A reasonable person would hear that threat, understand I'm serious about it, and help me with whatever job I've requested."

"No one's ever accused me of being reasonable." Samantha preferred to play dangerous games. It was something I'd have to encourage her to stop.

"Parker Johnson." He paced away from Samantha, beyond the wicker and glass table, toward a Grecian statue at the end of the room. "Jimmy Slater. Vincenzo Romano. Do you know what they have in common?"

"I'm not sure. Could you give me a few hints?" Her jaw was set tight. What was she thinking? "Their names don't all start with the same letter, I know that much."

Of course. She was delaying. She hoped Elliot would arrive and rescue us. But talking was *my* specialty, not hers. "No, bella. Johnson and Jimmy both start with the same letter. Maybe you're onto something there."

Fiori patted the cheek of his statue and continued his pacing. "All of them betrayed me by telling you what they knew. I don't know what it is about you—you're abrasive, lack humility, and you're not all that attractive."

"That's not true, at all," I said. "At least not the last part."

Samantha almost laughed at that.

Fiori continued, ignoring me. "I knew there was a leak in my organization and I've been trying to ferret it out for a year. Tighter security didn't work. Cameras and hidden microphones didn't work."

"Plus Mom wouldn't talk to you until you got rid of them," muttered Baptiste, while his father continued talking.

"The solution dawned on me when Vincenzo returned from his job in Cittavera. You were the key, Ms. Caine. I needed *you* to uncover the traitor for me."

That was why he'd given us the run of the place. He *wanted* us to attempt an escape.

"I was convinced it was Dr. Ivan. That's why we used the drugs. And when he went along with that ridiculous plan, I started marching everyone out in front of you, in case someone acted. If no one contacted the police or tried to help you escape here, you would have been moving along to my residence in France next."

That explained the changing faces in his staff on the yacht and then at the mansion through the day.

"It surprised me Cam-ron was brave enough to run with you, but truly..." He held his arms wide to the sky and looked up, a broad smile sweeping across his face. "I never would have suspected Jason, so thank you." He pulled the hands in, clasping them over his chest. "From the bottom of my heart, thank you for helping convince my traitor to reveal himself."

"No problem." Samantha forced her professional smile into place. "That tips our scales back into balance, right? Or would you like Antonio and I to go back to work? I have some information coming from a friend in Boston."

He neared Samantha, and she drew her head back. He took her face in his hands. "My only question is whether I should keep you alive until we find Jason and Cam-ron or dispose of you before you can turn one of my other men."

At least that meant neither of them had been found yet. There was still hope Cam-ron had contacted the FBI.

Baptiste leaned toward Bodyguard Three, the one who'd taken him after Zane's death. "Dispose?"

How long a delay could we eke out? Where was Elliot's team? "Pasquale, I'll do anything if you let her go. I swear, you'll have my complete loyalty. Forever."

He let her go and strolled the few steps to me. "As much as having you work for me would be a feather in my cap—and how much it would piss off your uncle–you're not that valuable. There will be a long line of conservators begging to take Cam-ron and Zane's place. Who wouldn't want to work on the pieces that come through my doors?"

This man had seemed so kind and genuine during our first meeting, all those months ago in Capri. But that was not the real him. This was not like my Zio Giovanni, who was concerned with money and power. Fiori genuinely believed the world owed him things. How did he make his money? Was he born into it? Did he have parents that created this monster in front of me, who thought human life was less important than his artwork?

That was it. His artwork!

I said, "What if I knew the identities of the people who took the fresco back from you?"

Fiori rolled his eyes. "Took it back? Stole it from me, you mean? Snuck aboard my boat and stole something of mine?"

"I know who it was."

"Please." He turned from us and walked to Bodyguard One, hand out. "I know exactly who it was. Those damn Reynolds Recoveries people. I've even hired them in the past."

The bodyguard passed him a gun with a suppressor attached.

Blood drained from my head, and the world shifted sideways. *What else do you have, Tony? Think fast or he'll kill her.* "The painting with the yellow flowers from Giovanni's. I'll get it for you."

Baptiste's voice quavered, looking anxiously at his father, Samantha, and back again. "The one you said was for my birthday?"

Fiori turned to face Samantha with the gun. "He'd never give it up."

Her breath increased. No matter what she said, the brave face she put on, she knew what was about to happen.

Focus on Fiori. Don't panic. "He would. If I told him the trade was that painting for Samantha's life, he'd give it to you."

"He doesn't care about anyone, least of all your snooping fiancée." He lowered the gun and looked at me. "Vincenzo told me she sent a photo of one of his stolen pieces to the authorities. I heard he had to pay a fortune in import taxes on it."

I leaned forward, testing the zip ties. Or the wicker of the chair. Or anything. "She's family. That means everything to him."

Fiori tapped the side of the gun against his forehead and paced the length of the room. When he returned, he said to Bodyguard Three, "Cut him free and give him your phone. I'm interested to hear this conversation."

I rubbed at my wrists once he removed the zip ties and I took the phone.

Samantha's attempt at a professional veneer had vanished, replaced by mottled skin across her throat, tight eyes, and a pinched mouth. I could only imagine the words running through her head; the same running through mine. *Please, Cristian. Answer the phone.*

"Don't get any ideas." Fiori waved the gun at me like a pointer finger. "There are too many weapons in this room to pull off a miracle. So call him. Right now."

I dialed the number and waited. One ring. Two rings. Three. *Please, please.* Four.

"Who's this?" asked Cristian.

"You're on speakerphone." I spoke quickly, no longer attempting to delay, but to convince. "I need your help. We have a new emergency. Do you remember the painting with the yellow flowers that Vincenzo tried to take?"

"I do."

"You need to ship it to Fiori or Samantha is dead." My muscles were practically as tight as when the stun gun's electricity jolted through me. They wouldn't say no. It was only a painting, and this was her life.

Cristian asked, "Is he there?"

"He is. You know I wouldn't be making this call unless it was serious."

"Pasquale, old friend." Cristian's voice was smooth and pure control. "You realize if you hurt a hair on either of their heads, you're dead. As are your pretty wife and your son."

Fiori marched over to me, speaking directly into the phone. "Spare me the warnings, you little whelp. Where's your father?"

"Don't you worry about my father. You're dealing with me now."

What did that mean? Had Giovanni gotten sick again? Another stroke? Another heart attack? "Cristian, it's only a painting. Please."

My cousin gave a wry laugh. "Nothing more than canvas and a little bit of paint, sì?"

"Canvas and paint?" Fiori spun from the phone, waving the gun enough that several of the guards flinched. "Canvas and paint? Is that all that masterpiece is to you?"

Baptiste slid behind Bodyguard Three. "It's alright, Papa. Get one of your guys to paint another one for me."

Fiori stormed over to his son, backhanding him. "Shut up, you pathetic little worm!"

My goal had been to distract him, but all it seemed to have done was agitate him. Make him angrier. This did not bode well for me, let alone for Samantha.

I'm sorry, I mouthed to her.

Her eyes widened, flicked to the window behind the guards, and back to me. She widened them again.

Fiori snatched the phone from my hand. "Send it to me."

Cristian responded, but I didn't make out the words. I was too busy looking where she'd indicated. Movement caught my eye. A figure next to the stone table on the terrace. Another next to the door, reaching for the handle. They were here. How many were there?

Fiori strode the few steps until he stood in front of Samantha. Bodyguard One grabbed me. *Oh no!*

"I have a gun pointed at your cousin's fiancée's head." Fiori lifted the barrel, pressed it to Samantha's forehead, and she closed her eyes. "Give me your word it's mine, or I—"

The crack of a gunshot sounded from somewhere outside and the glass shattered behind Fiori. A spray of blood burst from his temple and he collapsed in a heap, his gun and phone clattering to the ground.

Samantha's eyes snapped open, a splatter of red marring her face.

The guard's grip on me weakened, confusion washing over the group, as everyone but Baptiste drew a weapon, searching for the source of the gunshot.

Cristian asked, "What's happening?"

The door opened a sliver. A faint ping could barely be heard over the men's voices as a metal canister rolled into the room. I dove for Samantha, tackling her in her chair, wrapping my arms around her head as we fell, just as a blinding light erupted in the room. It was all I could do to hold on to her while pulling my head down so my shoulders covered my ears from the screaming pressure of the flash-bang grenade.

The pain. Cazzo Madre, the pain.

Just hold on to her.

Gunfire.

Screams.

A boot connected with my side.

Even so, I held onto her with everything I had.

Another boot knocked the air out of me and rough hands threw me off of her. Distant voices, hard to hear over the ringing in my ears, yelled, "Hands behind your head!"

Other voices pierced the confusion. "Drop your weapons!" and "You're under arrest!"

I blinked wildly, white flashes covering my vision. I could barely see, barely hear.

But I felt the zip ties going around my wrists again.

And finally saw Samantha's chair being righted by someone in tactical gear.

Elliot's SWAT team had arrived.

Just in time.

CHAPTER 44

SAMANTHA

Antonio and I sat on metal chairs by one of the giant stone tables on the back terrace. We'd been sitting for an hour in the cool evening, waiting until they cleared us to leave. Our chairs were as close as we could get them to each other, and our hands remained locked together. We'd forgone separate blankets around us for a shared one after an EMT had cleaned the bl—cleaned my face.

My head rested on Antonio's shoulder and he'd kissed it at least two dozen times.

FBI agents with their beautiful blue jackets moved through the space, along with police officers, detectives, and paramedics.

Police tape surrounded the yard, and the crime scene techs were placing their little flags around the garden room. Two bodies remained on the floor until the techs were done: Pasquale Fiori and Bodyguard One. Antonio had been on top of me when the SWAT team breached, so neither of us saw what happened, but the easy assumption was that Bodyguard One had presented himself as too big a threat. He must have been the only one completely loyal.

I gripped Antonio's hand tighter. Two more deaths over this smuggling ring. But only two and not his or mine. And not our families, either. We'd been in touch with Cristian who confirmed Cass and Sofia's families were safe and were being taken back to their homes.

Baptiste and everyone else in the room had been taken into custody, while officers interviewed the staff and remaining security personnel.

No one said a word about whether they'd found Jason—dead or alive. We'd circled back to the pond's edge, finding nothing more than a trail of blood by the water before we were told to sit still. And no one would talk about Cam-ron, either. Until Elliot showed up, we were little more than witnesses.

I let out a sigh. "What a shitty day." How had we only left the yacht this morning?

"Shall I call my travel agent now and book the flights to Tahiti?"

I sat up slowly, turning to stare at the ridiculous man next to me, and just laughed.

"You said we could go if we survived and here we are." He winked at me, that silly little move he'd been pulling since we met.

I'd shut the world off because I'd lost so many people. Antonio had taught me I should be grateful for them and grab onto every moment life gave me. Time to grab on. "I don't know about Tahiti. It sounds too much like a honeymoon destination."

He pursed his gorgeous lips, not cluing in. "Then Venezia?"

"I've gotta be honest, Antonio. I'm not enjoying this whole fiancée thing."

His teasing face fell. And good. He deserved that stress for a few seconds after how he proposed to me.

"What about Tahiti..." I paused, sinking in to my revenge for a moment. "With a layover for a day or so in Vegas on the way?"

He straightened, head pulling back from me, as though the flash-bang was still affecting his hearing. "Scusi?"

"It's still on the table, isn't it?" I tried to hold my smile down, but it was pointless. I was too tired.

"Are you saying what I think you're saying?"

"That depends on what you think I'm saying."

He blinked rapidly. "Flight to Vegas, get married, and go to Tahiti for a honeymoon?"

"So long as you promise I don't have to lie around on a beach."

He jumped up from his chair and flung the blanket around me. "I need to find a phone and call my travel agent."

I wrinkled my nose. "Your mother's going to hate me for this, isn't she?"

"Let me worry about my mother." He kissed the top of my head. "You just worry about not changing your mind."

"Yes, sir."

He dashed off. That smile. That excitement. My insides went all liquidy. I was clearly exhausted. And I was getting married again. I must have been hit harder in the head than I thought.

A chair on my other side scraped against the tiles, and I turned. "Elliot."

"I came straight from the airport. What are you still doing here?"

"No one's taken our statements yet." Camera flashes went off inside the garden room as techs photographed the scene. "Did you hear from Cam-ron Parker? He was here and we got him out, I told him to—"

"He called me. And he's eager to tell us about everything he's been doing here. He asked if his cooperation can help with his father at all, since from the sounds of it, his father's lawyer won't be around much longer."

"Parker can rot in jail." Two stretchers wheeled into the Basquiat room beyond the garden room.

"He probably will. But there's a lot of loyalty in that kid."

"Kid?" I snorted. "He's the same age as me."

"We are what our experiences make us." Cryptic answer. That was more like the Elliot I knew.

"How'd you know about the condo?"

"Foster Mutual's other prodigy. She called and told me about the message you sent her. Said she was worried you were in danger, especially since the message disappeared almost as soon as it popped up. We assumed if you were contacting her instead of me directly, there was a good reason for it. We knew Fiori took you from the yacht club but didn't get any information from the bodyguard we arrested. We spent far too much time mired in red tape to track the helicopter in time."

"I wanted to call you sooner, but I was afraid someone might be listening. Calling the FBI was too much of a risk." I ran my hands over my face, rubbing my eyes. "But Fiori killed one of the conservators after my message anyway, so that changed things."

"He threatened your family?"

I nodded. "My sister and niece, along with Antonio's sister and nephew."

"Lucy and I went to your condo and saw the pictures." He rubbed my upper arm, as though expecting me to share my feelings.

"What about Fiori's son, Baptiste?"

"I've only heard the high-level details on my way here. It sounds like he'll cooperate, as well as some of the other staff and security. The RCMP are preparing to take the yacht before it leaves the St. Lawrence. Interpol, the Carabinieri, and a half-dozen other organizations are digging in. Most of the worldwide effort over the coming months will be finding and seizing his properties. Like this one—we didn't know about it. It's going to take us a while to clean this up. I have a feeling the last few years we've been after him are just the start."

"Kelsey?"

"In custody."

"From the sounds of it, I'm guessing he has more people in place with the police here and elsewhere."

"I assumed as much." Elliot turned his chair to face me and leaned forward on his knees. "Three years, Sam. I've been trying to bring this thing down for three years, and you just step in and clear the decks like it was nothing."

"Nothing?" I let out a weak laugh. "I'm pretty sure I was almost killed at least a half dozen times in the past year."

"But if you rejoined the FBI, you would have had—"

"More red tape to deal with."

He sighed and sat back. "Fair. And you'd have been working alongside Kelsey, who'd be feeding info right back to Fiori, making sure he stayed ahead of us."

Footsteps approached, and we looked up at an FBI agent on his way with a tablet.

Elliot held up his hand and asked him to wait. "Once you and Antonio give your statements, you'll be free to go. As you may expect, I'll be in touch. Probably a lot."

I nodded. "We're going on our vacation for real this time."

"Good." He patted my knee. "Get some rest and when you get back, the contract position with Art Crime will be waiting."

How did I feel about that? Excited? Relieved? Terrified? "Really?"

"I just got word about twenty minutes ago. Apparently, Kelsey was the one whispering in a few people's ears about you."

"Huh." At least I'd been right about her on one count. "Rules?"

"Exactly the way you want it. The only catch is that you'll be working for me. We'll review cases and pick the right ones. You just need secure access from your home office, occasional visits to Detroit, and there may be some broader travel. This whole thing." He waved his hands, as though he could encompass the entire mansion and all its chaos. "It bought you pretty free rein, at least for now. As many or as few cases as you want."

"Elliot, good to see you." Antonio's rich voice soothed my tired nerves.

I looked up at Antonio and took his hand. "That was awfully fast. All the details taken care of?"

"Sì, I told you she's the best. I gave her the high-level plan and she's taking care of the rest of it. We'll have a hotel in New York tonight. Two new phones will be delivered and we fly out in the morning."

Elliot stood and waved the agent over, then shook Antonio's hand. "I hear you took good care of our Sam."

"I do my best."

I stood with them. "Elliot, I—I need to apologize for what I said after the letter."

"No need." He smiled, but there was something in his eyes that told me it he'd wanted to hear it. "It was a big shock, I know."

I tossed my arms around his neck. "Thanks for telling me. It means more than you can know."

Elliot hugged me back. He knew my father. Worked with him. Spent time with my mother. And then he watched out for her. And me.

"Maybe when we get back, do you think you could..." I let go of him. "Do you think you could tell me some stories about him? The stuff you're allowed to talk about?"

Elliot eased back, swallowing hard while he nodded. The man without emotions showed them again. "Special Agent Rivers is going to take your statements. I'll be in touch."

Antonio wrapped an arm around my shoulders as Elliot left. "You're becoming such a softie."

I mock-glowered at him. "Shut it, Ferraro."

"Never, soon-to-be-Ferraro." He shot me that smirk again. "Did he have news?"

"The contract position's a go."

He frowned, trying hard to push it into a smile. "So, the answer is no for my father?"

I nodded to the new agent and sat. "I don't know yet, Antonio. I need to think."

CHAPTER 45

ANTONIO

We parked in front of the wedding chapel in our red convertible the next evening. The beautiful white building had faux-stained glass and palm trees covered in lights. It was only half-past eight, but the sun had already set, so we'd have an evening ceremony. We were both exhausted, but I couldn't imagine being anywhere else.

Fiori's arrest and death were all over the news, which made explaining the safe house far easier for our families. Samantha didn't want to tell any of them what she'd been involved in, but I convinced her to give them enough of a story that it satisfied them for the time.

Cristian let us know Jason had evaded all the authorities combing the property and would be on his way to Italia soon. How he'd managed that after being shot was a mystery. The last time I'd been shot, I'd spent the night in hospital and had barely been able to fly a couple of days later.

"I feel underdressed." Samantha smoothed her hand over her outfit. She wore white pants and a blouse, while I wore black pants and a white dress shirt. The day in Vegas had been a whirlwind, including shopping, dinner, a tour of the strip, and sampling pastries from various shops.

"No cold feet. Remember, that was the only responsibility I gave to you."

"Yeah, that plus picking out our rings." She gestured to the small duffel I carried, where they were safely tucked away with our license. "I still say we should've just gotten our promise rings blessed."

This woman. So stubborn.

I'd forced her to two jewelry shops in New York and three more once we touched down in Vegas. "New promises, new rings."

A couple flew out the front door, laughing. She wore a short white dress and he was in a black suit.

"We should buy fancier clothes."

"Bella, I would marry you fully naked, if that's what it took. I don't care what either of us is wearing."

Samantha pressed her hands to her cheeks. She'd doubted this plan at least a hundred times but hadn't changed her mind. "I should have at least called my sister. She doesn't even know we got engaged."

I snatched those nasty hands from her face and kissed them. "We can celebrate with our families when we get home. They'll be happy for us, no matter what."

She looked at me, and the love in her eyes poured out. That and a touch of terror. "I really can't believe we're doing this."

"It might not be how you imagined it, but—"

"But what about you? Aren't you supposed to have a giant Roman Catholic service with all the trimmings? Shouldn't I be in a train that's twenty feet long?"

I pressed the button to put the top up and shook my head. "You've watched too many movies."

"This might be true." And she might be postponing the inevitable.

I got out and rounded to her side, where she allowed me to open her door without complaint.

"This is your last chance to get your head on straight and flee back to Michigan."

"If I haven't fled from you yet, do you really think I'm going to?" I half-walked, half-hauled her toward the chapel.

At the front door, she paused and drew in a deep breath. "This is perfect. Just the two of us."

Perhaps. At least, it was perfect because there was none of the pressure and stress of planning and preparing the ridiculously elaborate event my family would have insisted on. I placed my hand on the doorknob. "Well, Ms. Caine? Are you ready?"

"As ready as I'll ever be."

I'd been relatively calm all day, but the moment I turned that knob, my world changed forever. I was about to marry her. For real. "You say the most romantic things."

We entered and spoke with the woman at the reception desk to handle the paperwork. My travel agent—my mother's sister, in truth—had planned almost everything to the ultimate detail, so all Samantha and I had to do was get our marriage license and show up.

The older woman at the desk, with her dark hair and kind smile, said, "You've chosen our Star Chapel, where the evening sky will watch over your vows. It's directly through those doors. Everyone is already—"

"Grazie," I said before she could finish.

Samantha walked to the double-doors with me, eyes narrow. "What was that?"

I placed a hand on her back, ushering her forward. "I don't know what you're talking about."

She pulled open the door and froze in her tracks, mouth gaping wide.

Warmth and joy invaded my very soul.

Perfetto. This was exactly the surprise I wanted.

Her family, my family, our dearest friends, all smiled back at us.

Samantha covered her face as she laughed. "How did you do this?"

"I told you my travel agent's the best in the world."

The smile gracing her face was wider than any I'd ever seen on her before.

There were squeals of "Auntie Sammy!" from Emma, over-ly cool head nods from Sofia's boys, more squeals from Lucy—who was standing in front of Lorenzo, with his hands on her waist, what was going on?—and Cassandra came to hug her.

"You didn't think—" Cassandra suppressed a yawn. It was near midnight at home in Brenton, and given the night in the safe house, it was no surprise many of them were exhausted. "You didn't think we'd let you get married without us, did you?"

Samantha looked all around, unable to focus on one person over another.

"Alright everyone," I said, clapping my hands. "Save the stories for the reception. I need to marry this woman before she changes her mind."

"If only she had something appropriate to wear." Mario made his way to the front of the group, carrying a long white bag.

"Mario?" Samantha looked from him back to me. "How did he get here?"

Part of it was selfish. I wanted him there as my best man, but also knew she deserved to wear something as beautiful as she was. "That's why I had to delay you with all the shopping. Chiara picked out the dress and he was on a plane right away, but I needed a few extra hours before he landed."

Cassandra took Samantha's hand. "There's a changing room in back and we've got everything you need."

Lucy snatched her other hand. "And I need to tell you about my insane night last night! You're not going to believe what happened to me and Lorenzo!"

That was a story I'd need to have, as well.

The room emptied of its women, save my mother. She approached me slowly, raising one eyebrow. "This is how you tell me she said yes?"

I wrapped my arms around her and sighed. "We've been a little busy, Mamma."

"About that whole debacle." She stepped back, frowning. "Your father and I have been in touch with Giovanni to express our thanks for his assistance. I suppose it's time to practice some forgiveness?"

"Grazie mille, Mamma."

She followed where the rest had gone off with Samantha, leaving me with the men. My brother, father, two cousins, Samantha's brother-in-law, Sofia's husband, my nephews, Samantha's nephew, and Nathan. "Thank you all for coming. I know it was short notice."

Papa grabbed me by the shoulders. "Your mother would have killed you if you did this without her, you know this?"

"I know. Are the videoconference calls all set up?"

"They are."

CHAPTER 46

SAMANTHA

It was ridiculous. Then again, everything with Antonio Ferraro had a touch of the ridiculous. I'd thought it would be a small chapel with just the two of us and maybe an Elvis impersonator. Instead, I was in a stunning white sheath dress with a neckline that was far too low, a bouquet of lilies and gardenia, waiting for my flower girl to follow the bridesmaids down the aisle.

Nathan leaned close. "You don't think maybe you're jumping into this a little fast?"

When I married Matt, I didn't have anyone give me away. I'd always assumed my mother would take that duty, but the wedding was only months after her death and I was still reeling, so I gave myself away instead. This time, I was doing it right.

"You agreed to give me away."

"I mean, you were kidnapped two days ago and nearly killed less than twenty-four hours ago. Shouldn't you be under a doctor's care or something?"

I rolled my eyes at him. "They checked me over and I'm fine."

He blew upward, ruffling some hair which had fallen onto his forehead. "I still can't believe you brought the whole thing down."

"Can we hold off on talking shop until we get home and review the case?"

"I heard Dom Ferraro's opening an investigative branch. Any possibility of you working for them?"

Emma bounced up and down, peeking around the corner through the doors. Cass was on her way to the front. Then it would be Emma, then me and Nathan.

"Elliot offered me a job."

He nodded. Had he known? Or had he suspected? Elliot made no qualms about telling people he wanted me back in the fold, so maybe Nathan knew. "Private practice might be less dangerous."

I chuckled at the way he was bouncing between subjects like Emma bounced on her toes. "Are you trying to distract me or yourself?"

Emma grabbed my dress and whispered as loud as she could, "I going now, Auntie Sammy!"

I kissed the top of her head and glimpsed the plastic FBI badge under her little white dress with the pink bows. I'd given it to her for her third birthday last summer. The day after I met Antonio.

Once Emma was through the doors, Nathan gave a shake, like he was the nervous one.

"You know he's perfect for me, right?"

"I know." He smiled. "Are you happy?"

I was in a white dress, with the people I loved all around me, about to marry the man of my dreams. There were job offers from the FBI and Ferraro's, both the exact work I wanted to do. And I'd survived the smuggling ring. "More than I can remember."

'The Wedding March' streamed through speakers all around us.

"That's good enough for me." Nathan pulled down my veil and held out his elbow. "Let's get you married."

When we came around the corner, through the open doors, my breath caught. White walls, white folding chairs, and dim sconces. The ceiling above was dark, with a million pinpricks of light—either a huge skylight showing the stars or a projector.

My gaze settled on the front, at Antonio in a black tuxedo. The impeccable tailoring highlighted his broad chest and shoulders, but it was his face I couldn't get enough of. The cheekbones, the strong jaw, the hair I still loved running my fingers through. It felt like velvet at the nape of his neck.

"Sam," whispered Nathan.

A murmur spread through the crowd. Right. There was a crowd.

"What?"

Nathan chuckled in my ear. "We're supposed to be walking."

I bit down on my lip. The tackiness of my lipstick reminded me I was messing up my makeup. "I know. It's a little overwhelming."

Antonio's chest swelled with a deep inhale and he mouthed to me on the exhale, *Breathe*.

Easy for him to say. He knew this was going to happen. I was still busy with my head swimming. That was probably his plan all along, to ensure I didn't turn around and run.

When we reached the front, Nathan lifted my veil, kissed my cheek, and shook Antonio's hand. For the first time, the two seemed genuinely happy to see each other. Maybe my joy really was enough for Nathan, especially now that Antonio and I weren't watching over our shoulders anymore.

"Ciao, bella," whispered Antonio, as I took my place next to him. "Did you see the screens at the back?"

I craned my neck around, the veil catching on the dress. "Oh my god."

Another murmur rose from the crowd. I was apparently the entertainment for the evening. Huge televisions covered the back walls above the heads of the guests. Each screen was divided into squares, floating heads and smiling faces filling them. Janelle, Chiara, Giovanni and his family, a ton of people I didn't recognize—several bearing a striking resemblance to one or more of Antonio's family. "Are they live?"

"They are."

The officiant talked over us, as though disruptions were common in his chapel.

"I can't believe you did all this."

Antonio pressed a finger to his lips, then pointed forward. "Pay attention, amore."

Of course he did all this. Because that's what Antonio Ferraro did. He made miracles. Like cracking open the shell around my heart and bringing me back to life.

"I understand you've prepared your own vows?" said the officiant.

How did we get to that part so fast? For once, I didn't want the distractions. I wanted to focus on the moment and remember it all. I wanted to remember the twinkling lights on the ceiling. The energy zipping around my chest. And the way my heart beat so hard it felt like it would explode. I wanted to remember the smile on Antonio's face as he turned to look at me. On my sister's face as she took my bouquet. And the feeling of his big, powerful hands around mine.

"Twelve years ago, I had a crush on a quiet, serious girl, who always sat at the front of my class. It took me all semester to work up the courage to ask my Roman Art Girl out." He gave a dramatic sigh. "But she said no."

The crowd chuckled.

"Through some miracle, that same girl—then a woman—came back into my life last year. Still quiet. Still serious. And when I asked for her name, she again said no."

More quiet laughs rippled through the crowd.

"But through some sort of fate or coincidence—"

No such thing as coincidence, I mouthed.

"Shh, you." He feigned a frown, the little golden flecks in his brown eyes swimming in tears that hadn't yet fallen. He sniffled. "These are my vows. Let me get through them."

I squeezed his hands, my cheeks already aching for how much I was smiling.

He swallowed and I wanted to remind him to breathe, too. "Somehow, this woman ended up in my office, had coffee with me, and I was done for. I'm the luckiest man in the world to have you standing here with me, Samantha. It's been a wild ride, but I—" He wiped away a tear from his eye. "I wouldn't want to be on that ride with anyone but you."

He accepted a ring from Mario and slipped it onto my finger. An over-the-top platinum band with as many diamonds as he could cram onto it. "Samantha Caine, part of me has loved you for those twelve years. You were my guiding light, my north star, and I will always find my way to you. From this day forward, you're never alone."

A sharp sting behind my eyes had my gaze snapping heavenward. *Don't cry. Wearing too much make-up.*

"Samantha?" prompted the officiant. "Your turn."

The thickness in my throat was too much. It was a ball of tears ready to choke me or spill free. I whispered, "You did a really good job. Can I just say ditto?"

Antonio leaned closer, his amber and vanilla cologne surrounding me. That scent had carried me through so much. "Are those the vows you swore to me you'd prepared?"

I wrinkled my nose and shook my head. "No."

"Then...?"

"The ones I prepared were for you and Elvis. Not all these people."

"Do I need to find an Elvis, as well?" He raised his eyebrows, telegraphing how silly I was being.

It was just words. I could do words. I could push aside the squirmy ball of nerves in my stomach that tried telling me to hold it all in. For once, I could use Antonio's currency to show him how much he meant to me.

"A year ago, I felt alone. I'd lost too many people I cared about, so I kept my circle small. I was sure if I let anyone else into my heart, I'd just get hurt again. So I pushed everyone away.

Refused to set down roots." I swallowed hard. *You've got this, Sam.* "Until I met the most stubborn man in the world."

Antonio bit back his laugh, but the crowd didn't.

"You've been with me through..." I blinked up at the ceiling, then forced my gaze back to Antonio, despite the first tears rolling down my cheeks. Sofia swore the mascara was waterproof. Hopefully, she was right. "Oh my god, we've been through so much in such a short time. And you haven't backed down for a second. You stood up *to* me. You stood up *for* me. And when I needed it most, you even stood in *front* of me."

Always, he mouthed.

I took the simple platinum ring Cass handed me and slid it onto his finger—the one the promise ring had been on since September. "Antonio Ferraro, you've shown me a love I didn't know I was capable of. You're my rock. My partner. My everything." My voice broke, and I choked out the last. "And I can't wait to share every adventure of my life with you."

The officiant held his arms wide. "Now that Antonio and Samantha have given themselves to each other by solemn vows, with the joining of hands and the giving and receiving of rings, I pronounce they are Mr. and Mrs. Ferraro." He leaned closer and shifted to a stage whisper. "Now might be a good time to kiss."

I flung my arms around Antonio's neck, and our lips met. There was a cheer, some laughs, applause, and music started. But my entire world was the kiss. His arms. His body wrapped around mine.

When we finished, Antonio winked at me. "On to the next adventure, wife?"

"Lead the way, husband." I threaded my arm around his elbow before we headed through the crowd, still clapping. Whatever the world had in store for us, we'd be fine. Because we had each other.

Forever.

Epilogue

Samantha

"There's a spot." Antonio pointed two car lengths ahead of us. "Park there."

"I see several spots from here that are closer to the office." I waved my hand ahead of us but pulled into the parking space he'd requested. "Didn't get enough exercise in Tahiti?"

"I'm exhausted! I need a vacation from my vacation!" He snatched my hand once I'd put the truck into park, bringing my palm to his lips. "You didn't let me lie on the beach for more than a half hour."

"Don't complain." I winked at him. "You had fun."

"Best honeymoon I've ever had."

I rolled my eyes and reached for the door handle. "No complaints about me opening my own door?"

"You're driving. That's different." He placed a hand on my thigh, squeezing playfully. "Are you ready for this, Mrs. Caine-Ferraro?"

"Hey now!" I smacked his hand away. "That's only for work."

"Then are you ready, Mrs. Ferraro?"

The same goofy smile came over me that did every time I heard that. For the first week, I'd fought it, but Antonio forced me to say it over and over again, telling me how much he loved the smile that came with it. So I practiced giving it to him freely. "Yes, Dr. Ferraro."

We exited the truck and he took my hand once I was safely on the inside of the sidewalk. The flower baskets hanging from Via Calabria's black lampposts were in full bloom. Stunning reds and whites surrounded by greenery.

One more day until June, the month I'd moved back to Brenton last year. "I can only stay for a few minutes. I need to get to my meeting with Matt."

"Just come in and have Sofia set up your code, graciously accept my father's wedding present, then you can go on your merry way. Don't forget to take a breather and pick me up for lunch, though."

"Any idea what they got us?"

He hummed aloud, staring all around the street, but not at me.

"You totally know, don't you?"

"My new daughter!" Dominico stood on the sidewalk in front of the office, arms wide, waiting patiently for a hug. Sofia stood next to him, wearing a tight emerald green dress.

Antonio squeezed my hand and leaned close. "The welcome committee. How interesting."

I glanced at my husband from the corner of my eye. "What's going on?"

"So suspicious all the time." He raised a hand, avoiding my question. "Papa!"

"How was your trip?" Dom took me by the shoulders and pulled me in for the most enthusiastic cheek kisses he'd ever given me.

"Amazing." I switched to a hug from Sofia. "I even convinced Antonio to go rock climbing with me."

Antonio hugged his sister. "And I convinced her to come to the spa with me."

I held up my nails and all my diamonds sparkled in the sunshine. "First time they haven't been chipped in about a decade."

Dom clapped Antonio on the back. "Is she ready for the surprise?"

"Possibly?" I feigned a glower at Antonio, who was barely controlling his laugh.

Sofia slipped her arm around my elbow. "We can change it if you don't like it. I think it's too small."

Antonio nudged his sister behind my back, and her step stuttered in those sky-high stilettos she always wore.

We walked as a group past the front of the Ferraro's office and stopped at the glass door beside it.

"Look," said Dom, pointing above the door.

I sucked in a breath, free hand flailing behind me to find Antonio. They'd put the sign up and it was more beautiful than I could have imagined. Not the *Ferraro's Fine Art Investigations* sign Dom had originally shown us. Instead, this one had *Caine-Ferraro's* at the top.

"It's yours, my love." Dom rubbed my back, but I couldn't rip my eyes from it. "I only wish my father could have been here to see it."

I pulled Antonio next to me. "You knew about this?"

"I wouldn't say I *knew*. But he emailed me every day to find out if you'd take the job, so I had a feeling once you said yes, this might happen." He wrapped his arm around my waist. "Happy?"

What could I say? During our honeymoon, I'd decided to leave Foster Mutual. After a few dozen emails with Matt, we had a one-month transition plan in place that included an ongoing consulting role. Elliot had been easier to negotiate with, since he'd already assumed my FBI consulting would be part-time.

All I could do was nod and hold my husband close. I had everything I could want.

Sofia pulled open the door. "Let's set up your passcode for the security and you can go upstairs to make sure everything's the way you want it."

We made quick work of the security changes. Everyone else already had their own codes for the main office, with full access to the space upstairs through the studio. Once we were done, we passed through the second door into the new half of Ferraro's.

A small table had been added by the CFFAI doors, with another iris on it. I leaned in and took in the spicy scent, the one that reminded me of this place. And the music? "Classical. Vivaldi?"

"Chopin, today," said Sofia.

Antonio shook his head. "I need remote access to Sofia's musical selection."

"It's staying on my computer, troublemaker."

With a chuckle, Antonio ushered me up the stairs while Dom and Sofia returned to work. "Have you thought about your new job title yet? They want to order business cards and we need to add you to the website. And then we'll have to discuss hiring—"

He cut off at a popping noise from above. Then the sound of a wheeled chair moving. Someone was up there.

I crested the top of the stairs and halted before stepping into the office. Sure enough, Lucy Chapman sat at the desk she'd used three weeks ago, popping bubbles and shuffling in her chair to some unheard music—definitely not the Chopin from the way she moved.

"Sam!" She launched out of her chair and ran to us, throwing her arms around me. "How was the trip? I can't believe you won't get on social media and share photos. I would have thought Antonio would, but I'm guessing you—"

I broke free from the onslaught. "What are you doing here?"

"Dom called me." She gave Antonio a flyby hug on her way to the desk. "You remember Indigo Lake? Their customer, who thought they had a looted piece? Anyway, the documentation arrived and had my name on it. I got a little carried away and have been back a couple times. Dom said he didn't mind since you weren't here, anyway."

Antonio's gaze met mine, and from the way his face scrunched up, he was as lost as I was.

"I thought you were going to Greece with your family?"

"This sounded more interesting." She flashed a stack of photos in my direction. "Besides, Lorenzo and I were talking about going to Wisconsin Dells in June and he said his parents—your new parents-in-law—put on quite the barbecue for the Fourth of July."

"It's true," said Antonio.

Lucy dropped into the chair, looking more comfortable than she had at Foster Mutual last summer, when she was just an intern I took out on site visits. "I thought you weren't starting work yet?"

"Part-time next week." I meandered past her desk to the railing and looked down at the studio with the four conservators working.

Dom stood next to his newest hire—Cam-ron Parker—walking him through the selection of an adhesive for a repair. This was what he'd needed. A teacher. Someone to guide and help shape his talent, rather than leaving him to the wolves.

Alice had two of the worktables butted against each other, inspecting a ten-foot tall painting she hadn't taken off its frame yet. Frank and Zander sat at easels in the back.

Yeah, this was as perfect as things could be. Almost...

"Hey, Luce..."

"Yeah, boss?"

Exactly. "Have you ever thought about a career in art investigations?"

"Oh, Samantha." Antonio stalked over to me, drawing out my name on his lips. His gorgeous, full, kissable lips. He didn't stop until he'd pinned me against the railing. "You haven't even started work and you're already hiring?"

I slid my arms around his waist, down the curve of his exceptional ass. "You heard her. I'm the boss."

A rumble deep in his throat echoed through my body, and he dipped his head down, brushing his lips against mine.

"No making out in the public areas!" hollered Sofia.

He grinned and waggled his eyebrows. "Do you suppose Papa put that lock on the back door like you suggested?"

"Huh," muttered Lucy. "That's interesting."

Continue teasing your husband. Continue the flirting, Sam. "What's interesting Lucy?"

"At least you paused." Antonio winked at me. "That's an improvement."

I swatted his chest. His hard, muscled, tanned-after-two-weeks-in-paradise chest.

Lucy continued. "I think this painting was on loan to a museum in Berlin when it was confiscated."

"Berlin?" I cocked an eyebrow at Antonio. "I've never been."

"Perhaps we should have a discussion with Papa about your budget?" He took my hand, walking with me toward Lucy's desk and the mystery he knew I was now committed to.

"I'd need a translator." I pulled one of the photographs toward me. "I seem to recall you mentioning that you speak German, Dr. Ferraro?"

THE END

BONUS SHORT: Wondering what happened between Lucy and Lorenzo? What did she do when she got Sam's message? What brought the two of them together finally?

Join Janet's author newsletter and get
Forging Chapman plus behind-the-scenes details at
https://bf.janetoppedisano.com/d937hn8wk8

FREE NOVELLA: What was all that about Sam and Antonio in Boston, the conservator who found her father's letter, and a gunman? Check out the free novella *The Phoenix Heist,* the prequel to a new romantic suspense series, starring Scarlett Reynolds and her heist crew—and with cameos by Sam, Antonio, and Elliot.

Get *The Phoenix Heist* for FREE only at
https://bf.janetoppedisano.com/smbari40im

Acknowledgments

There you have it. Sam and Antonio finally have their happily ever after. Or do they? Don't worry, I'm teasing. These two lovebirds are together for life, even if they do get caught up in more adventures in the future.

It's been a long trek for them.

Antonio has gone from searching in vain for a woman who'd measure up to his ideal of Sam from college, to trying to shape her into someone who'd focus solely on him and their relationship, and finally into a partner working at her side to bring down Fiori.

Sam's story started with her five great heartbreaks and she's confronted each of them in a book. *Burning Caine* brought her and Janelle back together. *Chasing Caine* had her finally confess the impact her mother's death had on her. *Disarming Caine* convinced her it was time to get over her poor choice with Matt and confess her feelings for Antonio. *Enduring Caine* put her face-to-face with Vincenzo. And finally, *Forging Caine* provided her with the truth about her father.

Through it all, these two flawed people learned to lean on each other, be honest in ways they weren't even with themselves, and found the healing power of love. And isn't that why we read romance? For the way it demonstrates what the human heart is capable of, when given the right conditions?

Thank you for picking up this book—for joining me (and Sam and Antonio!) on this amazing journey.

To my husband and son, thanks again. For streaming Oppy Jr's hockey games when I was under deadline and unable to make it to the rink. For advising me on action sequences. For forcing me to the writing cave when I was procrastinating.

To my alpha (and at times beta) readers and first cheerleaders, Paula and Pat: Thank you for your support and for letting my books find a place in your hearts. And I apologize for taking so long to get to Ellis's book. It's coming soon. I promise.

To all my beta readers through the course of the series Colin, Missy, Kari, Cassie, Dianna, Gayle, Kim, Patty, Robbie, Sharron, Tracy, and Vivian (phew! What a list!): I appreciate your time and opinions. You've been a tremendous help in shaping my stories.

To my ridiculously amazing editor, Miranda Darrow: Thanks can't really convey my feelings. You took my "not quite a romance" first book and helped me mold it into an award-winner that gave me the confidence to follow this publishing dream, which wound up as a five-book epic love story. Your continued excitement for my books has been invaluable.

And finally, I'd like to thank you again, my dear reader. You're why I do this. At first, I was writing for myself, but every message any of you have sent me warms my heart and encourages me to keep publishing. Knowing someone out there is reading my words and finding some enjoyment or an escape for a few hours means the world to me. So yeah, thanks again.

About Author

Janet Oppedisano hails from Canada's East Coast and has lived in five provinces, from the Maritimes to the Prairies. Growing up with a Mountie for a father and marrying a Navy diver, it's no surprise she writes romance with a hint of danger and mystery in it. Not to mention strong heroes and equally strong heroines.

Prior to publishing her debut novel, she won awards for two of her unpublished works, including the Romance Writers of America's 2021 Vivian Award for Most Anticipated Romance, for *Burning Caine.*

When not writing, you can find her... thinking about writing. And indulging in her favorite pastimes, like baking, traveling, hiking, playing with her dog, and watching her hockey goalie son on the ice.

Oh, and it's pronounced oh-ped-ih-SAH-no. Exactly the way it's spelled. Honest!

You can find Janet and all her social media profiles at:
https://janetoppedisano.com

Made in United States
Orlando, FL
13 June 2023

34095896R00246